PRAISE FOR
WADE IN THE WATER

"Michael Oates revisits a tragic moment in American history with his novel Wade In The Water, a touching coming of age tale plunging the reader into the swirling waters of a devastating flood that destroyed the town of Johnstown, Pennsylvania in 1889 and took the lives over 2,000 men, women, and children. Perhaps overshadowed by more recent disasters such as 9/11 and Hurricane Katrina, the Johnstown flood has been forgotten by many. Oates brings its memory back with a gripping story that hooks you from the very start and flows on with identifiable characters and expressive narration, almost lyrical at times, exploring the choices people make as they survive or succumb to tragedy. Through vivid descriptions and well-developed characters with uniquely connected lives, Oates weaves for us a masterful story filled with harmony and conflict that twists and turns just as unpredictably as the raging floodwater intent on destroying it all. Wade in the Water pairs real people with real history. Hopes and dreams are challenged, and the will to survive is put to the test. The characters we are rooting for, as well as the one's we aren't, must literally sink or swim. And not simply in a battle of man versus nature, but in a battle of man versus a force so deadly, it threatens to annihilate every hope and dream they live for."

Debra Holland, *New York Times* **bestselling author of** *The Montana Sky Series*

"The 'Johnstown Flood' of 1889 survives as a dimly recalled phrase, but memory of the actual scope of the catastrophe has faded with time. In 'Wade in the Water', Michael Oates brings the drama and tragedy of the flood back with immediate, wrenching impact. Told through the eyes of memorable characters whose personal struggles are instantly erased by the immensity of the disaster, Oates conveys the terror of that horrible moment with meticulous historical accuracy. 'Wade in the Water' is the story of people – including real characters like Clara Barton of the Red Cross - caught in a nightmare of destruction comparable to the annihilation of Pompeii, with loss of life exceeding any American disaster up to that time. Oates tells a stirring story that highlights the fragility of life and the endurance of the human spirit."

John M. Adams Historian, Author of _The Millionaire and the Mummies_

"Michael Oates's _Wade in the Water_ is a triumph of historical fiction and a powerful parable for our time. In an age of heightened awareness of man-made natural disasters, ranging from Hurricane Katrina to the Fukushima Meltdown to Superstorm Sandy, Oates's finely crafted and emotionally haunting novel rekindles memories of an even deadlier natural disaster wrought by rampant greed and massive injustice. Grounded in historical fact and illuminated through the lives of owners and workers in industrialized western Pennsylvania, _Wade in the Water_ vividly recounts the week leading up to the apocalyptic Johnstown flood of May 31, 1889. On that day, a dam built to create a country club lake and fishing spot for wealthy industrialists burst and sent a fifty foot wall of water and tangled debris raging through a narrow valley, obliterating everything in its path, erasing a string of working class communities, and sweeping 2,029 people to their deaths. Remindful of John Dos Passos's USA trilogy, E.L. Doctorow's _Ragtime_, or Roman Polanski's film _Chinatown_, _Wade in the Water_ brings this event to life with a kaleidoscope of characters, both historic and fictional. From industrialists Andrew Carnegie and Henry Clay Frick to

Red Cross founder Clara Barton to black piano prodigy Blind Tom Wiggins to deeply compassionate portraits of ordinary steel workers, miners, cooks, and skilled craftsmen living in the shadow of impending catastrophe, Oates masterfully recreates the stark tragedy and deep injustice of this almost forgotten event. Filled with powerful prose and driven by the drum beat of impending disaster as the rain falls and the waters rise, *Wade in the Water* is a compelling and important novel, full of human tragedy and triumph."

Michael Steiner, Professor of American Studies, California State University, Fullerton Author of *Regionalists on the Left: Radical Voices from the American West*

"Michael Oates has written an absorbing work of historical fiction. Using thinly disguised historical figures (e.g. Andrew Carnegie, Henry Frick), he tells the story of the largely forgotten Johnstown flood of 1889. By creating well-developed characters enmeshed an involving tale, the Oates is able to convey the horror of being helplessly caught up in this unnatural disaster. The book is well researched and skillfully blends fact and fiction in a manner that reminds one of [Doctorow's] *Ragtime*. If one were teaching a course of history through fiction, this would be a strong addition to the syllabus."

Vince Buck, professor emeritus, California State University

"In Wade in the Water, Michael Oates creatively transforms the events and characters of the Johnstown flood into a wildly inventive and unpredictable tale."

Richard Burkert, President and CEO of the Johnstown Area Heritage Association

WADE IN THE WATER

A Novel of the Johnstown Flood

WADE IN THE WATER

A Novel of the Johnstown Flood

MICHAEL STEPHAN OATES

KNOX ROBINSON
PUBLISHING
London & New York

KNOX ROBINSON
PUBLISHING

34 New House
67-68 Hatton Garden
London, EC1N 8JY
&
244 5th Avenue, Suite 1861
New York, New York 10001

Knox Robinson Publishing is a specialist, international publisher of historical fiction, historical romance and medieval fantasy.

First published in Great Britain in 2014 by Knox Robinson Publishing
First published in the United States in 2014 by Knox Robinson Publishing
Copyright © Michael Stephan Oates 2014

A CIP catalogue record for this book is available from the British Library.
ISBN HC 978-1-908483-82-9
Cover art by Olga Dabrowska
Typeset in Sabon by Susan Veach
info@susanveach.com
Printed in the United States of America and the United Kingdom.

Download the KRP App in iTunes and Google Play to receive free historical fiction, historical romance and fantasy eBooks delivered directly to your mobile or tablet.

Watch our historical documentaries and book trailers on our channel on YouTube and subscribe to our podcasts in iTunes.

www.knoxrobinsonpublishing.com

For Liza

Wade in the water
Wade in the water children
Wade in the water
God's gonna trouble the water

- Negro Spiritual

PROLOGUE

The storm came out of Kansas, a whirling black anvil that whipped up a twister along the Cottonwood River, destroying three farmhouses and taking the lives of over a dozen men. After pounding Indiana and Michigan with hail and heavy snow, it crept into Pennsylvania and teased the town of River Fork with sporadic spitting and light showers until the early hours of May 30, 1889 when it unleashed its full force on the valley.

By day break, icy rain had flooded the mountain streams and filled the reservoir in front of the River Fork Fishing and Hunting Club. The winding boardwalk where valley gazers once strolled now lay toppled in the water, bent and broken, while white-fingered waves clawed at the shoreline behind it, scraping away the soil around the thin stilts holding up the patio deck.

Bennett Marsh wiped his eyes and stared down at the splintered wood jutting from the water. A clap of thunder shook the wooden planks beneath his feet, and a strong gust threw fat raindrops across the porch that bit at his face like a swarm of angry bees. He shielded his eyes, blew away the drops of water around his mouth, and gazed toward the dam. He had hoped to meet his father on the bridge that morning, but all he saw through the mist was a group of men, hazy images, straddling the broken planks and hacking away at the earth with shovels and pickaxes. He called to them with raspy, throat-burning shouts, but the swells were breaking loudly against the rocks, drowning out his pleas for help.

He left the porch and trudged through the floating debris littering the Clubhouse. Silver-rimmed serving platters and collapsed butler stands bumped against his shins as he slogged across the dining room and into the foyer. The front door would have made for an easy escape if it wasn't jammed shut. He dropped his shoulder and shoved, but it wouldn't give.

Water was now filling the foyer, leaking into the room through the ceiling, the walls, seeping up from between the floorboards. He retreated to the dining room and climbed atop the Steinway and untied a few of the Decoration Day streamers hanging from the chandeliers. He took the strands outside and fashioned a makeshift rope, tying off one of the ends to the patio door. His hands ached from the cold, and he quickly massaged his palms.

The rain beat down upon him as he stood on the edge of the deck, staring once more at the restless shoreline some twenty feet below. The waves were climbing higher, cutting away large chunks of the bank with every surge. He turned and peered through the streaked patio windows, hoping to find someone coming down the stairs, but it was clear, now, everyone in the Clubhouse that morning had already left. If only Blind Tom were there, he thought. But Tom was gone too.

With a strong grip on the canvas rope, he forced out a breath of steam, dropped over the edge of the deck, and climbed down, swinging over the troubled water like a pendulum. A wave crashed beneath him and shook loose one of the sagging wooden stilts. He wrapped himself around the rope, closed his eyes, and held on. With a sudden jolt, the patio deck dropped, and the canvas rope ripped apart.

1

The Number Eight rolled like thunder down the steep grades of the Allegheny Mountains, through dense forests where mountain lions hunted, past flowing brooks where black bears came to drink. It followed the rails alongside the Stone River in the skittering shadows of the white pines and balsam firs that had taken hold there and spread out across the hillsides in sweeping blankets of prickly bluish-green. Melting snow and heavy rain had fed the River early this year, and fallen leaves and deadwood collected where the winding waters bent and changed direction. A golden eagle circled above, dodging raindrops and floating high on the canyon's cool winds. Wild turkeys with plump bellies rested on the tracks until the engineer sounded the whistle and sent the fat birds scurrying off into the wet grass. Brisk morning air. Weeping clouds. Springtime in southwestern Pennsylvania.

Loaded with mail from as far away as New York City, the Number Eight was making stops in the valley before heading west to Pittsburgh. Mail clerks inside the number-one car were busy sorting and bagging while endless rows of sugar maples blurred past them through the windows.

Tightly packed in one of the mail bags was a letter destined for a town at the crest of the valley. It was from a man named Frank Damrosch, head of music education for New York City's public schools. A teacher and musician, Damrosch was in the process of establishing a music institute certain to rival any in Europe. American academies were not recognized for having the advanced

3

curriculum or the experienced instruction that European academies had, nor were they known for producing any artists or composers of any great significance. Europeans believed American artists lacked the experience of history and heritage, and their music was immature and uninspired. Damrosch intended to change this notion with his novel idea for a prestigious conservatory located here, in the United States.

It was with this intention that he had solicited requests for applications to the first class of his proposed academy. Colleagues believed an open enrollment was a ridiculous idea, contending the public schools and current music institutes in New York were full of prospective students. But Damrosch believed otherwise. He maintained the notifications he'd placed in community newspapers across the country would generate responses from hidden talent just waiting to be discovered. One such hopeful would find his letter today, in a mail sack coming down from the mountain.

The town of River Fork was spread out along the banks of the Lower Stone River, about a mile south of the reservoir. It had enjoyed the clean air and the pristine forests of the valley until the railroad, cheap land, and a fast flowing river brought the factories. Steel mills with black chimneys replaced the white pines, and dark clouds of smoke and ash now hung stubbornly over the town.

Up the hill from River Fork sat the train station, a simple two-story with a shake roof, built off the ground on short wooden stilts. Townsfolk were shuffling in and out that morning, doing their best to avoid the man on the ladder who was giving the factory-facing wall a fresh coat of bright white paint. Inside, ticket holders huddled on benches arranged back to back in the center of the room, and the constant murmur of their conversations echoed off the unpainted walls. A cool breeze blew in through an open window, and the seated crowd pulled together their coats and flipped up their collars. Passengers eager for travel stood with heads tilted back, pointing at the large chalk board behind the counter while the clerk scribbled on ticket stubs and collected money. Opposite the entrance, a pair of wrought iron gates opened to a wood-plank landing that extended toward the tracks and ran alongside the length of the depot. On the track-facing wall, a giant clock was striking ten.

A young man stood on the landing among the passengers and loiterers, rocking back on his heels and staring up toward the mountains. He was tall and lanky, his smooth face free from the signs of worldly troubles, and fresh with the innocence that favored a boy of his age. His baggy trousers fell short of his shoes, hand-me-downs from his father, same as the long-sleeve flannel and floppy tweed cap. A frayed knapsack hung loosely over his slouching shoulder, and a knitted scarf wrapped his thin neck, just tight enough not to choke. There wasn't anything special that could be said about him, nor was there anything special he could say about himself. He was a presentable, average boy of nineteen years. If he hadn't been thumping his heels and fidgeting about, he would have gone unnoticed.

The ride up the hill seemed quick. With the hope of the letter's arrival, and a brilliant Chopin polonaise in his head, he didn't remember passing the noisy factories, or bumping his rickety bicycle over the tracks. He did remember, though, the last bit of incline near the dam, for when he shifted his weight, his thighs burned from the heavy pedaling. Every morning, for the past month, he'd raced to the depot aboard his Safety Rover as swiftly as possible to greet the Day Express, hoping good news would arrive.

There was a luncheon scheduled that afternoon at the River Fork Fishing and Hunting Club. Jean Pierre had told him to be there at ten thirty, sharp. He restlessly took turns watching for the train and glancing up at the big clock.

Standing next to the boy was a short, healthy, middle-aged woman, holding hands with a younger woman of similar stature, both well-dressed in Victorian style. The mother twirled a fancy lace umbrella that matched the couple's lavender dresses and protected their ostrich-feathered bonnets from the rhythmic cadence of the raindrops. She rested the umbrella on her shoulder and caught the young man's attention. "Must be something important?" she said. "What's the Express bringing you that's making you nearly jump out of your shoes?"

At first, he didn't respond, but when the woman's wide eyes and even wider smile confirmed she was talking to him, he politely answered. "An application," he said, picking at his fingernails. "At least I hope it is. To a music institute in New York City. Gonna be the finest in America, maybe even the world. And I'm gonna study there. I just know it's on the train today."

"Isn't that something," the woman said, turning to the girl beside her, "Sarah Ann, here, is studying art in New York City, and simply having a wonderful time, isn't that right dear."

"Oh, yes," Sarah Ann said, peaking around her mother. "Simply wonderful."

A cool breeze came over the landing and blew the floral scent of perfume in the young man's direction. He breathed in the fragrance and locked eyes with Sarah Ann, her lips and cheeks glowing rosy red in the cool air. She smiled at him and his stomach dropped. Without any help from his aching thighs, his legs went weak. He wanted to say something clever to the girl, that she was pretty, or that at least her smile was lovely, but what came out was, "You smell really nice."

The mother scolded Sarah Ann for giggling, and brought her attention back to the boy. "I believe I recognize you," she said, twirling her parasol. "Not from one of the factories, but from the River Fork Clubhouse, isn't that right?"

The young man now realized the woman standing next to him was Louise Andrews. He had seen her before at the Clubhouse dinners with her husband, industrialist and Club founder, Charles Andrews. His chin quivered. "Yes, ma'am," he said, "from the Clubhouse."

"Then it must be you we hear playing the piano during our afternoon tea."

A feverish heat rushed into his cheeks. "I didn't know you could hear the piano from the sitting room," he said. "I'll be sure to check next time before I play."

The woman's smile grew larger. "Secret pleasures are hard to keep to oneself around the Clubhouse. The young boy who sneaks into the dining room and sits at the Steinway is a frequent topic. And I must tell you, I agree with what's been said about your music. It's lovely."

The boy's cheeks cooled, and the sound of a train whistle came echoing through the valley. A moment later he heard the bell. The women turned their attention to the track, and the young man moved closer to the edge of the landing. He curled one hand around the mail-catcher and swung out for a better look.

Funnel smoke fell over the landing in a mist of black rain as the Number Eight pulled into the station. The engine, tender, two mail cars and a Pullman bowed the tracks against the ties as the iron wheels, slowing in time with the bell, brought the train to a full stop. The engine blew a powerful blast from its side, spraying a jet of white steam across the landing, and the young man swung around the mail-catcher and settled in closer to the depot.

As the steam cleared, the door of the Pullman opened and the conductor hopped onto the platform accompanied by a shorter, rotund man wearing a frock coat and top hat. The young man didn't know much about Charles Andrews, just that he was a well-respected steel man who owned half the valley from River Fork to Johnstown and was one of the wealthiest men in the country. Around the Clubhouse, he came and went as he pleased, inspecting every aspect of Club affairs, and always concerned about the comfort of the members. He seemed odd and eccentric, but in an admirable sort of way. At times, he could be seen standing on the roof of the Clubhouse. The hired help said he did this to check on his steel factories and make sure all the chimneys were burning.

Andrews and the conductor walked down the landing, stopping intermittently to inspect the axels while the brakeman followed them atop the train. After some deliberate finger pointing and

7

consulting, the two men made their way to the engine and hopped into the cab. The young man hoped for a quick off-load, but Andrews and the conductor just stood inside the engine cab, transferring papers back and forth and talking with the engineer.

He bounced on his heels, pressed for time and needing to pee. He rubbed his thumbs over his fingertips and looked over his shoulder at the depot clock and mumbled to himself. "Hurry up, hurry up."

The local clerk came out of the depot, and the men in the cab began to move. The conductor stepped down and met the clerk on the landing, and as the two men exchanged documents, the well-dressed Andrews walked toward the depot. Though short in stature, Andrews strode with authority, one hand tucked in his coat pocket, the other stroking his well-groomed, snow-white beard. He doffed his hat as he approached his wife and daughter, and after kissing the back of their hands, paused and turned to the young man. "Expecting some mail today, son?"

The young man's stomach fell again, and he pushed out a reply through a lump in his throat. "Sure am, sir, just know it will be on today."

Andrews smiled and turned to Louise. "Be back in a minute dear," he said, and went into the depot.

The mail clerks kept sorting as the local clerk opened the door of the number-one car. One of the workers inside weaved around a mess of mail bags, grabbed a misconfigured gunny, and tossed it onto the platform.

"Wait, wait," said the young man, waving his arms, the tattered knapsack bouncing against his back as he ran. The flap popped open and his sheet music flew out onto the landing. He hurriedly retrieved the pages, shouting at the clerk to wait.

The clerk threw the mail sack over his shoulder and looked down. "Persistent young fella, ain't ya," he said. "Not even gonna let me get inside this time. And what is this, the third time this week?" He turned and started off toward the depot.

The young man buttoned up the knapsack and looped his arm

through the straps. "Can't we have a look right here?" he said, shuffling up alongside the clerk. "I just know it's in there. And you said it yourself...third time. Third time's a charm, right?"

The clerk stopped and regarded the boy. "Maybe you're right," he said, dropping the mailbag onto the landing. "Let's see what we've got. But if it ain't here," he shook a lazy finger at the boy, "you're helpin' me put all these letters back, no runnin' off on me, now."

The boy was so caught up in the arrival of the letter, he just now noticed Sarah Ann watching him over her mother's shoulder. "I promise," he said, "if it ain't there, I'll help you put 'em back."

The clerk stared at the boy. "It's Marsh, ain't it?"

"Bennett Marsh."

The clerk drew a set of jingling keys from his belt using an extra appendage on his right hand. It was a second thumb. Ben hadn't noticed before, and he stared at it curiously.

The clerk held up his hand for display. "Yup," he said, "two thumbs. Figured mail sorter was the perfect job for me."

They laughed, and the clerk with two thumbs unlocked the bag and sifted through the letters, reading the names aloud.

"Baker, Hoffman." He kept pulling letters out of the bag, two at a time, and piling them up on the landing. "Fisher, Howell... Aker, Singer."

The clerk mumbled a few more names and looked up, squinting to keep the funnel smoke from his eyes. "Marsh, right?" He reached in again and pulled out a large envelope clipped between his double digits. He brought it to his face for a better look, and back out again to verify the name. "What do you know, Bennett Marsh."

Ben snatched the envelope. Any more delay and he might have strangled the double-thumbed clerk. It had been three months since he'd first read the solicitation in the Tribune and decided to mail his application request, but holding it now, in his hands, all he did was stare at it. He looked up at the mountains where the train

9

had descended, and back down toward his hometown of River Fork, still covered with the dark haze. He was about to open the letter when Louise Andrews regained his attention.

"Is that what you were waitin' for?" she asked.

Ben nodded, rubbing his thumbs over the contents inside. Wedged in the corner was a small bulge. His fingers moved over the lump, but its shape was unrecognizable.

"Good news?" said Sarah Ann.

Ben took another whiff of her perfume and tried to respond without marking him a total fool. "I sure hope so."

Charles Andrews came out of the depot and called to Louise and Sarah Ann. "Our carriage is here," he said.

Louise turned to Ben. "Good luck with your music."

The two women walked away, Sarah Ann giving Ben an over-the-shoulder wave just as the door to the depot closed behind her.

For a moment, Ben forgot about the letter and the luncheon, but when the train whistle blew, his mind jolted back to the envelope in his hands. He hesitated opening it, afraid if it did contain good news, he would have to make a decision. New York might as well have been Paris. Except for his childhood years in East Liberty, he had never ventured beyond the rim of the valley. As he debated opening the envelope, the big clock on the depot roof sounded.

"Oh, no," he said aloud, "Ten-thirty, I'm late again." He ran to his bicycle leaned up against the depot wall.

The clerk pointed at the pile of letters still strewn about the landing. "You just hold on, now, son. You said..."

Ben stuffed the envelope into his knapsack and climbed onto his bicycle. "I said I'd help you if my letter wasn't there, remember." He sped away through the crowd and off the end of the landing, hoping to steal time on his way to the Clubhouse.

2

A haven for the privileged elite sat at the edge of the lake. Though the one hundred sixty-acre property boasted a sporting field, a boathouse, sixteen custom cottages, horse stables with box stalls, and several other free standing buildings, the Clubhouse was the main structure that defined the River Fork Fishing and Hunting Club.

Built in grandiose Greek-revival style that some said resembled an enormous southern plantation home, the three-story mansion was painted brilliant white, with thick fluted columns, burgundy trimmed eaves, and wood-shake gables. Forty-seven fully-furnished guest rooms lined the upper two floors, complete with indoor plumbing, fancy pull-chain toilets, and windows that opened to picturesque views of the valley. The ground floor featured a professional kitchen, a manager's office, a sitting room for the women, a smoking lounge and billiard room for the men, and a grand ballroom with floor-to-ceiling windows that overlooked a wide patio deck and gave the diners inside a breathtaking panorama of the lake. Joined to the end of the patio deck was a boardwalk, built high above the water's edge on thick round pillars, where members and their guests could stroll down to the dam, or up to the cottages where late night parties, some more elaborate than those at the Clubhouse, were held.

As Andrews's carriage was pulling into the driveway, John Parke stood under the dripping planks of the boardwalk on a mixture of wet sand and gravel, smoking a cigarette and staring out over the water. Dark clouds rested above the valley, and the landscape was in black and white. Towering pines surrounded the lake, and Parke followed their shadowy reflections until they vanished into the distance at the base of the foothills. A mirror image of the Clubhouse projected faintly onto the surface of the lake like a monochromatic Monet. He picked up a rock and pitched it into the water, sending out a set of concentric rings from one of the second-story windows.

It had been six weeks since his appointment as Club manager and resident engineer, a job he had accepted from Charles Andrews after a chance meeting in New York while studying engineering at the University of the City of New York. Andrews was there cutting the ribbon at the school's new library he had funded. Parke, newly married, and enticed by the handsome salary, had decided to forego his education to work for the second wealthiest man in America. He had hoped to begin his employment studying the architectural design of the dam, but since his arrival, most of his time had been spent repairing the damage caused by the season's unusually heavy rain.

A downpour the night before had eroded one of the stack fences by the sporting field, and Parke had sent out a group of Italian laborers to reset the fence posts and split rails. After a long draw on his cigarette, he flicked the butt into the lake and crunched over the gravel to where the Italians were working.

Andrews and the other club members put a tremendous amount of pressure on the twenty-eight-year-old to maintain the impeccable condition of the Clubhouse and its grounds. But although the position was stressful, it did offer a substantial perk: a master suite overlooking the lake, furnished with a comfortable spring-mattress bed, a handcrafted armoire, and a pedestal sink with an etched-glass shelf above it for his shave cream, straight razor, and hair tonic.

All week, Parke had been so preoccupied with the poor weather and the threat it posed to the upcoming Decoration Day celebration, he had neglected his shave cream and straight razor. Even the jar of Morgan's pomade he used to keep his wavy coif in perfect alignment had been untouched since Monday. He lit another cigarette and scratched at the stubble on his face while he watched the Italians work. Satisfied with their progress, he returned to the shoreline beneath the boardwalk.

A hundred yards from the Clubhouse sat the River Fork dam. Parke had read about it in the New York Times. The Times had labeled it an architectural wonder, an enormous embankment of piled rock and earth that stretched nearly a quarter-mile across and held back over twenty million tons of water. A wood-plank bridge for carriage and foot travel rested atop the crest on short round stumps. Under the planks, the rush of lake-water poured through a wide spillway and cascaded over the fifty-foot rock-face of protruding trees and vegetation that resembled more a part of the landscape than a man-made structure. Below, the Lower Stone River started its fourteen mile journey down the valley, winding through more than a dozen towns and boroughs until it met the Rock Creek River at the Stone Bridge in Johnstown.

Though it seemed of no concern to the Club members, Parke believed the dam's design was flawed, its structural integrity unsound. When heavy rain fell on River Fork, the lake would swell and overflow its banks, washing out a substantial portion of the grounds. It was a nuisance for Parke and the Italians, constantly repairing the fences, repacking the levees, and dry-sanding the carriage roads and walking paths. The annoyance Parke experienced was similar to what the townsfolk of River Fork endured every time the flooding raised the level of the Lower Stone River. In town, shop owners on Main Street would spend all day sandbagging their porches and moving displayed goods to higher ground. Parke often heard the Club members joking that the knee-high water in the streets was good for the townsfolk, saying, "They could all enjoy a good bath once and a while."

As resident engineer, it was Parke's job to question the safety and stability of the structures, be it fences, free-standing dwellings like the Clubhouse, or fifty-foot embankment dams. It hadn't been his job to build these things, but it was his job now to protect them. If he could understand why the lake didn't want to stay put behind the dam, maybe he could actually improve the look and safety of the grounds, instead of simply patching it up all the time.

Parke had been especially motivated to investigate the stability of the dam after reading an article in that morning's edition of River Fork's local newspaper, The Tribune. Jack Wisord, or "The Wisord of the Weather" as he signed his forecasts, had written a feature about the flood of '81, and how the reservoir at River Fork had nearly come out. Recently, there had been talk in town about a storm out of Kansas and the threat it posed if the dam failed to hold. Wisord confidently predicted the storm would bypass River Fork, and even if it did "happen to drop a good downpour," he wrote, "it would pose no threat to the dam, or to the towns below."

Something about the nonchalant manner of Wisord's prediction made Parke skeptical. He took the burning cigarette from his lips and used it to light another. After a deep pull, he ambled down to the water's edge and looked out over the lake. The water was restful and still, like an innocent child. But he had also seen it churning with waves and whitecaps whipped up from pouring rain and unpredictable canyon winds. It was those times that worried him, when the lake acted like an angry adolescent, incapable of controlling its innate urge for mischief. He glanced at the dam, then back at the lake, and sighed. "Jesus, that's an awful lot of water to hold back."

"Indeed it is," said a voice.

Parke looked over his shoulder at Charles Andrews.

"No use trying to hide it," said Andrews. "A job like this will do that to you."

Parke ran his fingers through his frizzed hair and stroked his scruffy cheeks.

"It's a whole lot different than textbooks and lectures, eh, John?"

Parke smiled in agreement.

"You're wondering how the dam was built, aren't you," Andrews said, walking up next to Parke. "How on earth it can hold back that much water?"

14

Though Andrews was an intimidating man, his voice was soft-spoken, permitting Parke to speak freely. "I'm actually wondering why the dam was built to hold back that much water," said Parke, "and why the people who built it thought it should." Parke scanned the lake from one end to the other. "This water wants to keep moving down the valley, and I'm afraid one of these days, it just might. Some things aren't meant to be held back."

Andrews nodded. "I had the same concerns when we were building the Clubhouse, but I was assured by the engineers that the design of the dam was sound." They walked under the boardwalk, across a grass-covered lawn, and onto the bridge. "See the width here?" Andrews said, making a sweeping motion with his hand from one side of the bridge to the other, "Enough space for two carriages to pass at the same time."

Parke's eyes measured the distance.

"It wasn't always like this," said Andrews. "After we bought the dam from the Pennsylvania Railroad, the entire embankment went through a series of retrofits. During one of the modification projects, the height of the crest was lowered in order to widen the breadth."

"And no one thought that might be a bad idea?"

"Again," said Andrews, "I was reassured the size of the spillway was sufficient to control the water flow." Andrews took off his coat and hat and handed them to Parke. He looked up the road for approaching carriages then lowered himself over the lakeside edge of the bridge.

As Andrews found his footing on the small rock ledge, Parke turned and gazed over the valley. Progress had spread out along the sloping hills as far as he could see – factories and foundries, homes and hotels, water towers and coal tipples, all dropped between a checkerboard of railroad track and split down the middle by the wide river snaking through the valley.

From the valley side, the spillway made a magnificent backdrop for photographs and picnics. Most of the oil paintings and stenographs hanging in the Clubhouse depicted it. Parke moved closer to the waterfall and looked over the edge. The near vertical drop-off made his head spin, and he quickly moved back to the lakeside of the bridge.

Andrews was still squatting on the rock ledge and pointing to the waterline behind the spillway. "See those metal grates down there?" he shouted, his voice barely audible over the rushing waterfall.

Parke looked down at the closely spaced rods that ran the length of the spillway and disappeared deep into the water. "I see them."

"That's a fish screen. Put there to keep the black bass we stocked the lake with from getting spat over the side."

Parke was bending over for a better look when he saw Morton Crick coming down the boardwalk.

Morton Crick was half as wide and twice as tall as Andrews, but his attire was the spit and image of the Club's founder, a pressed black coat and rigid top hat. He kept a quick pace, stomping off the sloping end of the boardwalk and onto the open area of level grass. With his hands cupped around his tapered mustache and V-shaped goatee, he shouted at Parke. "What the hell are you doing over there, those Italians aren't finished yet." He crossed the broad lawn and came onto the bridge. "Parke," he barked again, moving his hand to his hips, "I said, what the hell are you doing?"

Crick's long nose and ridged forehead made his eyes sink deep into his face, and Parke stared at their hollowness without saying a word. Meanwhile, Andrews had worked himself back onto the bridge.

Crick took his hands from his hips and quickly clasped them behind his back. His sunken eyes popped out like a pair of curious prairie dogs. "Oh, Charles," he said, "I didn't see you there."

Andrews brushed off his shirt and took his coat and hat from Parke. "We are having a discussion about the integrity of the dam, Mr. Crick, anything you would like to add?"

"No, no," said Crick, "I was just checking on the status of the stack fence."

16

Andrews put on his hat, holding on to the brim while he checked the sky. "You really think now is the best time for your croquet match?" he said, "Balls don't roll well in the mud. And repairing the stack fence won't make the field any drier."

"Nevertheless," said Crick, throwing Parke a resentful glare, "we need that fence repaired."

"I believe Parke and his Italians will have it ready by noon, croquet or not, won't you, John."

"Certainly, Mr. Andrews," said Parke, "We'll have it ready."

"You see," said Andrews, smiling at Crick, "ready by noon. Anything else, Morton?"

"No," said Crick, "that was all."

Crick ended the conversation with a respectful nod to Andrews, after which, his eyes sank back into his skull. He gave Parke a grimace and walked off quickly, and a bit more quietly, to the Clubhouse.

"Don't worry about him," Andrews said, once Crick had cleared the bridge. "You don't work for him."

"Don't I work for all the Club members?" said Parke.

"Technically you do," said Andrews, "But I assure you, don't worry about Morton Crick."

Even with Andrews's reassurance, Parke couldn't help but be concerned. He took his new position very seriously, and he wanted all of the members to be aware of his enthusiasm. After his first major improvement, installing new water pipes in the second-floor guest rooms, he had gathered a few of the members to witness the operation of a flush-toilet. He pulled the chain, and proudly pointed to the water as it flowed from the cistern, swirled around the commode, and disappeared down the drain. Morton Crick couldn't help bursting his bubble in front of the group by saying, as he unbuttoned his britches, "Wonderful job, John. Now, won't you all leave me in peace so I can put this device to good use."

Parke shook off Crick's intrusion on the bridge and asked Andrews if he could have a look at the dam's original construction

17

plans. Once he determined where the dam was flawed, he could make specific plans for repairs, and improve the water control and flooding issues at the same time.

"If there are any documents of interest to you, they would be in the office," Andrews said, "I'm not sure what you'll find, but you're welcome to have a look."

"Thank you, Mr. Andrews."

"It's Charles."

"Thank you, Charles," said Parke, acknowledging Andrews's request to make their relationship less formal.

After a short moment of silence, Parke looked out over the enormous reservoir. "Jesus," he said, "that's still an awful lot of water to hold back."

Andrews looked at the dam. "Indeed it is."

3

Ben came off the bridge and pedaled up the stone-paved road, weaving his two-wheeler through a grove of pines until he reached the clearing in front of the Clubhouse. He bounced across the cobblestone driveway and saw a man in brown overalls sitting on the wheel of an ice wagon, kicking his heels against the wooden spokes and chewing on a piece of straw. A thick brown tarpaulin covered a mound in the wagon bed, and nests of straw were tucked around the sides. Ben shot past the man, dropping his bicycle next to the porch stairs and hurrying into the Clubhouse through a small door marked Employee Entrance.

Except for an icebox against the far wall, the perimeter of the utility room was lined with shelves crammed full of pots, pans, dinner plates, dining utensils, cutlery, and cleaning supplies which included an aromatic jug of carbolic acid. The open container of disinfectant gave the room the sweet, tarry fragrance of perfume. Opposite a small closet, with one of John Parke's flush-toilets inside, an open doorway led into the kitchen.

Ben flung his knapsack on the shelf and went straight to the commode, leaving the door wide open. He sat and sighed in relief, staring at the envelope poking through a hole in his knapsack. He finished his business, tossed his scarf atop the knapsack, and reached for a long-sleeve white coat hanging from a hook on the toilet-room door. He was putting on the coat when the man from the ice wagon flung open the back door.

"Are you gonna take this ice, or not?"

Ben spun around. "What?"

"Ice," the man said. "For the ice box?"

"Yeah, right. Bring it in."

The man laughed, chewing his straw, obviously not interested in doing more work than necessary. "You want it, you come get it," he said, pointing to a thin hand-truck next to the ice box. "And I'd use that stack cart over there, if I were you."

Ben grabbed the cart and followed the man to the wagon.

The man slid out a sheet of plywood from the wagon bed and set it over the stairs. He climbed onto the wagon and threw back the tarpaulin, uncovering several columns of block-ice with tuffs of straw stuffed in between. He grabbed one of the blocks and handed it to Ben.

The weight of the block pulled Ben forward. He shuffled his feet, clutching the frozen brick against his chest for balance. "These are heavy."

The man laughed. "Five-gallon ice blocks, forty pounds each, wouldn't think water would weigh so much, would ya."

Ben turned to set the ice on the cart and the block slipped out of his hands and smashed onto the drive. He knelt and put the broken pieces onto the cart.

"You can't use that one," the man said, "not with all that dirt and mud all over it. I'll have to charge you for an extra one, now."

"How much?" Ben said.

"Two cents."

Ben reached into his pocket and pulled out an empty hand.

"Ah, hell," the man said, "I'll tell my boss it fell off the wagon. But if you drop another one... you're payin'."

Ben prepared himself with a slight bend in his knees. "I'll be careful."

The man handed him another block. Ben rested it on his shoulder, letting his legs absorb the weight. With a firm grip, and all the agility he could muster, he pivoted and set the block gently on the nose of the cart, a perfect placement.

Three more bends and pivots and Ben had four blocks stacked

neatly on top of one another. He moved around, gripped the cart with both hands, and tilted back the load. "It's too heavy," he said with a grunt.

The blocks began to slide, and the man hopped off the wagon, realigning the blocks and helping Ben tilt the cart backward. "Put your foot under the wheel," he said, "and pull it back."

Ben wedged his foot under the steel wheel, found his balance, and carefully tilted the cart. He pulled it slowly up the plywood ramp, and the man guided him into the utility room.

After the cart was set safely next to the ice box, the man wiped his brow, went back to his wagon, and rode away.

Ben transferred the first block from the cart to the ice box. His shoulder hunched forward and the block slipped. He straightened his back, bent his knees, and stabilized the block, hoisting it onto the top shelf. He set the other three in place, a bit more respectful of their weight, and when he'd finished, he twisted his body at the waist to work out the kink in his back.

He peeked into the kitchen. A combination of wall lamps and windows lit the room. Saucepans and stock pots, organized according to size, were stacked atop a long L-shaped table wedged in the near corner of the room. Barrels were shoved underneath with labels: sugar, salt, vinegar and flour. A copper saucepan simmered on the stove as Jean Pierre worked at the large wooden table that occupied the center of the room. Spread around the edge of the table was a collection of cutting tools, several jars of spices, and a few bunches of fresh herbs. The work table was a palette for Jean Pierre's culinary artistry, worn down and scarred from the cutting and chopping of many knives. He was using it now to slice a block of goose liver pâté into neat, uniform squares.

The tall, well-groomed Jean Pierre was trim and good looking, not at all what the diners expected to see when he emerged from the kitchen to receive their welcomed compliments. He kept his person and his kitchen unusually clean, and was seldom seen without his embroidered, bleached-white chef's coat and pleated toque.

When Ben came into the kitchen, Jean Pierre was at the work

table holding the copper saucepan tight against his hip while he whisked the viscous gelatin. "There you are," he said in a heavy French accent, "Where have you been?"

"Stocking the ice box. Just finished loading it in now."

Jean Pierre squeezed the corners of his mouth, tipping the curled ends of his wiry mustache up and down like a see-saw. "I tell you not to be late again."

"I got here on time," said Ben. "Had to wait for the ice man to settle his horse before we could unload."

Jean Pierre ran the whisk around the edge of the saucepan and poured the aspic into a shallow tray. "Take this to the ice box," he said, "carefully."

Ben carried the tray to the utility room and slid it into the ice box. As he returned, he glanced at the letter protruding from the torn corner of his knapsack. Maybe, he thought, he could ask Jean Pierre for a quick break so he could open it. Better not to ask, he'd only been at work for ten minutes.

Jean Pierre tidied up the wooden work surface. "Get me the oval platters," he said, "We need them for the pâté."

Ben started for the utility room. "No," said Jean Pierre, pointing in the other direction. "From the storage room. The storage room. Oval platters."

Ben left the kitchen through a pair of swinging wooden doors, hand-carved and painted bright white. He paused on his way down the hall and surveyed the dining room. The tables had been set with crisp white linen, polished silverware, and large white plates with the Club's insignia stamped on the rims. Freshly cut flowers in crystal vases sprang up from between the glassware, and Ben's eyes drifted over the black-eyed susans and sweet williams to the shiny black Steinway by the windows. If the luncheon finished on time, he might have a good hour to play before the men returned from their hunting excursion.

Ben returned to the kitchen with the platters. He set them on the work table next to the squares of pâté, and his thoughts drifted back to the piano. He began a Chopin waltz in his head.

"I will show you how to arrange the plate now," said Jean Pierre.

Ben would have liked the waltz better had Chopin begun in C major. Spending the entire introduction lingering in A minor seemed too depressing.

"Allo," said Jean Pierre, rapping his knuckles on the tabletop.

"What did you say?" said Ben, the third beat of his waltz cut short.

"I said, I will show you how to arrange the pâté."

"I'm sorry," said Ben, "I'm just a little distracted."

Jean Pierre gave Ben a knowing look and pinched off a bit of pâté with his fingers. "Ah... a woman," he said, twirling the end of his thin moustache with the goose fat.

"It's not a woman," said Ben.

Jean Pierre twirled harder. "A man?"

Ben straightened his coat and puffed out his chest. "It's a letter. In my knapsack."

"Ah, then a letter from a woman."

Ben closed his eyes and shook his head. "No. And not from a man either. It's from a music school in New York. Been waiting for it for nearly three months, and it finally arrived this morning."

A small door at the far side of the kitchen opened, and Morton Crick strolled over to where Jean Pierre and Ben were working. Even though Ben had worked at the Clubhouse for almost three years, he and Crick had never spoken. Crick seldom made an effort to interact with the hired help.

"Mornin', Jean Pierre," said Crick, bending over and sniffing the pâté. "Smells wonderful. What is it?"

"Des galettes, avec un morceau du merde," said Jean Pierre, running the words together quickly, his fingers held to pursed lips, the international sign for delicious.

"Delightful," said Crick, inhaling deeply.

"I am happy you like it," said Jean Pierre. "Now, if you will excuse us, we must finish preparing for the luncheon."

"Of course," said Crick, acting as if leaving was his idea. "Please carry on, then."

23

Crick went back into the office, and Ben looked at Jean Pierre with a curious grin. "What does 'day galet avek oon morso doo merd' mean?"

Jean Pierre snickered. "Crackers, with a piece of shit."

Ben laughed. "I suppose it's true what they say, everything sounds better in French."

"Sounds, looks, feels," said Jean Pierre, "I miss it every day."

The two continued working at the table, transforming the empty platters into an enticing display of pâté and brined gherkins.

"Why did you leave?" asked Ben.

Jean Pierre glanced down at his name embroidered on the pocket of his chef's coat. He rubbed at the fancy letters with his fingertips. "Opportunity," he said.

"And you couldn't find that where you lived?"

"Perhaps. But something told me it was time to...as you say, 'test the water'. Comprendre?"

Ben nodded

"So," said Jean Pierre, "Tell me about this music school."

"I've always wanted to study music," said Ben. "Playing the piano is the only thing I was ever any good at."

"I have heard you play, it sounds very good. But why do you need to go to this music school if you already know how to play?"

Ben thought for a moment. "You know I get to play with the musicians that come for the entertainment," he said, "when they're practicing, that is."

Jean Pierre bobbed his head in assent.

"They say I'm pretty good and all, but that I need experience and inspiration. I figure going to the academy is my best bet at finding it, since I haven't seen either of those things here."

"I see," said Jean Pierre. "And I believe you should do just that. But first, go and experience getting the aspic from the ice box. And bring that letter. We will see, right now, what you will do."

Ben went to the utility room and returned with the chilled aspic and the letter.

Jean Pierre cut the aspic in a crisscross pattern. He traded the knife for a spatula and flipped the cluster of the translucent diamonds onto the table and arranged them between the pâté and the pickles. "I will finish the platters," he said, "and you will read the letter to me."

Ben ripped open the envelope and pulled out a long sheet of paper.

"What does it say?" said Jean Pierre, interlacing the gelatin with the goose fat. "Read it to me. Stop staring, read it, read it."

Ben cleared his throat and gave Jean Pierre his best dictation, pronouncing the long words syllable by syllable.

TO ALL INTERESTED PARTIES
THE NEW YORK CITY ACADEMY OF MUSIC WILL HOLD AN
OPEN ENROLLMENT
ON JUNE 5, OF THIS YEAR
QUALIFIED APPLICANTS MUST BE PREPARED TO MAKE TUITION
AT THE ACADEMY CONSERVATORY
5TH AVENUE AND 12TH STREET, NEW YORK CITY, NEW YORK
Respectfully, Frank Damrosch (signed in ink)

"Does this mean I am a qualified applicant, or an interested party?"

"To me," said Jean Pierre, "it means you are interested, and qualified. You will go there, and you will be accepted."

"I don't know," said Ben, "June fifth is only two weeks from now, and New York City is a long way away."

A murmur of soft voices floated into the kitchen. Ben peeked over the swinging doors at a fluttering cluster of ostrich feathers. The women were filing into the dining room and settling into their seats around the fancy tables. A group of tuxedoed waiters shuffled past the women like a colony of mustached penguins and burst through the swinging doors. They raced past Ben, retrieved the platters, and waddled back to the dining room.

"New York? A long way away?" said Jean Pierre, "Nonsense. With a three-dollar train ticket, you could be there tomorrow. If this is what you want, you must go."

"What about my job? And my father? I know it would be difficult for him if I left."

"Not good enough reasons. Your job is just that, a job. You must do what you love. And as for your father, I wouldn't know. I never had one."

Jean Pierre took a garlic clove and flattened it on the table with the side of his butcher's knife. He directed Ben as he peeled and chopped. "Hand me that pan," he said, motioning to the cast iron skillets stacked on the corner table.

Ben grabbed the cleanest one.

"Not that one," said Jean Pierre. "Too new, too clean, worthless to me. Get me an older one, one of the seasoned pans."

Ben exchanged the new pan for one of the aged, weathered pans, and gave it to Jean Pierre.

The pan was blackened and burnt, coated with the remnants of the many recipes that had graced its surface. "You see?" said Jean Pierre, pointing to the bottom of the pan with the tip of the butcher's knife. "This one is seasoned. Food prepared in this pan cannot help but taste wonderful."

A waiter appeared at the swinging doors and called into the kitchen, "Les femmes demandent le chef."

"Une minute," Jean Pierre replied.

Jean Pierre dropped a stick of butter in the pan, set the pan on the stove, and added a scoop of the chopped garlic. Once the garlic had turned a speckled brown, he poured in a generous amount of white wine. As the mixture simmered, he dumped in a handful of large snails, shell and all.

"What is that?" asked Ben, scrunching his face.

Jean Pierre wriggled his moustache. "Escargot."

Jean Pierre added a pinch of salt, a few turns from the pepper mill, and a sprinkling of chopped parsley. "Ah...smell," he said, waving his hand in big circles above the bubbling mixture. He plucked one of the snails from the pan, twisted the meat out with a thin fork, and presented it to Ben.

Ben turned his head.

Jean Pierre moved the fork closer to Ben's mouth.

With eyes closed, Ben accepted the fork with the shriveled green snail on the end. Though the slippery morsel chewed like gristle, the taste was actually quite pleasant. The only flavor Ben could really discern was that of the garlic and the wine. "Not bad," he said.

Jean Pierre poured the rest of the shells, along with the boiling liquid, into a fancy porcelain bowl. "You see," he said, "Delicious. Now, I must go. My audience awaits. In a short while, the waiters will bring the plates. You clean the plates and straighten up the kitchen, and then you can play your piano until the men invade the lounge. Bonne? Au revoir."

Jean Pierre left the kitchen through the swinging doors with his arm held high, the fancy bowl resting on his fingertips.

Ben took a sip of water and swooshed it around to loosen the bits of chewy snail lodged between his teeth. After spitting out the remnants of the escargot, he picked up the envelope and squeezed at the bulge in the corner until the item slid out into his hand.

It was a lapel pin, about the size of a half-dollar, perfectly round and painted shiny gold. There was a black music note in the center, and in small black letters around the edge, the words New York Academy of Music. He held it over his head and rubbed the smooth surface with his thumb, admiring it the way an assayer might do when examining a precious stone. Pleased with its authenticity, he unhooked the clip and pinned the badge to his shirt.

4

The Club members who preferred a greater level of privacy when visiting the lake summered at the custom cottages built between the pines just beyond the boathouse – large two-stories, perched on the hillside, a stone's throw from the shore. After their morning hunt, the men would gather there under one of the covered porches, tipping back what was left in their hip flasks and arguing over who shot the largest buck before staggering down the boardwalk to the Clubhouse.

The only activity now on the grounds was a group of Italians dismantling the unused croquet equipment on the sporting field. One of the younger laborers held a small mallet in his hand and was jumping about, whacking the balls with poor aim at a wooden crate that had been tipped on end. An older Italian swiped the mallet and tossed it to another, and the two men taunted the boy with a game of keep-away. The boy hopped back and forth, spinning round in an attempt to steal the mallet until he became so dizzy he fell to the ground. Watching the boy struggle reminded Ben of his awkward adolescent years at the one-room schoolhouse in East Liberty.

At recess, when the children played kick the can or snap the whip, Ben was the one whose kick missed the can and whose body was snapped from the whip. Once, in a game of hide and seek, he thought he had chosen the best hiding spot ever, but after spending an hour and a half beneath the porch stairs, he realized the other children had simply forgot to look for him.

When a game called baseball came to town, all of the boys wanted to play. Ante-over and leap frog were replaced by a ball and a bat. Ben was determined to make friends with the new sport. He tried to pitch the ball, but he threw so wildly, no one was able to hit. He tried to catch the ball, but his lanky arms flailed as if he were swatting flies. And when he tried to hit, a fast-pitch caught him right on the knuckles. So instead of joining the rest of the boys outside, he spent his recesses inside the schoolhouse, sitting at his desk and listening to Miss Murray play the piano.

Miss Murray was in her early twenties, but she seemed much older to a ten year old. Matted black curls framed a pair of sweet, soothing eyes and a tight smile that could be turned down in an instant to discipline unruly behavior. One afternoon, during a lonely recess, she stopped playing and sat down next to Ben.

"Let me see your hands," she said, turning his palms up. "Long, thin fingers, I see. Not made for shooting marbles." She turned his palms down and Ben's fingers draped over hers. "And definitely not made for baseball."

She led Ben to the piano and set his hands on the keys. "These are the hands of a pianist," she said. She took a long brown feather, with a patch of white at the tip, and waved it like a baton. "This is how you play, like the golden eagle, thin, and light as the air."

At first, Ben was nervous during his recess piano lessons. But the more time he spent with Miss Murray, the more comfortable he became. He learned quickly, and was soon playing full pieces in front of the class. And although the baseball players snickered, Miss Murray would always stand next to him with her encouraging smile, waving her golden eagle feather to the beat.

Ben left the piano, and Miss Murray, at sixteen, when his father was transferred to River Fork as foreman of The Morton Crick Foundry. Ben tried to make new friends, but when he discovered River Fork's favorite past time was also baseball, he searched for other ways to occupy his time.

The job at the River Fork Clubhouse rewarded him when he saw the perfect piano sitting in the corner of the dining room. When he was hired, he agreed to give up half his weekly salary for the chance to practice on it once a day. Instead of a pal who could pitch and play second base, the Steinway became his new best friend.

Ben's mind raced back to the present, and after checking the cottages once more, he went inside the dining room and sat at the piano, a nine-foot grand painted obsidian black, buffed to a glossy shine, and tuned to perfect pitch. With the lid raised, it looked like a giant, black butterfly opening its wings. Some days, he imagined himself flying with it out the window, over the lake, and beyond the hills.

Ben raised the fallboard and removed the red velvet scarf covering the keys. He retrieved a small metronome from his knapsack and set it beside him on the bench. After a few minutes of scales and finger exercises, he took the printed notes of a Beethoven Sonata to the keys with a strict adherence to the 'tick-tock' of the metronome – right hand cadenza up, then rest, left hand cadenza down, then rest, quarter-notes on the beat, eighth-notes in between.

The notes were correct, and in perfect time, but the mechanical melody made him stop. His hands felt heavy on the keys, like the ice blocks he had lifted earlier that morning, cold, and difficult to control.

He went to his knapsack, took out a long brown feather, and set it in the crease between the pages. "Light as the golden eagle," Miss Murray would have told him. He let out a deep breath, drifted into fond memories of East Liberty, and let his hands glide lightly across the keys. His new melody found its way onto the patio deck, and out of the corner of his eye, he saw Sarah Ann and Louise Andrews strolling down the boardwalk and stopping in front of the big windows to listen.

5

Percival Marsh was twelve years old when one of the bricklayers told him there had been an accident at the construction site and his father had been killed. His sisters broke down in a trio of sobbing. His mother, sick with a disease no doctor could diagnose, sat in her rocking chair, stoic and unmoved. Even though two other men, sober men, had also died when the roof-rafters of the Mayfield/Jones Building collapsed, Percival always thought things might have been different had his father not been stricken with such a fondness for drink. Percival never forgot the smell, for when they wheeled his father to the house that evening, dead for six hours, the body still reeked of whiskey.

Maybe this was why Percival could detect a liquor-tainted canteen from across the foundry floor. Maybe this was how he could smell the breath of a drunken laborer whose mouth was covered with a water-soaked handkerchief. Maybe this was why he kept such a keen eye on his crew.

He started his morning in the usual way, sniffing water flasks and spot-checking the steam engines. Afterward, he went to the office and reviewed the safety logs. It had been three weeks since the last factory accident, and he was surprised when he heard the piercing wail of the mill whistle. Recently, the men were getting careless, preoccupied with talk of unionizing, or exhausted from working too many 'long turns' – all day Sunday and into Monday morning. He did his best to look after the men, especially his friend Don Crawford, one of the engine oilers. Crawford's presence at the foundry was cherished. Pourers and pullers alike rejoiced when he came onto the floor. It meant time to rest, since the only break for food or water came when the steam engines needed maintenance or oiling.

Percival had seen Crawford earlier that morning out by the tracks talking to a group of day laborers gathered behind the foundry looking for work. Men in dirty brown overalls and equally filthy caps walked up and down the rails, peeking into the mills and trying to get the attention of a foreman while those who had been seeking jobs the night before lay sleeping under wool blankets atop the ballast of crushed rock.

One of the scruffy men broke off his conversation with Crawford and approached the only man whose face and overalls weren't covered with soot.

"Anything for us, today?" he asked Percival. "We'll take anything you got."

Percival dusted off his bowler. His beardless face made it hard for him to negotiate with authority, but he tried to be firm. "I've got two tons, needs to be loaded by midday," he said, replacing his hat and pointing to a stack of razor-wire piled alongside an empty flatbed. "Pay's a dollar."

The laborer swept his hand around his mouth and stared at the barbed wire, groaning in contemplation. "I got a dozen men here," he said, "A dollar ain't enough."

"The way I see it," Percival said, "since half your men are sleepin', you've only got six. Anyway, I don't care how you split it up, the pay's a dollar. You can do it yourself and keep it all, if it suits you."

"I'll kick in a dime," Crawford said.

Percival turned to Crawford. "That's comin' outta your pocket."

Crawford nodded and called to the man. "Take these," he said, tucking his rusted oil can under his arm and tossing the man a pair of heavy mitts.

"Thanks again, mister."

"You didn't have to do that," Percival said to Crawford as the men began loading the flatbed. "They would have worked for a dollar."

Crawford took a soiled handkerchief from his hip pocket and wiped a layer of soot from his forehead. "That group's been hanging around here for two weeks," he said, "and nary a day of work."

"That's what they choose to do," said Percival, "What about you and your family? How many kids you got now, six?"

"Soon to be seven, Mary's pregnant again."

"Again?" said Percival. "I can't imagine you got much time for impregnatin', less Mary's got an oil can of her own with somethin' special in it."

Crawford laughed. "Even workin' six days and a long turn," he said, "there's still time for love makin'." He stuck the oil can in front of his crotch and squeezed out a stream of chain lubricant.

Percival shook his head. "Yeah, well I wouldn't know."

The day laborers had formed a bucket brigade and were passing rings of wire when one of the pullers came out of the foundry. He was dressed like all the other factory men, soot-covered cap and dirty bib-and-brace overalls pulled over two pairs of long johns. A chaw of leaf tobacco made his cheek bulge like a chipmunk's. He spat out a mouthful of black juice, rubbed it into the mud with his boot, and wiped his mouth with his sleeve. "What's this bunch doin' loadin' wire?" he said, spitting again. "I've got a full crew in here, Marsh."

"Your crew ain't got time to load, Morgan," said Percival, "I've got an order for two more tons of wire. Need it by the end of the week. Stock handler says the material will be here within the hour. You'uns kick-in ten cents apiece for them laborers, and maybe Crawford will shut down that engine for another oiling, give you'uns a decent break." Percival wagged a finger at Crawford, "And make sure you shut it down. I don't want to see them gears eat up another oil can."

"Speakin' of decent breaks," Morgan said, spitting, rubbing and wiping, "You give Marsh the list?"

Crawford stared at his feet the way a boy does when his mother asks him about his marks at school. "Not yet."

"Ah, hell," said Percival, "You signed it, didn't you."

"I had to." Crawford exchanged his handkerchief for a folded square of paper and waved it in front of Percival's face. "Everyone's name is on here, Crick can't fire us all."

Percival put his hands on his hips. "He can, and he will," he said. "You've read rule number nine. Hell, it's posted all over the shop floor. Anyone who even mentions the idea of unionizing will be 'promptly discharged'." Percival wrinkled his forehead and stared at Crawford. "You really want to risk your job over this? You get fired here and you won't be able to find work at any other mill in the valley, maybe even the state. And that goes for you too, Morgan."

"God damn it, Marsh," said Morgan, "We got to do somethin'. No way we can keep workin' like this. Twelve hour shifts, seven days a week in these hell holes? Take a look around, ain't no one here over forty." Morgan pulled up his sleeve, exposing a road map of lumpy razor cuts on his forearm. "Ten dollars a week ain't worth this. And I heard you the other day, Crawford, sounded like you were coughing up a lung." Morgan flapped his arm and the dirty sleeve fell to his wrist. "If we don't demand some better wages and workin' conditions, getting fired will be the least of our worries."

The day laborers stopped loading when they heard the word, 'fired', and looked over at the three men.

Percival walked Crawford and Morgan away from the flatbed. "It ain't that I disagree with you," he said, speaking in a soft whisper. "I know things got to change. But now ain't the right time. Hell, look what's happenin' over in Homestead. Crick's got them workers locked up like prisoners. For all we know, this load of wire is being shipped over there to make sure none of them try to slip out when the guards ain't lookin'." Percival felt the sting of chimney soot in his eyes, and he moved the trio further from the mill. "I even heard the governor's threatened to call in the State Militia, for Christ's sake. Crick won't think twice about firing all of you just to nip this thing in the bud. And the worst of it is he'll have me do it." He swiped the letter from Crawford's hand. "Now get back to work, both of you. Those rods should be here any minute. And Crawford, I think that steam engine is gonna need another oiling, soon."

Morgan and Crawford went into the foundry and Percival unfolded the paper. Sure enough, all the melters, puddlers, casters, drawers, and oilers had signed it. At the top of the page were the words Petition for Inclusion in the Amalgamated Association of Iron and Steel Workers. Underneath were a few sentences requesting acceptance into the union, followed by a list of names, one hundred twenty-three in all.

Percival looked at the day laborers who had loaded half the stack of razor-wire onto the flatbed. Out of the six men that had started the job, only four were still working. The two quitters were sitting on the ballast, their hands and forearms cut-up and bleeding from the sharp barbs.

Percival tucked the letter in his pocket and headed into the foundry. A blast of hot air hit his face as he walked into the open-ended mill, a two-thousand foot long, thirty-foot high structure of steel girders and corrugated sheet metal atop a floor of poured cement, stained black from burnt metal and tobacco spit. At the far end, giant egg-shaped Bessemer hearths filled with molten pig iron shot vermillion plumes of fire toward the ceiling, scorching the underside of the creased metal roof. Just below the roof, giant hooks powered by massive steam engines rode on hanging rails, carrying iron cauldrons to the casters who poured the liquid metal into rail-spike and fishplate molds. The busy room echoed with the clanking din of the steam engines and the pounding on the casting molds, and Percival covered his ears.

He hurried to the office, wondering how he should approach Crick about the union petition. He could start off by inquiring about the status of the Homestead strike and find out Crick's current position on the matter. Then he would have a better idea of how to bring up the notion of creating a set of labor standards for the River Fork foundry. Talk of unionizing was grounds for termination, and if Crick was still hell-bent on keeping the Union out of it, Percival would change the subject and remind Crick of his request for promotion to junior executive, a position Percival had applied for earlier that year. The company preferred to promote from within, and having climbed the corporate ladder from common laborer to foreman, junior executive was Percival's next logical step. Twenty years in the factories was taking its toll on him the same way it had been beating down on the rest of the men, and the executive position would get him out of the foundry.

The office was next to one of the Bessemer hearths, and the bitter smell of melting iron burned Percival's lungs. Workers around the base of the cauldron were shooting blasts of compressed air into the open hearth, and bits of slag were spewing over the top and falling to the ground like fiery rain. Percival stood before the office door, the letter clutched behind his back. After taking in a hot breath of vaporized coke, he exhaled strongly, knocked twice, and entered.

The office was empty. He closed the door and sat behind the heavy oak desk. Though he shared the office with Crick, and was allowed to handle paperwork and hold employee meetings there, he contributed nothing to its décor. The desktop was covered with Crick's regatta trophies and archery medals. On the walls were photographs of Crick posing confidently outside his steel mills and flaunting his hunting trophies in front of the River Fork Clubhouse.

Percival had been foreman for three years and had never been invited to the prestigious Clubhouse. At one time, he had considered asking Ben to take him just to see what it looked like on the inside. But he wouldn't need Ben's help after his request for junior executive was approved. As an executive, he would be asked to attend as a guest, or better yet, join as a member.

Mixed with the clutter on the desk was a large envelope. Percival set down the petition letter and picked it up. Typed on the front, in bold black letters, were the words Junior Executive Job Description and Contract, the employment package Crick will present to the new junior executive. He looked up at a photograph of Crick standing on the porch of the Clubhouse, one hand holding a cigar, the other resting firmly against the front door, guarding the mystery that lay behind it. Percival imagined standing at the door step and wondered if the members had to knock to get inside.

He stared at the envelope, thinking about all the time he had given to the company, the dedication he had shown by moving to River Fork, and the perks that came with the executive position – the comfortable hours, the private office, the Club membership, the security of a steady salary. When he received the promotion, he and Ben would move out of the low-rent company-shack and buy a plot. He'd build a nice brick two-story in town, maybe next to Morrell's place on Main Street, or Mellon's place on Prospect Hill, painted bright white, with a flower garden and shade trees.

Percival's dream vanished when the foundry whistle sounded. He dropped the envelope and ran out of the office to find a group of workers huddled around one of the steam engines. A man's hand was wedged between the gears and the engine chain. "Oh shit, Crawford," he shouted, running to his friend.

Blood was gushing from the wound in pulsating spurts. Crawford was gripping his arm at the wrist, blubbering in a ceaseless moan of obscenities while the rest of the workers stood motionless, staring at the man caught in the machine.

"Shut it off. Shut it off," hollered Percival.

The chain was wrapped around Crawford's wrist, and even with the engine stopped, the wheel continued to turn, pulling his arm further into the gearwheel. Percival motioned to a pile of ingots stacked next to the engine and yelled at the workers. "Quick, take one of those rods and set it against the pinion."

Three men grabbed a length of steel, lifted it onto their shoulders, and lined it up with the gearwheel.

"Now shove," Percival commanded, "Push. Push."

Three more men positioned themselves behind the rod and shoved. Slowly, the gearwheel reversed. Percival gently pulled on Crawford's arm as the machine released his hand.

Crawford tucked his bloodied, disfigured hand under his armpit, gritting his teeth and sobbing.

37

"I'm takin' him to the hospital," Percival said, "You'uns keep on workin'."

The men stood silent.

Then, as if nothing too important had happened, Morgan fed the chain onto the gearwheel and signaled to one of the pullers to restart the engine.

As Percival led Crawford out of the foundry, he saw Morgan eyeing Crawford's rusty oil can lying in the pool of blood beneath the engine. Percival watched as Morgan picked it up, spat out a splash of tobacco juice, and went back to work.

6

It wasn't until Percival reached the end of Main Street that he realized he was still clutching the sleeve of Crawford's bloodied long-johns. The doctor had cut it off with the same razor-sharp surgeon's knife he'd used to remove what was left of his friend's shredded hand. Percival had plenty of work waiting for him at the foundry, but the foundry was not where he was headed.

The woodshop was just up the hill from Main Street, on a road with no name. Painted dull green, its low-pitched roof was flattened on top, giving it the shape of a small barn. A layer of factory soot covered the peeling walls, thick enough for boys to scribble their names in, and for girls to draw hearts around them and write their names alongside. A pair of wide double-doors marked with flat-timbered X's faced the street. To the right was a smaller door with a pinewood shingle hanging overhead, the words Clem's Woodworks carved into each side by the shop's owner.

Percival knocked on the small door out of courtesy, and entered. A hodgepodge of chairs, bedroom pieces, and dining tables filled the room. He craned his neck over an oak dresser and peered toward the back of the shop.

"Percival," a voice said, "Is that you?"

A tall man in baggy coveralls came out from behind an unfinished cabinet. His long, stringy hair was pulled back and tied with a small cord of twine, exposing the tan, leathery skin of his forehead. The size of his ears and the speckling of moles around his sagging cheeks gave Percival the impression he was in his mid-seventies.

There were no bells or chimes on the front door like at Howell's General Store, but James Clement always knew when someone entered his shop. Maybe, Percival thought, it was because of his big ears.

"Afternoon, Clem," said Percival. "Got time for a visit?"

Clem invited Percival in with a hand-wave. He took a ball of steel wool from the work table and bent back to the cabinet. "But I do have to finish this piece today," he said. "Might even try to give it a bit of stain and shellac, too, take advantage of this dry heat that's come up all of the sudden. I've been puttin' off poor Mrs. Green's cabinet now for two weeks, but you know how stain and shellac don't like the humidity, bubbles up on the wood, somethin' awful."

Percival walked cautiously to the back of the shop, minding his steps around the unorganized arrangement of bare-wood desks, dressers, and armoires. He lifted his feet to keep from kicking up the layer of sawdust and wood shavings covering the floor, Crawford's bloody sleeve still dangling at his side. "I'd love to help," he said.

With the wide front pocket of his overalls stuffed full of small tools and rags, Clem looked like a skinny kangaroo. He stared at Percival holding the blood-stained long john. "Rough day at the foundry?" he said, reaching into his pouch and tossing Percival a tack cloth.

Percival shoved the bloodied sleeve into his hip pocket, and began wiping the cabinet in small deliberate circles with the tack cloth, cleaning off the dust and preparing the bare wood for a coat of stain. "Ol' Don Crawford went and got his hand cut off this morning. He tried oilin' the pinion wheel while the engine was still runnin'."

"He gonna be all right?"

"Doctor says he's fine. 'Cept now he's got only a stump for right hand. Won't be throwin' the ball around with his kids no more."

"Maybe he'll learn to be ambidextrous."

Percival shrugged. "Maybe."

Clem took a carving chisel from his kangaroo pouch, pried off the lid of a tin can, and stirred the mahogany colored sludge inside with a long rusted nail. The fumes escaped into the air.

Percival stepped back. "That's strong," he said, covering his nose. "Never seem to get used to it." He opened another set of barn doors, copies of the ones facing the street, and stepped out into Clem's backyard, filling his lungs with fresh air and gazing about the property.

Set a good distance from the shop, between two bushy maples, stood a pair of two-story homes with unfinished walls and shake roofs. To the right was a long wooden table with benches on either side, and next to it, atop a wooden sawhorse, was a large metal drum split open lengthwise, a metal grate set over the top. "You use that metal drum for cookin'?" Percival said, coming back into the shop. "Where'd you get that?"

"The men at that fancy Clubhouse asked me what I wanted for all the work I'd done, and I said a metal cookin' drum. A big one. And they obliged, being steel men and all."

"Nice. My son works up there."

"Right," said Clem, "How is Bennett anyway?"

"Still talkin' crazy 'bout goin' to New York. Waste of time if you ask me." Percival rolled up his sleeves and looked around, marveling at the quantity of Clem's inventory and spying a wicker bassinette hanging from the ceiling. "Don't know how that boy could count on supportin' a family by studying music."

Percival had the authority to speak about raising a family. After his father died, it was he, a twelve-year-old carpenter's apprentice, who had fed and clothed three sisters and a dying mother on a salary of only two dollars a week. Each time a sister married, Percival hoped the new brother-in-law would help add to the kitty, but as soon as the ring went on, the new brother and the new bride went away. Eventually, though not with a suitor of this world, so did his mother.

Clem dipped a rag into the tin can, soaking it with the black liquid. He worked the stain into the pristine pine, applying the color in smooth strokes and following the grain until the raw wood glowed a rich, mahogany brown. "Sometimes," he said, "you got to let the bird leave the nest. Make their own choices. And hope they're good ones like you taught 'em."

"Ben's still a boy."

"Is that so?" said Clem. "And how old were you when you got married?"

Percival answered reluctantly. "Nineteen."

"And you did all right, didn't you?'

Percival wilted and stared at the floor. He took a deep breath. "I'm still here, I suppose."

Clem put one hand on Percival's shoulder and lifted up his chin with the other so the two men looked eye to eye. "You never told Ben about his mother?"

Percival felt the urge to pull away. But Clem's touch soothed him, and he spoke remorsefully. "I told him she left us," he said, bowing his head. "I never thought it would do any good to tell him otherwise."

"He's old enough now."

"Maybe so. It just never seems to be the right time."

Clem went to the work bench and dipped his cloth into the tin can. "I think the right time is coming soon. Especially if he heads off to New York."

"Anyway, how's he gonna make do in New York City? He'll never be able to survive so far from home. They'll crush him in a place like that."

"He might surprise you. Besides, you'll never find out if you keep him sheltered here."

Percival grabbed his own stain-soaked rag and worked it into the inside corner of the cabinet, pressing down so hard his fingernails poked through the cloth and gouged the soft pine. He thought about what Clem had said, and wondered what it was Ben was really looking for, and why he had to leave River Fork to find it.

Clem grabbed Percival by the wrist and pulled him away from the cabinet. "First," he said, "you didn't want him to work at the foundry because it's too dangerous. Now, New York City is too far away. What's he supposed to do?"

Percival pulled away. "How 'bout minding his p's and q's at that Clubhouse and workin' his way up the company ladder to manager. Manager. Now that's a respectful, successful position."

"Like you've done at the foundry?"

"Damn right, and I'm about to make executive. I've become a part of that company. Almost twenty years. It's my life."

Clem nodded. "But you're not spendin' the rest of the day up there, you're spendin' it down here with me, burnin' your nose hair on shellac and messing your hands with wood stain."

"The foundry," Percival said, "is my job, my responsibility. Woodworking's just somethin' I enjoy doin'."

Clem looked at him with a soothing stare. "Shouldn't your life be something you enjoy doin'?"

Percival threw his staining rag onto the work bench. "Maybe so. But enjoyment don't pay the bills."

7

All was quiet except for the sound of a barking dog coming from somewhere in the street. Ben had heard its faint whimpering earlier that afternoon on his way home from the Clubhouse, probably a whippet or a coonhound.

He felt cold and cramped in his small bedroom, confined by its low sloped ceiling, bare walls, and un-planed pinewood floor. A rickety platform bed and a weathered nightstand sat on one side, a sitting desk that doubled as a chest of drawers on the other. Above the bed, an open window let in a misty breeze that cooled the room. He sat on his sagging mattress resting a cigar box on his lap. While growing up in East Liberty, he'd kept boyhood treasures in it, smooth skipping stones and squirming earthworms. Once, he'd used it to hide a frog he found in a nearby pond, but later that night, its incessant croaking gave it away, and his father made him return it to the lake.

There were no rocks, worms, or frogs in the box now. Instead, there was a folded letter from a music academy and thirty-three dollars. He figured forty would be enough for a train ticket, tuition, and maybe three months room and board somewhere close to the academy. After his savings ran out, he would get a job at a local restaurant or hotel. Jean Pierre had promised to write him a recommendation.

He set the box on his bed and peeked down at his music pin, admiring its shine and smooth surface while he contemplated a journey to New York. The whine of the dog came into the room,

44

and he propped himself up on his knees and scooted to the window. A reddish-orange burn filtered through the mixture of rain clouds and chimney smoke, and through the mist he saw his father coming slowly down the road. He closed the cigar box and slid it under his bed.

Downstairs, the front door opened and shut with a thud. "Bennett, you home?"

Ben hurried to his chest of drawers, more than a hundred pages of sheet music strewn atop it. Miss Murray had given them to him before he left East Liberty. "I've memorized them all," she had told him, "They won't do anyone any good hidden inside the piano bench." He put the pages into his knapsack, mindful not to rip or crease the thin parchment, and hid them under his bed.

He clomped downstairs to a single room illuminated by an oil lamp hanging loosely from the ceiling. A round dining table and two high-backed chairs were the only furnishings, along with a cast iron stove and an oak icebox set against the far wall. The small fireplace kept them warm in winter, but recently, spring rain had found its way down the chimney and soaked the floorboards, leaving a dank, musty odor inside the room. He saw his father outside the back door tossing something into the scullery.

After a "whoosh" from the flush toilet, Percival came inside with a handful of twigs and a pine log. "You hungry?" he said, "I'm gonna heat up some stew."

Ben sat at the table. "I ate at the Clubhouse."

Percival shoved the log and the twigs into the belly of the stove. "I forgot," he said lighting a fire, "You eat like a king up there."

Ben laughed. "If kings eat leftover goose liver and aspic."

"High society food. Not too many folks in this town eat food like that." Percival opened the ice box and took out a cast iron pot and set it on the stove. "I see you're movin' up over there, climbing the company ladder, that's good."

Ben looked at his father, confused.

"The nametag," said Percival, pointing at Ben's chest. "They only give those to employees with potential."

45

Ben covered the pin with his palm and twisted it round. "It's not from the Club," he said. "It's a music pin, from the academy in New York I've been tellin' you about. Classes start in two weeks, and I want to go."

Percival put a finger to his lips and bent his ear to the window. "There's that barkin' again," he said, "heard it all the way home. I think its Miller's retriever from across the way."

Ben turned toward the front door and shook his head. "It's a coonhound," he said, "probably a stray, been wanderin' round town all afternoon."

Percival took a long wooden spoon and stirred the stew, now bubbling over the stove's fire that warmed the room. "We don't get strays around here," he said. "It's Miller's gun-dog, must be searchin' for a dead rabbit or a wild turkey." He checked the temperature of the stew with his finger and licked off the broth and wiped his finger on his trouserleg. "Suit yourself about supper. I've gotta eat, though, it's been a rough day."

Ben hoped for a more interested response from his father instead of a debate over the breed of a barking dog. The way his father had changed the subject reminded him of the time they spent Thanksgiving at Reverend Beale's home. After dinner, Mrs. Beale, who played the psalms at Sunday service, sat at the piano while Father Beale led Percival, Ben, and the Beale's three sons in a medley of standard hymns. While Percival complimented Mrs. Beale on her wonderful playing, Ben asked Father Beale if he could play. Before Ben made it through the introduction of a Chopin waltz, Percival and the rest of the group had wandered back to the table for pumpkin pie. When Ben finished, he expected at least some praise, but all his father said was, "Hurry up, Ben, you're missin' out on Mrs. Beale's fine pie."

This time Ben wasn't willing to give up. "So what about New York, Pa?"

"What about it?"

"New York. The music academy. I want to go."

"Waste of time goin' to New York," Percival said. "I've told you that already. Playing around on the piano is fun for impressin'

46

girls and all, but you'll never be able to support a family doin' it. Keep workin' that club-job of yours. Put in your time, and you can make manager. Manager of the River Fork Club." Percival wagged the dripping spoon at Ben. "Now that's a fine job. A secure job, impressive too, one that can support a family."

Ben wasn't concerned with impressing anyone, nor did he care too much about supporting a family. "Maybe I don't want to stay in River Fork," he said. "Maybe what's right for me ain't in this town. It's only New York, pa. It's really not that far away. I'd come back when there's a break in the classes, like at Easter, or at Christmas time. I wouldn't leave forever like mother did."

In his entire life, Ben had only seen two emotions in his father, 'everything's fine' and 'hoppin' mad.' He braced himself for the latter.

Percival threw the spoon to the floor and pointed a stiff finger at Ben. "Don't you ever talk about your mother like that," he said, "You never knew her. She was a fine woman. The best woman I ever knew." He picked up the spoon and used it to point again, the veins on his forehead bubbling under his skin like the boiling stew behind him. "Now I'm gonna get that promotion, and we're movin' to Main Street, not New York. You work at that Clubhouse, you put in your time there until they give a you pin to wear on your chest, and that's the last I'll hear of it."

The barking dog was much louder now, as if it were just outside the front door.

"Dammit, that dog," said Percival, "I'll shut that thing up myself. I'll give Miller a piece of my mind, too." He stormed out, leaving the pot of stew boiling on the stove.

Later that night, Ben lay in bed holding his music pin and staring up at the dark swirls running through the pinewood ceiling. Outside, the same dog was barking loudly. A stray, he thought, probably a whippet or a coonhound. He leaned over to his nightstand and blew out the candle. Two more weeks and he'd be in New York, and his father could have the house on Main Street and the River Fork Clubhouse all to himself.

8

Rain fell throughout the night, and by morning the roads were pitted with pools of sticky mud. Ben mounted his Safety Rover and pedaled hard between the puddles to where the factory homes ended and the road turned sharply toward the river. At the top of the hill, he peered through the stale greyness covering the town like cigar smoke over a poker table. Smoldering factory chimneys stabbed the landscape in two's and four's, surrounding the homes and buildings like inefficiently spaced prison bars. The view from Laurel Hill was a depressing sight. Ben had never seen it in any other way.

The trail into town was split down the middle by a ridge of patchy grass. He rode inside the wagon tracks through gusts of ash-filled wind. He squinted and kept his mouth shut tight, bouncing his bicycle over the muddy divots until he reached a stretch of level ground near James Clement's woodshop. The barn doors were propped open, and Clem was outside milling about the front of the shop.

"Fine day for a ride, ain't it," said Clem, his ponytail dangling against his back as he appraised the sky.

Ben hopped off his bicycle and wiped the stinging soot from his eyes. "Sure would be nice to see the sun now and then."

Nearby, a train raced alongside the river, and Clem waited for it to pass. "What brings you to my neck of the woods?" he said,

"You ain't returning that bicycle, are you? I told you it's yours to keep."

Ben recalled the first day he'd heard those words, after a long walk home from a trying day at the Clubhouse. He'd been dragging his feet in the dirt when he came upon Clem standing in the middle of the road. They walked together, Clem preaching words of encouragement until they reached the barn doors in front of the shop. "Workin' with people is tough," Clem said, disappearing behind a stack of piled wood. "Everyone's dealt a different hand. And how they play their cards has nothin' to do with you, so don't take it to heart. They say life's a journey, and I've got somethin' here that might make yours a little easier." He came out from behind the woodpile with a brand new bicycle. Ben never knew why, but after that day the weight of his modest troubles didn't seem as heavy.

Now, Ben gripped the handlebars and ran his fingers over the seat. "I wouldn't think of givin' it back," he said. "It's a Jim dandy. But the chain's stickin'. Can you take a look?"

Clem grabbed the bicycle by the seat and lifted the back wheel. He gave the pedal a hard push with his foot and the chain spun round with a series of loud clicks. "Looks like all she needs is a little gear grease," he said, dropping the wheel to the ground. "Why don't you take it up to your father? I'll bet he can fix her, lickety-split."

Ben took back the bicycle, his only possession of any monetary value, and something his father always seemed to forget he owned. If he took the bicycle to the foundry, his father would ask him again where he'd got it, and then he'd stare off into nowhere and ramble on about something he couldn't afford, like the new Victoria carriage Andrews rode around in. Ben would be back down the road with the broken bicycle before his father realized he was gone. "He's too busy. I don't want to trouble him."

Clem set one hand on his hip and scratched his chin with the other. "Give me a minute." He went inside and returned with a handful of gear grease. He bent down and spread it around the chain links. "Now give her a test ride," he said, wiping his hand on his overalls.

Ben rode around in a wide circle. The clicking sound was gone, and the chain spun freely around the gears. "Better now," he said, straightening out and heading down the road. "Thanks, Clem."

When Ben reached the drop-off toward Main Street he bore down hard, pumping his legs and picking up speed with the help of the freshly greased chain. Maybe, he thought, if he pedaled hard enough, he could make it all the way to New York.

In the spirit of River Fork's love for baseball, the natives called the porch benches in front of Henry Howell's General Store, 'the dugout'. It was the perfect place to gossip and discuss the town's affairs. The men would camp for hours, the lucky one arriving early, claiming the rocking chair and earning him the right to pick the conversation. The only hitch was that he'd better have something interesting to say, otherwise, he was sent back to the benches.

It was mid-morning, and the dugout was full. A quick breeze was blowing the smell of fresh Chase & Sanborn's across the porch, and the old-timers sat back in their seats, taking in deep breaths of the fresh-roasted beans.

"I thought that joker from the Tribune said a storm was comin'," the man in the rocking chair said, hoping the familiar talk of weather would pass muster with the group.

Someone in the dugout responded. "I read that, too. Ol' Jack Wisord says it's gonna be the biggest storm of the season. I heard it already stirred up a tornado along the Cottonwood."

"He says it's headed south," said another. "We don't need any more rain around here anyhow."

All heads turned when the screen door opened and Henry Howell stepped out onto the porch. A tall, sturdy man with a round face, he held a flat spatula in one hand and a folded up newspaper in the other. A soiled apron draped over his healthy belly and down to his knees. "You'uns fixin' to order any food?" he said. "Dry toast, griddle cakes?"

"I don't believe so, Howell," said the rocking chair man, a balled fist pressed to his stomach. "But I'll take some of that rheumatic oil you sell in there. I believe the omelet you made me yesterday has started my kidneys to fail."

The ribbing sparked a contagious laugh that spread down the length of the dugout.

"Now that's funny," said Howell, "But don't you know not to insult the cook before you order your food."

The laughter settled, and Howell had no takers for breakfast. He took the newspaper and slapped it against the shoulder of the old-timer closest to him. "Here," he said, "an out-of-towner left this. Thought it might keep you'uns busy for a while." The man took the paper and Howell pointed to the top of the page. "This article here might help stimulate the conversation."

The man on the bench followed Howell's finger and read aloud, "Decoration Day comes early for Cass City. On Thursday, a dinner will be served in the Red Front store by the wives...."

"Not that one, the one beneath it, the one about the weather." Howell shook his head and went back into the store.

As the old-timer searched the front page, Ben rode up on his Safety Rover and leaned it against the hitching post as if it were a horse. After greeting the men with a tug of his cap, he folded his arms over the stair rail and listened in on their conversation.

"The Cass City Enterprise," the man read, dropping the paper into his lap. "Cass City...where is that, Ohio?"

"Michigan," Ben said.

"Michigan, right," the man said, returning his attention to the Enterprise. "Say's here, the rainstorm on Sunday, I believe they mean yesterday, wouldn't you think?" Silence meant the rest of the men agreed. "Was a very severe one, as it was accompanied by both wind and hail, heavier than any time on record, but from all accounts it did more damage east and south of here." He set the paper in his lap again. "Michigan…ain't we east of Michigan?"

Ben lifted his head and grinned as the dugout mulled over River Fork's relative position to each of the Great Lakes. He waited for a lull in the grumbling. "Southeast."

"Yeah, don't you know your geography," another old-timer said, elbowing the newspaper-reader in the ribs. "Southeast, like the kid says."

The newspaper-man lifted a finger and plotted the course of the storm in the air. "That means it's headin' our way, don't it?"

"Straight our way," a woman said, trotting up the porch stairs in a fragrant burst of perfume. She stopped one step above Ben and leaned on the rail next to him, her eyes level with his, her wavy, ginger brown hair brushing against his shoulder. Ben couldn't help but stare.

"Operator in West Virginia says heavy rain flooded out the tracks from Parkersburg to Marietta. A tower operator along the Muskingum River confirmed it, says it's the worst storm she's ever seen. I'd be prepared to take cover when it moves into the valley."

The dugout went quiet save the slow creek of the rocking chair. The man with the newspaper swung his head toward the porch stairs. "Not sure I'd trust the opinion of a woman."

She looked at Ben, and Ben gave her a look that said he'd trust anything her pretty face had to say. The old-timer's insult seemed to have struck a nerve in her, and the wood began to creak beneath her fingers as she tightened her grip on the stair rail.

"But if you'd like to join the conversation," the old-timer said patting his knee, "I've got a good spot for you right here."

The woman's jaw clenched. She appeared to be formulating a response but she held it back. She whipped her head round and glazed the old man with a sarcastic grin. She'd chosen not to play into his game, which made Ben even more curious about who she was, and what was behind her smooth, olive skin and sweet honeysuckle scent.

"I'd offer you the rocking chair," the old-timer said, "but I don't think the slowpoke sittin' in it can move fast enough to vacate. You might end up squashin' him."

The rocking-chair man smiled and rubbed his palms together. "Fine by me."

The old-timers laughed until winded, exchanging elbow jabs and knee slaps.

Ben shook his head, hoping the woman would take notice of his disgust. When he saw she had hurried into the store, he scooted up the stairs after her while the old-timer with the newspaper caught his breath and read on about the Cass City cornet band and a ten-cent dinner at the Red Front store. The rest of the men leaned forward in their seats, craning for another look at the woman.

Ben slapped open the screen door and made his way past a big wooden display table piled high with hats, crockery, and cooking utensils. He slung his knapsack over a tall high-backed chair and sat at the counter. Howell's boy, Doc, came from the back room, a sack of flour resting on his shoulder. He dropped the bag next to a barrel of cider vinegar and cleared his throat.

"Good morning, sir, may I help you."

"My good man," said Ben, pushing his voice down deep, "One sarsaparilla, if you'd be so kind."

Doc shook his head. "All out, dear sir," he said, motioning to the amber Hutchison bottles lined up on the shelf behind the counter. "May I offer you an alternative?"

Ben pounded his fist. "Sarsaparilla. Now." He hopped off the stool and extended a straight arm at the clerk, pointing his hand like a gun. "Pow, pow, pow."

Doc slipped sideways and spun around, drawing his own finger-gun and firing back. The two boys ducked and dodged, exchanging fake pistol-fire and parroting quick bursts of exploding bullets and pinging ricochets until Ben bumped into the perfumed woman he'd followed into the store.

"Having fun, boys?" she said.

Ben regained his composure and assumed a proper stance.

Doc tucked in his shirt and stood up tall. "May I help you?"

The woman gazed around the room. "Work pants."

Doc replied straight-faced. "Along the back wall, ma'am."

Ben slunk with embarrassment back to the counter trying not to laugh. Doc shared his amusement only after the woman had disappeared behind a tall rack of woolen coats and trousers.

Doc straightened his cap, and his demeanor returned to store clerk. "How come you ain't workin' up at the Clubhouse today?"

Ben grabbed a seat at the counter. "They're all out on the lake with their brand new yachting clothes and homemade picnic lunches. Jean Pierre doesn't need me till later tonight, some fancy dinner they've got planned. Now how about that sarsaparilla."

"I've got somethin' new," said Doc, setting a tall glass on the counter and filling it with a brown liquid from one of the Hutchison bottles. He slid the drink to Ben like they did at the saloon next door and emptied the rest into his own glass.

Ben took a decent sip. The sugary beverage tasted sweet on his tongue, and its bubbly effervescence tickled his nose. "That's good. What flavor is it?"

"They say it's got twenty-three. They call it a Waco."

Ben repositioned himself, resting one arm on his knee, the other on the counter. "Say," he said, sipping his beverage, "how's that gal of yours?"

"Pretty as ever. Takin' Jennie to the Stone Bridge this Sunday for the Decoration Day parade. Gonna be some fireworks that night, for sure," Doc said with a wink.

Ben was picturing rings of fiery sparks in the sky when a roar came from the front porch. "Sounds like someone got kicked outta the rocking chair."

"The weather's always a good starter," said Doc, "but you can only talk about somethin' for so long."

Ben was gulping his Waco when the sweet smelling woman came up beside him. She set a pair of folded pants and a flannel button-down on the counter and asked Doc if he had any hats. Doc pointed to an arrangement of feathered bonnets on the display table.

"Men's hats," she said, resting her hands on the counter.

54

"Yes ma'am," Doc said, hurrying into the back room.

Ben set down his glass and shifted his eyes to the woman's hands. No ring. Not shopping for her husband. He leaned back, trying to make eye contact while he thought of a clever way to start a conversation. The only women he'd ever seen shopping for flannels and men's hats worked at the telegraph offices or on the rails. "You work for the railroad?" he said.

The woman drew her attention away from Doc's progress only to glance briefly at Ben. "Something like that, yes."

"I work at the Fishing and Hunting Club."

"That's nice."

It seemed the woman favored silence to chit chat, but Ben was feeling brave. "Them clothes you're buying, they required for your job?"

"Not required," she said, holding up the button-down and pillowing her cheek against the flannel. "Preferred."

"I know what your mean," said Ben. "I have to wear a long, scratchy kitchen coat for my job, sometimes a funny hat, too, though I'd much prefer a pair of comfortable flannels. But Jean Pierre says we have to look sharp for the members. Says people pay more attention to you when you look sharp."

A slight nod indicated she agreed with Jean Pierre's theory. "Sometimes," she said, "you have to wear the uniform if you want to play the game."

Before Ben could think of a cleaver response, Doc returned with a dozen men's hats stacked neatly on top of one another. The woman thumbed the brims, and Doc helped her fish out a brown bowler near the middle. She tried it on and Ben nodded approval. After a quick exchange of folding bills for coins, she was on her way.

Ben admired her as she left the store.

Doc let out a low whistle. "That," he said, toasting the woman's exit with a tip of his glass and a quick drink, "was Emma Ehrenfeld. The new telegraph operator at the Number Six tower."

"Pretty gal," said Ben, his eyes following her every step as she strode down the stairs and into the street. "So they're lettin' women work along the river now?"

"She's the only one. And at the busiest tower from here to Johnstown, too."

"Guts, and looks," said Ben. "Hard to find a combination like that."

The two went back to sipping their Waco's, and Doc pointed at Ben's music pin. "What's that," he said, "some kind of badge?"

"It's a music academy pin," said Ben, pinching it away from his chest.

Doc strained to read the inscription. "Does that mean you gonna leave us?"

Ben sat back and folded his arms, a big smile pasted on his face. "Gonna buy me a ticket," he said. "And in two weeks, me and my knapsack full of sheet music are headin' off to New York City."

Doc twirled his glass around in circles. "I'm plannin' on leaving this town, too," he said, "once Jennie and me get married."

Ben sprang up onto the counter. "This store has been in your family for forty years," he said, "ain't no way your father's gonna let you leave. He's probably just shy of givin' it to you."

"I've got plans of my own," said Doc. "When Jennie and me get hitched, we're movin' to California. A fella there found a new way to grow oranges. Valencia oranges, he calls 'em. I'm gonna get me some land, plant a grove, and start a business." He took a sip and pointed at Ben's glass. "Now, tell me what flavors you taste."

"Sarsaparilla. Maybe sassafras, too."

Doc grabbed his log book and found the stub of a pencil. He slapped the book on the counter. "All right," he said, "I'll put those two flavors down here. Every time we agree on another one, I'll write it down."

A short, fat boy and his mother came up with a handful of items and set them on the counter.

"I've got a basket here, ma'am," said Doc, "if you'd like to buy one, might make it easier to carry your things."

"That'll be fine," she said.

Doc added up the sundries, including a sassafras stick and a fistful of Lancaster caramels the fat boy had pinched from one of the candy jars. He and Ben resumed their flavor-find as the boy and the mother left the store.

"I taste a little vanilla," said Doc.

"And black cherry, too."

"Uh huh."

While Doc scratched down the flavors in his log book, Ben looked away at a flatboard shelf and a pyramid of imported Chinese teaboxes, each one lacquered and hand painted with sweeping strokes of foreign calligraphy. "How do you know you're doing the right thing?"

"Doing the right thing with what?"

"Heading off to California. How do you know you're makin' the right decision?"

Doc took the empty Hutch bottle and set it back on the shelf with the others. "You know just as well as I do, a man ain't a man till he makes it on his own. I figured you'd be happy for me."

"Sure I am. But what if that orange growin' idea of yours doesn't pan out, then what?"

"Guess I never considered it wouldn't. But if it don't, I'll think of somethin'."

"Not a very safe plan. I'd like to have somethin' to fall back on. What if you get there and everyone's eating apples?"

"Then I'll grow apples," said Doc, closing the logbook. "I wrote down caramel too, long as you don't have any objections."

Ben sipped and shook his head. He always thought Doc would be a fixture in River Fork, a familiar face forever there if he needed him. "Just seems risky, unpredictable. Such a long trip, too. Who knows what trouble you'll run in to along the way. You got a good job here, and a girl. You sure it's worth it?"

Doc twisted his arms across his chest and cradled his chin in his hand like some ancient Greek philosopher. "You remember that Columbus fella we learned about in school," he said, "in fourteen hundred ninety-three Columbus sailed across the sea, and all them

57

explorers from Spain, or France, or wherever it was? Everyone said they were gonna fall off the edge of the earth. But that didn't stop 'em. They sailed on anyhow. Scurvy, crickets, sea monsters. And after a while the wind and the waves dropped 'em off here."

"I ain't sure that's exactly how it went."

"Well it was somethin' like that. Anyway it doesn't matter. Point is, they weren't worried about what they didn't know, weren't afraid of fallin' off the earth neither. And even if they did, oh well, at least they tried. But they didn't fall off. They made it to the new world, and all that trouble getting here was worth it."

"How do you know it was worth it, maybe when they got here they just turned their boats around and went home."

"You and I are sittin' here, ain't we? Reckon one of them boats carried over our great grandpa, or great, great grandpa, or great, great, great...."

Outside, a commotion broke out. Ben turned to see the fat boy pressing his hand to his stomach, the upper half of his body jolting forward. In a concentrated stream, a mixture of undigested food slopped from the boy's mouth and onto the porch. The smell of Chase and Sanborn's vanished, and the dugout cleared. Even the man in the rocking chair relinquished his prominent position.

Doc put away the log book and went to the storeroom for a bucket and a wet-mop. Out front, he filled the tin pail at the spigot next to the stairs. The mother and the boy had already hurried off when Ben came out.

"You need some help swabbing the deck?" Ben asked.

"Wouldn't mind it," said Doc, handing Ben the mop.

As the two cleaned off the porch, Henry Howell opened the screen door and peeked out. "Quit foolin' around with your pal and get down to Johnstown," he said, wiping his hands on his stained apron. "We've got a load of dry goods waitin' for us at Olson's place."

Doc cleared away the rest of the vomit with a toss of the water bucket. "Guess we're headin' to Johnstown."

Ben stared at his buddy. "I ain't got time to go to Johnstown."

Doc grabbed the mop from Ben and leaned it against the wall. "You don't expect me to go alone, do you? Besides, you said you didn't have to work till tonight."

Before Ben could think of another excuse, Doc hurried into the store and returned with Ben's knapsack and a lumpy canvas bag. "Hold on to these," he said, and ran off behind the store.

A sturdy Belgian pulling a work wagon came around the side of the store with Doc at the reins. At one time, the wagon had been a handsome prairie-schooner, with a box bed and a flatboard seat up front for the driver, but Henry Howell had removed the bows and the canvas bonnet to haul a recent shipment of fancy gas lamps. Doc slowed just enough for Ben to hop on and they rode off.

Doc stopped the wagon at the end of town, where a single-arch viaduct spanned a deep, seventy-foot wide ravine. Although the block-bridge was built for rail traffic, carriages used it to avoid the sweeping oxbow bend in the river and trim six miles off the trip to Johnstown. It marked the end of River Fork and the beginning of Mineral Point Borough.

Ben swiveled round, scoping out the unfamiliar part of town. "Why are we stoppin' here?"

"Pick up a couple of friends."

"You said we were going alone."

Doc gathered the reins and handed them to Ben. "Did I say that?"

Doc hopped off the wagon and ran to the house at the end of a long footpath, sneaking around porchside and disappearing behind a pile of stacked firewood. After a few uneasy minutes, he returned with two giggling girls, their long dresses and feathered hair bouncing behind them as they raced to the back of the wagon. Doc helped them into the bed, hoisted himself up front, and set off across the bridge. When they had lost sight of the viaduct, Jennie climbed over the headboard and traded places with Ben.

Ben had only met Jennie once, when they happened to cross paths at the General Store. She was friendly and pretty. Ben approved of her. "Too good for you, Doc," he had teased. Jennie's friend was rougher around the edges, tom-boyish in her slate-grey dress, but still round in all the right places. She scooted along the headboard until her shoulder rubbed up against Ben's. "Ain't you gonna introduce yourself?" she said.

"Maybe he don't want to, Dixie," said Jennie. "I know a lot of other boys wished they never had."

Dixie reached over and thumped Jennie on the top of the head. "That's a lie, and you know it."

Doc leaned back, keeping one eye on the road. "This is my friend, Ben Marsh," he said.

Dixie put her hand on Ben's shoulder. "And where have you... 'Ben'...all my life," she said, tickling him behind the ear and giggling.

"Behave yourself," said Doc, "We got a long ride to Johnstown."

"Dixie always behaves herself," said Dixie.

"Where'd you get a name like Dixie, anyway," said Doc.

"My father loves the South," she said, glancing at Jennie then returning her attention to Ben's shoulder. "You ever been down south, Ben?"

Jennie and Dixie sniggered. Ben figured it was something girls did when they got together with a couple of boys. "I've never been down south," he said. "But I am goin' to New York this June."

"My uncle lives there," said Dixie. "Next to some ancient Indian mound."

"That's Newark, Ohio," said Jennie. Ben's talking about New York, as in the Statue of Liberty."

Ben pulled his shirt flat against his chest, separating the music pin from the folds in the flannel. "This is my academy pin."

Dixie stared at the badge with one eye asquint. She perched up tall on her knees and gave the group a military salute. "My grandfather was in the academy," she said, "West Point, 1859."

"It's a music academy pin," said Doc, handing Ben the grocery sack.

Ben set the bag in his lap. Inside were four Hutch bottles and two oranges. He took out one of the Hutch bottles.

"What instrument do you play?" asked Jennie.

"Piano," Ben said, fidgeting with the stopper.

Dixie snatched the bottle from Ben and stuck the stopper in her mouth and bit down. With a twist and a pull and a jerk of her head, she popped the cork. She gave the bottle back to Ben, spat out what was left of the stopper, and opened the rest of the bottles the same way. "So why do you have to go to New York to play the piano?" she said, biting and spitting. "Can't you find one you like around here?"

"It's a special school," said Ben, "The best in the nation. I'm gonna study piano, orchestra instruments, voice, and how to be a true musician."

"Can you play chopsticks?" said Jennie.

Doc grabbed one of the bottles from Dixie and took a big swig. "Of course he can. He can play Mozart, Brahms, all them classical fellas. Ben's a damn near professional, ain't that right, Ben?"

Ben slouched and picked his fingernails, staring at the puddles pitting the road and the dirty mix of mist and factory smoke trailing off in the distance behind them. "I'm pretty good."

"Then how come you ain't gone yet?" asked Jennie. "It's nearly the end of May."

"Maybe he's scared," said Dixie. "My brother was so afraid to go to middle school he hid under his bed for a whole week."

Ben sat up. "I ain't scared," he said. "I just need to buy my ticket," he slouched again, "and tell my pa."

Dixie drained her Waco in a few quick gulps and pitched the bottle over the sideboard. After concealing a small belch, she snuggled up next to Ben and looped her arm around his. "If I wanted to go," she said, "I wouldn't be botherin' with what my pa had to say, that's for sure. I'd just go."

61

With his head pitched sideways and eyes averted, Ben never made a beverage last so long. For the next half-hour, he took small sips, and wondered. Was his father keeping him from leaving River Fork? Or was it the fear of being out on his own? Maybe it was something inside he was missing. Some inner strength those sailors Doc was talking about had that he hadn't found yet. He wasn't sure. His thoughts swirled around as he pondered the reasons, distracted only slightly by the tug of Dixie's arm. Pretty girls ran through his mind too, just not this one, for each time Dixie leaned over to kiss him, he moved the bottle to his lips and nursed on it like a newborn.

They passed through the small town of Moxham, and Ben checked the road. He could see the borough of Johnstown through a gap in the trees, and the towering mountain peaks surrounding the town, forming a giant bowl were the valley ended. Factory chimneys lined the river flats like giant cigarettes tipped on end, and clusters of homes and other buildings filled the gorge, growing taller and multiplying as they funneled down the sloping hillsides toward the river. At the far end, the enormous Stone Bridge with its castle-like arches of speckled granite connected the two sides of the town and made the viaduct at Smith's Crossing look like a child's toy. Ben thought the haze from River Fork must have followed them, for when they pulled onto Main Street, the air turned black and rancid with chimney smoke.

The winding dirt road they'd followed through the valley turned into a straight, brick-laid street filled with tall three-stories and the cacophony of busy pedestrians, trolley cars and wagons. Ben kept the Hutch bottle glued to his lips until they stopped beneath the scalloped grey awning of Olson's Dry Goods.

Doc climbed off the wagon and headed into the store.

Ben got up to follow, but Dixie grabbed his arm and brought him down with a forceful tug. She took the two oranges from the grocery sack, handed one to Jennie, and kept one for herself. "You ain't gonna leave us girls all alone now, are you?" she said, staring at Ben while she peeled the orange.

Ben looked over the part in Dixie's hair. The front door of Olson's dry goods was propped open with a rusted oil drum, and men in brown overalls and bowlers were moving in and out pushing wheelbarrows full of lumpy burlap sacks. Ben lost sight of Doc and sat back against the headboard and stared up toward the lake at River Fork. The broad gully of the valley stretched out before him like a trough dug in-between the mountainsides, ready for the water behind the dam to wash through if given a chance. Ben turned to Dixie chomping on an orange wedge, the juices spurting and spilling over the back of her hand. "Either of you'uns here in '81 when that dam broke?" he said.

Jennie twisted round and hung her arms over the headboard. "I was," she said. "Our basement flooded. Ruined all my summer dresses."

Dixie slurped on the orange, lapping up the pulp that had collected between her knuckles. "I spent three nights at the First Baptist sleeping next to my brother," she said, shuddering. "I thought we'd at least get out of our school work, but Miss Orr came in with her books and pencils and paper, and Father Beale made us wheel out the old chalkboard they kept in the sacristy, can you believe it."

"I heard there's a big storm comin' our way," said Ben, "and that it might happen again."

"Not a chance," said Jennie. "The men at that River Fork Club fixed up that dam real strong."

"Besides," said Dixie, "We'll need a lot more rain for a flood."

Doc returned with a wheelbarrow piled high with sacks of flour, sugar, salt, and black pepper. He set the burlap pillows on the wagon's bed, and Ben dragged them to the headboard, stacking them between him and Dixie and covering them with a heavy tarp. After they finished loading, Doc went up front and turned the wagon around.

As soon as they rolled off the brick road and onto the dirt trail toward River Fork, ball lightning lit the sky above Johnstown, followed by a crisp thunderclap not a second after. Heavy drops began to fall and Doc slapped the reins and rose up. The horse heaved forward and Doc looked back. "Hold on," he said, setting off to outrun the thunderhead, "we're in for a wet and bumpy ride."

9

All John Parke wanted was recognition. The most glorious reward he had ever received was when his wife, Lily, accepted his offer of marriage. The success of their union hinged on a vow and a promise, Lily vowing to have and to hold, as long as John fulfilled his promise of a better life. Parke hoped that by bringing Lily to the River Fork Club, the mere association with affluence would prove his ability to do so. He was concerned, however, that the lavish lifestyle he'd so quickly thrust upon his new bride would be too much for the poor farmer's daughter to handle. But Lily, with her voluptuous figure, charm, and beauty, took to the socialites like an understudy who'd just been gifted the leading role. Not a day after settling into the Clubhouse, she was hobnobbing with the member's wives, enjoying fancy luncheons and late night dinner parties with a newfound affinity for debauchery that made Parke more of a housemaid than a husband.

While Lily was upstairs, sleeping off an all-night soirée at the cottage of Morton and Ada Crick, Parke stood patiently beside the office window, handing out reassuring looks to the men in the room, and drawing on his machine-rolled Duke of Durham. At one time, he had preferred to roll his own cigarettes, but recently switched when he discovered Lily favored the clean look of a manufactured brand. He watched with clenched fists as Andrews took the telephone receiver off the candlestick and cranked the handle. A crackling sound came from the earpiece, like the rustling of dried leaves, and the crowded office grew restless and skeptical.

"Is anyone there?" Andrews said, pressing the receiver to his ear. "I say, is anyone there?"

The bystanders grumbled, and Parke's forehead beaded with sweat. He wiped away the drips with a sticky palm still reeking of pitch oil from handling the utility pole. At least Mr. Crick had more pressing business matters to attend to that morning and wouldn't be adding to the pressure.

Andrews backed away from the device and glared at Parke. After another crank of the handle, he returned the receiver to his ear and spoke again, slowly and clearly into the mouthpiece. "Can anyone hear me? Is anyone there?"

The crackling was the only reply.

Helpless now to affect the outcome of Andrews's communication attempts, Parke resorted to prayer while he mulled over the possible problems with the line. Was it the utility pole? Had it shifted after they'd set it in place? Had the wire been pulled from the relay? He looked out the window to check. The twenty-five foot pole tapered upward, perfectly straight, supported by an angled push-brace of solid pine. The cement hadn't fully set, but that wouldn't have any effect on the wiring. The cross-arm appeared solid too, and the wires fed neatly into the relay box, with a clean run over the driveway straight into the office. Maybe there was a defect at some other relay or transfer station along the way. If so, the problem was out of his hands. He did everything he could to secure a clear transmission.

Except for his quasi-triumph with the flush toilets, recognition had been scarce lately, and in addition to the success of Andrews's telephone call, he added another prayer that included a small appeal for accolades.

Every town in the valley had at least one speaking telegraph. Johnstown was the first, with one at City Hall, and another at Union Station, after which, each borough up the valley followed suit. The telegraph poles ran alongside the tracks by the river, with relay stations at all the crossings and communication towers. Earlier that morning, Parke had been given the charge by Andrews to set the last 'dead end' pole in place at the River Fork Clubhouse. Parke had chosen an area beyond the driveway, on a hillside next to a thick line of white pines. It was his decision to blend the pole in with the rest of the forest, another idea that had gone unnoticed.

He cut short his prayer when he saw Andrews's eyebrows rise. The white-bearded industrialist seemed to have a renewed interest in the crackling line.

"Harland," said Andrews, raising the corners of his mouth. "Is that you? Harland, can you hear me?"

Andrews had made contact. The installation of the pole and the connection of the wires was a success. Parke let out a sigh of relief and waited for praise.

"Marvelous," said Andrews, "excellent job." Andrews looked at Parke who received his favorable glance with beaming pride.

Andrews's gaze quickly returned to the wooden box. "Excellent job Harland...yes...very good. Put the merger documents on my desk, and I will sign them the coming week." Andrews set the receiver onto the candlestick to a generous round of applause.

Two men pushed Parke aside, vying for a better position to congratulate Andrews.

"Splendid," said one man, softly patting his palms together then shaking Andrews's hand, "Just splendid, Mr. Andrews."

"You, sir," said the other, "definitely have the Midas touch."

Andrews addressed the group. "Let us adjourn to my cottage and freshen up before dinner. Oh, and Parke," he said, "Won't you join us?"

Parke settled himself, content with providing a working telephone line for Andrews's amusement and convenience. If praise from Andrews didn't come today, he thought, it would surely be bestowed upon him later in private. He watched the group exchanged smiles and pats on the back. "No thank you, sir," he said. "A good deal of the members haven't checked in yet, and I still have work to do."

"Very well," said Andrews, as the group left the office. "Oh, and one more thing."

Parke lifted his chin. "Yes, sir."

"Give yourself a shave. You look awful."

Parke went to the window and angled his head against the glass and looked out. The ash trees skirting the footpath sawed in the wind. He could see the group led by Andrews marching off toward the cottages oblivious to the brooding cumuli overhead. Parke watched the ashen clouds swallow up the pale blue voids and transform the sky into an infinite field of grey. If he had learned anything during his time at the University, it was that neglected embankment dams patched with loose gravel and horse manure had a penchant for bursting under conditions of extreme rain. With such a tremendous amount of pressure already built up in the lake, the dam wouldn't stand a chance if the coming storm turned out to be as powerful as predicted. If the looming stormfront raining on Andrew's parade provided any indication of what was to follow, the dam would surely fail, and God help the thirty thousand people living below it.

10

Three miles from the River Fork Clubhouse, past the shops and businesses along the river, Main Street snaked up to what the locals referred to as Prospect Hill, where some of the town's wealthiest and most influential moguls had built their extravagant homes – three-story revivals with wrought iron fences, thick grass lawns, and big white-ash trees that shaded manicured flower gardens like giant parasols. The mayor of River Fork lived there and so did Milton Morrell, president of both the Savings Bank and the First National. Even Andrews and Crick had built homes on Prospect Hill, and stayed there frequently until the construction of the Club's cottages by the lake.

Though out of his way, Percival walked the upper side of Main Street that morning, admiring the homes with the high-pitched roofs and the shaded front yards. He walked with his shoulders pressed back, past a woman tending her garden. He nodded politely, and she responded with a mechanical wave. He had allowed plenty of time for a casual stroll. Not a chance he'd be late. Not on the day he was to receive the executive position. Not on the day he'd pick out his plot. Not on the day he'd finally get an invitation to the Club.

At the end of Prospect Hill, he caught the road to the foundry, and as soon as the fancy homes had disappeared behind him, he heard the clank of the steam engines. The River Fork Clubhouse sat off in the distance across the river, and he squinted to bring it into focus, taking a moment to watch Parke and his men tilt the utility pole into place. "And modern technology too," he said to himself, "Boy, it's gonna be nice."

With a confident gait and a bright whistled melody, he walked past the day laborers loitering behind the foundry.

"Any work for us today?" one asked.

Percival hurried by. "Not today," he said.

Executives didn't deal with day laborers, and Percival was more than ready to be done with the annoyance. He walked into the mill and took a deep breath of the scorched air, holding it in for a moment then forcing it out his lungs as if to give it a pleasant farewell.

Production was flowing as usual, with the casters molding fishplates, and the pullers coiling razor-wire. He observed the frantic bustle for what he hoped would be the last time. Executives didn't labor in the mills; they sat in armchairs behind oak desks.

Morgan came up to Percival and walked with him across the foundry floor. "Where's Crawford?" Ain't he comin' back to work? We've been missin' them oilin' breaks."

Percival kept his pace, glancing left and right and nodding to the workers. "It's only been a day since he lost his hand, Morgan. And from what I've heard, it don't look like he's comin' back."

"Done give up, huh," said Morgan, "pansy. Hell, I knew a fella once, a logger, done chopped his hand off with a machete, cuttin' branches, wrapped it up tight with a handkerchief and kept on workin'."

"Fella like that might have been in a different place," said Percival. "He's bitter. Crawford I mean. Bitter at the company. Blames the company for the accident, for not havin' the proper conditions and safety regulations. Says he ain't comin' back to this hell hole. To be honest with ya, can't say I blame him."

A voice came across the floor. "Marsh." Then again without allowing time for a response. "Marsh." It was Crick.

Any sentimental feelings the mill had given Percival that morning were relieved by his brief conversation with Morgan. Percival had spent a long time laboring in the rolling mills and foundries, but he certainly wouldn't miss it, especially sitting behind an oak desk or enjoying a fine cigar in the Clubhouse lounge. He moved toward the office, patting Morgan on the shoulder and smiling. "You take care of things around here."

Crick allowed Percival to enter first. "Sit," he said, closing the door behind him.

Crick adjusted his coat and sat in regal posture behind the desk, meshing his fingers together like engine gears. His coarse mustache slanted toward the corners of his mouth, giving him a permanent frown. Percival tried to decipher Crick's state of mind, but Crick was a hard man to read.

Crick removed a thick envelope from the drawer, slid out a loose packet, and thumbed through the pages. "You know what this is?"

Percival tilted his head to indicate uncertainty, though he'd already seen it the day before when Crawford lost his hand.

Crick straightened the papers like an oversized deck of playing cards, laid them on the desk, and patted the stack with his fingertips. "This is the job offer and contract for the new junior executive position. It outlines the responsibilities and benefits of upper management."

Percival nodded.

"You know what a position in upper management means, Marsh?"

"I have a general idea, sir."

"It means you assume more responsibility," Crick said with a smile. "And more accountability. It means taking the credit when things are goin' well, and taking the blame, and sometimes the punishment, when they're not."

Crick leafed through the pages, pausing every so often to review some of the text more purposefully. "But, now, with this responsibility comes exceptional benefits. It means better hours, better pay, an opportunity for private housing, hell, maybe even a plot on Main Street." Crick gave Percival another smile. "It even means an invitation for membership at the River Fork Club. You'd like that, wouldn't you?"

Percival squirmed in his chair. "I would, sir."

Crick leaned over the desk, his folded arms smothering the stack of papers. "I would truly like to offer you this position," he said.

"And I would be truly happy to accept it, sir."

Crick looked at Percival the way a hunter might look at a deer as it struggled for its last, dying breath. "I don't think you heard me correctly, Marsh," he said, easing back in his chair. "I said I would like to offer you this position. Truth is, I'm not going to do that."

"Sir?" Percival's head dropped, and he stared at the stack of papers he'd hoped would take him out of the foundry and into the Clubhouse.

Crick opened the drawer, took out a long sheet of paper and dropped it on the desk. He slid it in front of Percival. "You recognize this?"

It was the foundry worker's petition for union inclusion, the name of every laborer under Percival's charge signed in ink. In his haste to help Crawford, he had left it on Crick's desk in plain view.

Crick laid into Percival hard, not allowing him a word in edgewise. "Here's your crew," he shouted, leaning forward and stabbing at the paper with his middle finger. "Your men, all asking for union membership, the outright grounds for the termination of 'em all." He sat back in his chair and interlaced his fingers. "Here's your lesson in upper management, Marsh. Who do you think should accept responsibility for this? Huh? You want to be a leader? You want to be an executive? Who do you want I should fire, the Indians, or the chief? Looks like you've got a choice to make. Is it you, or do I fire the bunch of 'em?"

Percival stared silently at the paper.

Crick stood and stabbed at the petition again. "Laborers here, Marsh, laborers. Hell, I see the tracks every day, crowded with 'em, ready to work the mills. Any one of those dullards can be taught to pull wire or pour metal. These men here," he stabbed more firmly at the names, "are dispensable. Who do you want I should fire, Marsh, who?"

Percival sat quiet.

Crick's shouting had carried out onto the foundry floor. Except for Morgan, who kept coiling wire, all the men stopped working and stared at Percival as he came out of the office and gently closed the door behind him. The men went back to work, watching over their shoulders as Percival made his way across the foundry floor. Outside, he was approached by one of the day laborers waiting by the tracks.

"Any work for us today, mister?" the laborer asked.

Percival kept walking, "Not today," he said. "Not today."

11

Two minutes was his record, but after only a minute and a half Ben was fighting the urge to breathe. The rotten smell had overpowered the sweet perfume of the carbolic acid. Fresh air was another ten, maybe fifteen seconds away, and he forced himself to hold on. How, he thought, could someone who prepared such wonderfully smelling food for one end, produce such a foul stench from the other? And how was it every time he needed to use the flush toilet, Jean Pierre had used it just a moment before.

Finally finished, he raced outside. After several deep breaths with hands on knees, he returned to the toilet pinching his nose and pulled the chain. It must have been all that Waco drink, he thought. He and Doc had identified ten of the twenty-three flavors, but now, Ben wished they'd stopped at five. Doc warned him drinking too much could have laxative effects. He grabbed his white coat and fled to the kitchen where Jean Pierre stood over the stove working a wooden spoon around the sides of a copper pan.

"Sauce Béarnaise," said Jean Pierre, waving his hand over the pan and taking in a deep breath of the classic accompaniment. "Smells wonderful, no?"

"Oh yes, wonderful." Ben gave Jean Pierre a grimace. "And where do you need me tonight?" He hoped it would be far away from the utility room.

"You will help serve the courses. The guest-list is at one hundred fifty, and I need you to work with the waiters."

"I've never served courses before, but I'll help with whatever you

74

need." Ben reached into his hip pocket and took out a train ticket. "Anyway, have a look at this," he said, handing Jean Pierre his one-way ticket to New York City.

"Ah, you've decided to go to the big city," said Jean Pierre.

"Bought it today. Only cost me three dollars, too. And I was hoping you could write me that recommendation? Maybe help me find a job at your friend's bakery? Haven't given much thought as to where I'm gonna stay, either."

"I like that," said Jean Pierre, "No plan at all, the way of the free spirit."

Two men came into the kitchen through the back door dressed like Jean Pierre, in bleached white coats and floppy toques. They didn't notice, or didn't seem to mind, the smell in the utility room. Jean Pierre spoke to them in French, and they quickly went to work at the chopping table.

"Let us see how you do tonight," Jean Pierre said to Ben. If I give you a recommendation, especially if it is to one of my colleagues, it has to be sincere. What about your parents? They will not help you?"

"It's just my father," said Ben, "Anyway, I'm not sure I'm gonna tell him. He probably wouldn't even take notice if I did."

"You are lucky."

"Lucky to have a father who wants me to stay here?"

"Lucky to have a father," said Jean Pierre. "My parents, I never knew them."

Another group of impeccably dressed Frenchmen entered the kitchen and assembled around the wooden table. They pushed Ben aside and waited for direction. Ben didn't realize there were so many Frenchmen in River Fork. Apparently, along with Jean Pierre, Andrews had imported an entire kitchen and serving staff. Ben laughed at the banter of oui, oui's and ooo-la-la's. "Where did all of these French chefs and French waiters come from?" he asked Jean Pierre.

Jean Pierre looked around the room, leaned over, and whispered in Ben's ear. "From France."

Ben left the kitchen and found one of the waiters who spoke the most understandable English, a tall thin man who pronounced his name "Awn-ree." Henri wore a stunted black jacket buttoned only at the top, concealing half of a full-length white apron. He spoke in a heavy French accent, substituting 'z's' for 'th's', and swallowing every 'r'. "This is your first night serving courses, no? Where is your jacket? Where is your apron? Come with me." They passed a group of waiters setting out the butler stands, and Ben's mentor made eye contact with them and snickered. He led Ben into the storage room. "Here," he said, handing Ben a tuxedo jacket and a long, white bistro apron. "Put these on."

The dining room and the ballroom were usually separated by large accordion-style doors, but that evening the divider was opened wide to accommodate seating on both sides. Ben shadowed the slender waiter to the center of what was now one giant, over-furnished room.

Gas chandeliers hung from the high ceiling of ornate, bronze-colored panels. A thick band of crimson crown-molding wrapped the ceiling, and below, oversized portraits of the Club's most prominent members hung on the walls, their frowning faces staring downward, ready to supervise the guests and make sure each one kept his elbows off the table and his napkin in his lap.

Ben and Henri weaved through the tables to the far corner of the room where a heavy pine log crackled in a massive alcove large enough for a man to stand in. Reflections of the vibrant plumes danced over the Steinway and onto the fogged windows overlooking the lake.

"This is your station," Henri said, pacing around an oval-shaped dining table draped with floor-length, pleated linen.

Set in front of each cushioned chair was an excessive arrangement of china, cutlery, and stemware, the unused space in the middle of the table consumed by an enormous arrangement of freshly cut flowers.

Henri pointed while describing the various dining implements. First to a ceramic plate, hand painted around the edge and stamped in the center with the club's insignia. "This chop-plate is for decoration," he said. "Remove it when the guests are seated." He continued around the table. "These are the game shears, this is for water, this for wine, this for sherry, this...." He went on for what seemed like an hour, spending twenty minutes alone on the significance of eight different forks. Finally, he asked Ben if he had any questions.

Ben could think of only one thing to ask. "Where do you put the food?"

Henri gave Ben a look just shy of disgust. "I will be serving the table next to yours, just do what I do. Le sommelier will serve the wine, le maître d' la table will describe the courses. All you need to do is bring the food. Besides, I do not believe anyone important will be sitting at your table, so do not worry."

Ben was straightening the chairs and polishing the stemware when a quintet dressed in tuxedos passed behind him and took its place upon the small stage next to the fireplace. The leader propped up the lid of the Steinway while the others rosined their bows. Ben was listening to the violinist tune his strings when the maître d' came out of the kitchen and signaled with a quick whistle. Ben left the table and followed Henri, joining the rest of the waiters queued up in front of the kitchen's swinging doors.

As Ben approached the lineup, he saw a herd of people swarming in the foyer. Behind the mingling socialites, shiny black carriages crowded the drive. A cool breeze rushed into the dining room, and the heat from the fireplace sent it quickly back out the front door.

Just as the railroad brought people together, so did it divide. And as the meager town of River Fork went about its mundane matters, an elite crowd of business tycoons and fortunate guests spilled into an exaggerated display of luxury. Women in long silk dresses, white gloves, and Victorian bonnets were escorted by men in black coats, white pocket squares, and top hats. The couples scattered around the room in a parade of black and white, bowing, curtsying, and handshaking until their graciously exhausted bodies demanded they sit down.

One by one, the waiters made their way to their respective tables. Henri's table was seated, and he left to attend to them. Ben followed.

"No, no," Henri instructed, "wait here until your guests are seated. Then go and greet them with a pleasant 'bon soir monsieur, madame,' remove the charger plates, and meet me in the kitchen. Watch, and imitate what I do."

Ben waited as Henri and the other waiters disappeared from the line. Soon Ben was alone, every table seated but his. Perhaps, he thought, a fortunate bit of luck would fall upon him and his table would remain empty.

Chatter faded, and the diners turned in their chairs as the final group made their way across the room. Three couples and a single man successfully found their seats, stopping briefly along the way to shake hands with some of the guests. Two of the men Ben knew from the Club as Morton Crick and John Parke. He had never seen the single man before.

Only two empty chairs remained, and the entire room stood and applauded as their occupants entered the room arm in arm. Ben recognized them immediately as Charles and Louise Andrews.

Ben wasn't familiar with elegance, but it was obvious the two exuded the true meaning of the word, the refinement of Andrews's chesterfield only slightly surpassed by Louise's satin dress and understatedly sophisticated bonnet.

The applause settled, and the two aristocrats took their seats. As a rite of passage unbeknownst to Ben, the new waiter was given the most important table. The Frenchmen figured if Ben could survive an evening serving the most important guests, he was suited to serve anyone. Ben's test was to be with a group of truly important persons.

Charles Andrews and his wife Louise always attended the first dinner of the season with Morton and Ada Crick. Parke, who sat next to his wife, Lily, had invited Lane and Stella Addison. Ben had seen Parke welcoming them in the foyer the day before. Addison was an architect from New York whom Parke had praised for his work on country homes in the Long Island area, and his design of a custom resort in the Adirondacks. Ben felt his stomach drop as he stared at the table of achievers. "No one of any importance, huh," he said to himself, glaring at Henri who looked back with a wide smile.

Commotion settled, and the quintet started in with a Brahms' nocturne. Chamber music filled the room, and the season's first formal dinner at The River Fork Fishing and Hunting Club had begun.

Ben made his way to the table and found his guests engaged in introductions. His hands shook as he removed the charger plates. "Bon soir monsieur, madame …."

Parke went first. "May I present Mr. Lane Addison and his lovely wife, Stella."

"And I'd like everyone to meet Mr. Frank Damrosch," Andrews said, presenting his guest to Crick, Parke, and their wives. "Mr. Damrosch is the godson of Franz Liszt and the founder of the New York Academy of Music."

"…Monsieur, madame…monsieur, madame…" Ben almost dropped the stack of charger plates in Parke's lap. He moved around the table and darted toward the kitchen.

Crick twisted in his chair and called to Ben. "Monsieur… monsieur, we would like the wine, right away."

Ben turned slowly, half-paralyzed, a blank stare on his face.

"The wine please?" Still no response from Ben, and Crick said it again, this time in sarcastic French, "Doo van, see-voo-play?"

Ben tried to speak, but could think of nothing to say.

12

Henri bumped the sommelier on the shoulder and sent him in to rescue Ben. The tuxedoed sommelier stepped in front of Ben, cradling the wine bottle in his palm, "Le vin, monsieur," he said, "Château Lafitte dix-huit cent cinquante-cinq." Crick pretended to read the label. The sommelier popped the cork and gave Crick a quick pour. Crick swirled the glass, brought it to his nose, and breathed deeply. He took a generous sip, swishing the wine in his mouth the way he'd seen Jean Pierre do, and after granting approval, the sommelier poured the Bordeaux around the table, first to the ladies, then to the gentlemen.

As Crick fed the group a tall tale about his knowledge of fine wine, Ben fled to the kitchen where Henri was assembling the first course on a large tray.

"Carry it like this," said Henri, hoisting the tray onto his shoulder. "Set it down on the butler stand. Serve from the left, ladies first, then the gentlemen. When they are finished, remove from the right, comprendre?"

With a serious face, Ben lifted his tray as Henri had done, using a slight bend in his legs. Now he was focused. He made it to the table and served the first course of turtle soup without incident. He even passed a quick smile to Louise Andrews and a formal nod to Mr. Damrosch, and the two acknowledged his politeness.

In choreographed unison, the group dipped their spoons into the steamy broth. Though the flowers obscured Ben's view of the far side of the table, he could see each diner clearly except for Crick whose back was to him. Ben stood patiently by the butler stand, listening, unnoticed, to their conversation.

"…So I explained to him that Pennsy is the shipper," said Crick, "and no matter what the Union in Pittsburgh is doing, if they want my business, their men will unload the freight, not mine. I told him we have…" he held up his fist, ready to extend a finger with each choice, "…the Union Pacific, the ATSF. Hell, even the B&O to choose from, and if his company wouldn't unload it, I'd find another one who would."

Andrews tilted his soup bowl and scraped at the sides for the last bit of broth. "No need to preach to the converted, Mr. Crick," he said, "I'm in perfect agreement. We pay for freight on board to the plant, not to the tracks behind it." Andrews eyed the bowl as if he desired to lick it clean, but instead, followed proper etiquette and set down his spoon. "And how did he respond?"

"Off-loaded it quicker than greased lightning," said Crick, "And offered a ten-percent discount, to boot."

Polite laughter allowed Ben to remove the plates and return to the kitchen. The conversation was intriguing, and Ben hoped the group would allow him more time to listen by slowing down between courses as the dinner progressed. Upon successful placement of a salad niçoise, and a visit from the maitre'd, Ben returned to a conversation led by Mr. Addison.

"…the unveiling of Gustave Eiffel's tower at the world's fair," said Addison, "A fascinating piece of architecture."

Parke dabbed at the corners of his mouth with his napkin. "Very impressive, half a million rivets, and over a thousand feet tall. However, some are unaware that Eiffel was not the only designer. Three others, an engineer and two architects assisted in the…."

"I've seen photographs in the Pittsburgh Press," Crick interrupted. "An eye sore, if you ask me. I have no interest in it at all. Besides, what's its purpose?"

Addison answered the way an artist might respond when his work is insulted. "Its purpose, my dear man, is the achievement of beauty through architecture. Creating something that has never been thought of before."

Parke nodded.

"Is that so," said Crick, slugging back a gulp of wine. "Still doesn't interest me."

"It's made from puddled iron, Mr. Crick," said Andrews. "Doesn't that interest you?"

"Only if it was my company that sold it," said Crick.

The table erupted with laughter. Ben found moving under its cover the best way to minimize detection. He continued to use this strategy, hurrying back and forth with the courses during moments of levity, playing mainly off Crick's crude repartee. Ben maintained a speed quick enough not to miss too much detail of the conversations, but careful enough not to drop any of the food. With each trip to the kitchen and back, he moved the butler stand closer to the table, giving himself a successively better position to eavesdrop. After his most recent trip, Parke was addressing the group. Henri's table was chattering and toasting their glasses, and Ben strained his ears to listen.

"Even though the expert from the Tribune has assured us otherwise," said Parke, "I strongly believe major flooding will occur. Hopefully, with the help of Mr. Addison here," he extended an open hand across the table, "I will be able retrofit the dam and avoid any major damage to person or property. And with the heavy rains we've been having, the sooner my improvements are made, the better."

Parke's wife, Lily, had been keeping up with the men in food and in drink, and the men were enjoying watching her do so. Full featured and full figured, Lily attracted the attention of every man in the room. Ben hadn't been the only one to notice that after a taste of the upper-crust lifestyle, she had become a bit too much for Parke to handle.

As Parke rambled on about the dam and its stability, Lily gazed up at the crystal shimmer of the chandeliers and fanned herself, spreading the scent of bergamot orange perfume around the table.

"Well I do hope, dear," she said, cutting her husband short and patting him on the shoulder, "that you are successful in your efforts, for all of our sakes." She paused, making eye contact with the men at the table. "Heaven forbid that lake empties into the valley and takes this beautiful clubhouse with it. Where then will we hold such lavish occasions?"

The brief laughter in response to Lily's mocking died, denying Ben the chance to flee to the kitchen. However, it did give him the opportunity to watch Crick drop a hand under the table and onto Lily's knee.

"Successful, Mr. Parke," said Andrews, "We all hope your efforts prove to be just that."

"But what if it did happen?" asked Addison. "What do you believe the result would be, Mr. Parke, if the dam did indeed fail?"

Parke pressed his hands together and set them under his chin, prayer-like. "If the dam broke," he said, "the water would cover this valley, hill to hill."

It was apparent, from the uncomfortable silence, that dams breaching and towns flooding were not proper topics for such a cheerful event. And in order to transition to a more pleasant subject, Damrosch offered up a cleaver crumb of praise to Andrews for his latest bit of philanthropy.

"I must say, Mr. Andrews," said Damrosch, clearing his throat. "My colleagues and I are grateful that you have shared a portion of your success with us in the form of such a generous endowment to the School of Music, especially for the construction of the new concert hall."

Ben's ears perked. His unfortunate placement at the head table, he thought, might in fact yield good insight into his chances at attending the music academy.

Andrews smiled. "After learning how interested Augustus Julliard is in the establishment of the academy," he said, "I couldn't resist being a part of it. It is my intention to give as much as I can to as many worthy causes as possible. A man who dies rich, dies disgraced."

Andrews's wit sent Ben away with empty plates and back with

another course, escargot. When he returned to the table, Damrosch was speaking about the music academy.

"No, not entirely, Mr. Andrews. Of course, natural talent is something we look for in all potential students, but I would say that there is something else, an intangible quality if you will, that must be present when considering one's acceptance to the academy."

Except for Crick, each guest removed a tiny, two-pronged fork from their array of cutlery, and with the aid of a specialized set of tongs, began skillfully twisting free the garlic-infused snails from their shells.

"And what is it that you look for in your students of music, if it isn't musical talent," said Crick, finishing his wine and immediately searching for the sommelier.

"Heart," said Damrosch. "Passion."

Ben saw Crick give Lily's thigh a firm squeeze that made her posture straighten.

"Passion, eh?" said Crick.

"In business," suggested Andrews, "we might call it character. Just as character gives the entrepreneur the ability to become a great leader, passion gives the artist the ability to create inspirational music."

"Or the architect the means to conceive a thousand-foot tower of puddled iron?" said Parke.

"Precisely," said Andrews.

"And what about the musicians this evening, Mr. Damrosch," said Louise, "Would you say they are playing with passion?"

Damrosch bent an ear toward the stage as the lead violinist worked through a difficult passage. "It's pleasant," he said, returning to proper position at the table.

"A difficult man to impress, I see," said Stella Addison.

"Most men of character are," said Andrews. "They are aware of a professional's passion, and appreciate it when they see it."

"I most certainly stop and take notice," Damrosch said.

Crick, preoccupied with legs and liquor, summoned the sommelier and traded the empty bottle of Chateau Laffite for a full one. "And how do you measure a man's character, Mr. Andrews?" he said, filling his glass.

"Integrity," said Andrews.

"Integrity?" said Lily, holding up her glass for a re-fill. "And all this time, my husband's led me to believe a man's character was measured by the size of his architecture."

The men snickered. The women covered their mouths.

"And how would you define integrity, Mr. Andrews?" said Crick.

Andrews gathered Lily and Crick into his gaze and leaned in to the table. "Integrity," he said, softening his voice, "is what you do when no one else is looking."

The sommelier was flagged down again, this time by Addison, and the conversation moved away from integrity and architecture. Ben kept his routine, removing empty plates, bringing full ones, and allowing enough time in between for an interesting dose of upper-class anecdotes.

The caramelized crust that covered the cool vanilla custard bubbled hot as Ben served the final course. He took his position beside the butler stand, and when everyone had finished his dessert, the sommelier, who had just received secret instructions from Addison, returned to the table. The sommelier gracefully unfolded a butler stand and lowered a large tray from his shoulder. On the tray was an assortment of items: a set of beveled reservoir glasses, a pitcher of chilled water, a row of fancy slotted spoons, and a small bowl of sugar cubes. In the center was a tall, clear, hand-blown bottle with a wax seal, the bright green liquid inside obscured by a small, hand-painted label. Ben leaned forward to see.

Addison took the bottle and held it up. "La fée verte, the green fairy," he said. "A fine pernod fils from my recent trip to Paris."

The sommelier set one of the beveled glasses in front of Mr. Addison. He took a slotted spoon from the tray, rested it across the rim, and carefully set a sugar cube upon it with a small pair of tongs.

"And what might this be that you've been so kind to share with us, Mr. Addison?" asked Parke, as the sommelier readied the glassware similarly for the others.

85

Addison uncorked the bottle, and without upsetting the sugar cube or the fancy spoon, gave himself a healthy pour. "Absinthe, my dear man, a favorite libation of artists, musicians, writers... perhaps even architects and steel magnates, eh?"

"Oh, dear," said Ada Crick, slurring, "I've heard it's been banned for having hallucinogenic effects?" She pushed the glass away. "Didn't Gauguin go mad from drinking it? One sip and I'd be done for the night. I don't feel comfortable drinking that."

Crick slid the glass back in front of her. "On the contrary, my dear," he said, his eyes fixed on Lily's chest, "I imagine drinking it would make you feel quite comfortable."

"It was Van Gogh," said Addison, handing the bottle to the sommelier and allowing him to fill the other glasses. "He committed himself, no absinthe, and all he did was cut off his own ear."

As more of the green fairy left the bottle, an explosive blossoming of herbal aromas released into the air, overpowering all the other smells at the table, even Lily Parke's citrus scented eau d' toilet.

"May we have the plates cleared?" said Addison, removing the water pitcher from the tray. "We require plenty of room for this."

Ben removed the dessert plates, freeing up space for what appeared to be the start of a religious ritual. To Ben, the smell of the absinthe was a medicinal combination of floral and chemical that fell somewhere between an improperly mixed witches potion, and a recipe nightmare where fennel and anise had freed themselves from the pantry and run amok.

Addison poured the chilled water over the sugar cube, through the slotted spoon, and into his glass. As if by magic, the aromas softened to a refined perfume, and the clear green absinthe turned milky white. He passed the water pitcher around the table, and each took turns transforming the sterile elixir.

Addison tapped the rim of his glass and set the slotted spoon on the table. He stood tall and raised his arm high in salute. "To success," he toasted, "in business and in art, to the stability of dams and of character, to passion, and...and to heart, for absinthe makes the heart grow fonder."

After responding with an emphatic, "cheers", the group sipped the bohemian spirit while Ben continued clearing the unwanted utensils and stemware from the table.

Damrosch tipped his head for another taste and lifted a finger pointedly at an opening in Ben's jacket. "I see you have one of my music pins. Will you be joining us for an audition?"

Ben looked at Parke, the only person at the table he knew well enough to solicit permission to reply. Parke gave him an affirming nod. "I hope to," said Ben. "I've been practicing very hard."

"A waiter who is also a musician, how amusing," said Lily, belittling her husband with a crude look for allowing Ben to speak.

"Well, let's hear," said Damrosch, still gripping his glass. "Who is opposed to a private serenade from a future student of the New York Academy of Music? No one, very well then."

Damrosch got up from his seat, bumping the table with his portly belly and half-staggering to the platform stage where the quintet had just finished a bit of Bach. "How about a quick break?" he said to the pianist, "I have someone here," he looked over at Ben fidgeting with the butler stand. "What was your name, son?"

Ben raised his head and answered quietly.

"This aspiring young man, Ben," Damrosch said, "would like to play a short piece, if you don't mind."

The musicians left the stage, and Damrosch signaled Ben over with a circular wave of his arm.

"You're putting the poor boy on the spot, Mr. Damrosch," said Andrews. "Come back, sit down, and enjoy your last bit of drink, Mr. Crick's about to finish the bottle."

Ben sauntered to the piano as Damrosch reclaimed his seat at the table.

He reached for something short, and not too busy. Beethoven's Sonata Pathetique Third Movement, that's it. Not flashy, but well-known. What a chance, he thought, to impress Damrosch and secure his acceptance to the academy. Maybe, he hoped, Damrosch would ask him to enroll tonight.

Ben's hands shook as he took his seat at the Steinway. He adjusted the bench and set his fingers on the keys. Against the underside of the lid, he could see the blurred reflection of the dining room and the elongated images of the group patiently awaiting his performance. He was about to start playing when he heard a loud thump. He scooted to the edge of the bench and peered around the Steinway.

Ada Crick had fallen out of her chair. Andrews and Parke left their seats and hovered over her. Parke knelt beside her and cradled her head. "Are you all right, Mrs. Crick," he said, fanning her face with an open palm. Parke reached up past Crick, who sat sipping his beverage, and took a glass of water from the edge of the table. He tilted Ada's head back and brought the glass to her lips. Her glossy eyes slowly opened as she sipped the water.

"Maybe a little too much of your green fairy, eh, Mr. Addison?" said Crick, scooting back in his chair and making room for his wife who was sprawled out on the floor. "Where was that asylum you were talking about?"

Louise Andrews and Lily Parke got up and grabbed the inebriated Ada by the arms and lifted her to her feet. Ada's head flopped to her chin. She stumbled in an attempt to stand, her swollen ankles buckling under the weight of her thick legs.

Louise grunted, unable to support the limp drunkard. "Will you be so kind, Mr. Crick, and accompany us to your cottage so we may put your lovely wife down for an early night's rest?"

Crick, who seemed troubled with the inconvenience, pushed himself up from his chair after swallowing his last bit of absinthe.

"Oh, Louise," said Lily, locking eyes with Crick who had suddenly become more interested in helping, "the two of us can manage. You show Mrs. Addison the drawing room, and I'll join you shortly."

Crick exchanged places with Louise, and he and Lily left the dining room by way of the patio door. They shuffled up the boardwalk toward the cottages, Crick's poor wife hooked under their arms and flopping between them like a marionette.

"Gentlemen," said Louise, taking Stella by the arm, "will you excuse us, please? I believe we've had enough talk of architecture,

Mr. Addison. Allow me to show your wife the wonderful décor of our drawing room." The men stood when Stella Addison rose from her chair. "And the savors of our soothing aperitifs, each one guaranteed, free of hallucinogens." Louise circled the table, passing by the piano and whispering to Ben, "It was nice to see you again, good luck in New York."

After the women left, Ben worked his way through the Beethoven Sonata.

"Ah, Beethoven, pleasant choice," Damrosch said, his attention focused on the men at the table.

"Now, Beethoven," said Andrews, "there's an example of passion."

"Cleary a master," said Damrosch. "He wrote this sonata when he was twenty-seven, and already suffering from tinnitus. Twelve years later, he was completely deaf. But his heart still heard the music clearly. He felt it. When Beethoven touched the keys, he didn't play the piano, the piano played through him."

"And where do you suppose passion and inspiration like that comes from?" said Addison.

Damrosch stroked his beard. "Look at the masters," he said. "Beethoven was deaf most of his life. Mozart, for instance, wrote some of his most famous works from his death bed. And it wasn't until our good friend Van Gogh went crazy, committed himself, and cut off his own ear that we've taken notice of him."

Parke leaned back and stretched his neck toward the boardwalk. "It would appear, then," he said, "adversity and tragedy create the best recipe for inspiration and creativity."

Addison gathered the beveled glasses and emptied the bottle of Absinthe equally among them. Ben kept an ear on the table, his sonata drifting further into the background. "Methods for inspiring passion and inspiration in architecture," said Addison, "seem to be much less gruesome than those in music or in art. Perhaps, Parke, it would do us both some good to check into an asylum as Van Gogh did."

"I'm not certain that would be necessary," said Andrews. "One may find inspiration in good fortune and tragedy alike, if he chooses to do so. How a man responds to those events is what makes the difference."

Parke twirled his glass and stared at the milky liquid. "I believe any more of this, and I will have to check in to that asylum."

"I agree," said Damrosch. "Where is this lounge you've told me about, Mr. Andrews? A game of billiards and a belt of single malt sounds most intriguing."

Andrews pushed his glass aside. "I do believe, Mr. Addison, it's time for me to retire, but Mr. Parke, here, would be happy to join you. Billiards is his forte. And Parke, please have the decency to whoop Crick in a game of carom if he decides to come back."

Parke glanced at the boardwalk again. "It would be my pleasure."

Ben approached the end of the sonata, concentrating on the last theme, and pausing before playing the final cadenza. After a run of sixteenth-notes, he struck the last chord strongly and waited for applause. The pianist from the quintet startled him with a tap on the shoulder.

"Some of the guests are still dining," the pianist said. "We need to retake the stage."

"I'm playing for the table," said Ben. "I'd like to finish with one more piece."

Ben followed the pianist's eyes to where Andrews and his guests had been seated. Except for a disorganized arrangement of empty glassware and crumpled napkins, the table was empty. Ben stared for a moment and stepped down from the stage.

As he returned to the table, the pianist called to him. "Is this yours, son?" he said, holding Ben's music pin pinched between his fingers.

Ben patted at the empty spot on his chest. "Yes, it's mine," he said, taking the pin.

Ben was pinning the badge onto his shirt when Henri startled him. "Tres bien," Henri said, "very well done. I believe you have passed the test." He congratulated Ben with a pat on the back then threw an open hand at the table. "Do not worry about cleaning this. The Italians will do it. You may go. And welcome to the team."

Ben looked at the empty chair pushed out further than the rest, and wondered why Damrosch had left so soon. Was the piece he'd chosen too simple, uninspiring? Did he not have the passion Damrosch was looking for in the students of his academy? But a formal dinner was not the place to praise a musician for providing entertainment. Not the right time, he thought, to be recognized.

The Italians quickly moved in and cleared the table just as Henri had said, and before the pianist had finished the Minute Waltz, all evidence of Damrosch's presence was gone.

The sweet smell of jasmine followed Ben as he escorted his bicycle along the boardwalk gazing up at the collection of celestial fireflies that filled the sky. He breathed in the flower's bouquet and focused on a cluster of bright stars that resembled one of Jean Pierre's giant soup ladles.

"Isn't it pretty?"

Ben turned around, nearly losing hold of his Safety Rover. He tightened his grip on the handlebars and stared deep into a pair of sparkling eyes that had captured the crescent-moon's reflection off the water. "Very pretty."

She wore the same periwinkle dress that she had at the train station, and her silky curls matched its softness. Sarah Ann lifted her head to the heavens. "The stars, silly," she said.

Ben's heart pounded, and his eyes followed hers over the lake to the bright grouping above the hillside. "Oh, yes, the stars," he said, "very pretty."

She sidestepped the bicycle and sidled up to him until her leg brushed against his. She raised one hand to the sky and lightly touched his shoulder with the other. "That's Ursa Major," she said, "the Big Dipper. Slaves used to call it the drinking gourd.

'Follow the drinking gourd,' they used to sing, to help them find their way under the cover of night."

Ben searched for something interesting to say, something that would really impress. He knew nothing about stars, but he could tell her about the music academy. He knew nothing about slave songs, but he could ask her about the art school in New York. He struggled to find the right words, but Sarah Ann's touch filled him and his mind went blank. His legs went limp, and if it hadn't been for his firm grip on the bicycle, he would have fallen over. "I've never paid much attention to the stars," he said. "Except that they seem so far away."

Sarah Ann slid her hand down Ben's arm and gently peeled his fingers from the handlebars. The bicycle fell to the ground, and the two now stood hand in hand, face to face. Ben stared at Sarah Ann as she ran her thumbs over the back of his trembling hands.

"I know what you mean," she said, swinging his arms out and back as if she were playing an intimate game of ring around the rosy. "Before I left for school, my father told me to aim for the stars. But sometimes, searching for things so far away, I've felt I may have missed what was standing right next to me."

A silence passed that seemed to go on forever. Ben didn't mind. He would have held hands with her on the boardwalk all night long. He wished, though, he could pause and dry his sweaty palms, but he didn't dare risk letting go.

The eternal bliss was interrupted when a woman's voice came across the boardwalk. "Five minutes, dear."

Sarah Ann looked over her shoulder.

"Do you need to go?" said Ben.

"I don't want my mother to worry."

"Maybe I'll see you tomorrow?"

"Maybe. But I'm sure my mother will keep me busy this week. And we leave for New York on Friday, and then for Scotland on Monday to see my grandparents in Dunfermline. And then it's straight back to school."

Ben's fingers slipped free, and the two separated. Sarah Ann moved away, and Ben quickly took his hands to her waist.

Sarah Ann tilted her head to the side and looped her arms around his. "Are you really going to New York?" she said.

Ben nodded, resting his hands on her hips like he was at a junior cotillion. Sarah Ann moved her hands up his arms and pulled him closer. They exchanged smiles, and a rush of wind pushed them together. With his chin quivering, Ben leaned down to meet her. He closed his eyes, breathed her scent, and brought his lips closer to Sarah Ann's.

"Sarah Ann, dear. Time to come in."

The two froze, and Ben backed away.

Sarah Ann slowly pressed her lips together and gave Ben's arms one more playful swing. "Follow the drinking gourd," she said, and skipped off toward the cottages.

Ben watched her until she left the boardwalk and disappeared into the woods by the cottages. He was going to New York, and that was that. He had his money, he had his ticket. He would catch the train Sunday morning and be at Grand Central Depot before the Decoration Day parade in River Fork reached the dam. And his father, busy mingling with his newfound friends at the Clubhouse, would never know he'd left.

13

Clem's shop was dark, the windows and the small door shut and latched, the barn doors strapped and locked with a rusty chain. He had worked all day staining a small oak end-table, and after a hearty meal of venison stew, he sat on the porch to watch the stars. When he finished his coffee, he went upstairs to read the Good Book by candlelight.

Every evening, Clem ended the day with a verse or two. Between pages he'd stop and massage his hands, working a thumb around the palm and up through the fingers. Years of cutting and sanding wood had made his hands stiff, and they ached with a steady pain. He looked out the window at the empty house next door, vacant now for almost a year. It was when the house was empty that the aching returned. When he had guests, he didn't feel the pain. He did, however, feel his eyes weighing heavy in his head, and he set down the Book, curled up next to his bedside candle and pinched out the flame.

As Clem drifted off, three hunched figures moved alongside the shop through the cool air, the crunching of leaves under their feet masked by a chorus of chirping crickets. A tall, thin boy carrying an iron pipe reached the end of the wall next to a woodpile. He dropped the pipe and hunched in front of a haystack. Like a jack-in-the box, he sprung and pointed toward the second floor window. "Hey Slug," he called, "he's put out his light."

A heavy-set boy with bloodshot eyes came up from behind.

"Quiet, stupid, you'll wake him up." Slug punched the scrawny boy in the arm and pulled him down behind the haystack. "We wait a bit, till he's good and asleep."

A short boy, red-faced and freckled, crawled over a pile of scrap wood and sat against the haystack with the others. "Go easy on Skinny," he said. "That old man can't hear us down here."

"Yeah, you tell him, Red, he can't hear us down here."

Slug punched Red in the shoulder. "The hell he can't. That ol' timer's got ears like a nervous jackrabbit. We wait here for a bit, till he's good and asleep."

"Are you sure he's got turpentine in there?" asked Skinny, "'cause my pa's got a good bottle of ether we could swipe."

"It's a woodshop," said Slug. "The old man's got tin cans full of that shit in there."

Red leaned forward. "I need to get movin'," he said, scratching his back, "this haystack's aggravatin' my sunburn."

Slug pulled Red by the collar and slapped him on the back. "Serves you right, swimmin' round in that lake all afternoon. Ha, you get sunburned even when it's rainin'."

"How come you never go in?" said Skinny.

Slug pushed Red into the haystack. "Splash around naked with you two nancies?" he said, "Hell, I've even seen nigger families washin' in there. I ain't swimmin' in no nigger water, thank you."

Red was still cringing from the slap when a rustling came from under the woodpile. Red kicked his feet out. A snake lay motionless, hidden under a thin cover of maple leaves. "It sure is fun," he said, "You should try it sometime."

"Jesus," said Slug, "I really need that turpentine now. You two marys are givin' me the shivers. Grab the pipe, let's get to work on that barn door."

Red reached for the pipe, and the snake shot out from under the leaves, coiling itself into a tight ring, tongue-spitting arrowhead at the front, segmented rattle shaking vigorously at the end of its tail.

The boys inched themselves away.

"Get it, Slug," said Skinny. "Give it a whack."

Slug grabbed the pipe and drew it back over his shoulder, his hand jittering at the wrist.

The snake jabbed its head forward, feinting a strike.

Slug flinched and grabbed Skinny by the shoulder. He shoved the pipe against Skinny's chest and scooted back. "You do it, you pansy."

Skinny brought the pipe down hard, flattening the snake's head against the leaves in a series of blows that left a clump of red mush where the spitting tongue had been. He threaded the pipe under the snake's belly and flung its limp body into a puddle of mud.

Slug had already jumped to his feet, and was hurrying to the big barn doors that faced the street. Red and Skinny got up and followed.

It was quiet, except for the crickets and the distant sound of rolling water from the river. Slug looked around. He separated three pieces of straw from a bundle he'd pulled from the haystack, threw the rest to the ground, and held up the strands in a closed fist. "You pick one, Skinny. All right Red, now you," he said, pinching off the bottom half with his thumbnail as Red pulled it out.

The boys compared straws. Red's was the shortest. "Bad luck," said Slug, taking the pipe from Skinny and slapping it into Red's hand. "Now jam it in between the lock and the chain, and prier her open."

Red slid the pipe into the chain where Slug had shown him. He gave the pipe a strong twist and the lock snapped. The chain loosened around the door handles and slid to the ground.

Skinny went to the corner of the shop and checked the house. "Nothin'," he said in a coarse whisper. "Looks like he's still asleep."

Slug checked the road once more, and with a slow creek from the barn door hinges, they went inside.

Just past the threshold, Red knocked over a chair that was balanced on a small table. Slug grabbed Red's sunburned neck. "Watch where you're goin', you'll wake up the old man."

"I can't see a thing," said Red.

"Let your eyes adjust a bit," said Slug, "Give it a minute, then look for those cans."

As the room came into focus, they listened for movement from the back-house. When Slug gave the go-ahead, they weaved their way singlefile around the silhouette of furniture to the far corner of the room and a tall cabinet stocked with tin cans.

"I think I see one," said Skinny. He took a can from the shelf and handed it to Slug. "Is this the stuff?"

Slug popped the lid with his pocket knife and took a sniff. He set the can on the shelf and smacked Skinny in the back of the head. "Shit," he said, "this ain't nothin' but water, stupid, look for one that says turpentine on it."

They searched the shelves until they came to a row of cans striped with rust. "How about this one?" said Red. "There's a word on the front, starts with a T".

Slug pried off the lid and confirmed it with a sniff. "This is it. Now, each of you grab one and get out of here."

Following orders, they each took a can. Red turned and lost his footing on the sawdust-covered floor. He grabbed hold of the shelf and the entire rack fell with him to the ground. The loud crash was followed by movement inside the back-house, then the unmistakable 'chick-chack' of a shotgun.

"Who's in there?" the voice called.

The boys got to their feet, but the darkness and the clutter of Clem's shop made for a difficult escape. Clem burst through the back barn doors, and Slug, Red and Skinny fled with cans under their arms, knocking down shelves and furniture until they found the front door. Clem followed them through the shop, gaining ground.

Outside, Red and Skinny had made their getaway, but when Slug reached the road, he collided with Ben and the Safety Rover. The handlebars twisted, and the bicycle came to an abrupt halt. Ben launched into the air, slamming into Slug and the turpentine can and falling face first to the ground.

Mineral spirits dripped from Slug's forehead, but his eyes remained wide open. He scowled, spitting out the turpentine that had splattered into his mouth. "If I get caught," he said, running his sleeve across his face, "I'm blamin' you. You better watch your back." He said it again as he threw the empty can to the ground and ran off down the road and out of sight.

Ben pushed himself up to his knees and was wiping the mud and turpentine from his face when a strong hand gripped his shoulder. He spun around, scooted back on his heels, and broke free.

The moon sat directly behind the tall figure, wrapping the man's silhouette with a radiant glow that intensified around the top of his head, encircling it like a halo. The figure held a shotgun in one hand, and reached out to Ben with the other. Ben took the shadow's hand and was swiftly lifted to his feet.

"You all right?" said Clem.

Ben bunched his shirt together and rung out a good drip of turpentine. "I think so."

Clem fanned his face. "I'll be sure to hold off on my late-night cigar till you dry out."

Ben pulled his bicycle off the road and leaned it against the shop. The front of the frame was cockeyed, sitting at a right angle to the back end. The chain had snapped and twisted up between the metal spokes of the rear wheel.

"That bruiser sure did a number on her," said Clem. "Good thing she was there to take the brunt of it. Let's get her inside and fix her up."

Ben searched his shirt for a dry spot to wipe his face. "Don't bother," he said, "We can't fix it."

"Well," said Clem, "unless you only want to make left turns, I reckon we ought to give it a shot, come on."

Clem went into the shop, righting the toppled furniture and the storage rack and returning the tin cans to their proper place on the shelves. He lit a gas lamp and set it on the work bench. "Bring'er on back," he shouted.

Ben dragged the bicycle across the floor to an open area in front of the work bench. Clem helped him flip the bike end over end, resting it upon the seat and the crooked handlebars. Clem gave the front wheel a spin. "That looks good," he said, moving to the back of the bike and fiddling with the rear wheel. "I was surprised to see you this morning. Thought you were headin' off to New York."

It was a good thing he'd purchased the train ticket, Ben thought; bike riding to New York was no longer an option. "I'm planning to."

Clem rattled the back wheel until the chain zigzagged free of the spokes. "And how long were you figurin' on plannin', before you figured on doin'?"

It was a strange question. One Ben had never been asked by his father. Though Ben had been schooled in the art of planning, he'd missed his father's lessons on doing.

Clem took the chain and looped it over the sprockets. The broken ends swung out and back and knocked against the frame. He went to the work bench and rummaged through the drawers, pulling out handfuls of furniture latches and door hinges and piling them on the tabletop.

"Ain't this a woodshop?" said Ben, "This bicycle is made out of metal."

Clem fished through the clutter of hardware. "We just need a bit of ingenuity, that's all." He found a brass hinge that seemed to interest him and held it up to the lamp. "You ever heard of a fourth season proposal?" he asked.

"No."

"I knew a fella once, never heard of it either."

Clem set the hinge on the pile and searched for another. "See, this fella wanted to ask his gal to marry him. So he planned out the whole thing, with a poem, a song, a ring, and a secluded spot by a perfect lake where he was gonna ask her." Another hinge caught

99

his eye, and he examined it next to the light. "Anyway, winter came and he was all set to ask her, but it was so cold, the lake had frozen up. Then spring came and it rained so hard, the shoreline around the lake flooded." He went back to the pile and found another hinge. "Now it was summer, and it was so damn hot, the roses he'd bought her had plumb wilted over." Clem spun around, holding a thick, brass door-hinge between his fingers. "Here's the one," he said, pinching it around the top and removing the pin.

"So what about this fella?" said Ben, "Did the gal say yes?"

"He never asked her. Turns out, by the time fall changed the color of the leaves, someone else had stolen her away. I suppose she didn't feel like waitin' any longer."

"Too bad for him," said Ben. "But I ain't looking to get married, not yet that is."

Clem bent down and studied the broken chain. "No," he said, "I suppose not."

Ben knelt opposite Clem so the chain was at eye level.

"Feed those two ends together," said Clem. "We're gonna splice her right where she broke off."

Ben took the open links and meshed them together, lining up the holes where the rivet had been. "You really think we can fix her?"

Clem stuck the hinge pin through the hole and went to the work bench for a hammer and a small block of wood. "You can fix almost anything with a splice," he said, "ropes, wires, chains, all you need is something strong to hold the two ends together." He slid the hammer under the bicycle and braced the wood-block against the chain. "I'm gonna set the block on this side, and you're gonna ram the pin with the hammer. We'll flatten it round the link like a rivet."

Ben drew back the hammer while he held the splice in place with his thumb and index finger. He brought the blunt end to the chain in a full swing, smashing the back of his thumb. In a reflex, he yanked his hand away and dropped the hammer. "It's no use," he said, grimacing from the sharp pain and checking the damage to his thumbnail that had already turned purple around the quick. "This ain't gonna work. Even if we can fix the chain, we'll never get that frame straightened out. Might as well just get a new one."

"Don't give up on her so soon," said Clem. "Just because she's beat up don't mean she ain't worth fixin'. It's like one of them bare-knuckle boxers who gets his clock cleaned in the first round. It don't make him quit. It makes him tougher for the next round. We're gonna fix up this Rover just like them spongers and bottle-holders patch up them prizefighters in the corner of the ring. When we get done, she'll be better than new, ready for the next fight." Clem slid the hammer to Ben. "Now try it again."

Ben gave the hinge pin a whack, and the makeshift rivet flattened against the chain link. Clem did the same on his side while Ben used his good hand to hold the block of wood.

Clem tugged on the chain. "Nice and taut," he said. "Now let's have a look at that frame."

Ben set the bicycle down as flat as the bowed metal would allow. The thin frame stuck up like a dinner triangle. "If that boy bent her out," he said, "maybe I can bend her back."

"That might not be the best approach," said Clem. "I'll bet your father could straighten her out up at the foundry. You sure you don't want to let him have a look?"

"I'm sure," said Ben, stepping onto the peak and balancing with arms outstretched as if he were walking a tightrope. Ben bounced on the bicycle, pushing the curved frame closer to the ground with each hop.

"If you force that thing too hard," said Clem, "she's liable to...."

Ben's foot came down on the frame and the metal snapped. The bicycle slid out from under him and he fell backward onto the freshly stained end-table. One of the turned legs splintered off and caught Ben square in the back as he hit the ground.

Ben's face tuned beet red. He sat up and massaged his back where the table leg had struck him. "Shit," he said, "Now it's busted for good. Ain't no way we can fix it now. I reckon I never deserved anything this nice anyhow."

Without a word, Clem went to the workbench and put away the hinges and the hardware.

"I'm sorry to have caused you so much trouble, Mr. Clem," said Ben, waiting for a response.

Clem was silent.

Ben stood and brushed off his shirt. "I'm gonna leave now," he said, "before I ruin the rest of your shop." He left the broken Safety Rover on the floor and walked away, shuffling through the sawdust and out the door.

When Ben arrived home, he found his father slumped at the edge of the porch with his elbows on his knees, a small piece of paper in one hand, a half-empty whiskey bottle in the other.

Percival took a big swig and looked up. "You're home late," he said, "Where've you been?"

Ben took off his knapsack and sat next to his father. "Big dinner at the Club," he said. "Had to work late."

Percival grunted, took another gulp of whiskey, and leaned back on his elbows. "The Club, huh? To hell with that place."

Ben had never seen his father so haggard, and at the moment, hell was exactly the place Percival looked like he belonged. "Pa," said Ben, "What happened?"

Percival swung his head toward Ben. "I done got fired, that's what happened. After twenty years with the company. Fired. And all because Crick won't let the Union come in. All I wanted was what's fair for the men, and I get fired over it." He leaned to one side and brought the bottle to his lips for a quick drink. "That son-of-a-bitch Crick, got laborers working twenty-four hour shifts in those hell holes for ten dollars a week, arms scarred up from razor-wire and hands chopped off from steam engines. And there's Crick, shittin' in high cotton and wipin' his ass with the whitest bolls."

Ben waited to respond until Percival finished another visit to the bottle. "Jeez, pa, fired? That ain't fair. You said they were gonna give you that executive job."

"I reckon Crick done found a way to save some more money instead."

"They at least give you your owed pay?"

"My owed pay?" said Percival, holding the whiskey high over his head, "Here's the last of it." He dropped the bottle to his lips and took a swig.

"All of it gone at the saloon?" said Ben. "That must be expensive whiskey."

Percival gathered himself and sat up, hanging his legs over the porch. He kicked at the dirt and shrugged. "They sell more than just whiskey at the saloon."

Percival held up the paper he was clutching, a photograph. From the pale light of the porch lamp, Ben saw the faded image of a young woman. She was posed by a staircase like a statue, one arm bracing herself on the banister, the other hanging loosely at her side. She wore a long flowing dress and a soft smile. Her eyes stared straight at Ben.

Percival set the bottle down and touched the photograph with his fingertips. "You know, I told you your mother left us."

Ben remembered agreeing not to talk about his mother. He kept his promise and nodded.

A tear ran from the corner of Percival's eye, and he gave the photograph to Ben. "That weren't entirely true," he said, staring into his lap. "We met at a town dance, fell in love right away and got married. I wanted to take care of her on my own, so we left her family and moved to East Liberty. I heard there were big money jobs in the steel industry. She didn't want to go, but I packed us up anyhow."

Ben folded his hands in his lap like his father had done, and thought back to his childhood in East Liberty. "I don't remember her at all."

"You wouldn't have. She died the day you were born."

Heavy drops thumped in the dirt, and Percival kicked at the dark splotches with both legs. "The doctor knew it; said only one of you would survive. Your mother wanted it to be you. Last thing she said to me was to make sure I took good care of you. Then she died."

Ben recalled being teased at school and picked on after Sunday service, the boy whose mother cared so little about him she left without a saying a word. "Why didn't you tell me?"

The rain fell harder, and Percival rested his head in his hands. "I guess I thought by not tellin' you, I was doin' what your mother wanted. Maybe I was wrong."

Ben stared at the puddles pooling in the dirt. He was in no mood to be saddled with the emotions of East Liberty, and the memories of a mother he never knew. Not now. Not when thoughts of music, and the lure of New York City filled his mind. He pulled himself out of the past and focused on more relevant matters. "What about the house, pa?" he said. "Don't the company own it? Reckon they won't let us stay here if you don't work for the company no more."

"Where are we gonna get the money?" said Percival, seizing the bottle, his hand shaking as he brought it to his mouth.

"I'm talking about the house, pa. Where are we going to live?"

"No money left," said Percival, "what are we gonna do about money?"

Ben was losing his father between thoughts, and figured it best not add insult to injury. "I've got some saved," he said. "Not much, but we'll find a way to make do."

Percival hiccupped a small belch. "Two days," he said, "one to clear out, and one more because Crick's such a swell guy." He took a drink. "Then, I don't know where I'll go."

"Where you will go, pa. What about me?"

Percival's eyes fluttered and his words began to slur together. "I know you've got plans to leave this town," he said with a heavy breath, "and study your music. You don't need me holdin' you back. Do what you need to do, and don't worry 'bout me none."

In the battle with the bottle, the booze had finally won, and

Percival swayed out and back as if he were sitting in a rocking chair. He fell forward, taking himself and the whiskey bottle over the edge of the porch and into a shallow puddle. He tried to stand, but fell face first into the mud, what was left of the whiskey spilling onto the ground.

Ben grabbed his father around the waist and helped him into the house. He set him in front of the fireplace and dropped a pine log onto the fire. With a long poker, he worked the embers beneath the log, and the flames sprung up and warmed the room. He tucked the photograph into his father's muddy shirt, covered him with a flannel blanket, and went upstairs to fetch a blanket of his own. He curled up next to the fire and stared into the flames. The rain fell in a soothing rhythm, tapping out a peaceful melody on the roof. Ben shut his eyes and played a perfect version of Beethoven's Tempest with the rain.

While Crick's absence would have typically made for a pleasant evening, Parke grew suspicious when he failed to return to the lounge. It wouldn't have bothered him had Crick's disappearance been solitary, or with the purpose of attending to pressing business matters, or even to answer the unpredictable call of nature. But Crick had no business of either kind, and moreover, he had gone missing in the company of his wife, Lily.

Addison and Damrosch were enjoying the Club's fine selection of aged whiskey while Parke, the effects of the absinthe wearing off, sipped on a glass of water. Although his expertise was in pocket billiards, he had no trouble embarrassing both men in various games of carom pool. Between visits to the table, he had hoped to gain some insight into the potential problems with the dam, but as it turned out, Addison's work had been limited to sketching and drawing, and he knew nothing about engineering or embankment dam construction. His willingness to help Parke had only been a means to secure an invitation to the Club.

After Addison and Damrosch retired, Parke practiced straight shots and cut shots until he was sinking two-carom banks with his eyes closed. When his arm began to throb from pounding breaks so hard the sound of cracking ivory could be heard on the boardwalk, he returned his cue to the rack and went upstairs.

No longer flying with the green fairy, he sat at the end of his bed, listening to footsteps in the hall moving swiftly past his door and finding their place in different rooms. It was boredom, anticipation, or curiosity, he didn't know which, that took him from his waiting spot and into Lily's side of their adjoining rooms. A globe lamp burned on the nightstand, throwing the long shadow of a wine glass and a half-empty flask of whiskey onto the unmade bed.

The shelf above the pedestal sink was cluttered with an assortment of unfamiliar perfume bottles, a few of which had fallen onto the floor and now sat in a pool of sticky resin. Inside the wardrobe, Parke found a trove of long dresses and lace corsets, all borrowed, he supposed, or on loan from the member's wives. He searched the drawers for the matching dress and bonnet he'd gifted Lily on their wedding day and found them crumpled beneath a stack of neatly folded bodices and undergarments.

An odd, syncopated thumping in the hall drew his attention away from the dresser. The handle rattled for a moment, and the door opened. Parke was stunned when Lily came into the room, ragged and disheveled. Her bonnet was missing, the side of her dress was torn, and in her hand was one of her shoes, its heal missing, the frayed strap broken off at the buckle. When she shut the door, the smell of alcohol wafted across the room. Parke winced, and before he could ask her where she'd been, Lily hurried to the washbasin. She dropped the broken shoe into the wastebasket, kicked off its mate, and wet a small linen towel. Then, as if Parke were invisible, she marched right past him, plopping herself onto the bed and draping the cool rag across her forehead.

Parke waited for at least an acknowledgement of his presence, but when none came, he put his hands on his hips, hoping to draw Lily's attention. "It's late," he said.

Lily turned away and stared at the bedside table. "Is it?"

"Very," said Parke, picking up the good shoe and tossing it into the wastebasket next to its ruined partner. "Where have you been?"

Lily groaned and put a hand to her head. "I was helping Ada Crick, remember," she said, slouching against the headboard and taking deep breaths. "Helping Ada Crick."

Parke went to the bedside table and spun around the table clock, facing it toward Lily. "And for the four hours after that?"

Lily dropped her hand and the towel fell into her lap. Beads of water ran down her matted hair and into her face. Her eyes glistened in the light of the globe lamp a glassy, bloodshot red. "Ada needed a lot of help," she said, laughing to herself.

Parke shook his head. "And your hat, your dress, your shoe?"

Lily giggled. "Ada's a big woman."

Parke pulled out a red satin dress from the armoire. "These dresses," he said, holding the flowery gown folded over his arm, "and bonnets...gifts, I suppose?"

Lily stared at the dress. "So this is the thanks I get?" she said. "Here I go out of my way to help someone, and I get scolded for my trouble. I'd expect at least a 'Thank you, Lily', or, 'I'm so happy for you, Lily, that now you have such fashionable clothes to wear'."

Parke paced at the foot of the bed. "I'm not scolding you," he said, "I'm simply asking you where you've been. I was worried."

"And what are you worried about, John."

Parke took the whiskey bottle and held it up to the globe lamp. "I'm worried about losing the woman I married."

Lily turned away.

Parke went to the array of perfumes above the sink. "I'm worried about losing her to this place, and to all of these...things. This was not what I intended when I brought us here."

Lily slapped her hands on the bed, sagging even further down the headboard. "And what did you intend, John, if it wasn't to offer me a chance at a life of luxury."

Parke returned to the foot of the bed. "I intended to share the luxury with you, not to have it steal you away. Lately, I've been playing second fiddle to everyone and everything. Is this how you want to spend your time?" He balanced the whiskey bottle and the dress in his hands as if he were weighing them on a scale. "Gallivanting with the member's wives into the wee hours of the night?"

"Don't tell me you don't imbibe," said Lily, "in your billiard lounge and your..."

"Within reason, yes," he said, "but I've never 'misplaced' my hat, or broken a shoe because of it. And I most definitely didn't bring you here for the soirées. I brought you here to spend time with me, not the member's wives."

Parke went to the sink and poured out the whiskey.

Lily tried to get up but teetered backward, knocking her head against the headboard.

"I'd like it if just once," Parke said, dropping the empty flask into the wastebasket, "you'd put me over a luncheon. Just once, choose me over a dinner party."

Lily rubbed her head as she slid onto her back and stared at the ceiling. "And what do I do while you're working all day and into the night, fixing and repairing, and investigating who knows what about that rotten dam. What do I say when they ask me to join them for a luncheon at their cottage, or for a sailing trip on the lake, or for a dinner party. And what do I say when they tell me you're just the hired help, and that the only reason you were given this job is because they couldn't find anyone else. And what do I say when all of this goes away. And it will, John. It will all go away. And what do I say, then."

Parke was taken aback, and a sting of sadness welled inside him. He stared at Lily in her torn dress, the smooth material of which he'd never felt against his skin. "You say, Lily, that I'm your husband. That's what you say. And unless these 'things' can provide for you something more than I can..." he threw the satin dress to the floor, "...you say, that you're my wife."

14

Ben expected to see his father asleep beside him. Maybe, he thought, he had awoken during the night and moved himself to bed.

The ceiling in Percival's room sloped to a spring box-bed and an open window just as it did in Ben's room. Yesterday, the chest of drawers was full of undergarments, overalls, long-johns, trousers, and button-down shirts for Sunday mornings. An assortment of wood carvings Percival made before his steel days had sat atop the dresser, including a hand-shaped wooden bowl for his billfold and pocket watch. But this morning, Ben found the room and the chest of drawers empty, the bric-a-brac gone. The only thing indicating his father had ever lived there was the picture of Ben's mother lying on the floor in the corner of the room. Ben picked up the photograph, folded it into a small square, and slipped it into his hip pocket.

Back in his room, Ben stuffed a pair of pants, two shirts, and a roll of socks into his knapsack. He took the cigar box from under his bed and reviewed the contents: thirty dollars, a train ticket, the enrollment invitation, and the academy pin. He fastened the pin above his shirt pocket, and stuffed the box, with the extent of his possessions, into his pack.

Outside, he stared at the vacant house. He felt its emptiness, greater than simply the absence of its inhabitants. Maybe he would return tonight; maybe he wouldn't. If only he had time to find his father. But searching for him now would mean certain tardiness, and he couldn't afford to be late, not with such an important request of his employer to make.

When he arrived at the Clubhouse, Jean Pierre was at the chopping table, thumbing through a copy of Francatelli's The Cook's Guide, and Housekeepers & Butler's Assistant. "A must", he had told him, "for professionals of the food service trade."

Ben put on his coat and walked over to the chopping table. "You think I could start putting in more work?" he said.

Jean Pierre took his head out of the book. "Why, because this place is just too much fun, eh?"

"I need to make some extra money."

"For what?"

"I just need it."

"All right, all right," said Jean Pierre, "We all need extra money, I understand." He closed The Cook's Guide and folded his arms against his chest. "Problem for you is that I don't make those decisions. You need to speak to Mr. Parke."

Ben marched to the small door and knocked on it hard with a balled fist. The door creaked open.

Parke was sitting at the desk with his head in his hands, holding down a mess of loose papers with his elbows. He popped his head up and glared toward the door. "Damn," he said, "I told them to fix that lock a week ago. It's letting anyone and everyone in here." Parke moved his attention away from the door and focused on Ben. "And what do you want? Storage room's out the swinging doors and down the hall."

"Don't need the storage room sir, just a brief moment of your time, if you can spare it."

Parke rubbed a palm over his stubble, and sighed. "I can, as long as it's truly a brief one."

Ben took a deep breath. "I'd like to ask for more work, sir."

Parke leaned back in his chair. "More work generally means more pay, and we just can't afford that. Now pull that door shut on your way out."

Cowardice told Ben to obey Parke's orders, but courage kept him in the room. "I only ask for my regular pay," he said.

Parke took a moment to respond. Apparently he had forgotten about the arrangement of Ben's salary. "You're forgoing half of your pay to play that piano, aren't you." he said.

"Yes, sir."

Parke examined one of the papers, tapping on it with his pencil. "And what do you propose to do to earn your full salary?"

Ben grabbed the office door and swung it back and forth. The mortise lock was off kilter, rubbing against the door jamb where the lock met the strike plate. "I know a little bit about carpentry," he said, realizing the idle time he'd spent at Clem's woodshop might actually pay off. "I could fix this door if you'd like."

"Is that so," said Parke. "And how would you do that?"

Ben analyzed the door, running his fingers along the jamb and the mortise lock. "Tighten the locking mechanism and the strike plate," he said. "Maybe put a little grease on the hinges too, so the door swings nice and smooth."

Parke was more interested in the paper on his desk, and he continued tapping, whispering numbers in the thirties until he reached the bottom of the page. "I don't think so," he said. "Any one of the Italians can repair it. I don't need to bump you up to full salary just to fix a door."

Ben looked around the room, hoping to find something else that was broken. "I really need the money, sir. I'll do anything."

Parke stared at the paper, making checkmarks and scribbles next to the names. "What I really need is more help on the grounds," he said. "Big project comin' up. Can you do heavy lifting with the Italians?"

Laboring in rock and earth was not the work Ben was looking for, but he had no choice. "I can, sir."

"All right," said Parke, slapping the pencil on the desk. "You tell Jean Pierre that when he doesn't need you, you'll report to me."

"And the pay?"

"Depends on you. Full pay for a full day. No more playing around on that piano."

"Sir?"

"If you want your full pay, there will be no time for messing around with music. Besides, how dirty and smelly you'll be from laboring all day, no one is allowed in the Clubhouse like that. That's the deal, take it or leave it."

Ben stood quiet. With a bit of reluctance, he agreed.

"Good," said Parke, returning to his pencil and his paperwork. "And that door you've been fiddlin' with, shut it on your way out."

When Ben came into the kitchen, Jean Pierre had his head in The Cook's Guide again, flipping a grip of pages back and forth. "The duck...or the filet?" Jean Pierre posed the question to the air.

"What difference does it make." said Ben.

"It makes all the difference," said Jean Pierre. "The decision will determine the rest of the meal. Le canard requires sauce a l'orange and a smooth Bordeaux. Le filet demands sauce béarnaise and a rich Burgundy. Once you begin preparing the entrée, you cannot go back."

"Never?" said Ben.

Jean Pierre twirled his mustache in contemplation. "I suppose if you started with the wrong entrée you could go back and change it. But that would mean different mis en place, time to make the correct sauce, perhaps different herbs, a different wine, possibly you might need to..."

"I understand. A lot of work."

"So what do you think, the duck or the filet?"

"I'm through making decisions today."

Jean Pierre smiled. "Did you get what you wanted in there?"

Ben picked at the edge of the work table. "Sort of."

"You do not look so happy for someone who is getting extra money."

"I've got to give up playin' the piano, and work maintenance with the Italians...when you don't need me, of course."

"I will do my best to keep you in here," said Jean Pierre. "Anyway, you will be off to New York soon. Away from this town and this job. You will be able to play the piano every day."

Ben feared, now, that soon might actually mean never. If only June could wait until Christmas. "Yeah," he said. "I suppose."

"So tell me which one. The duck or the filet?"

"I don't know," said Ben, "the duck."

"And why do you say that. Tell me why you would choose the duck."

"I've tried it before. It was pretty good. And there's a lot of that Bordeaux wine in the storage room. Besides, you made beef last night. Better to serve something different tonight."

"Le canard it is," said Jean Pierre, tossing Ben the copy of The Cook's Guide. Take this, use it when you start your job at my colleague's patisserie. Make sure he sees this book in your hands on your first day, it will be all you need to impress him."

Ben smiled and took the book to the utility room and packed it into his overstuffed knapsack.

15

The Number Six Bridge was the last railroad crossing before the dam. Up trains used it for Mineral Point, Moxham and Johnstown, down trains for Millville, Grubbtown and Sonman. It was a sturdy deck-bridge with thick wooden trusses and an open roadbed, built by the Pennsylvania Railroad some twenty years earlier when the river ran slow beneath its heavy-timber frame and the only activity around it was the pushing and pulling of levers by a lone flagman who stood at the water's edge and worked the semaphore.

When the factories were built, traffic over the bridge increased ten-fold. Now, more than fifty trains a day crossed the 250 foot span. A coal tipple stood on the south side, a massive weave of wood beams over thirty feet high, with a double-bucket hoist, a fifty-ton bin, and a swiveling iron chute that could fill a tender in less than two minutes. On the north side, the flagman's job of flipping levers had been replaced by a right-angled signal scaffold that extended high over the tracks, with sliding gas lamps and a small deck where the controller could stand while he worked the pulleys. Behind the scaffold was a twenty-foot high tower of crisscrossed wooden planks that looked like a giant garden box-lattice.

Along the side of the tower, a narrow stairway zigzagged up to the telegraph office, a small square shack with a flat roof, windowed on all sides and attached to the valley by an umbilical cord of twisted wires draped between wooden crosses. On a clear day, the operator could see for miles, westward to the viaduct at Smith's Crossing, or eastward to the dam, where the black Victorias crawled across the carriage road like tiny spiders.

The man in charge of the Number Six tower was determined, strong, and quick on his feet. However, the man in charge of the Number Six tower was a woman.

Emma Ehrenfeld was twenty-seven years old. She had worked at Union Station in Johnstown for six years until Eddie Hunt, a man, asked to be transferred out of the busy Number Six tower, the 'rats nest', as the valley operators called it. The supervisor at Union Station had come to Emma one day and told her to "pack her things," there was an "opportunity" to work at the Number Six Bridge. Apparently, none of the men had volunteered. Today was her third day in the rats nest.

She was six hours into her twelve-hour shift when a flagman came up to the tower on horseback. He clomped up the stairs, and she could hear him mumbling to himself. "Jesus, the smoke is thick, I almost rode into the river, can barely see the bridge from the siding." He burst through the door. "Eddie boy," he shouted.

Emma stared straight ahead, arranging papers on the small desk and straightening the telegraph and telephone machines against the window. She sat upon a stack of log books and procedure manuals giving her a better view out the window.

The flagman spoke with a twang in his voice as if his nose had been pinched shut. "You're not Eddie," he said, dipping into a pouch of leaf tobacco and stuffing a fistful into his mouth. "But I ain't complainin'. You're much easier on the eyes. What's your name, darlin'?"

"Emma Ehrenfeld, I'm the operator at this tower now."

"Well isn't that fine." He laid a smile on her, revealing a sparse row of stained, crooked teeth, and paced around the room with a lopsided swagger that suggested he'd spent more time on the saddle than at the signal station. A breeze blew through the tower and moved his stench around the room. "I'm Kinney," he said, "Fastest flagman on the rails. If you ever get scared up here all alone, darlin', you just holler. Maybe I'll even switch places with them books of yours, let you sit on my lap." Kinney roamed, looking behind the hat rack and inside a box of unclaimed overcoats. He went to the desk and examined the stack of papers, trying to act nonchalant.

Emma could tell the only thing he was interested in 'examining' was her. "I'm fine with the books, thank you."

Kinney stood over Emma while he picked at the tobacco between his teeth. "You got a bag in here for me?" he asked, "Or am I gonna have to keep searchin' for it myself." He reached down between Emma's legs. "Maybe you got it hidden under your seat."

Emma pushed herself away and grabbed a canvas bag she had shoved under the desk. "This what you come in for?" she said.

Kinney took the bag and untied the drawstring. "Ah, torpedo detonators," he said, "These little fellas will give you quite a bang. What do you say, sweet thing, you interested?"

"Not interested in little fellas from fast flagmen," said Emma.

"Oh," said Kinney, pointing at Emma's attire, "So that's it. Man's pants, man's flannel, even a man's bowler. You ain't one of those types, are you?"

Emma learned long ago not to answer questions that led to more questions, especially when they came from pesky men. She was in a man's world, though, and had accepted that from time to time she would have to deal with men being men. "You got what you come in for," she said, "Now get on down to the signal."

Kinney put the bag on the floor, took out one of the torpedoes and set it on the desk. The poufy red pouch, used to warn engineers of trouble on the track, was the size of a bar of soap, something Emma thought might do Kinney a bit of good. The leather straps on either end gave the small flour-sack the look of a fat, square belt buckle. Kinney went to the toolbox and came back with a ball-peen hammer.

"What are you gonna do?" said Emma.

Kinney raised the hammer and brought it down on the detonator with a thud.

Emma turned away.

116

The pouch split open, throwing a puff of white powder into the air.

Kinney dropped the hammer on the desk and burst out in a convulsion of laughter, "Only pressure can set 'em off, honey," he said, "Boy, I got you on that one."

Kinney's stench was right on top of her. "The railroad is a man's job," he said, "It ain't no place for a jumpity woman." He knelt, took Emma's bowler from her head and put it on his. "Why don't you let a real man wear this."

Kinney held on to Emma's chair, keeping her pinned against the desk as he nibbled on the back of her neck. She raised her shoulders and leaned forward, but Kinney stuck on her like a hungry horsefly. Emma gripped the hammer. "You stop it now, you hear. I'm warnin' you." She drew back the hammer and was about to sink it into Kinney's skull when a train-whistle blew. The Limited was pulling up to the bridge. Emma dropped the hammer. Kinney stood up as if a drill-sergeant had called him to attention.

A set of heavy footsteps came up the stairs, and the conductor and the engineer stomped into the office. Emma knew them as Deckert and Hess. Deckert was the cleanest conductor on the rails, sporting a double-breasted jacket and a tight waistcoat, clad with brass buttons and matching cufflinks. A square black hat with a shiny bill rested atop his head.

Engineer Hess was a short, pudgy man who wore thin rimmed glasses and light blue coveralls. His clothing and his pin-striped cap were stained with streaks of grease and engine oil.

"Ma'am," said Deckert, tugging on his handsome hat, "Any reason we've got a red light?" He took out a gold pocket watch clipped to a beaded chain and checked the time, making especially sure Emma got a good look at it.

"Well," said Emma, "Mr. Kinney here…"

Kinney stepped in front of Emma and finished her thought, "…just came up to show this gal how to work the new telephone," he said, shaking his head, "'women'. I'll be down in a jiff and have her to green, lickety-split."

117

"Why don't you go, now," said Deckert, polishing the pocket watch on his lapel.

"Yes, sir," said Kinney. He grabbed the bag of torpedo detonators and left.

"You got orders for the Limited?" asked Deckert.

Emma sifted through the paperwork. "Only for her to head on up on track number three."

Hess went to the window. "A lot of haze out there," he said, "Can't tell if it's storm clouds or factory smoke. Any news about the weather?"

"Just porch-talk about the storm that's comin'," she said, stretching her neck for look. "It was spittin' when the sun come up. But since then, it's been dry."

A thick black smoke had settled over the river. Even the Limited, sitting right below the tower, was covered in a soupy fog. Emma looked down at the train and could barely see Kinney kneeling in front of the engine with his torpedo bag.

"Well, all right then," said Deckert, "Reckon we'll head up the hill after we fill up."

Emma flipped through the papers again. "I don't have any orders for the Limited to fill up here," she said.

"I'm sure they're in there," said Deckert, "Why don't you have another look."

Emma went back to the papers as Hess and Deckert clomped out of the office and down the stairs.

A shout came from below the tower. "Can you give me a hand down here, darlin'," said Kinney, "This contraption is stuck. I can't seem to get her to budge."

The last thing Emma wanted to do was help Kinney. But with Hess, Deckert, and the rest of the Limited crew present, she couldn't think of a good enough reason not to. When she came down to the signal, the Limited was still held up shy of the bridge. Hess was in the engine cab. Deckert and Kinney were twiddling with the lamp-lever at the signal scaffold.

"I think it might need a woman's touch," said Kinney, backing away with Deckert and letting Emma take a look on her own.

Emma tugged at the pulleys. The lamps slid and swiveled with ease. "Seems all right to me," she said.

Hess moved the Limited across the bridge, rolling over a torpedo detonator Kinney had strapped to the rail. The pouch exploded with an ear-ringing blast, shooting out a huge cloud of white smoke from under the train. Emma jumped back and screamed. Kinney's horse kicked its legs and stomped at the ground. The men laughed. Even the proper conductor Deckert joined in.

Kinney was buckled over, holding his side with one hand and flapping Emma's bowler against his leg with the other, "I told you this ain't no place for a woman," he said.

"Enough horse play," said Deckert. "Move her under the tipple Mr. Hess, and fill her up."

Emma had already shaken off the practical joke and was back in front of Deckert. "I couldn't find any orders for a stop here," she said, dusting off her trousers. "You need to head on up the hill and fill up in Sonman." She added one more demand, "And tell that dirty, filthy flagman, I'd like my hat back."

Deckert ignored her orders, and her plea for the hat. He rested a hand on her shoulder and walked her back to the tower. "I know you're just doin' what you're told," he said, "And I can appreciate that. But if we wait, and fill up in Sonman, they'll be six trains ahead of us, and that will put me way behind schedule. Now you go on, get back up to your desk and look pretty. We've got it from here."

Deckert left Emma at the tower and walked alongside the rails as the Limited lumbered across the bridge. Procedure said to pull off to the siding, but Hess left the tender and the six boxcars on the bridge.

The brakeman climbed onto the engine, and with the help of a long-handled pole, he fetched the coal chute and swung it toward the tender. When it reached the train, it scraped against the boiler and fell into the open space between the engine and the tender.

The tipple operator came onto the deck and shouted down at the brakeman. "What the hell are you doing," he said, "you can't fill up from there."

The chute was wedged against the tender. Hess moved the train, and the chute was dragged forward and the wooden beams at the base of the tower began to split.

"Stop, stop," the operator shouted, "She's gonna break."

For a moment, Emma thought about helping them. But instead, she let the men do as they will and went up to the office. At the desk, she peered out the window. Now, every man at the bridge was working to free the stuck chute.

Emma was wiping the torpedo powder off the desk when a call came over the speaking telegraph. It was the yardmaster at Mineral Point. "Where have you been?" he said, "I've been trying to reach you."

"Problem with the semaphore," she said.

"The Day Express left here ten minutes ago," said the yardmaster. "She's headed your way. Orders are to clear the bridge and hold all trains on the siding till she passes."

Emma looked out the window. Kinney and the brakeman were on top of the train attempting to lift the chute over the engine. Hess and the fireman were trying to uncouple the engine. Deckert was pacing and pointing.

Emma went back to the telephone, "Ten minutes ago?" The line crackled. "Wait, wait," she hollered, "Tell the Express to hold up. I've got a train stuck on the bridge." There was no answer; the line was dead. Emma stuck her head all the way out the window and yelled to the men. "Get that train off the bridge. The Express is coming. Clear the track."

The men were arguing over what to do with the chute and paid her no mind.

She got on the telephone and called to the roundhouse for a helper train. If the men could get the engine out of the way, she thought, a helper could move the cars quickly off the tracks once the chute was freed. "You've got to send a helper down, right away," she told the man at the roundhouse.

"Sorry," he said, "I don't have any orders for a helper. You'll have to call the yardmaster at Mineral Point for approval."

Before she could tell him why she needed the helper, he dropped the line. Emma slammed the receiver on the desk and hurried down the stairs. She could see the Day Express, with its five mail cars, running in the distance behind the factories at the base of the hillside. It was about a mile from the sweeping turn that would take it into the valley and straight toward the river.

She hollered to the men now trying to unhook the chute from the tipple. They were barely visible through the thick smoke, and still uninterested in what she had to say. Once the Express made the turn, she knew the engineer would never see the Limited until it was too late.

She went to Kinney's horse. Fortunately, sharing a bit of humiliation with the torpedo explosion had made them instant friends. After a firm but comforting pat, she took the pony up the hill through a small neighborhood and a patch of pine trees until she caught the Express about a half-mile from the turn. She rode above the saddle, racing alongside the train, shouting and waving her free arm high above her head. The men inside the cab waved back, whistling and blowing kisses at her.

She kept up with the Express until it came to a bridge above a narrow ravine and disappeared behind one of the factories. Emma couldn't follow, so she took the horse straight through the rolling mill. The men stopped working and stared with empty faces as she came in one end, wove around the machinery, and blew out the other side, snatching a red handkerchief from one of the workers as he was wiping his brow.

Outside the mill, she found the train. She waved the handkerchief over her head and shouted at the men to stop.

The engineer waved his cap out the window. "We're comin' for ya, darlin'," he yelled.

121

As the train came to the turn, Emma slapped the reins to the right and took the horse toward an old distant-signal about a quarter-mile from the river.

She jumped off the horse and ran to the semaphore, a small signal-station that had been abandoned several years ago when the carriage-road it protected was moved closer to the river. She pulled on the blade, but it was locked in place with an old, corroded rail-spike. There wasn't time to search through the ballast, so she took the biggest rock she could find and hammered out the spike. She tried to move the arm down to horizontal, but even when she hung on it with all her weight, the blade wouldn't budge. It had been left up for so long it had rusted stuck.

The train was making the turn. She checked the river, then the train, then the river again. All she saw was a black haze wrapping the bridge. There was no way to tell if the Limited was still there.

Kinney's horse waited, patiently, unaware of the danger, the saddlebag full of detonators still draped over its hindquarters. Emma ran to the bag and pulled out one of the torpedoes and raced back to the track and strapped it to the rail.

The Express had finished its turn and was picking up speed, pounding down the hill like a sprinter on his last leg. The whistle blew, and the sound of the churning wheels grew louder and louder. Emma looked at the puny pouch, then back at the bulging bag on the horse's hip.

When the engineer finally saw her, she was still working, bouncing back and forth on the rails, pausing only briefly in between hops to dip into the canvas bag. The engineer let out another long whistle-blow, and Emma jumped off the tracks just as the train rolled over the first detonator. She could hear the faint sound of the men shrieking as the train ran over the entire contents of the torpedo bag. Emma had even stacked a few of the pouches on top of one another for good measure.

Smoke billowed from both sides of the train in a series of explosions that rang out across the valley like cannon fire at

Gettysburg. The engineer slowed the train, bringing it to a stop just shy of the Number Six Bridge.

When Emma rode up, the men were standing around the Limited with their jaws hung open. She could even see Deckert's hands shaking as he checked his watch. After the third try, he found his pocket and tucked it away. He went to Kinney and swiped the bowler from his head. He dusted it off with a gentle sweep of his palm, walked across the bridge, and handed it to Emma. Emma wiped the headband with her shirt, fixed the hat square on her head, and went up to the office.

From then on, all the men on the rails listened to Emma Ehrenfeld and followed her orders with a polite, "Yes, ma'am."

16

Ben watched from the swinging doors as a sparse group in casual dress filed down the narrow staircase and found their seats in the dining room. The tables had been stripped of the fancy plates and flowers. There was no grand entrance, no quintet. The flames that had roared in the fireplace the night before were gone, leaving behind a pile of dusty grey ashes. Ben was ready for table service, and found Henri in the center of the room closing the accordion doors.

"Where are the people from last night?" said Ben, "The ones I was serving."

Henri latched the divider, closing off the ballroom, and returning the ground floor to its normal size. "Dinner tonight," he said, "is for the leftovers."

"Stale bread and cold escargot?" said Ben, "I believe Jean Pierre is serving duck."

Henri laughed. "The leftover guests. Those not invited to the cottage parties."

"And me?"

"No hired help at the cottages, members only. You stay here and bring the courses just as before. Then you may go."

Ben brought and retrieved the courses, and before he knew it, the dinner was over. When he returned to the kitchen, Jean Pierre was tidying up the work table.

"C'est tout," said Jean Pierre. "Now go home and get some rest. With the extra work you have taken on, I have a feeling the rest of this week will be... how do you say...trying?"

124

Backbreaking was more like it, and Ben wasn't ready to go home. If and when he did, he wasn't sure he still had a home to go to. He stared over the swinging doors at the piano.

"Why do you not go and play?" said Jean Pierre, pointing toward the dining room. "There are only a few guests left, no one of any importance. I will not tell Parke or the others, they are all up at the lake, anyway, half-drunk by now."

Ben ran to the storage room. "All right," he said, "One last time."

He grabbed his knapsack and hurried back through the dining room past the remaining guests who were spread out over a dozen half-empty tables. Most of the men had moved on to cigars while the women still nibbled on cheeses and sipped aperitifs. All of them ignored Ben as he sat down behind the Steinway.

He chose Beethoven's Sonata Pathetique, first movement. There was no one to impress tonight, no need for a cheerful melody. He played. The slow, grave progression of minor chords resonating throughout the room the feel of a funeral march. He struck the notes hard, staring at his hands until his fingers blurred against the background of black and white. During the chromatic cadenza that led to the main theme, he caught the subtle fragrance of jasmine over his shoulder.

He stopped playing and turned to a woman of seventy. Her powder-white face was filled with deep, shadowy wrinkles. She wore a bargain-basement bonnet set atop a coiffure of flattened silver swirls that resembled a poorly made bird's nest. Perhaps his melody had touched the old woman, he thought, and she had come to pay him a compliment.

The woman bent down and engaged Ben at eye level. "Excuse me son," she said, breathing a hint of bitters into his face, "Do you mind playing a bit softer, it's becoming difficult for us to hear our conversation."

She retreated before Ben could respond, her question more a demand than a request. He gathered his sheet music, closed the fallboard, and left the stage.

It was a slow walk across the dam that evening, and Ben's

knapsack hung heavy on his shoulders. The sun had dipped well behind the hills and could no longer burn away the drops of rain that had begun to fall. He pulled on the side-straps, lifting the load high on his back. Half-way across, he stopped and looked behind him at the boardwalk, hoping to catch a glimpse of Sarah Ann. His eyes followed the walkway up the shoreline to an assembly of partygoers huddled on one of the cottage porches. Light from the gas lamps danced over the socialites, throwing their disfigured shadows onto the roof of the boathouse. He could hear glasses clinking and swells of sporadic laughter.

He imagined himself mingling among them, Andrews coming up right away with a firm handshake, "Bennett Marsh, my good man," he said, pulling Ben inside, "your music was so inspiring, won't you sit and play for us?" Damrosch found him and pleaded, "Oh yes, Ben, amazing, consider yourself accepted to the academy, no audition required, of course." As Ben fantasized, he didn't notice the movement coming from the dark side of the bridge. When he finally heard the footsteps, the three boys were right on top of him.

Ben turned to Slug who was already within arm's reach, staring at him with glazed eyes and rocking unsteadily. Red and Skinny came up from behind, reeking of turpentine, and slithered around Slug, flanking Ben.

"You're the one," said Slug, aiming a finger at Ben, "that almost got me nabbed last night. Made me spill a whole can of good sniffin' oil, too."

Ben hugged himself, pulling the pack tightly against his back. "Just leave me be," he said, "I don't want any trouble with you."

Slug stumbled closer. "Well maybe I, want some trouble with you," he said, pointing at himself, then at Ben, as if the giver and the receiver of the trouble needed clarifying.

Ben looked for a path of escape, but the fumes from Slug's turpentine-soaked shirt made him lightheaded, and all he could do was stand his ground.

"What do you got in that pack?" said Slug, hooking a curved

finger around the strap of Ben's knapsack. "Let's have a look, eh."

Red and Skinny closed in, and Ben twisted to avoid their grabs, the knapsack strings flinging loosely at his side. The two boys grabbed hold of the straps and took turns yanking Ben one direction, then the other.

"Let me help you out," said Slug.

Red and Skinny stopped their game of tug of war and Slug reared back and punched Ben straight in the stomach. Ben buckled, releasing his grip on the pack. Red ripped it off and flung it into the air, landing it at the edge of the bridge.

Ben crawled on all fours, gasping for air and searching for his pack. Slug stomped hard on his hand, and he felt his fingers crush under the weight of Slug's heavy boot. Slug pulled back his leg and kicked at the pack, sweeping it over the edge of the bridge and into the river.

"No," screamed Ben, reaching in vain for the pack.

The pack disappeared into the void and landed in the water with a quiet splash.

"Now we're even," taunted Slug.

Red and Skinny ran off laughing. Slug followed, but not before giving Ben's hand another stomp. "I told you to watch your back," he said, swinging his leg like a croquet mallet and putting the toe of his boot to Ben's head. He let out a sinister laugh and ran down the bridge and disappeared.

Ben stood, but dizziness quickly returned him to prayer position. His head and hand throbbed, and he struggled for air. He sobbed with what energy he had left, pounding his healthy fist on the marred planks.

"Damn it...damn it," he shouted.

He could still hear the clinking glasses and the muddied laughter rising from behind the boathouse. With glassy eyes, he tried to focus on the people up the shoreline, but the flicker of the gas lamps and the fog over the lake blurred his vision. His head began to spin.

"Damn it, damn it, damn it."

His cursing and pounding softened as he ran out of fight. Hunched over on all fours, he caught his breath. "Damn it."

Sobbing turned to anger and he ripped off his music pin. He staggered toward the edge of the bridge and threw the pin as far as he could into the lake. Then, as if in a dream, the bridge suddenly tipped on its side. He spun around, and the soggy planks came up and hit him square in the face.

17

A clap of thunder rattled the window, so loud Parke felt as if it had come from inside the room. He sat up and rubbed his eyes, but his bedside candle only illuminated a blurry portion of the bedroom. He blamed the distortion on his third glass of wine, one too many, he thought. Rain blew sideways, and heavy drops thumped on the window and called to him, beckoning. He crawled over an empty bed and went to the window. He pulled aside the curtains and pressed his face to the glass. Swells and white caps churned the water. At the dam, waves were leaping up and spilling between the wooden planks of the bridge. Along the shoreline, broken strips of wood floated in the water where the boardwalk used to stand. He stood motionless at the window, watching the lake come alive. The water crept up the shoreline and encircled the Clubhouse. Suddenly, the foundation broke free and the Clubhouse floated away. He swayed as it drifted along the shoreline and rose into the air, hovering before the dam like a ghost, bringing him closer and closer to the rocky face and the enormous body of water swelling behind it. He looked up the shoreline where the boathouse should have been, and found men and women standing on the cottage porches, laughing and drinking wine as giant waves washed over them. He tried calling to them, to warn them to move to higher ground, but no sound came from his mouth. The disfigured bodies turned and stared at him with blank faces as a churning sheet of water rushed down the hillside behind them, uprooting the cottage and washing the oblivious onlookers into the lake. Then the

Clubhouse tilted forward, drawing Parke's attention to the center of the bridge and a crowd of people marching back and forth waving American flags. The boulders at the face of the dam shook, and one by one they broke off and fell into the river. Water poured over the face of the dam, and the bridge folded at the center. He could hear the wood cracking, the men and women screaming as they plunged over the edge. Then the heavy rocks and the muddied earth gave way, and a wall of water gushed through, hissing louder and louder as it raced toward him. He crossed his arms and turned away as the tidal wave consumed the Clubhouse and exploded through the window.

John Parke sprang out of bed wide awake, breathing hard and sweating. He could hear Lily snoring through the walls of their adjoining rooms, no doubt passed out from red wine. He lit a cigarette, went to the window, and ripped open the curtain.

The boardwalk and the boathouse were still standing, and only a light drizzle fell on the water. The stillness of the lake and a long draw from the cigarette calmed his nerves.

He went to the washstand and splashed himself with cool water, inadvertently dousing his smoke. He dried his face and lit another cigarette, this time lighting a candle lamp with the same match. No time for his shave cream or straight razor, he dressed and went down the hall, passing a series of closed doors and a solitary portrait of huntsman Crick standing over a three-point buck. Parke smirked at Crick's posed bravado, and with a small circle of light at his feet from the lamp, he inched his way down the stairs to the first floor.

The dining room was quiet and dark. A ticking of raindrops atop the porch awning drew him to the window and the silhouette of the dam, where a soft wind was blowing moonlit peaks of black water against the rocks.

Avoiding the tables, chairs, and butler stands, he crossed the dining room into the office, and the most concentrated amount of the Club's affluence. Andrews was there, represented in the heavy oak writing desk and paneled mahogany walls, Crick in the two oversized Louis XIV armchairs and the tufted leather settee, Melon

130

in the three-tiered bookcase, Knox in the Oriental rug, and the rest in the blue ribbons and regatta trophies proudly displayed atop the Duncan Phyfe étagère of the same rich-stained Jamaican wood.

Parke's contribution was in the two small wall-lamps that flanked yet another self-indulging portrait of Crick, this time wearing a fishing vest and holding a drooping string of black bass. He leaned in to light the lamps, and the cigarette hanging from the corner of his mouth brushed against the photograph, spreading a thick strip of ash above Crick's forehead. As he wiped away the cinders, the picture sprung from the wall on a pair of concealed hinges, revealing a small combination dial and a horizontal handle built into a flattened door. He inspected the seam around the safe and jiggled the handle, locked as he expected.

He was re-securing the picture when he heard the creak of footsteps coming off the carpeted floor of the dining room and onto the bare-wood planks of the hallway. He crouched down with his back to the door and held the candle low. The footsteps stopped in front of the office. Parke held his breath, ready to taste the burning end of his cigarette, when the early-morning wanderer continued down the hall and up the east stairs.

Parke stumbled to the desk for an ashtray and extinguished his smoldering smoke. After lighting the sconces, and another cigarette, he went to the opposite wall and searched the bookcase.

He found his old University textbooks stacked behind a row of more prominently displayed volumes such as Archery Accuracy, Running the Perfect Regatta, and The Official Rules and Etiquette of Lawn Tennis and Other Popular Field Games. He had hoped the books would provide him with more information about the construction of the dam, but all he found was a review of structural engineering basics and one of Crick's regatta medals tucked inside the jacket of an unused yachting handbook.

He examined the desk drawers. Each moved freely except one, secured with a cylinder lock. He took a letter opener from the desktop, and with a small steel ingot Crick used as a paper weight, he hammered the thin blade into the keyhole. One twist and a sharp 'click', and the drawer popped open. Inside was a large, overstuffed envelope, the top flap folded over a brass grommet and fastened with a strand of twine. Scribbled on the front were the words River Fork Dam Retrofit, 2-29-85. Parke unwound the twine and pulled out the papers. He set them on the desk and began reading, pausing only to blow away the ashes falling from his cigarette.

The ashtray was nearly full when he came across a dozen separately bound packets of original drawings, building plans, seismological calculations, labor schedules, and inspection reports, all pertaining to the original construction of the River Fork embankment dam. He hoped this was the treasure he'd been looking for, and that somewhere within the pages he would find the information he needed to prove the dam was unstable. If he could figure out what was wrong with the dam, he could figure out how to fix it. However, after an hour of reviewing the documents, he learned nothing new.

He looked back at the envelope. Something about the date bothered him. February 29, 1885, was wrong. 1885 was not a leap year. Lily's birthday was February 29th, and he was still in debt to Andrews for the extravagant surprise party he'd thrown for her in the Club's ballroom the year before as an enticement for his bride-to-be. 1884 was a leap year, not 1885.

He marched to the picture of Crick, swung it open, and tried the numbers on the wall safe – right 2, left 29, right 85...left 2, right 29, left 85...right 29, left 2, right 85. Nothing. What could a backward fella like Crick have been thinking when he set the combination? "Backward," he said out loud, then whispered to himself, "That's it." Right 85, left 29, right 2.

He pulled the handle. This time the door swung open. Inside a deep pocket in the wall was a stack of loose papers.

Back at the desk, and the ashtray now overflowing with cigarette butts, Parke studied the documents, encountering page after page of projects detailing changes made to the dam after the completion of the Clubhouse; titles such as Obligatory Repair and Aesthetic Modification. Buried in the content of one project description was the authorization for a substantial structural change to the dam. A work order entitled Carriage Convenience showed the dam's height had been lowered by five feet in order to widen the bridge and allow two carriages to pass at the same time. Parke knew that lowering the dam's height meant raising the water level, thereby leaving very little distance between the surface of the lake and the top of the dam. With the recent rains, the water level was rising quickly, already dangerously close to the crest. The work order also revealed that after the dam's height was lowered, work to secure the rock-face and compact the earth was never finished, and the minimal effort employed to plug any seepage was limited to tossing loose rock over the face, and packing leaks with mud, gravel, and manure.

The most troubling of all was a project titled Pipe Removal. It revealed the two lower discharge pipes, installed during the original construction, had been removed. Attached to the project page was a purchase order for two sections of iron pipe. The buyer and seller's names were blacked out, but it was clear that the pipes had been excavated and sold to a local steel company as scrap iron for the sum of two dollars.

Parke thumbed through the rest of the documents, all revealing more evidence of oversight, incomplete work, and cutting corners. At the bottom of each project and work order was the signature of the same man, Morton Crick.

Parke returned the papers to the safe and spent the rest of the night formulating a plan to secure the dam. Re-reading the original construction plans and re-calculating structural requirements, he determined the quickest and most efficient way to stabilize the dam was to cut another spillway, allowing more water to flow out of the lake. More rain was expected this week, and he needed to move fast. A dam breach would mean catastrophic disaster, the likes of which no one in this town, or anywhere else for that matter, had ever seen.

Rain in the driveway got him up from the desk and to the window. He drew on his cigarette and watched the moonlit drops strike the earth around the utility pole. The needled branches of the pines swayed in the wind, but the pole held strong, straight and tall, fixed solid by the brace-pole and the hardened cement. He returned to the desk and wrote out specific job responsibilities for each man involved in the project he entitled, The New Spillway. He was so absorbed in his planning, he hadn't noticed the night slipping away. The next time he looked up, the sun was peaking over the hills through a patch in the cloudy sky.

Across town, a clear beam of light shown through an unfamiliar window. Still dressed in his clothes from the night before, Ben was regaining consciousness to the sound of a crackling fire, and the smell of freshly brewed coffee.

18

Ben got up from the cushioned sofa and followed the smell of coffee out the front door. He came out into the yard and saw Clem standing over the oil drum. A fire crackled under a tin pot and a glistening skewer of ham hocks sizzled on the grill. Fat from the pork knuckles fell through the metal grates and made the fire hiss. Clem lifted the pot from the fire and offered Ben some coffee.

Ben eased himself down at a wooden table next to the oil drum and looked around the property. His lips were caked with dried blood, and he licked at the crust tickling the corners of his mouth. Factory smoke mixed with the grey clouds, and a sprinkling of dirty mist fell into his face.

"Nothin' like a hot cup of coffee to start off this beautiful day," said Clem, filling two cups and returning the pot to the fire. "Sure is one hell of a bump you got there. Must have been quite a spill you took on the dam last night. Gotta be careful walkin' that bridge after dark, what with the rain, and all."

Ben felt at the side of his head. His hair was wet, and the knot above his ear was tender to the touch. His nose was sore and his hand ached, but the dizziness had passed. When he saw the green garage and his broken Safety Rover inside, he realized he was behind Clem's woodshop.

Opposite the garage, a pair of two-story homes with covered porches and high-pitched shake roofs stood beside each other like

135

mirror images. The house Ben woke up in was without adornments, the other had a small garden in front with a low picket-fence and a brick path running down the middle. The windows of the simple house were empty, but the windows of the other were framed on the inside with ruffled, white curtains. Two giant sugar maples sat on opposite ends of the property, and spread around the yard between them, Ben counted at least fifteen more wooden tables with long benches tucked underneath.

"I say," said Clem, "gotta be careful out on the dam after dark."

"Oh, yeah," said Ben, "I'll be more careful next time."

"How ya feeling?"

Ben surveyed the houses and the yard once more. "What happened? How did I...?"

"Lucky," said Clem, "Lucky I was out for a stroll. Looked down the bridge and saw you lying there, not movin' a muscle. We picked you up and brought you here, chipped some ice from the ice box and set it on your head while you were sleepin', you know, to keep the swellin' down. Gotta be mighty careful out on that dam after dark."

"We?" said Ben. "Who's we?"

A voice from behind replied. "Me."

Percival walked to the fire and dropped a stack of pine logs next to the oil drum. "Will that be enough?"

"That ought'a do her," said Clem, fanning the bacon smoke from his face. "Now, go sit. I know you ain't gonna show it, Percival, but I can tell you were worried. You don't have to say nothin', just sit. I'll fix you'uns up a hot plate, and top that coffee off, to boot."

Clem loaded three plates with ham hock, and took a cast iron skillet full of biscuits off the fire and set it on the table. After he mumbled a short prayer, each man ripped off a biscuit and dipped it into the hot pork grease dripping off the meat.

"We sure are much obliged, you takin' us in and all," said Percival, his mouth half-full of pork knuckle and biscuit. "As soon as I get to workin' again, I believe it'd be right to pay you for your trouble."

136

"It ain't nothin'," said Clem, pointing to the unadorned two-story. "That house there's been empty for so long, I could almost hear it askin' for someone to move in. Anyway, it'll be nice havin' some company. Sure glad I decided to stay."

"Well, we sure are obliged," said Percival.

"Yeah, Mr. Clem, much obliged," said Ben, washing down a chewy mouthful with a gulp of coffee. "By the way, what do mean, you decided to stay?"

"Ben," said Percival, "we don't need to be prying into this man's affairs. He's been more than kind already."

"It's all right," said Clem, lifting a leg onto the bench. "Seems like I've always done better movin' around. Spend too much time in one place and you tend to wear out your welcome. Make a difference somewhere then move on to the next."

Ben set down the pork knuckle and stretched his injured hand, working his fingers out and back. "You never wanted to settle down?" he said. "You know, like with a family and all?"

"Ben, please," said Percival.

"Naw, naw, the boy's just curious." Clem took sip of coffee and repositioned himself square to the table. "I've got family."

Ben ripped off another biscuit. The pork fat had completely separated from the ham shank, and he soaked the biscuit in the pool of drippings. "Where are they?"

Percival raised a finger, about to admonish Ben again for being so stubbornly intrusive. Clem waved him off and Percival went to the oil drum for the coffee pot.

"All over, I reckon," said Clem, "Up north, out west, down south, don't know for certain, to tell ya the truth. Just spread out all over."

"I'd be worried," said Ben, "not knowin' where my family was."

"The way I figure," said Clem, "You teach 'em right, and they'll be just fine when you let 'em go. Ain't that right, Percival."

Percival stared at Clem for a moment then divvied up the rest of the coffee. "And how is it you come to River Fork, bein' you ain't got any family here."

"I came into Pennsylvania from the east, through Montgomery County," said Clem. "Set up a shop between Fort Washington and Camp Hill a few years before the war. I stayed there, uninvolved by the way, till a good time after, till I heard about the big steel factories goin' in near Pittsburgh. When my time in Camp Hill came to an end, I picked up and headed west."

"Camp Hill?" said Percival, "Ain't that where..."

Clem cleared his throat and stopped Percival's line of questioning.

"But you ain't in the steel business," said Ben, scooping up the last bit of greasy meat with the biscuit.

"No," said Clem, "I ain't. But the steel factories meant lots of work, and lots of work meant lots of laborers, and those laborers and their families needed places to live. And who do you think they called on to build and furnish them houses? Until they start makin' homes outa steel, the good ol' carpenter is a downright necessity. But now, since the cleared land's already full of homes, and since I've been so long without neighbors, I was about to move on again. That is until you'uns come round."

"We're glad you decided to stay," said Percival, "and if I hadn't said it already, we sure are much obliged."

Ben looked inside the workshop at the stacks of furniture crowding the floor. "Looks like plenty of work in there, keep you busy for quite a while."

Clem gathered the empty plates. "I suppose it would," he said, "but these digits don't work with the skill they used to." He set down the plates and held up his fingers, stained and bumpy and swollen like knotty twigs. "You know, I've been thinkin' 'bout what you said, paying me for my trouble, that is."

"Of course," said Percival, "I wouldn't think of acceptin' such generous hospitality without us payin' our way."

"I reckon you still got skills from your time in the wood trade," said Clem.

"I still got the skills, but I ain't got the tools."

Clem laughed. "Don't worry 'bout that, none. The garage over there's fulla tools, it's the hands I'm missin'. How's about in lieu of any monies, you help me with Mrs. Green's table, Mrs. Hartman's armchair, and all the rest, and you're welcome to stay as long as you like."

Percival leaned back and looked inside the garage. "What about Ben," he asked.

"For a short while," said Clem, "But Ben tells me he's got plans of his own."

Ben didn't say a word.

"Is that so, Ben?" said Percival, "You've got plans of your own?"

Ben picked at the edge of the table. "Don't know about that, now. Situation's changed. I've… I've lost my tools as well, so to speak, and unless there's a stack of sheet music and a train ticket in that garage, it looks like for the time being, I'm stuck here."

"Then you're welcome to stay too," said Clem. "Long as your father can keep us in business."

"That oughtn't to be too hard," said Percival. "Like Ben said, plenty of work in there."

"And what about your work, Ben, up at the Clubhouse, shouldn't you be on your way?" Clem retrieved a pocket watch from his overalls. "It's nearly a quarter to eight."

A splinter had found its way into Ben's thumb, and he worked at it with his fingernails, trying to pinch it out. "Don't start till ten," he said.

"Well you better get movin," said Clem, "and that bicycle ain't gonna do you no good, now."

"I can make it with a swift run in less than forty, got plenty of time."

Clem handed Ben a dollar. "Not if you're gonna stop by Howell's for some coffee and flour."

Ben stared at the bill. "Geez," he said, "how much coffee and flour do you need? I'll never be able to carry that much."

"You just order it and pay for it, split it up fifty cents for each. Howell's boy will bring it up." Clem slapped Ben on the shoulder. "Now go on, get."

Clem led Percival through the shop, pointing at the furniture and spelling out the customer's specifications for each piece. "Dark stain with a heavy shellac for this one," he said, "light stain with a rub of steel wool here. Oh, and put a little scrollwork around the edge of this one."

Percival nodded as he followed Clem around the stacks of cabinets and armoires, dining tables and sitting chairs. "You say you spent some time in Camp Hill?" he said.

"I did," said Clem.

"You stopped me earlier. You knew what I was gonna ask you about, didn't you."

"I did."

"Then you were there when it happened?"

Clem stopped in front of an old roll-top desk. "Never really felt like talkin' 'bout it with anyone but, yeah, I was in my shop window when the down train come runnin' up the hill just out of the Camp Hill station. The Picnic Special, full of children headed to Shaeff's Woods was comin' down, runnin' quick, and the two engines collided head on, just shy of the Camp Hill bridge, so hard it made the ground shake." Clem shuddered as if a sudden chill had swept through the room. "Women and children screamin'. The cars by the engines were torn up pretty good. I ran to the first car of the up train and seen an elderly man bleeding, howling for his daughter. The car had already caught fire, and I ran in and pulled the girl out. Clara was her name. I'll never forget." He set his hand on his hips and massaged his back with his thumbs. "More people were screaming inside, and I tried to go back in, but the flames were too hot."

"She survive?"

Clem nodded. "And can you believe it, the gritty young thing went round tending to the injured until the Congress Engine and Hose Company arrived. Turns out she went on to become a nurse, or somethin'. I could'a figured that."

When they had made their way in a full circle back to the barn doors, Clem asked Percival if he had any questions. "If you mean

140

about the train wreck," said Percival, "I got plenty, but as far as the staining and finishing, naw, I believe I've got her."

"Good," said Clem, "Now no more talk about train wrecks, time to get to work."

Clem walked out of the shop, and took the cups and the plates to the house.

Percival went to work staining the legs of an oak table, and after a few minutes, Clem returned dressed in a heavy brown jacket, faded britches, and a wide brimmed hat. In his left hand he held a shotgun. With the two empty haversacks thrown over his shoulder, he looked like a skinny draft horse.

"I'm off for some game," Clem said, "Be back before dark." He smiled as he watched Percival work. "I'd sure like to get Mrs. Green that dining table tomorrow."

"I'll get it stained," Percival said, "But a full day of sunshine would sure be nice for the shellac."

Clem trotted off between the two houses and up toward the hills. He turned and called back to Percival. "I'll see what I can do."

19

Every year, the people of the valley celebrated Decoration Day with emphatic patriotism, congregating in every town and borough to march and wave their American flags. They gathered along the river, from the bridge at the River Fork dam, to the Number Six Bridge, to the viaduct at Smith's Crossing, all the way to the Stone Bridge in Johnstown. News of the upcoming celebration had spread as far as Sonman, and larger than normal crowds were expected this year since the holiday fell on a Sunday. On the benches in front of Howell's General Store, the old-timers were discussing their participation in the festivities.

"You'uns marchin' in the parade this year?" the man in the rocking chair said, staring up at the porch awning.

"Wouldn't miss it. Marchin' all the way to the dam bridge this year."

"Reckon I will too, heard there's gonna be one hell of a shindig up there."

"I'm headin' to the Stone Bridge," said another, "gonna watch my niece play the clarinet in the middle-school band. They're fixin' to whoop up a Louisiana-style barbeque too, a nickel, all you can eat. And how's about you, you headin' up, or downriver?"

"Hell," the rocking chair man said, "I ain't headin' neither. Stone Bridge is too far away, and I ain't goin' one step closer than this porch to that River Fork Club, even if it is 'love thy neighbor' Decoration Day. Besides, that shindig at the lake is for members only. Ain't no way in hades they'll let me, or the likes of you'uns in there."

The men looked at each other and agreed in unison, "sour-puss", and sent the rocking chair man back to the benches.

The next in line moved swiftly from bench to chair, rocking as he stroked the armrests. After he'd warmed the seat, and enough silence had passed, he took out a piece of paper from his shirt pocket. "Got a telegraph from my brother in Ohio this mornin'," he said, unfolding the paper, "Says here there's a terrific rain storm headin' our way, a regular old-time northeaster." He folded up the paper and tucked it away. "I'm sorry to say, fellas, but if this storm hits us, there won't be any Decoration Day festivities this year."

A man from the bench waved his arm. "Tribune don't say that."

"Even so, best to stay away from town the next few days. You'uns know every time we get hit, that river overflows. Even on this porch, water be up to our knees. And I don't trust that dam neither. Folks been talkin'…say she's gonna burst this time."

"Tribune don't say that."

The previous rocking chair man chimed in. "And what makes you think that Wisord fella's got it right this time, on both accounts. I tell you, that boy don't know nothin' 'bout weather, or dams. Weather forcastin', hell, ain't no other job in the world you can be wrong so many times and still get paid."

As the men debated the accuracy of Jack Wisord's weather forecasting, and his knowledge of embankment dam stability, Ben moved unnoticed up the porch stairs and into the store. He grabbed a stool at the counter and waited for Doc who was selling a young woman on the advantages of a grocery basket.

"Much easier to carry," Doc said, holding the basket by the straps, "See? Easy to carry." The woman agreed, and Doc added two cents to her bill. "Have a nice day, ma'am, bye now." Doc waved goodbye and the woman walked past Ben, basket under her arm out the screen door.

Ben slapped his dollar on the counter. "Coffee and flour," he said. "Fifty cents of each."

"You must be hungry," said Doc. "Thirsty, too." Ben was stoic, and Doc went to serious. "What do you need all that coffee and flour for, anyway?"

"It's for Mr. Clement," said Ben, looking through the walls of the general store toward Clem's house on the hill, "you know, the cabinetmaker."

"Yeah, I know him. Is it that time again?"

"Not sure. What time would that be?"

"Well, every week ol' Clem comes in, orders up a load of coffee and flour, sometimes sugar, pork knuckle or brisket too, enough fixings for half the town. Don't know what he does with all of it, but every week he comes back for more." Doc reached under the counter and pulled out a basket. "How about a few of these, much easier to carry."

"I ain't carrying it back," said Ben, "no matter how many baskets you try to sell me. Clem said you'd deliver it."

"Oh, yeah," said Doc, dropping the sarcasm. "I suppose I can do that. 'You want the sale, you deliver it', that's what he always says. And believe you me, I do want the sale." Doc put the dollar into the cash box and scribbled the order in his log book. Ben turned to leave. "Wait, wait." Doc flipped to the back of the log book. "We've still got a few more to figure out."

Ben stopped. "A few more what."

"Flavors." Doc took two Hutch bottles from the shelf and popped the stoppers and set them on the counter. "Doctor Pepper."

"Doctor who?"

"That's what they call it. Found out yesterday from the delivery man. Named it after a real doctor, I reckon. Says it'll give you pep when you drink it. Doctor Pepper, see." Doc showed Ben the front of the bottle.

Ben gripped the bottle and ran his thumb over the raised lettering. "Don't know about pep, but it'll sure give you the runs."

Doc put his hand on his stomach, "I noticed that, too. Anyhow, let's have a look at them flavors." Doc pointed with his pencil and read the flavors he had recorded in the log book. "Sassafras,

144

sarsaparilla, almond, caramel, root beer, black cherry, licorice, vanilla..."

"I ain't in a tastin' mood," said Ben. "I gotta get."

"Where you gotta get to?"

"Clubhouse. Took on extra work."

"Well good luck with that. That's something I won't be joining you in."

"How so."

Doc looked around, making sure no one was looking, and rolled up his sleeve. He showed Ben a rawhide band tied round his wrist, the name 'Jennie' burned into the leather. "It's like a promise," he said. "This Sunday, the two of us are gonna sneak away and get hitched. We ain't too sure how our folks are gonna take the news, so we've been keepin' it a secret."

"Now you're leaving me?" said Ben.

"I can't stay here no more. My life is somewhere else."

"California?"

"Yeah," said Doc, nodding his head with certainty, "California. Jennie says she'll stay on the farm and keep the books while I work the field. I've been in this store since I was eight years old, saved up over two hundred dollars. It's time for me to move on."

"Well congratulations to you. Now, if you expect me to get the two of you a weddin' gift, you'll let me head off to work so I can make some money."

"Extra work, huh," said Doc, "I never thought I'd hear you say that."

"No choice. The company done kicked us out of our home after pa lost his job. I was needin' the money to get us a place to stay."

"You find one?"

Ben put the bottle to his lips for a quick sip. "We're staying with Clem. He opened up his back-house for us, ain't chargin' us rent neither, long as pa helps him with his jobs, that is, real kind of him, too."

"Is that right, stayin' there? You mean, like sleepin', all night long?" Doc took a swig, "Caramel?"

"I think we got that one already," said Ben, "And yeah, we're sleepin' there, why shouldn't we be?"

"Folks who lived there before stayed just shy of a year, then one day they up and vanished. No one's seen hide nor hair of 'em since."

"That don't mean nothin'. Maybe they just moved away. Lots of folks up and move away, that don't mean nothin'." Ben took another sip of the Doctor Pepper, "birch beer?"

"How'd I miss that one," said Doc, penciling 'birch beer' in the log book, "Only two more to go. Maybe them folks did just move away, but be careful, that Clem's an interesting man, and maybe a bit unstable."

"How do you figure?"

"Anyone who drinks fifty cents worth of coffee a week has got to be a little nervous."

"I ain't seen nothin' fishy," said Ben, taking another drink. "How about anise and fennel?"

"Amos and who?"

Ben sniffed around the top of the bottle again. "Yeah, anise. It's like licorice, but a bit more…medicinal."

A bluebottle fly had found its way into the store and was circling above the counter. Ben swatted at it, but it kept coming back, each time dropping closer to the sweet scent of the soda pop.

Doc stuck his nose into his bottle. "All right, smarty, if you say it's like licorice, but we've got to agree for certain on the last one, fair enough?"

"Fair enough," said Ben. "Now I really got to get, I can't be late."

"Why do you have to take on extra work if you're livin' free and clear with Clem?" said Doc. "Besides, ain't you going to New York?"

"Can't now. Ain't got no sheet music, no train ticket, no money… all of it, gone." Ben gulped the last of his drink and turned the bottle upside down. "All of it…" a drop clung to the rim then plopped onto the counter, "…gone."

Ben set down the soda bottle and the fly went straight to it, landing on the rim and crawling down into the neck. He slapped his hand over the top, trapping the fly inside.

"What do you mean, gone?" said Doc, "How?"

"Out on the dam last night. Slick...or Slag...."

"Slug?"

"Yeah, Slug. Payback, I reckon, for bumpin' into him durin' a turpentine heist the night before."

Doc laughed. "His real name's Weldon, you know. And he ain't nothin', not without his two sheep. You know why they call him Slug, don't ya."

Ben watched the fly buzz round inside the Hutch bottle, ramming itself into the sides of the thick amber glass. "Tell me."

Doc set his arm on the counter and leaned in. "One mornin' Weldon was out huntin' with his pa... didn't have no dog with 'em so his pa used his boy as the retriever. Anyway, Weldon was a little too anxious and a lot too stupid, and went after the game before his father had taken the shot. When his pa let go the Winchester, Weldon caught a ball of buckshot right in the ass. He cried and cried when they tried to take it out, so the doctor told 'em it'd be best if they just left it in. Except for Weldon and his pa, only two boys in River Fork don't know that story."

Ben looked at Doc.

"All right, three," Doc said. "But let me tell you, he ain't nothin' without them two cohorts. You give him a one-for, knock him on his buckshot caboose, and he'll cower like a broken mule."

"Broken or not," Ben said, "that mule done kicked everythin' I owned over the side of that dam, and now that's why I need the extra work."

"Well as long as you'll be at that Clubhouse, you can keep practicin' your piano until you save up enough."

"Lost that, too," said Ben. They've done taken away my playin' privileges."

"No more playin'? Jesus, Ben, that's the only thing you ever talk about doin'. How you gonna get your privileges back? You just gotta."

147

"Maybe if I work real hard they'll let me play again. I can't think of any other way. And now, it's really gettin' late, Doc. Ain't no way I'll get my playing privileges back if I show up late."

"Tell you what," said Doc, "I'll get my pa to watch the store. You help me load up the wagon, and I'll take you up to the Clubhouse before I drop off that order." Doc set down the log book, "That last flavor can wait."

"As long as you promise not to invite that crazy Dixie," said Ben.

"I promise," said Doc, leading the way out the back door.

After loading the coffee and the flour, Doc moved the wagon to the front of the store. Ben sat at Doc's side, picking his fingernails and tapping his heals on the floorboards. They waited at the corner of Main Street for a carriage to pass, a fancy Concord painted solid black, with gas lamps on the sides and red velvet curtains drawn over the windows. A groomed black Shire slowed the coach and stopped in front of the porch benches. The coachman called to the dugout, and the men looked blankly at each other.

Doc drove alongside the carriage, and Ben's eye caught the detailed scrollwork around the edge of the frame, and the brilliant shine of the thick door handles. He could see his reflection in the polished brass knobs as they passed.

Doc waited until they had cleared the black coach by a good fifty feet then snapped the reins, kicking the horse into a four-beat gait. They trundled up the windy road and Doc turned to Ben. "Reckon they must be lost."

Ben looked back, curiously eyeing the coach. "Reckon so."

Back in front of Howell's, the coachman shouted to the men on the benches. "I say, can any of you gentlemen tell me the way to the River Fork Fishing and Hunting Club?"

The dugout concluded it was the man in the rocking chair's responsibility to answer. "Dad gummit. Last time I sat here, interrupted by vomit, now this." He scowled at the men on the benches then turned to the coachman with a forced smile, "And how can I help you, sir?"

"Directions," the coachman said, "To the…" he looked down at a folded sheet of paper, "…River Fork Fishing and Hunting Club. We're comin' up for the Decoration Day show, don't know these parts too well."

"You don't say."

For a moment, the rocking chair man contemplated turning them around and sending them back downriver, but fearing he'd lose his position on the porch, he changed his mind. "Ah, the River Fork Club," he said, holding his chin in his hand. "Well, you stay on this road to the end of town. When it forks, take the high road alongside the river…low road will take you right into the water. Follow the road up the hill. It'll wind round close to the factories, but pay no mind, just follow her till you reach the dam, three miles, or so. You'll catch some bumpy spots, especially over the tracks, so take 'er slow. Across the dam you'll hit a stone path, laid down smooth. Head up through the pines and you can't miss it. Oh, a beauty of a place it is, if you ask me."

"Much obliged," said the coachman, clicking his mouth and sending the horse off in a good clip up Main Street.

The old-timers watched in silence as the black coach rolled up the road and out of sight. The rocking chair man began to rock again, gently stroking the arm rests. "Looks like that storm ain't the only thing headed in to River Fork."

20

Parke paced in front of the office window without the comfort of a cigarette, wearing down a smooth line in the Oriental rug. He was breathing heavily, almost hyperventilating. The small door to the kitchen wouldn't stay shut, and the sweet smell of boiling rhubarb leaked into the room. The pie filling mingled with the rich odor of the leather furniture and made Parke's stomach turn. He went to the door and fidgeted with the handle.

"Damn it, Parke," said Crick, sitting comfortably behind the desk, "With all your attention to detail, I thought you'd have that fixed by now. That lock best be repaired by the end of the day."

"Yes, sir," said Parke, pushing the door shut. He pulled out his pocket watch and checked the time. "Two o'clock. They'll be here any minute."

"And why are you so nervous?" said Crick, "They're coming to see us, remember."

Even though Parke made all the arrangements and did all the work, Crick had led the other members to believe he was in charge of the Club's entertainment, everything from boat parades and regattas, to lawn-bowling and archery tournaments. Recently, when Parke brought the well-received showing of Gilbert and Sullivan's Pirates of Penzance to the Clubhouse, Crick took all the credit. For the Decoration Day entertainment, Crick turned to Parke for suggestions.

Parke knew of a Negro slave, an idiot savant from Georgia with a most amazing musical talent. Blind at birth, the man was a virtuoso pianist. It was claimed he had the innate ability to reproduce any musical composition perfectly, after only hearing it once. The Negro had amazed crowded opera houses and theaters in New York and Philadelphia, and Parke thought it would be a most impressive act to bring to the River Fork Club.

He had seen the act once at the Bijou Opera House in New York City. No one had ever heard of the so-called prodigy, and the audience was skeptical of his proclaimed supernatural musical abilities. So when the blind, burly, retarded Negro fumbled awkwardly onto the stage, the crowd hissed and guffawed for several minutes. After the snickering subsided, the man, who called himself Blind Tom, plopped down on the piano bench and hunched over the keys like a clumsy bear.

As Blind Tom played, his posture straightened, his head lifted, and his body swayed gracefully with the music. He played Beethoven and Bach, flawlessly. He played Chopin and Debussy, again without errors. Then he launched into a medley of varied genre, many of which were his own compositions, some with patriotic marching rhythms, others with melodies that mimicked the sound of howling wind or falling rain. The spectators sat amazed as he continued non-stop for over an hour.

At one point, Blind Tom stopped playing. He stood and addressed the crowd, returning to his cockeyed posture. In a slow, torpid voice he shouted, "Tom weel now pafom tree songs at da same time." He melted back into the piano and played a Chopin nocturne with the left hand, Yankee Doodle with the right, while singing Oh My Darlin' Clementine. He finished with an original piece he wrote when he was five years old entitled Falling Rain. It was an unprecedented performance that brought the astounded audience to its feet. Reverting to the form of his awkward entrance, Blind Tom stood and cheered with them, imitating the clapping, stomping his feet, and hollering back to the crowd. The uncanny musical ability, and the odd mannerisms of Blind Tom had left a standing impression on Parke, and he was certain that the amazing, inimitable act would fascinate the Club members.

151

Crick scooted back his chair and kicked his legs under the desk. "Don't worry about the General and that idiot circus freak of his. We'll have them entertaining us for pennies."

"I don't know," said Parke, "I've heard they command a hefty price. Every venue from Boston to Baton Rouge has paid it. And this Blind Tom fella is worth it, too."

"We ain't a run-of-the-mill theater, Parke," said Crick. "We're one of the most prestigious private clubs in the country. Hell, they should be payin' us."

Outside, a polished black coach rolled into the driveway.

"You've never met this General," said Parke, "I've heard he's a hard-headed curmudgeon, especially when it comes to booking his talent."

"I don't care how much of an ornery son-of-a-bitch he is, or how much money he demands for his 'act', neither him, nor his sideshow nigger is gonna intimidate me. General, my ass. If he'd a fought, he'd be in politics by now."

The doorman met the two men at the front porch, brought them into the foyer, and directed them down the hall toward the office.

"He did fight," said Parke, "In the Indian War, and for the South, lost his leg, even."

"He didn't fight in no Indian War," said Crick, "That was sixty years ago."

"He's eighty-six," said Parke, "and still tough as nails, they say."

"Eighty-six and buckled over from bending bones, I imagine." Crick leaned back and folded his hands across his chest. "You can't let people intimidate you, Parke, whether their eighteen or eighty-eight. When you're in a position like mine, tough decisions are made on a daily basis. You learn to be strong and assertive. Watch how I handle them…take notes. You might even learn how to motivate those Italians of yours."

A loud thump thump thump on the office door made Parke jump. He brushed his lapels, adjusted his coat, and opened the door.

The General stood in the doorway, his erect posture absent of any degenerative bone disease, only reinforced by the use of a long, tapered wooden cane. He was tall for a man in his eighties. His wavy white hair showed no signs of receding, and flowed evenly over his head, grazing the collar of his confederate-grey jacket. His face was leathery, his eyes stern, denoting a look more of experience than age. Dark splotches on his cheeks and chin were obscured by a coarse white beard, the thicker hairs around his chin formed a goatee.

The General scanned the room, taking in deep breaths of the dark wood and leather. "Ah, mahogany," he said in gruff baritone, "A nice, rich wood. Not as strong as oak, though." He rapped his cane against his wooden leg, and in a bellowing voice addressed Parke. "Afternoon, son, General James Bethhume."

Parke didn't remember extending his hand, but the General already had hold of it and was gripping it hard. "Pleasure, John Parke," he replied, longing for a puff of tobacco. "Please, come in." Parke extended an open palm, offering the General one of the small-backed Louis XVI chairs facing the desk. He intended to make the introduction to Crick, but the General interjected.

"Morton Crick Jr., I presume," said the General, "son of the innovative steel-man, Mort Crick. I've heard a lot about you, son. I hope you're takin' good care of your father's business." The General sat, raising his head toward the ceiling in reflection. "You know, I represented your father back in fifty-nine on a personal injury claim." He brought his head down and looked Crick in the eye. "Them workers should never have been standing so close to the rails." He laughed and hacked up a cough from the bottom of his lungs.

Crick had slumped so far down in his chair he had to push himself up with his feet to regain eye contact. Parke stood against the bookcase and watched as Crick attempted to lead the conversation. The General, who had assumed a presidential posture in his chair, struck his cane on the floor before Crick could speak. "All right, gentlemen," he said, "here's how it works."

While the men talked business in the office, Ben was busy in the kitchen pressing pastry dough into pie tins with Jean Pierre. Behind him, a pot of cane sugar and rhubarb stalks boiled on the stove.

"Bring me another stack of pie tins," Jean Pierre said with a wave as he checked the oven.

The smell of sweet rhubarb followed Ben into the hallway. Sitting on a tufted-leather settee next to the office door was a large, heavy-set black man. He wore a fitted suit that mimicked the stretched leather covering the settee, pulled taut and pinned down with small brass buttons. He was humming a soothing tune and swaying side to side, his individual girth occupying most of the bench designed for two. The aromas from the kitchen filled the Clubhouse, and the man rubbed circles around his stomach, taking in deep breaths of the freshly baked pies.

Ben smiled and tugged on his cap. The man lifted his head as Ben clomped past him, but said nothing. His face was disfigured, not in a grotesque way, but in a manner Ben was not used to seeing. His eyelids were folded over, closed so tightly they appeared as if they had been glued shut, his hair matted down like steel wool. Smooth skin, dark as chocolate, covered a flattened nose, puffy cheeks, and a swollen neck. His mouth hung open, and the crimson flesh of his lower lip curved outward and folded down toward his chin.

Ben hurried to the storage room and returned to the kitchen with the pie tins. He stared at Jean Pierre. "There's a large black man sitting in the hallway."

Jean Pierre lifted a wooden spoon from the stock pot to taste. "Is there, now," he said, engrossed with the consistency of the pie filling.

"I wonder what he's doing here."

"Je nais se pas, I do not know."

Jean Pierre didn't appear to be concerned with the man's identity, but he left the stock pot and peeked over the swinging doors down the hallway. He turned to Ben and shrugged.

Ben heard the voices inside the office rising. "Sounds like an argument in there," he said, joining Jean Pierre at the swinging doors.

154

The last shout was clearly audible. "Before we decide to play here, you have to make the star happy first."

The General flung open the hallway door and stepped out. He called to Ben and Jean Pierre. "Bring this man some pie," he said, slamming his cane on the floor.

Jean Pierre despised releasing his culinary creations at any time other than his own, and was about to deny the old man's request when Parke came into the hallway, nodding in vigorous affirmation.

Jean Pierre bit his lip. "Go get him a pie," he said to Ben.

Ben went to the cooling rack and grabbed a pie. "Ooo, ooo, that's hot," he said, dropping the tin and blowing into his palms.

"Here," said Jean Pierre, tossing Ben a kitchen towel. "Put that under it."

Ben slid the hot tin onto the towel and carried the pie to the small, broken door.

"No, no," said Jean Pierre, "go around, go around."

Ben hustled out the swinging doors and down the hall. He gave the pie, with towel, to Parke. Parke gave the pie to Blind Tom who followed the men into the office, twisting himself sideways and ducking his head to fit through the doorway.

Tom sat on a leather sofa behind the General and ate his pie. Despite Tom's threatening physique, Crick considered him, at least for the moment, harmless. Parke was frozen.

"Now that we have that settled, General," said Crick, "let's get down to details. We would like to book your virtuoso for three nights." He spun a calendar end over end and slid it in front of the General, circling the 28th, 29th and 30th of May. "Friday, Saturday...then Decoration Day, for the grand finale. I believe this will give you ample opportunity to capture the interest of the high society that enjoys membership in this Club."

The General stood and thumped his cane on the floor. "Son," he shouted, "I was rich in high society before your mother squeezed you out of her baby biscuit. We don't book for three nights." The General waved his hand above his head. "We give 'em one show, one show only." Blind Tom raised his arm, imitating the General's wave.

"One night only," exclaimed the General. "Two hundred dollars. Take it or leave it."

The General produced a hand written contract, flinging it theatrically from his hip like a magician performing the never-ending scarf routine.

Crick, running low on vigor, tried one more time. "I believe, good sir, at least two shows are appropriate. That is an agreement we can...."

Tom rose from his seat, his body absorbing the unused space in the room and stealing any presence Crick was attempting to achieve. He pointed in Crick's direction with a rhubarb-covered finger and said in a voice so low it shook the window pane. "Tom only plays for one night, like da General says."

Now both hands went up, and the General's cane struck Parke in the face. "One show only...a Memorial Day celebration."

Tom flapped his hands together, clapping and casting bits of pie crust and rhubarb around the room.

Crick signed the contract as Parke made his way to the door.

The General nodded in approval and snatched the contract from Crick's hand. He surveyed it, quickly confirming the signature and the two hundred dollar price. "Now we have it, my good men," he said, waving the contract. "A one of a kind show, hallelujah."

Crick, dumbfounded, confirmed the details. "So, Sunday, Decoration Day, correct?"

The General folded up the contract and tucked it inside his coat pocket. "Lord willin' and the creek don't rise," he said, lighting his pipe and holding out an open palm. "And that two hundred dollars, if you'd be so kind."

Blind Tom, still clapping said, "May I have another pie?"

156

21

Ben stepped off the bridge and headed down the road toward River Fork. The wagon ride that morning was nice enough, but Doc wasn't a chauffeur, so he took his usual route into town on foot. It was just past dusk, and the sky glowed in streaks of yellow and burnt orange. The clouds were spitting, and he hurried past the factories, or 'open ovens', as the locals called them, slowing down in the fresh air between them to catch his breath.

On one pass, a man came off the tracks and found his way to where Ben was walking, a day-laborer, late twenties, maybe early thirties, dressed in brown trousers and long johns. He was covered with a dark layer of soot and ash and looked like a chimney sweep in a tweed cap. Patchy stubble grew around his thin jawline, filling the depressions in his sunken cheeks and extending all the way down his neck. A big cloth pack hung over his shoulder, and he reeked of sweat and burnt metal.

"M...m...mind if I join you?" the man said, hacking up a chunk of phlegm and spitting it over his shoulder.

"I don't mind," Ben said. "Where are you headed?"

"Into town. A man d...done come up to the tracks the other day...invited me for a m...meal. I ain't had a good meal in a long time, and since there ain't no work for me tonight, reckon I'd take him up on his offer."

Ben scooted ahead as they passed an open oven, but the man kept his steady pace, unaffected by the heat of the factory furnace.

Ben had every intention of taking a job at one of the factories instead of at the Clubhouse, but Percival wouldn't have it. He had heard stories from his father about how terrible factory conditions were, but had always been curious to get another's perspective. Ben waited for the man to catch up. "What's it like?" Ben said. "Workin' in the factories, I mean."

"Hell," said the man. "That's the only way I can put it, hell on earth. 'Cept Satan's droppin' melted p...pig iron on you instead of p...pokin' you with a p...pitchfork. The factories will sweat the damn life outta you. I've lost nearly forty p...pounds already. I don't know if my family would even recognize me."

"Where's your family at?"

"P...Pittsburg. They're coming in to town this Saturday. My twin girls have their hearts set on m...marchin' in the parade to the dam. My wife even made them a matchin' p...pair of p...pretty dresses to wear, red, white, and blue. Oh, I hope they recognize me."

As Ben waited for the man again, he noticed the absence of the day laborers. Usually the tracks were covered with them, playing cards in the dirt or inventing gambling games with the ballast rock. It was raining, but not hard enough to have sent them into their wedge tents in the woods.

When they came to the fork at the top of Main Street, Ben expected the man to head off along the path by the river, a much faster way to town, but the man stayed at Ben's side. "Fella told me to take the wagon road," he said, 'follow it round till you see the big sugar maples.' Boy, I sure hope I can find it."

"Sugar maples?" said Ben. "What's this man look like."

The dirty day laborer hiked up his pack. "I dunno know, tall, thin, white hair p...pulled back and tied off with a bit of twine."

"Well," said Ben, "I believe I can help you. That's where I'm headed, too."

They walked across the knoll, and Ben asked the man his name.

"Owen," he said, "Owen Ahl."

Ben shook Owen's callused hand.

Up on a ridge, Ben could see the wide canopy of the sugar maples. "There it is," he said, pointing to Clem's property.

"Oh, boy," said Owen, "I can't wait for that home-cooked meal."

They started toward the house, and a crisp gunshot stopped them in their tracks, exploding from under the sugar maples like a whip cracking in an empty canyon. Before the echo had faded, there came a loud commotion, a ruckus of hollering and cheering. Ben ran up the hill. Owen followed with an awkward trot, lopsided from the weight of his pack.

Ben came around the woodshop and found Clem's backyard crowded with more than a hundred men, some milling around the back houses, others seated at the benches between the sugar maples. His father was standing in the middle of the yard holding a smoking pistol. Two men dressed like Ben's new friend were patting Percival on the back and laughing.

At the far end of the yard, a man was milling around a haystack. He found what he was looking for and set the tall Hutchison bottle on top of the straw wall. He made sure the target was set firmly in place and moved away. "How 'bout ten out'a ten?" he shouted.

Percival cocked the pistol and took aim.

The men went silent, and shifted their eyes from bottle to barrel.

With his arm straight out, and one eye shut, Percival fired.

The ringing blast sent a perfectly aimed bullet across the yard, shattering the bottle into a million pieces. Bits of amber glass flew into the air like sparkling confetti. The audience erupted, hooting and hollering like school boys at a three-ring circus.

"That's my pa," said Ben, clapping his hands.

Owen nodded, sharing a bit of the group's amusement.

Across the yard, Clem came out from behind the oil barrel. "All right, all right," he shouted, "enough sharp shootin', you'uns get settled now, supper's just about ready."

The crowd obliged, and marksman Percival, after receiving a few more pats on the back, brought the Colt to Clem who stuck the pistol into his kangaroo pouch.

Every day laborer in the valley must have been packed into Clem's yard, Ben thought. Most were seated, huddled around the wooden tables. The rest were perched atop the haystacks or spread out on the ground using their bindles for back rests. The rain had slacked off, and the yard and the men were dry. At the tables, they played cards in between their coffee cups, laughing and ribbing each other. By the haystacks, a few had found some cockroaches in the straw and were racing them across a length of canvas. All were filthy, soot-covered, smelly, and emaciated. If a strong wind had blown through the yard, it would have taken the cards, the cockroaches, and a good number of the men with it. Clem's yard was a civil war camp, save the Sibley tents and horizontal refreshments.

The table next to the blazing oil barrel was crowded with cooling turkeys and baskets of corn bread, but the benches on either side were empty. Ben led Owen to the table, and they sat and watched as Clem turned a long skewer of wild turkeys over the fire.

"I see you brought a friend, Ben," said Clem, "Glad you could make it."

"I sure am g...glad you invited me," said Owen, removing his cap, "Much obliged."

"Well, you are welcome," said Clem, "Owen, isn't it."

"Yes, sir. And I'd be g...glad to offer my help, if'n you need it."

"Ben," said Clem, "grab the end of that spit."

Ben came round the opposite side of the barrel as the flames teased the turkeys with unpredictable pokes of fire.

"Best way to help now, Owen," said Clem, "is to get outta the way."

Ben and Clem shouldered the long skewer, and Owen scurried off the bench as they dropped the charred turkeys onto the table. Ben held tight as Clem stripped the birds from the stick.

Clem reached into his apron, retrieved a handful of serrated knives, and jabbed one into each of the turkeys, right between the shoulder blades. He went again to his pocket like a magician to a top hat and pulled out the revolver. He held the pistol high and fired into the air. "Come and get it," he shouted.

The camp-men formed a line, the way church parishioners line up to receive communion, anxious for the feast, but still minding their Sunday manners. The procession snaked around the maple trees, bindles, and benches to the turkey table, each man filling his plate with a big cut of meat and a grip of corn bread. Those who could manage it filled their coffee, wedging the tin cup between the fixings on the way back to their place in the yard.

When all of the men had passed through the line, and were busy messing their faces and fingers, Clem divvied up what was left for Percival, Ben, Owen, and himself. After a brief bow of his head, he joined the others who had already dug into the turkey. "Fine work on Mrs. Green's table," he said.

"I reckon I would have done all right as a cabinetmaker," said Percival.

Or a lawman, thought Ben.

"Would have?" said Clem, picking at one of the carcasses. "Why do you say, would have?"

"I've got myself trenched into steel," said Percival, "It's too late to go back now."

"Is it?" said Clem. "The way I figure, losing that job at the foundry's the best thing that could have happened to you. Now you're free to do whatever you want. And if that's cabinet makin'... then the hell with the steel."

Percival popped his head back and took a swallow of coffee. "I sure do enjoy it."

Ben wasn't paying much attention to the talk about cabinet making. He was too busy chomping on his turkey leg and humming the song he'd heard the black man humming in the hallway.

"Wade in the water," said Clem between bites.

"What?" said Ben.

"That tune you're hummin', those are the words," said Clem, finishing the rest of the lyrics half talking, half singing. "Wade in the water children, wade in the water, God's gonna trouble the water."

"Never heard of it," said Percival.

Clem pushed his plate to the center of the table and rested a leg n the bench. "Don't expect you would have. It's a slave song."

"How was it all them s...slaves could s...sing so good?" said Owen, "Over a hundred men in the s...steel factories, not one of them can carry a tune. And why'd they sing so much, anyway?"

Ben set his leg on the bench the way Clem had done. "Maybe it was to pass the time," he said, "I'm sure they got awful tired and lonely."

"I heard them songs had secret meanings," said Percival. "You ever hear that, Clem?"

Heavy sighs and long belches came from the men on the benches. Most of them had had their fill of the turkey meat and were washing it down with what was left of their coffee.

Clem leaned into the table. "Don't know for sure," he said, "but this one comes straight from the Bible. John five: four, for an angel went down to the pool and troubled the water, whosoever stepped in first was cured of all illness. Kind of like a baptism. Though I have heard some say it was meant as a message, telling the slaves to run through the water to throw the bloodhounds off their trail."

"You mean they'd try to run away?" said Ben.

"Wouldn't you?" said Owen.

"I don't know. I'd be too scared of what might happen if I got caught."

"What about the things you'd miss out on if you never tried?" said Clem.

Owen looked over the yard toward Johnstown. "I'd take the chance."

Clem lifted his chin and motioned to Percival. "What about you, would you run through the water, or stay on dry land?"

Percival picked at his turkey wing. "I suppose each man's gotta make that choice when the time comes," he said.

Everyone had finished his supper and coffee, and the rain was back on. The day laborers filed out of the yard in groups of six and eight and headed to the tracks or to their wedge tents between the trees.

Owen left with the last group. And after thanking Clem for

his hospitality, he stood at the edge of the property as if he were waiting to be invited back.

"Every Wednesday," said Clem.

Owen waved goodbye and left the yard with a smile so wide it cracked the soot-caked, turkey-glazed corners of his mouth.

Clem slapped Ben playfully on the shoulder. "You want to do me a favor?" he said, pointing to the cluttered tabletops. "Gather up them turkey bones into the fire, and run them coffee cups and plates to the scullery."

Percival swung himself round on the bench and faced the oil barrel and the burning logs still sending out a good flame. "You put this shindig together once a week?" he said, "I never knew, never heard a peep, neither."

Clem spun around as Percival had done, and the two men faced the fire and sat with their forearms bent behind them on the table, parallel and selfsame like a pair of contemplative crickets. "That's because you ain't a day laborer," said Clem, "and as for the noise, tonight was our first game of sharpshootin'."

Percival smiled and held out his palm and captured some of the rain drops. "You reckon we're gonna get hit by the storm?"

"If we do," said Clem, looking up and catching a big drop between the eyes, "reckon we better sandbag that shop real good. Shame if it got washed out now."

Clem leaned back and looked beyond the garage toward the river. Though the property sat on a hill, a good distance from the banks, they could still hear the faint sound of moving water. "That river's got a mind of its own," he said, "and I don't trust it. Don't trust that dam, neither."

"Fella from the Tribune's been writing stories all week," said Percival. "First he says the storm's headin' south, then he says it's comin' straight toward us, then it's headin' south again. Then he's goin' on and on about how there's nothing to worry about, and how them industrialists spent all kinds of money fixin' up that dam so even if the storm does hit us, it won't breach like last time. I wish he'd make up his mind."

"Folks were lucky in '81," said Clem.

"Come to think of it," said Percival, "he got it wrong back then, didn't he?"

"He did. And washed out shops and flooded homes ain't nothin'. When she goes again," Clem shook his head, "let's just say, I'd start headin' for higher ground." He took a turkey carcass from the table and tossed the stripped bones into the oil drum. "Let's get these into the fire before the rain puts her out."

Percival stood at the oil drum and worked a stick around the fire, punching at the charred ends of the logs and moving the fresh parts of the wood to the flames. "You really think that storm's comin', and that dam's gonna breach?" he said, hoping if Clem had any information from some source other than the Tribune, he'd be kind enough to share it.

Clem looked up, gazing at the clouds as if they would answer for him. The only response was another drop between the eyes. "All I know is there's an awful lot of water up on that mountain that wasn't meant to be there. And it don't matter what that weatherman says, or how much money them steel men spent, ain't no pile of rocks gonna hold it back forever. Things of these kinds generally give way. Might not be this time, but sooner or later, it's gonna go. All of it."

"Well, if it does," said Percival, retaking his seat, "I say we tie Crick to the dam, maybe that Wisord fella from the Tribune, too. He's another one I'd like to give a good thumpin' to."

Ben was hustling around the yard, tossing turkey bones into the fire and making trips to the back side of the houses with armfuls of coffee cups and plates.

"Wonder if I went wrong," said Percival, "lettin' Ben see that pistol so comfortable in my hand."

Clem grabbed a pine log from under the bench and dropped it into the barrel. The log was moist and it crackled as it burned, shooting up pellets of orange fire that glowed brilliantly then vanished in a curl of grey smoke. "Ben's a grown man," he said, "I believe he can handle it. Besides, you show him a little bit of you, he might show you a little bit of him. Soon he's gonna decide to go to New York, or some gal's gonna come along and sweep him off his feet. Before you know it, he'll be long gone. It's a sad thing, father and son going through life never knowin' each other."

A steady drizzle began to fall, and what was left of the daylight had disappeared behind a cover of black clouds. Percival stared into the hypnotizing flames dancing in the oil drum. "I was sixteen years old when my father died," he said. "We never did see eye to eye. Even the morning of the accident, I tried to convince him not to work on the rafters, but ain't no kid was gonna tell him what to do. Hell, long before I started workin' with him, we fought. I wanted to stay in school, he said it was a waste of time. I wanted to start my own cabinet makin' business, he said it was too risky. I wanted to go one way; he'd always pull me the other. The only time we ever connected was when we went huntin'. The only time my father was ever sober, too."

"And how'd you manage that?"

Percival laughed. "We'd pack a bag with knives, tin pots, extra shells, all the tools for field-dressin', and my mother would take it to the kitchen and swipe my father's whiskey bottle while she packed our lunches. He wouldn't check the bag till we were out on the mountain, and by then, it was too late to go back."

Percival sat in front of the oil barrel, the hollow bones popping and spliting apart as the rain put out the last of the glowing embers. He leaned back, eying the Colt Clem had tucked in his coveralls. "You think I could borrow your hunting gear and a couple of guns?"

"Why," said Clem, "You ain't thinkin' about shootin' the weather man, are you?"

22

"Damn it, Ben," said Percival, swatting away the nose of the shotgun, "Never point that thing at anyone, hold it straight up, or straight down. The only one who should ever lock eyes with that barrel is the deer, understand."

The melody of Vivaldi's Four Seasons played in Ben's head. He tried to push it out and listen to his father's instructions, but the string concerto kept creeping in. He took the shotgun and leaned it against the oil drum.

Ben watched Percival assemble Clem's hunting gear on the table, packing the two haversacks so quickly he could only remember a few of the items stuffed inside: a knife, some extra shells, and a tin canteen. Ben took one of the packs, draped it over his shoulder, and patted it against the long brown duster Clem had loaned him. With the loose fitting coat and the oversized hat, he looked like a gangly Texas outlaw.

Percival, whose build was similar to a more youthful Clem, wore his hunting get-up well. Even without the Winchester, his long jacket and wide-brimmed hat told any deer that wanted to live to run the other way.

On the table was a stretch of canvas tied at the ends and sides to a pair of long wooden poles. To Ben it resembled a large scroll. "What's that for, pa?"

Percival rolled up the canvas and handed the sticks to Ben. He

166

took the other pack from the table and looped it around his neck. "You don't think the buck is gonna walk back with us, do you?"

Percival shouldered his rifle, and Ben went for the double-barrel. Percival snatched it away before Ben could take it. "I'll carry the guns," he said.

Ben tucked the sticks with the canvas under his arms, and with a crescendo from Vivaldi, he followed his father out of the yard and up the hill. A scattering of clouds filled the crisp, pre-dawn sky, and the only evidence of daylight approaching was the thin bands of florescent red and orange that glowed around their edges.

"I say we head over the dam," said Percival, pointing up toward the mountains, "Then around that Clubhouse. The forest is thick back there, lots of streams too where the deer like to drink."

Ben fumbled with the sticks to the quickening tempo of Vivaldi's Primavera. The canvas stretcher slipped from his hands and fell to the ground. His jacket flopped about him as he bent over to retrieve the sticks, and he stepped in a deep puddle. He kicked off the mud, but the insides of his shoes were now soaked.

Percival waited, looking up toward the mountain in anticipation. "Come on Ben. Set it on your shoulder and let's get going."

Ben had just finished Vivaldi's Spring when they came to the dam.

Standing on the rock ledge at the far side of the bridge was John Parke. He was studying the spillway under the faint light of the dawn.

Ben moved on to where Parke stood crouched over the edge of the bridge. He turned his head away and hurried past, but it was too late, Parke had seen him.

"What brings you out here so early?" said Parke.

"Deer," said Ben.

Parke stood and rested his arms on the bridge. "Must be slim pickings in that kitchen for Jean Pierre to send you out to shoot our dinner."

Ben twisted around, motioning to his father coming up with the guns. "Just out hunting with my pa," he said.

Parke pushed himself onto the bridge. His pants were soaked and his shirt was stained with streaks of mud. Ben could see clumps of black soil caked around his fingertips.

"Will you be needing me on the grounds today?" Ben said.

Parke dug at the dirt beneath his nails. "What I really need is for someone to fix that office door. You think you can manage that?"

"You bet I can," Ben said, "better than new."

"Today, no later. And make sure it locks."

"Today, yes sir."

After Percival exchanged 'mornin's' with Parke, he and Ben left the bridge and walked up the cobblestone road toward the Clubhouse. At a signpost that read Club Members Only Beyond This Point, they turned onto a muddy path, winding through a grove of pines and circling the backside of the Club's property. Percival walked along the tree line, stopping at each no trespassing sign to gaze at the Clubhouse. Ben kept moving with his head down, carefully avoiding the puddles while he balanced the sticks on his shoulder. In his head, the third movement of Vivaldi's Summer, with its scratchy violins and presto arpeggios, played in full orchestration.

The cottages and the horse stables were quiet, and Ben and Percival moved past them unnoticed. They cleared the last property marker and headed across a wide swale fringing the entrance to the forest. Just as Ben moved into Vivaldi's Autumn, Percival called him to a spot under the trees where a thick covering of pine needles had been turned over.

"See this activity here?" Percival said, pointing to the disturbed needles.

His symphony interrupted, Ben sauntered over to where his father was standing and studied the clump of loose debris. To Ben, it looked exactly like all the other random patches of dead needles.

Percival waved Ben on, and they moved into the lush thickness that covered the sloping hills.

Like an expert tracker, Percival crept along in front of Ben, glancing left and right, up and down, paying close attention to bent branches and broken pinecones. After the entrance to the forest had closed behind them, and the senseless arrangement of the trees made it impossible to walk a straight line, Percival dropped to one knee and brushed aside another collection of loose needles. "Here, Ben," he said, "Over here."

Ben set down the sticks and leaned in with hands on knees. "Deer tracks?" he said.

Percival picked away the twigs and studied the print. "No," he said, drawing an imaginary circle in the air above it. "See the oval shape. And the front toes, lined up evenly. It's a dog. All the activity around here, the farms, the trains, the factories, drives the deer up the mountain. Keep your eyes peeled. Soon we'll find a set of tracks we can follow."

They walked for an hour, the concentration of trees growing thicker, and the sounds of the valley, and Vivaldi's concerto, fading further into the distance. Every so often an indentation in the mud, or a disturbance in the ground-cover would catch Percival's eye, and he'd stop to show Ben the details of the animal's print: wild turkey, quail, rabbit, and more dog. Then he'd pop up and move quickly through the trees, twisting around the trunks and hopping over the fallen branches that bumped up from the ground like knobby knees. Ben struggled to keep up, all the while staring at the ground, hoping to impress his father by finding a set of tracks they could follow.

At the base of a tall maple, a grouping of dead tree limbs fanned out over the ground like bony fingers. Ben studied the open space between them. "Over here, pa", he shouted, "I think I've found somethin'."

Percival tiptoed back with a finger pressed to his lips.

Ben pointed to a track in the mud.

Percival peeled away the needles as he'd done before, exposing a clean print. He studied the edges, paying close attention to the spacing and shape of the front toes. He took his finger and traced around the three-looped heel-pad. In a quick, almost graceful manner, he set down the shotgun, rose to his feet, and flattened the rifle across his chest. "These are tracks, all right," he said, "But not from a deer."

169

Ben looked at the four-toed, clawless pad sunk deep into the mud. "What's it from?"

Percival looked back over his shoulder. "Mountain lion." He reached down and handed Ben the shotgun and raised his free arm and pointed toward the hills. "Looks like it headed that way," he said, "come on."

"Aren't we lookin' for a deer?" said Ben.

"We are. And if you were a hungry lion, which way would you be headed?"

Percival ran off in a swift jog, weaving through the trees and purposefully changing direction every twenty yards or so. Ben followed, the long sticks bouncing on his shoulder, the double-barrel pointed straight to the ground. They trekked over dirt mounds, gullies, and ravines until they came to a fast flowing stream.

Otto Run started high in the mountains, snaking through the canyon and feeding the reservoir just east of the Clubhouse. With all the rain and melting snow, the water moved quick over the shallow bed of fallen branches and river rock. At the edge of the creek, Percival lost the lion tracks, but found something, or rather someone, whipping a cane fly-rod over his head.

The fisherman threw out the flimsy line as if he were a ringmaster, setting it gently on the surface of the water then gracefully drawing it back in one quick motion, teasing the fish with the shimmering silver hook at the end. The current ran strong against the man's legs, throwing a splash of whitewater against the back of his boots. He raised an open hand to Percival and Ben.

"What are you fishin' for," asked Percival, "Musky, pike?"

"Black bass," the man said. "They come up from the reservoir to spawn here."

"You catch any?" said Ben.

"Not yet. But I think they're startin' to warm up to me."

The man drew back the rod and threw a side-armed cast, skipping the sparkling lure across the water and sinking it just below the surface. Ben saw something move under the water, close to where the man had landed the fly. A shadow came up and darted back, and the man yanked the pole with a clean jerk. An agitated black bass popped out of the water, its mouth chomping on the silver hook that had pierced its upper jaw. The fisherman spun the reel with a smooth turn of his wrist and grabbed the line and pulled the fish from the water. "That's a little sucker, ain't it," he said, holding up the tiny black bass for display.

The man worked the pole into his armpit while the fish struggled and twisted round. He gripped it below the gills and smiled at it, as if it hadn't been the first time this particular black bass had dangled from the end of his line. He pulled the hook from its mouth and set the fish in the water. It flopped in his hand for a moment and swam away.

"You mind if we pass by?" said Percival.

The man made a big overhand cast, landing the fly a good distance from where he'd caught the frisky juvenile. "I don't mind," he said, "But watch your footing. It might be shallow here, but if that current sweeps you off your feet, you'll be down at that lake in no time."

Percival stepped into the creek and took a deliberate path, lifting a foot from the water, and setting it down on the river bed where the rocks were flat and absent of loose debris. Ben copied his father's big steps, and the two made their way to the opposite side of the river.

Percival plotted their course through the dense pines. They moved further into the woods, and a mist fell through the trees, sprinkling the prickly branches with dew and drawing out the fresh scent of the pines. The only sounds were the squishing of loose needles and the occasional crack of a semi-dry cone under their feet as they tramped through the wooded maze.

After another hour, Ben stopped. His legs and back ached from carrying the canvas, now dripping wet from the mist in the air. He dropped the sticks, leaned his gun against a rotting log, and sat. "I need to rest for a bit, pa," he said.

Percival had moved well ahead and had to backtrack. "All

right. But I wouldn't sit there if I were you." He took his rifle and stabbed at a patch of rotting bark. A hole opened in the trunk, and a mound of black ants spilled to the ground. Ben bounced off the log, but the ants had already found their way onto the top of his shoe. He lifted his leg and chased them off with a few quick slaps.

"Let's move on," said Percival, "Looks like there's a good spot up ahead."

Ben retrieved the canvas and let his father carry the gun. He kept moving through what looked like the same set of trees and the same brown carpet of needles and cones they'd passed hours earlier. Suddenly the thick forest opened to a broad meadow of tall grass, forty yards deep and twice as wide. The wind brushed the field with a quick stroke, sending a wave of green hues up one direction then back down the other.

Percival set down the guns, pulled out a canteen from his sack and took a swig. "We'll rest here," he said.

Ben dropped the canvas and sat in the thick grass. He pulled his knees to his chest and reached into his pack for his canteen. The ground was sticky with dew, and he felt the dampness soaking through the seat of his pants as he drank. He was ready to move on when his father crouched down beside him and grabbed the back of his head, slowly turning it toward the tree line across the meadow. Between a narrow spacing of pines and a drooping limb of thick-needled branches, Ben saw the russet-brown profile and the crooked antlers of a stout, white-tailed buck.

Percival handed Ben the double-barrel and helped him wedge the butt against his shoulder. He set Ben's hand under the stock and brought his index finger to the trigger. "Line her up," he whispered, "and take the shot."

Ben had only shot a gun once, when he and Doc 'borrowed' Henry Howell's .22 rifle and took it behind the General Store to shoot at tin pots and vinegar barrels. Even then it had taken him five minutes to gather up enough nerve to pull the trigger.

The deer disappeared when Ben squinted into the gun-sight. He opened his eye and the buck returned, dipping down for a chew of grass then up again. Ben lowered the barrel and dropped the gun from his shoulder. "You do it, pa. I don't think I can get a good shot at it."

Percival lifted the gun and jammed it against Ben's shoulder, putting the sight in perfect line with the buck. He let go and moved away. "You can do it, Ben. Go ahead now. Knock it dead."

Ben closed his eyes and held his breath. He pulled the trigger, and the blast put a ringing in his ears so loud he felt as if he'd been standing next to the Sunday morning bells at the First Presbyterian. The rifle-butt pounded against his shoulder and sent him falling backward into the wet grass, soaking the backside of his duster. He sat up on his elbows and looked across the meadow. The deer had vanished into the woods.

"Damn it, Ben," said Percival, shaking his head, "I had it all lined up for you, too." He checked his rifle. "I'm gonna head around to the other side. I might still have a chance at it."

Ben rubbed his shoulder and started to follow.

"Wait here," said Percival. "And don't move from this spot, neither. I don't want to end up shootin' you by mistake."

Ben sat in the grass as Percival traced the tree line to the other side of the meadow and into the woods where the buck had made its escape. Time passed slowly as he waited alone, long enough for the back of his coat to dry, long enough for the rain clouds that had dropped in on them earlier to pass, and another, darker set to move in. Except for the patter of the raindrops and the rush of the wind blowing shades of green across the field, all was quiet.

Ben waited for the sound of a rifle shot and for his father to come running back calling for the canvas. He waited, but no shot came. Between a cluster of trees that stood so high they seemed to touch the clouds, he heard the sound of rustling branches.

He took the shotgun and followed the sound to the edge of the meadow and into the trees. He dropped low and listened for its direction. How impressed his father would be, he thought, if he could take the buck all by himself. He crept along and stopped at an opening where he thought he heard the crackling of twigs.

173

Behind a fallen trunk were several tall pines, their soggy branches drooping over the dead tree. Movement came from behind the log, and Ben tiptoed over the blanket of needles to the middle of the clearing. He saw it now, the muscular body, the thick tawny coat, the long curved tail flicking up and down and round and round in small, tight loops.

The cat came through the trees, peeling back its mouth yawn-like and baring its teeth. Slowly, it lifted a front paw, revealing a row of tapered claws hooked over the end of a thick, padded foot. With a short hop, it jumped onto the log and paced its length with perfect balance, sweeping its tongue around its face, its eyes, like glistening black almonds, fixed on Ben.

Ben wanted to run, but even if his legs hadn't been frozen stiff, he knew it was the wrong thing to do. He snapped open the shotgun and went to his sack. His hands shook, and the shotshells slipped through his fingers.

The cat halted and cocked its ears and purred in a low rumbling growl. Ben took a slow breath, and a cold shiver ran down the back of his neck. He fumbled for a shotgun shell and finally found one, pulling it out of the bag but dropping it when the lion snarled. The cat bent forward and crouched, setting his front paws over the edge of the log, ready to spring. Ben dropped the gun and ran.

The lion jumped from the log and was almost on top of him when a blast came from across the meadow. A bullet whizzed past Ben's ear, and the lion dropped lifeless on his back, knocking him to the ground.

Percival came running up and pulled the lion off. He grabbed Ben by the arm and lifted him to his feet. "You all right," he said, checking for cuts and bruises.

Ben nodded, dazed, staggering to keep his balance.

Percival knelt over the cat and poked it with his rifle. Blood oozed from a fist-sized hole in the side of its head. Its eyes were shut tight, its mouth, full of white daggers, hung open. Its hindquarters had evidence of a previous scattergun wound, and when Percival lifted its paw, Ben could see the ridge of a thick scar running down the back of its leg.

"Must have been caught in a bear trap at one time," Percival said.

Ben felt a shiver pass through him, and he pulled his jacket tight against his chest. "I reckon it's made its way out of a lot of close calls," he said.

"Well it ain't walking away from this one, that's for sure."

Percival grabbed the shotgun and walked off toward Otto Run, flipping the two firearms onto his shoulders with a military flair. "Come on, Bennett," he said, "Let's go home."

Ben stood over the dead lion, and the comforting violins of Vivaldi's Autumn flowed softly into his head. He watched his father disappear into the woods, and hurried to catch up.

It had been raining all afternoon, and both the yard and Clem's cooking drum were full of water.

"Looks like this is it," said Percival, staring out the screen door while he sipped his coffee. "It's coming down good, and doesn't look like it's lettin' up."

Clem moved around the fabric-covered couch in the center of the room and set a tray of ham hocks on the low table in front of it. He sat next to Ben who had already started eating. "Come on now, Percival," he said, "get yourself some supper before it cools off."

Percival grabbed a pork knuckle and sat in a high-backed chair by the window and gnawed on the chewy meat, taking breaks in between bites to drink his coffee. "Venison sure would have been nice," he said.

Clem set down his plate and took his coffee to the screen door. He stared across the yard, slurping from the tin cup and stroking the sparse, grey stubble around his neck. "Sometimes you get the deer, sometimes the deer gets you."

"Or the mountain lion," said Percival. "Lucky for you, Ben, that deer made a clean get-away. If I'd have picked up its trail, I might not have come back so soon."

Ben kept his eyes on his plate. "I know."

"I've been thinkn'," said Clem, pointing toward the shop with his coffee cup, "If we start addin' value to those pieces in there, I'm gonna need to fix the lock on that barn door. Mineral spirits is one thing, but finished furniture; we can't have that walkin' out of here."

Ben's stomach dropped, and so did the pork knuckle he had pinched between his fingers. "The office door …at the Clubhouse," he said, getting up from his seat. "I'll be fired for sure if it ain't fixed by mornin'."

"I wouldn't head up there tonight," said Percival. "Dark, and late, and raining so hard. I'll bet it's dumping even heavier up by the dam."

"Parke told me to have it fixed, today. I promised."

"Your pa's right," said Clem, "Not a good idea to go tonight. Head out early morning. Early-morning rain is easier to manage. Fix that door before they wake up. And considering the time them socialites go to bed, that shouldn't be too hard."

"I can't," said Ben, pacing, "I need Park's tools. I've got to go tonight."

"Trust me," said Clem, "Wait till morning. You can take my tools. Get her fixed lickety-split, and no one will be the wiser."

Ben worked his fingers around his forehead in tiny circles. If he was going to have to stay in River Fork, he couldn't afford to lose his job at the Clubhouse. He needed to be near the Steinway, and at least have something to look forward to. Clem had never steered him wrong before. "All right," he said, "But early, I mean early, before the sun come up, early."

"Don't worry," said Clem, "I'll get you up."

23

FRIDAY, MAY 28, 1889

Ben waited on the porch stoop and caught his breath. He had made good time getting there, and was certain the Clubhouse was still asleep. Above him, raindrops pelted the narrow awning, tapping out a syncopated rhythm like corn popping in a hot skillet. The liquid kernels dripped off the edge of the canvas and onto his cap. He set Clem's tool bag on the porch and removed a skeleton key from his pocket. Jean Pierre had given him the key to lock up after late nights of piano playing, but this was the first time he had used it to break in before dawn.

A blue sliver of predawn light followed him inside to the hook on the back of the toilet door. He hung his cap, and fat drops ran off the rigid brim and dripped to the floor. He put the skeleton key into his pocket, grabbed Clem's tool bag off the porch, and shut the door. As he stepped into the darkness, he heard a crunch under his foot. The roach was so thick and hard, he felt like he'd stepped on a rock. He kicked up his leg and sent the flattened bug into the corner of the room. A scampering of tiny feet, like the scratching of sandpaper, raced across the floorboards and up the walls. Even on his best day, he could never get the kitchen clean enough to keep the rats away. How disappointed they must be to find only snails and goose liver to eat.

He felt his way into the kitchen and lit the gas lamps. The work table was free of Jean Pierre's cutlery and spices and made a good place to set the tools. He sifted through the bag, careful to avoid clanking metal against metal and to keep from stabbing his fingers on the rusted nails at the bottom. Clem had stocked the bag with an assortment of tools: a file, a rasp, a chisels, a prick punch, a set of lineman's pliers, and a brand new HD Smith & Co. screwdriver. Ben knew the screwdriver better from the advertisement he'd seen in the Tribune that referred to it as the 'perfect-handle' screwdriver. He was already familiar with the damage to the door, and knew all he needed was the perfect-handle. The lock was a simple fix, a loose screw.

He made his way to the broken door, stopping to steal a quick peek at the Steinway. Too bad the piano wasn't the reason for his early morning visit. He was close to the door and the broken lock when he heard noises coming from inside the office, a high pitched squeak, then a muffled, methodic thumping. Maybe the rats had fled to the office after he lit the gas lamps. Vermin always seek cover in the dark.

With one quick motion, he threw open the door. Standing at the desk was the backside of Morton Crick. Ben had seen him there many times before, although never with a pair of high-heels hooked over his shoulders and his pinstriped pants crumpled around his ankles. The kitchen lamps barely illuminated the office, but Crick's rear-end shined like a cracked train lamp in a dark tunnel.

Crick twisted his head around and locked eyes with Ben.

Ben stared back with chin to chest, the way a young boy stares at his older sister after catching her in the nude.

Fumbling to pull up his pants, Crick bent over and knocked his head on the corner of the desk. He fell over backward, dragging the woman to the floor. Ben caught a good look at Lily Parke as she scrambled on hands and knees searching for her undergarments. She scurried out of the office, and Ben heard her quick footsteps racing up the stairs and across the second floor. Crick lay on the ground, cursing his trouser buttons, and Ben entertained the idea of offering him the perfect-handle.

Crick got to his feet and shuffled to Ben. "Not a word of this to anyone," he said, pointing at Ben with a trembling finger. "Not a word."

Ben expected his knees to start rattling or his stomach to plunge to the floor. But instead, he felt calm. Even the urge to pick at his fingernails was gone. The only thing twitching was the clump of hair on Crick's upper lip. Crick stormed out of the room, and Ben smiled, enjoying the position of importance he'd just inherited.

By now, daylight had found its way into the kitchen, and Ben went to work on the lock. Ten minutes to reposition and tighten the mortise, two more to straighten the strike plate against the jam, and the lock was fixed. He greased the hinges, swung the door out and back a few times, and took the tools to the utility room.

As he set the bag on the shelf, he noticed a set of papers pinched between the wall and the jug of carbolic disinfectant. He slid out the Beethoven piece he'd played the night before, the one that seemed to have left Mr. Damrosch unmoved. Somehow it had fallen out of his pack. He pushed aside a stack of dinner plates and rifled through a box of cutlery, hoping by chance Jean Pierre had stumbled upon a train ticket and a wad of cash too.

Ben rolled up the sheet music and put it inside the tool bag. Since the fight on the bridge, he hadn't given much thought to the academy and his valley exodus, but this unexpected discovery rekindled his interest.

He was putting on his kitchen coat when he heard a wagon rolling to a stop out back. He rung out his cap and went onto the porch. The iceman he'd dealt with before was perched atop the canvas tarp, puffing on a piece of straw as if it were a fine cigar.

The man pulled the hay-stogie from his mouth. "Look who's here so bright and early," he said, throwing back the tarp and uncovering the pyramid of block ice. "And I thought I was gonna have to wait till ten o'clock."

Ben came off the porch, hands on his hips. "No waitin' today," he said, "Go ahead and get started."

The man put the straw cigar in his mouth and leaned against the ice blocks. "Son," he said, "we've had this conversation already. You want ice, you unload it, simple as that."

Ben walked closer to the wagon, scanning the tower. "Lotta ice here," he said. "First stop of the day?"

The man went back to puffing straw. "And a lot more to make down the valley, too, so you better get movin, less you want to pay for cold water."

"I've been thinking about that," said Ben. "And I'm pretty sure it's you who should do the unloadin'."

"I told you boy, I don't ..."

"And the stackin' in the ice box, too."

The man hopped off the wagon and hiked up his pants. He was taller and wider than Ben, and used his size to intimidate. "Listen," he said, leaning into Ben, "this is the last time I'm gonna tell you. You want ice, you get it now, or I'm headin' straight outta here."

Ben scrunched his eyes and tilted his head the way a father does when he's about to scold an unruly child. Having just gone toe to toe with Crick, he was full of confidence, and now he was the one leaning. "You think you're the only ice man in the valley?" he said, ticking off on his hand the competition. "I've got Union Ice, Doc's ice company, Owen ice, and a hell of a lotta others to choose from, too. So if you want the business, and I'm sure you do, you'll get movin', less you want to be the one stuck with the cold water."

The iceman backed up until he hit the wagon, the piece of straw dangling from his lower lip. He spit out the straw and pointed a finger toward the utility room. "Mind if I use your stack cart?"

While the man loaded the icebox, Ben went to the kitchen and boiled a pot of coffee. He climbed atop the corner table and watched through the window. It took the iceman four trips to fill the icebox, and when he rode away, Ben could see him wiping his brow with his sleeve.

Ben came down and poured himself a cup of coffee. He went to the dining room and sat at a table near the Steinway, easing back in the cushioned chair and crossing his legs the way he'd seen the Club members do, the true way to relax after a hard day of labor management. The surge of adrenaline had settled, and he leisurely sipped his coffee, gazing out over the lake and enjoying the peacefulness of the empty room. Even though the day had just begun, he felt he deserved a rest.

24

Parke and his interpreter, Damato, were talking by the shoreline a good fifty feet from the dam. Damato was six-foot four, with a chest round as a locomotive boiler and arms thick as cannons. He towered over Parke who was holding his project notes in one hand and pointing to various areas of the rock face with the other.

Parke stood on tiptoes, arching his arm out in front of him, indicating to Damato several locations along the crest of the dam. After Damato recited back Parke's instructions, they walked across the lawn and joined a group of forty laborers waiting on the bridge.

Lined up behind the laborers were six work wagons hooked to big, brown draft horses and filled with large chunks of bedrock. Three rail cars, loaded with granite boulders, sat on the siding below the dam, and Parke was sending the wagon teams back and forth from the gondolas to the bridge.

Damato bellowed Parke's plan to the men, pointing and reaching as Parke had done. After a little head scratching, and a few questions about pay and break times, the group went to work, unloading the rocks from the wagons and setting them along the embankment where Damato had indicated.

On the far end of the bridge, another group of men armed with shovels and mattocks and pickaxes were chipping away at the face of the dam, a stretch of over fifty feet where Parke had determined the new spillway be located. Parke watched the Italians put his plan into action. Satisfied, he went back to the Clubhouse. Hot coffee would keep him alert while supervising, especially when the spillway crew broke through. He remembered from his investigation that a dozen men had gone over the edge during the original construction, and he did not want that to happen again.

No luncheons or sporting events were scheduled that day, but the Clubhouse still buzzed with activity. The chambermaids and the hired help were busy cleaning and decorating for the Memorial Day festivities, scurrying around the dining room with flags, banners, and canvas streamers. Parke was making his way through the sea of red, white, and blue when Crick caught up to him in front of the swinging doors.

"What the hell do you think you're doing?" said Crick, blocking Parke's way into the kitchen.

Parke was taken aback, never before having to ask permission for a cup of coffee.

"You've got every last Italian pissing around on that dam," said Crick. "I need to get this place ready for Sunday. Streamers round the Clubhouse, flags in the yard, not to mention that stage set up outside where that idiot nigger of yours is gonna perform. You ain't got time right now to put them laborers to work on your foolish projects."

Parke grit his teeth and clasped his hands behind his back, fighting the urge to throw Crick a few choice words and a fist to the mouth. "If I don't get that dam fixed," he said, "we're gonna have bigger problems on our hands than hanging those steamers."

Both men turned as Andrews came down the stairway and headed straight into the office.

"Let me get the work on the dam finished," Parke said. "Forty men can do it in a day. And besides, I'd feel better if we held the festivities inside the Clubhouse."

"If you hadn't noticed, Parke," said Crick, "The storm's already passed. And for Christ's sake, the drizzle out there right now, it's only water."

Before Parke could say another word, Ben came out of the kitchen with a sheet of paper rolled up in his fist.

"If you're finished in the kitchen," Parke said to Ben, "get outside and help the Italians."

"I was thinking," said Ben, moving closer to Crick but looking straight at Parke. "I'd rather spend the afternoon at the piano."

Parke was startled by Ben's dismissal of a direct order. "We had an agreement," he said. "When you aren't in the kitchen, you're out on the grounds with me. And I say I need you at the dam. Now."

Ben didn't move.

Parke raised his arm and pointed toward the big windows as if he were sending Ben to his room for misbehaving. "Put down those papers and get out there."

Crick stepped forward and inserted himself between Ben and Parke. "Mr. Parke," he said, resting a hand on Ben's shoulder, "Don't you know this young man is a musician? He needs to be practicing at that piano, not out on the dam stacking rocks, for God's sake. We need to be encouraging the proliferation of the arts, Mr. Parke. I've spoken to that music expert, Mr. Damrosch, and he says this boy has talent. According to him, all he's missing is a little inspiration. Now how do you suppose he's going to get that by swinging a pickaxe into a pile of rocks?" Crick guided Ben toward the piano. "Now go ahead, son, you play to your heart's content. We wouldn't want a promising pianist smashing his fingers on one of them boulders, now would we, Parke?"

Parke threw his hands up in defeat. "Play the piano then, for all I care," he said, punching open the swinging doors. "All I came in here for was a cup of coffee."

Parke found the coffee pot warming on the stove. He poured out a ladle-full into one of the ceramic mugs reserved for club members, and was about to take a sip when Andrews burst through the newly repaired door and into the kitchen.

"I've got no connection," Andrews shouted. "No connection at all."

Parke followed Andrews into the office to the telephone table by the window.

"I tried to reach Pittsburgh," said Andrews, "then the depot, and I can't get through, no connection at all." He lifted the bell and flicked the cradle and slapped the bell against his palm like he was emptying tobacco from a pipe. He set the bell against his ear and shrugged.

Parke reached behind the box and tugged on the wires. "Seems to be secure on this end," he said, "I'll head around back and check the pole."

Parke went outside and marched across the drive and the back lawn to the tree line where the utility pole stood solid in the ground like a stripped pine. The relay box strapped beneath the crossbar blended into a backdrop of dark grey clouds, but Parke could clearly see the black wire running from the forest to the top of the pole. Drops of rain fell into his face. Squinting, he traced the wire across the driveway and down the side of the Clubhouse until he lost it behind an old Buckboard wagon the Italians had used when they laid the cobblestones.

Parke jogged across the drive. Behind the buckboard, hanging loosely against the wall, he found the severed wire whipping about like a lizard's tail. At his feet was the other half, pressed deep into the thick mud by what looked like the heel of a shoe.

He studied the muddied end of the wire, matching it with his eyes against the dangling end. It appeared as if the wire had been intentionally cut. He ran inside the Clubhouse and searched the storage room for his tools. All he found were serving plates, butler stands, and bistro aprons. He took his hand and swept away a shelf-full of platters.

Andrews stuck his head into the hallway. "Parke," he said, "what the hell is going on in there?"

"Found the problem," said Parke, "have her fixed, lickety-split."

Parke went to the kitchen and saw Ben's tool bag sitting on the shelf in the utility room. He played with the idea of opening it without permission, but reconsidered, uncertain of Ben's newfound position in the Club's hierarchy. He found Ben at the Steinway enjoying the reinstatement of his piano playing privileges.

Parke's first attempt, "Excuse me," went unnoticed like a child attempting to attract the attention of a preoccupied parent. He added, "I'm sorry to bother you," on his next try, but Ben had just started a run of sixteenth notes and continued playing. After, "I'm terribly sorry to bother you, Ben," Ben stopped playing and spun around.

"I realize you are busy practicing," Parke said, trying to keep the sarcasm from his voice, "but it would be wonderful if I could borrow just a moment of you time."

"As long as it's truly a brief moment," said Ben.

Parke led Ben to the kitchen. "If that's your tool bag over there," he said, pointing to the utility room, "grab it and meet me outside."

Parke met Ben at the back door and led him to where the wires had been cut. "Cut clean through," he said, pointing at the two ends, "sabotage." He poked the tool bag with his finger. "I hope you've got somethin' in there that can fix it."

Ben looked at the wires, the bag, then at Parke.

"You do know how to fix it, don't you?" said Parke.

Ben set the tool bag on the buckboard and took out a towel and a pair of lineman's pliers. There was a canvas tarp in the back of the wagon and he pulled it over the bag to shield it from the rain. "You can fix almost anything with a splice," he said, "chains, wires. We just need a little ingenuity, that's all. Step aside, and let me have a look."

Ben took the muddied wire and brushed the frayed end over his palm. He took the towel and cleaned off the end. "Hold on to this," he said, handing Parke the wire and the towel. "Keep it dry and don't let her drop."

Parke raised his hands in surrender.

"Don't worry," said Ben, "It ain't gonna shock you."

The other end of the wire was still flopping against the wall, and Ben caught it as it slithered by. He took the lineman's pliers and cut back the cotton sheath and tin foil, exposing a pair of twisted copper wires. He exchanged ends with Parke, and did the same cutting and peeling with the other wire.

186

Ben twisted the two exposed ends together. He went to the bag and grabbed a small rag that smelled of shellac, and wrapped the sticky cloth around the bare wire. He gripped the splice and squeezed, creating a tight seal around the ends. He pounded a rusty nail into the wall with the side of the lineman's pliers and hung the loose wire over it, keeping the repaired section under the eaves and off the wet ground.

Just then a shout came from inside the office. "Hallelujah," said Andrews. "Hallelujah, I've got a connection."

Parke looked at Ben. "Where'd you learn to do that?"

Ben smiled and returned the lineman's pliers to the tool bag. "I know this cabinetmaker in town," he said. "I just did what he would have done."

Parke thanked Ben with a smile and a sticky handshake, and sent him back to the piano. Having missed his chance for coffee, Parke ran around the back of the Clubhouse to check on the progress at the dam.

When he came to the shoreline, he noticed the bridge deserted. The wagons, most still full of bedrock, had been moved off the far side, and where the spillway was supposed to have been cut, an abandoned pickaxe jutted from the rocks.

He heard a commotion at the far side of the Clubhouse, and when he came up the hill, he saw the Italians spread across the sporting field hanging red, white, and blue streamers along the stack-fence. One of the wagons he'd filled with rock was now loaded with lumber, and the laborers were using the planks to build the base of an enormous bandstand.

Crick was standing on a wooden box in the middle of the field, twirling a black umbrella and smoking a cigar. A group of Italians had gathered around him shouldering American flags. Crick pointed with his cigar at various places in the yard where he wanted the flags placed. "Carry those flags with pride, gentlemen," he shouted.

As the Italians dispersed, Crick left the sporting field and strolled merrily up the boardwalk, whistling. Parke was certain it was

187

Crick who had sabotaged the phone line; now he had stolen his laborers, too. Parke hurried over the grass lawn and onto the bridge, stomping hard across the wooden planks all the way to the far end where the lone pickaxe stood anchored in the rocks. He hopped onto the lip of the dam and pried out the axe.

At one of the near cottages, he saw Crick standing on the porch, stretching his arms and patting his mouth as if he were suppressing a yawn. Crick opened the door of the Queen Ann Tudor and went inside.

Parke raised the axe over his head. "I hope you enjoy your nap," he said, swinging the curved blade hard into the solid face of the dam.

25

While Parke picked away at the dam, Ben was kneeling beside the backdoor stoop scrubbing his hands under the water spigot. Even with borax and a bristle brush, it took him nearly ten minutes to scrape the spoiled shellac from his palms. He was drying his hands on his trousers when he heard music coming from the dining room, a perfect rendition of his beloved Beethoven sonata. For a moment he thought his mind was playing a trick on him, and that Beethoven himself was taunting his meager attempts at imitation. But the sonata went on, flowing with an alluring completeness and perfection Ben had never been able to achieve.

When Ben heard an elderly man shout from inside the dining room, the perfect melody stopped. He shut off the water spigot and raced into the kitchen.

Between the crackle of a hacking cough, a voice called out, "Anyone in here?" The General spread apart the swinging doors with his cane and came into the kitchen. His left hand held a hand-carved pipe, and he drew on it in a series of short puffs. He rapped his cane on the floor. "I say, is anyone in here?"

Ben popped his head around a tower of pie tins stacked at the edge of the cutting table, bringing himself far enough into open space to be seen, but still well outside the reach of the General's cane.

"Mr. Parke said there was someone in here that could be trusted," the General said, pointing the chewed end of his pipe at Ben. "Now, son, would that be you?"

Ben straightened his posture. He felt as if he were back in school, called up to the front of the class by Miss Murray's great grandfather. Ben considered himself trustworthy, and to his knowledge, he hadn't done anything that warranted a scolding. "Reckon it is, sir," Ben said, "And yes, I can be trusted."

"I'm headin' into town," the General said. "Heard there's a saloon with a fine selection of...spirits, that I'd like to...sample."

Even at the ripe age of eighty-three, the General still had a hankering for whiskey and women.

"You keep an eye on my property," he said, throwing his head back toward the dining room. "You make sure he stays put in this Clubhouse till I get back. Agreed?"

The General puffed on the pipe until a cloud of smoke floated above his head. He wiped his palm against his trouserleg and stuck out his hand like he was drawing a gun. Ben instinctively shook it, not certain if the General was asking or telling, and simply answered, "Yes, sir."

The General peeled back the swinging doors with his cane as he had done before. "I will see you tonight. Oh, and just to let you know." The General turned and gave Ben a wink. "He loves his sweets."

The General made his way out of the kitchen while Ben remained standing, confused. Tonight, he thought, would that be dusk, or midnight? Ben was uneasy with the commitment he'd just agreed to, but before he could clarify the specifics of their arrangement, the General had hobbled through the foyer and out the front door.

Ben ran out the employee door and onto the driveway. Apparently, the lure of the saloon had given the General an extra pep in his lopsided step, for when Ben came to the front of the Clubhouse, the General, his pipe, and the black Victoria were halfway to the bridge.

A parade of chambermaids nearly ran Ben over as he came back into the kitchen. They were laden with all things red, white, and blue and rushing out the back door. Ben fought his way toward the center of the room like a salmon swimming upstream. One of the women passed by the cutting table and bumped the stack of pie tins. Ben reached out and kept the pile from toppling over. Caught between two of the tins was a small piece paper. He slid it out, careful not to unbalance the rest of the stack, please take to storage room – J.P., the note read.

Ben tucked the top plate under his chin, slid the tins off the table, and braced the pile against his chest. With slow, cautious steps, he backed his way out the swinging doors and into the dining room.

The first floor of the Clubhouse was once again a giant ballroom, although now it looked more like the floor of the continental congress than a Victorian-style dinner hall. Tall American flags adorned every corner, and a continuous swag of thick, tri-colored banner encircled the room, forming tiny peaks of red, white, and blue where it was pinned to the wall. Patriotic streamers hung from the chandeliers, dangling off the crystal branches like tails on a kite. The entire room had been transformed. Even the ivory table cloths had been replaced with the colors of old glory.

The dining room was empty, except for a lone black man sitting behind the Steinway. It was the blind Negro Ben had seen in the hallway, the one with the hankering for rhubarb pie. His Chopin polonaise filled the room.

Ben moved quietly with the pie tins for a better view of the man who had just recently been placed in his charge. The man sat poised at the piano. Not hunched over, misshapen or awkward, but upright and carefree, his head tilted back as if he were gazing into a summer sky. He smiled as he swayed with the music, the way a tree bough bows and bends freely in the wind. His large hands moved effortlessly over the keys as if they were playing independent and unaware of their master's direction.

Ben closed his eyes, and the tune became more than just padded hammers hitting strings. The melody filled every part of his body, taking him to a perfect place in his mind, to a river. A river where he floated peacefully, whisked one way, then another by the cool flowing currents of the water around him.

Ben's muscles relaxed, so did his grip on the pie tins, and the cool water of the flowing river suddenly vanished. Both men jumped at the sound of metal crashing to the floor. When Ben opened his eyes, the piano bench lay overturned, and the man was standing against the wall, rubbing his hands on his trousers and stomping on the floor. His head twitched, and his mouth opened and shut like a gasping fish.

"Who dare? Who dare?" the man hollered, pacing behind the piano with short, quick steps.

"My name's Ben, Ben Marsh." Ben stumbled forward, his clumsy feet slamming into the fallen mess of pie tins. The clanging set the man off again, and he pounded on the wall with his fists.

"Ben? Ben? Who dat? Who dat?"

Ben hopped to an empty space away from the clutter, and approached the man slowly, with arms outstretched, as if he were attempting to calm a wild animal.

"The old man," Ben said, "with the cane and the pipe. He told me to look after you. He put you in my charge."

The man stopped his pounding, and his body relaxed as if he'd been shot with a tranquilizer dart. A big smile returned to his face. "Da General take care of Tom," he said. "Tom and da General... we's friends." He fumbled around the stage, feeling for the piano bench. "Is Ben and da General friends?"

"Yeah," said Ben, "we're friends."

Tom wandered toward the big windows. "Den if Ben and da General is friends," he said, "Tom and Ben is friends, too."

Ben righted the piano bench. "So that's your name?"

"Yessir. But bein' dat Tom can't see nothin', some folks call him 'Blind Tom'."

"And which do you prefer?"

Tom stopped hunting for the piano bench and followed Ben's voice, "I suppose, Tom pafers...Tom."

On the stage, Ben got a good look at Tom's size, amazed that his own six feet came just shy of Tom's shoulders. Ben took Tom by the arm and sat him on the bench. "You mind if I sit with you?"

Tom patted at the small open space next to him. "Bein' dat we's friends and all, Tom don't mind."

There was barely enough room on the bench for Tom, and Ben pulled up a chair.

"Your music sure sounds nice," said Ben, "How'd you learn to play like that?"

Tom tilted his head and rubbed his ear on his shoulder. "I never really learned," he said. "Folks say it was a gift from da Lord."

"So you've been playing your whole life?"

"It's da only thing I's ever any good at," said Tom, pecking at the keys with random chords and improvised melodies.

"And how is it you've come to River Fork?"

"Da General," Tom said. "He takes Tom all over. Tallahassee, New Orleans, Boston, New York City. Now he says we have to go to Pennsylvania, and put on a show for some rich folk at a fancy clubhouse."

Ben looked out the big windows, imagining all the possibilities beyond the valley. "It must be exciting," he said, "playin' in front of all them people."

Tom raised and lowered the fallboard, toying with it the way Ben used to do with the lid of his cigar box. "I reckon," Tom said. "But sometimes we go places and people throw things and say mean words, and Tom don't want to go, but da General says he has to on account of da rich folk pay money to hear Tom play his piano and sing his songs."

"So why do you have to do what the General says?"

Tom shrugged. "Playing da piano is all I know. And da General helps Tom find da pianos, because Tom can't find 'em on his own. And Tom has to play da piano. He just has to."

"Why, Tom? Why do you have to play the piano?"

"To feel," said Tom, "da happy and da sad. Like when mammy and pappy'd argue, or when I's scared or lonely. I'd just sit and listen to what was round me. If'n I'd hear da rain," Tom played a low running base line against a fast-falling minor arpeggio, "I go and play a song 'bout da rain, dat's da sad. But when da sun come out, and we go play in da yard," Tom changed to a major key and played a light flowing melody against it. "I go and play a song 'bout da sun. Dat's da happy."

"And that's why you play, for the happy and the sad?"

"Mostly, but being my talent was a gift from God, I figure if I didn't play…" Tom sat up straight and grabbed his lapels, "…dat would be downright, "ir-ri-spon-sa-ble.""

"And where are they now? Your mammy and your pappy, I mean?"

Tom rubbed his hand against his legs and chewed on his lip. "Mammy went to work on a farm in Alabama, and pappy went to work on a farm in Mississippi. They say I's too young to go with 'em, so da General, he took me, he's my family now." Tom wiped the corner of his eyes with his knuckles. His hands went to his knees again, and his neck stretched toward the kitchen.

"What is it?" asked Ben.

Tom took a deep breath and licked his lips. "Boy," he said, "Tom sure is hungry."

The smell of rhubarb pie filled the dining room. Ben gave Tom a pat on the shoulder and got up from his chair. "Be right back."

Tom returned to the keys, this time with a Chopin nocturne. The melody began softly, with a fluttering minor trill trapped near middle C. In forte, it leaped up an octave to a single note, countering the introduction with a forceful response of triplets, then falling back to the root and softening in quiet resolution.

Once again, Tom's music took Ben away from the Clubhouse, to the steel mill, and the suffocating burn of the factory furnace. He couldn't believe how Tom, God given talent aside, could evoke such emotion from such a simple tune. Ben remained in the mind of the millworker until Tom finished the piece, and wondered if he would ever be able to attain the same level of musical perfection. "Tom," he said, "can you teach me to play like you?"

Tom smiled and leaned toward Ben like he was getting ready to tell a tall tale. "If'n you only want to play da notes," he said, tapping a finger on the side of his head, "dat's in here. And maybe Tom can teach you dat. But if'n you want to feel da music," he put his hand over his heart and patted his chest, "dat's in here, and ain't nobody can teach you dat but yurself."

26

"Fine work. And I do mean fine work," said Mr. Green, running his thumbs under his suspenders. "Now Mrs. Green can have that fancy dinner party she's been naggin' me about." Mr. Green put his hands on his hips and did his best Mrs. Green impersonation. "Can't have a dinner party without a table to put the dinner on." He wagged his finger in the air and continued in a twanging voice, drawing out every vowel, "I need that table," his finger froze, then started wiggling again, "You tell Mr. Clement, I need that table."

Clem laughed. "It's all yours," he said, pushing the table flush with the headboard.

Percival threw a canvas tarp over the wagon bed and tied it off at the corners. "In case she starts spittin' again," he said.

"Much obliged," said Mr. Green, slapping a five-dollar bill into Clem's palm and climbing onto the driver's seat. "Reckon you won't see me till Mrs. Green hops onto my back again."

Mr. Green flicked the reins, but the mule didn't move. After slapping it on the rear a few times, he took a barbed stick from under the seat and jammed it into its hindquarters. The mule jumped forward, and the wagon churned through the mud. "Fine work," he said, goading the mule up the road, "mighty fine work."

Percival hurried into the shop. "Come on Clem," he shouted, "let's get back at it. I'm sure there's another Mr. Green out there whose back is aching too."

He went straight to an unfinished cherry-wood armchair next

to the work bench. With the headrest removed, the turned-wood spindles stuck out from the seat like arthritic fingers.

"Over here, Clem," Percival called, "let's work on this one."

No answer.

"Clem," Percival called again. Still no answer.

Percival trotted back to where he and Clem had loaded up Mr. Green's dining table and found Clem bent over on one knee, clutching his chest. It was as if he were being knighted by some cruel king who instead of resting his sword on Clem's shoulder had thrust it through his heart.

"Clem, Clem, what happened?" Percival shouted, running to his fallen friend.

Clem took a big gulp of air, "I'm all right. Just give me a minute."

Percival knelt beside him.

"Just don't have the energy anymore that you young'uns do," said Clem, taking in a series of deep, controlled breaths. "I'm all right. I'm all right."

Percival lifted Clem to his feet. "Come on now, let me get you to the hospital. Hell, as many times as I've been there, they'll put us at the front of the line."

"Naw," said Clem, "I ain't gonna be one to cut in front of a factory accident. Let me walk it off. I'll be all right."

"Come on into the shop anyway, and have a sit," said Percival.

Percival sat Clem in the unfinished armchair with the crooked-fingered backrest. He went to the house and returned with a cup of water. "You sure you don't want to go the hospital," he said, handing Clem the water. "They can check you out, and maybe I can find out what's been happening up at the foundry. Pretty sure they'll be someone there I can ask."

"Then I reckon," said Clem, taking slow sips, "you missed the other night's conversation while you were playin' musketeer."

"And what conversation was that?"

"The one about that Morton Crick fella," said Clem, "finding out them workers still had their minds set on joinin' the union. He went and fired the bunch of 'em."

"Everyone?" said Percival.

"Casters, puddlers, pullers, every last one of 'em," said Clem. "And on the day your friend, Crawford I think it was, had mustered up the nerve to return to work."

Percival shook his head in disgust. "What happened?"

Clem took a drink of water and let out a relaxing breath. "So Crick gathers everyone on the foundry floor like he's gonna give poor Crawford a big 'welcome back', and with half a dozen men from the Pinkerton Agency behind him, he fires 'em all. Crawford comes at Crick with a haymaker that misses on account of his stub for a hand. The hired thugs pin him down and drag him out by the heels, kicking and screamin' the whole way. Then they shoo everyone out of the factory with guns drawn. And that's why there was such a big turn out the other night. No more time for shindigs in my yard after all them day laborers land fulltime positions."

"Damn that bastard," said Percival, popping out one of the spindles from the back of the chair. "Lying, conniving son-of-a-bitch. Pretty soon, he's gonna get what's comin' to him." Percival thrust the knobby stick upward from his hip. "Maybe this Sunday when they shoot off them fireworks, one will find its way into his britches and explode up his ass. Then he'll see what it's like gettin' fired."

Percival went to the work bench and grabbed a square of sanding paper. He held the spindle up to one eye and stared over its length as if he were peering down the stock of a rifle. "And there I was," he said, working the sandpaper over the wood, "all set on goin' up to that Clubhouse this Sunday and lettin' bygones be bygones."

"You still gonna go?" said Clem.

"I don't know. Ben told me about it, the big Decoration Day celebration and all. But Ben and I ain't on too good of terms right now. I'm not sure he'd like it if I tagged along."

"I don't suppose he would have told you about it if he didn't want you to go," said Clem.

Percival exchanged the sanding paper for a clump of steel wool and ran it down the spindle, smoothing out the rough spots and paying special attention to crevices between the fancy spirals. "I'm not sure what he wants," said Percival, hammering the spindle into the seat with a block of wood. "You'd think a father would understand his son well enough to know. I wish I could figure out how that boy's put together."

Clem raised a finger and got Percival's attention then disappeared behind an oak chest of drawers and came back with a hand-carved maple toolbox. "Take a look at this piece," he said, setting it on the work bench. "Tell me what you think."

Percival studied the toolbox. Its slatted sides meshed perfectly, with no noticeable seams. Fancy chiseled flourishes adorned the curved lid, with brass hinges at the back, and a thick, cast iron clasp in the front. Its deep rich stain glowed against the background of unfinished furniture. Percival followed the smooth grain of the wood with his fingertips. "Beautiful," he said, "don't believe I've seen anything finer."

"And I didn't have to tell you I used a dovetail chisel for the joinery," said Clem, "or a round-file for the detail on the lid, or a handmade mix of stain and lacquer for the finish for you to appreciate it, did I."

"I suppose not. But what's that got to do with Ben and me."

Clem clasped his hands round the back of his neck and looked up at the ceiling, "Lord in heaven," he said, "ain't the two of you a pair. Hardheaded and stubborn as Mr. Green's mule, neither of you willing to give the other one a chance."

"I've tried," said Percival. "For twenty years I worked in the factories, trying to show Ben the meaning of dedication and hard work. Every day I tell him he's got the perfect opportunity up at that Clubhouse, and that he can make manager someday if he puts his mind to it." Percival sat in the cherry-wood chair and rested his head in his hands. "I've tried to set a good example, at the foundry, at home. Hell, I even took him hunting." He stared off into nowhere. "I've tried, Clem, believe me, I've tried. There ain't nothing more I can do. I think I've lost my chance with him."

Ben kept still behind the haystack, not sure how long he should wait before coming into the yard. At least, he thought, long enough to put the conversation he'd overheard out of his mind. He picked at the haystack until Clem got a good fire burning in the oil drum and his father was well into the staining of the armchair.

He scooted around the haystack and came into the yard, feigning shortness of breath. Clem was at the table, drinking coffee and staring at the flames in the oil barrel. Percival stood inside the shop, wiping his hands on a rag soaked in mineral spirits. Ben could smell the lacquer thinner all the way across the yard.

"Grab yourself a cup," said Clem, "and one for your father too. I'd hate for him to set himself ablaze over a cup of coffee."

Ben poured two cups and sat next to Clem, mindful of how to start the conversation. "Big celebration up at the Clubhouse on Sunday," he said, "They've really outdone themselves this year."

"That right?" said Clem.

Percival came to the table and sat opposite Ben.

Ben took a sip of coffee and turned to Clem. "They've set up a big stage for a band. My friend Tom's gonna put on a big-city show, right there on the sporting field. They're gonna wheel out the grand piano. I might even get a chance to play, too. Then a big dinner inside the Clubhouse. The way they've dressed up the place, you'd think the president himself's gonna be there."

Clem went to the fire and refilled his cup. "I reckon Harrison already has Decoration Day plans at his own white house."

"President or no president," said Percival, "I'd sure like to head up there."

Ben perked up in his seat, surprised at his father's interest. "Sure, pa," he said, "Maybe you can watch me play a little before the show."

"And maybe," said Percival, "I'll finally get a chance to peek inside that fancy Clubhouse."

Ben's smile flipped back on itself, another chance to connect with his father swept away like water over the falls. "About getting into the Clubhouse, pa," he said, "they're keeping the main group on the bridge. Mr. Crick's only letting members and their guests on the grounds. Except for a few of the Italians and the hired help, ain't no one else allowed."

Percival sat back and shook his head. "If that don't beat all," he said. "Ain't nowhere I can go where that fella isn't standin' in my way. I'll say it again, one of these days, someone's gonna give that son-of-a-bitch what's coming to him."

Ben knew his father had no chance getting into the Clubhouse on his own. He also knew half of what he'd told him was a lie. The Clubhouse was private, but at a nickel a head, Crick was letting everyone on the grounds. What if, he thought, he could sneak his father inside the Clubhouse, and show him how much the Club members valued music, maybe then he'd be able to convince him studying piano was a legitimate pursuit. "We can meet on the bridge, pa. I'll bring down a bistro apron and slip you in with the kitchen crew."

Clem laughed. "Where there's a will there's a way," he said, shuffling across the yard. "I'll see you'uns tomorrow." Halfway through his front door, he turned and called to Percival, "Finish as much as you can on that chair tomorrow. Oh, and I'd line up some more sand bags round the front of the shop. We can't have any of our fine furniture washing away."

Ben took Percival's nodding as an acceptance of both his and Clem's requests, and while he mulled over their scheduled meeting on the bridge, Ben's eyes wandered around the yard to a pile of sand bags stacked next to the haystacks. "What's he talkin' about, pa, bags around the shop?"

"Clem thinks that storm's gonna hit us hard," said Percival, "and that squirrelly river's gonna wash us out."

Ben swirled his cup like he was getting ready to throw dice and a bit of black coffee sloshed over the sides. "You think he's right, pa, about the storm and the dam?"

"I don't know, Ben," said Percival. "Lately he's been right about a lot of things."

The past few nights sleep for Ben had been quick, closing his eyes to the dark and suddenly opening them to the morning light as if there had been no nighttime at all. But this night the night lasted, and Ben dreamed.

He dreamt he was in the Clubhouse performing a Beethoven sonata for a dining room full of members and guests. Waiters in black jackets carrying silver trays traipsed around the room setting food and wine on the tables while diners laughed and toasted their glasses.

He was playing his melody, following the peaceful currents of the river Blind Tom had taken him to, when the lid of the Steinway began to flutter, and the piano floated off the floor.

Across the room he saw a young woman, pretty and petite, dancing through a sea of tuxedoes and ostrich-feathered bonnets toward the stage. She was strangely familiar, yet mysterious in the way of dreams. Like a graceful apparition she glided onto the stage, sweeping her flowing dress beneath her and sitting next to him on the bench.

"Your music is beautiful," she said, tucking a loose bunch of chestnut curls behind her ear. "I'm studying the stars in New York City."

Ben had no voice. His hands were frozen, too. But his melody played on as he stared into her eyes.

She touched his shoulder and ran her fingertips down his arm. "Maybe," she said, "when you get there, we can…"

Ben awoke. The floating piano, the river, and the girl, were gone. He sat up and rubbed his eyes. Through the window, the black sky was thick with haze and factory smoke, but a small bit of light flickered in the yard.

He went to the window. A pile of ash smoldered in the oil barrel and the barn doors to the shop were opened wide. He cupped his hands against the glass and saw his father inside the garage holding the Colt revolver and working a small rag through the barrel. Percival took a fistful of cartridges from the work table and pushed them, one by one, into the chamber. He flicked the cylinder, gave it a quick spin, and holstered the loaded pistol in his belt.

Ben's eyes widened and locked on the back of his father's neck. Percival tilted his head and started to turn. Ben leaped in a swan-dive back to bed. "Did he see me?" he thought. "Oh Lord, I hope he didn't see me."

Ben tried to shut his eyes, but it was as if they'd been glued open with spoiled shellac. He slipped beneath the covers and pulled the flannel blanket up under his chin. He thought about the recent trouble his father had had with Crick. "Pa wouldn't... pa would never. No, no...no way pa would ever..." Ben tossed and turned, trying to forget what he had just seen, and what he had considered his father might do. He stared at the wood-grain swirls in the ceiling and waited for the night to end. But tonight, the night dragged on, longer than it ever had before.

27

The nighttime was gone, and so was a good part of the morning. Ben put on his shoes and hurried into the yard. The barn doors to the shop were closed, and there was no sign of his father. He tucked his shirt into his trousers, matted down his hair with a closed fist, and scanned the breadth of the property. Clem was sitting at the turkey table, warming his hands around a steaming tin cup and staring into the flames.

"Where's my pa?" said Ben.

Clem stood and met Ben at the oil barrel. He filled a cup and held it out. "Hold your horses," he said, "How 'bout some fresh coffee to start this peach of a day."

"Where is he?" Ben said, dismissing Clem's cheerful offer.

Clem pulled back the cup and set it on the table. "Left early."

"Where? Where did he go?"

"Don't know," said Clem, hiking up his britches and plopping himself back down at the table. "Just said somethin' 'bout shootin' himself a turkey, and headed up the road."

Before Clem's backside hit the bench, Ben was out of the yard and onto the road, racing up the hill in a full sprint toward the Clubhouse.

He made it to the dam in record time, flying across the bridge, through the sporting field, and past the bandstand with over a hundred blue folding chairs set up in front of it. Two Italians had pitched a red and white canvas tarp over the bandstand that resembled a circus tent and were tying down the sides with thick ropes and long cast iron stakes. The big Italian was swinging a sledgehammer. He stopped his pounding and looked up as Ben went rushing by.

Inside the kitchen, Ben found Jean Pierre at the stove directing a crew of Frenchmen busy chopping, slicing, sautéing, and hustling back and forth to the ice box. Jean Pierre was giving orders in French and pointing around the room with a wooden spatula. Ben scooted against the wall to where Jean Pierre stood conducting his culinary concert.

"Where's Crick," said Ben.

"What?" said Jean Pierre.

"Crick. Where is he."

Jean Pierre went back to his symphony, pointing and waving his spatula like a baton. "I believe he is in the office," he said, thrusting the spatula toward the office door as if he were calling for a cymbal crash.

Ben darted between the sous chefs to the newly repaired door and rattled the handle. A muffled shout came from inside the room, as if the speaker's hands were clasped over his mouth. Even through the distortion, Ben could tell it was Crick.

"What the hell do you want," Crick said.

Ben replied in his best French accent, "There is no problem in there, monsieur?"

"No," shouted Crick, "But there will be one out there if you keep rattling that door."

"I am sorry monsieur, it won't happen again."

Ben retreated and asked Jean Pierre if he had seen anyone that morning who didn't belong at the Clubhouse.

"Only the Italians," said Jean Pierre, "to get supplies for the grounds."

Ben peeked over the swinging doors. On his tiptoes he could see all the way to the Steinway. The front of the Clubhouse was empty.

"Oh," said Jean Pierre, "and one other man...said he brought the metal stakes for the tent."

"What did he look like?"

"He was dressed in the type of clothes..." Jean Pierre ran his fingers down his chin, stroking an invisible goatee, "...like...like they wear at the steel factories."

"Where did he go?"

Jean Pierre used his spatula again to point to the back door. "I sent him to where the Italians are working."

Ben ran outside and found the two Italians still hammering the tent-supports into the wet ground. He looked up and down the sporting field then ran to the lawn in front of the Clubhouse. The bridge, the shoreline, even the boardwalk was empty.

He came back into the kitchen just as the waiter, Henri, bolted through the swinging doors, sweating and out of breath. "There is a man," Henri shouted with hands on knees, "He has a pistol." Henri raised his arm and pointed to the office. "He has found his way into the office with Mr. Crick."

Ben ran to the small door. He rattled the handle, but the lock he'd fixed so well was holding strong. "Go around, and try the hall door," he shouted to Henri.

"I have already. It is locked as well."

Ben called back to Jean Pierre. "Go get the Italians. Tell them to bring the hammer."

Jean Pierre dropped his spatula and ran out the back door.

Ben let go of the handle and pressed his ear to the door. The room was silent. He closed his eyes, straining to catch even the faintest whisper. Then in quick succession, he heard the click of the hammer and the explosion of the packed gunpowder behind the bullet.

"No," Ben screamed.

The big Italian yanked Ben away from the door and shoved him against the cutting table. Henri and the other Frenchmen fled. Ben covered his face and watched through his fingers as Damato drew back the sledgehammer and smashed open the door.

The smell of gunsmoke came out of the office, followed by a hysterical shout from Crick, "Get him out...get him out."

The Italian went in and dragged the facedown corpse from the office. Ben took his hands from his eyes and looked down at the dead man. The back of the man's head glistened in a halo of bright red clumps that encircled a gaping crater where his scalp had been. A stump of a hand, crusted with flakey dried blood, stuck out from the man's sleeve and dragged along the ground. It didn't tell Ben anything about a new baby, or a petition for unionization. All it revealed was that the dead man on the kitchen floor wasn't his father. He let out the breath he'd taken in after he'd heard the gunshot, refilled his lungs, and sighed with relief.

Crick came out of the office, brushing off the lapels of his sack coat as if he'd just excused himself from the breakfast table. He took off a virgin-white yachting cap and looked it over for stray blood-spatter, outwardly relieved the incident hadn't ruined his sailing outfit. "Take the body to the mortician," he told Damato. "Let him deal with it, then get back here and clean up this mess, and be quick about it, too. The General and Mr. Addison will be here any minute, and I can't have an incident like this lingering around the Clubhouse all morning."

Damato carried Crawford's body out the back door, and Jean Pierre returned to the kitchen, tapping his spatula on the cutting table and calling his helpers back from the intermission. In less than a minute, the Frenchmen had resumed their cutting and chopping, and except for the office door now dangling by the hinges, the kitchen was back in order.

Over the swinging doors, Ben saw Mr. Addison coming down the stairs holding his arm out for the General. Instead of taking it for balance, the General batted it away and whacked Addison on the shin with his cane. Blind Tom followed, dragging his feet down the stairs like he was being pulled by a leash. Crick adjusted his yachting cap and met the men at the bottom of the stairs.

Addison and the General sported brand new double-breasted coats and bright white yachting caps. Addison scratched his wrist under the coarse fabric of the jacket and adjusted his cap. "We heard a ruckus," he said, "is everything all right?"

Crick told the men everything was fine and steered them toward the dining room. "Just a disgruntled ex-employee," he said, "a little upset with the conditions of his dismissal."

Ben looked down at the smear of blood trailing across the kitchen floor and wondered how anyone could have been more upset with Crick than his father was.

"Being quite familiar with the sound of a service revolver," said the General, "I'd say he was extremely upset." With a cane-push against the floor, the General twisted around and peeked over the swinging shutters. "Must be quite a mess in there."

Crick came around in front of the General, shepherding him the other direction.

A man in a tattered brown coat and an equally experienced porkpie hat came through the patio door and into the dining room. Ben knew him as Club member Able Marring, owner of the agile skiff, Wind Tamer, and the winner of last year's Decoration Day sailing regatta.

Marring called to the men with a wave of his arm. "Come on gents," he said, "We're ready to set sail."

"And the libation?" shouted Crick.

"Ready, as well."

Addison stepped next to the General and pointed subtly at Blind Tom. "He isn't going with us, is he?"

"Heavens no," shouted the General. "If that behemoth wandered too far port or starboard, he'd tip us over."

The General grabbed Tom by the arm and led him toward the kitchen.

Ben backed away from the swinging doors and held his breath.

"I see you in there, son," the General said, punching open the doors with his cane.

Ben's attempt to conceal his eavesdropping had failed, and he acknowledged the General's call with a subordinate, "Yes, sir."

The General complimented Ben on the job he'd done watching

over his property the day before, and demanded his services again. "I hereby leave my Negro in your charge," he said. "And make sure he spends plenty of time at the piano – classics to patriotics, contemporaries to originals, you hear me."

"Yes, sir."

The General reached out and shook Ben's hand, officially passing him Blind Tom's invisible leash. "Make sure," the General reiterated, "plenty of time at the piano."

Although Ben was uncertain he could "make" Tom do anything, he repeated his two-word mantra and smiled. He was prepared to watch over Tom and follow the Generals orders, but not cooped up inside the Clubhouse. This time he was taking Tom into town.

28

As the men greeted Able Marring, Parke was still on the far side of the bridge, chipping away at the dam. A glimmer of sunlight washed over the patio deck, and Crick put a curved palm to the side of his face and shouted toward the dam. "See, Parke," he said, lifting his head and spreading his arms out like a Baptist preacher, "Sunshine. You can relax now and stop wasting your time."

Parke kept swinging the axe into the rock.

"I suppose he won't be joining us, then?" Addison said, as the men followed Able Marring to the boathouse.

"Not a chance, son," said the General. "Can't change the course of something with that much determination."

Ben watched from the big windows as the General, Addison, and Crick got into the Wind Tamer, and Able Marring untied the moorings and pulled the sailboat from the dock. After the sails snapped open and the boat vanished behind the trees, Ben ran to the swinging doors and grabbed Tom by the cuff. "Stay right behind me," he said. "We gotta move fast."

Ben raced out of the Clubhouse dragging Blind Tom behind him like an overstuffed cuddly bear. Just beyond the bandstand, the Italians had fashioned a makeshift coffin out of the leftover timber and were loading Crawford's body onto a flatbed wagon. Ben used a combination of sign language and confident shouting to convince the driver to take Tom and him into town. "New clothes," he said, tightening an imaginary necktie. "For Sunday's show." Ben lifted

Tom's arm and pointed to a split seam in his jacket. The big Italian needed more convincing, and Ben threw a different pair of words at him, "Crick's orders."

Not willing to risk losing his job, the Italian agreed to take Ben and Tom into town. The three men rode together at the front of the wagon with Tom occupying most of the space. The Italian and Ben rode side-saddle, on opposite ends, one half of their rear-end hanging off the edge of the bench.

Ben stared at the muddy road, batting the rain drops from his face as if he were swatting flies. He tried to forget about the morning's incident, but having never been so close to a dead body before, the lifeless millworker in the box behind him put a knot in his gut. He cringed every time the wagon took a sharp turn or bumped over a section of railroad track and the limp corpse thumped against the wooden slats of the casket.

They rolled through the neighborhoods and onto Main Street, past a dozen shop-owners who stopped their holiday decorating and flag hanging to stare at the coffin. Ben finally broke the long silence.

"Thank you for giving us a lift, Mr...."

"Damato," the Italian said.

"Thank you, Mr. Damato," said Ben, realizing the Italian had a better understanding of English than he'd thought. "And please make sure the undertaker informs this man's family. Tell him to give him a good burial as well, and to send the bill to the Clubhouse, care of Mr. Crick."

Damato leaned around Tom and looked Ben in the eye. "And Mr. Crick told you this?"

"After you left with the body," said Ben, "Crick was real shook up. Told me to make sure we took good care of the deceased and his family."

Damato nodded.

"He also said you could pick up a new set of duds for yourself at Howell's when you're finished at the undertaker's. I heard they've got a nice new selection of work jackets."

211

Ben and Tom hopped off in front of Howell's store, and the wagon axel sprang up and popped Damato off the bench. The men on the porch were engaged in a debate about the weather, but they stopped, and every head turned as Ben and Tom came up the stairs and into the store. Even Doc, who was rarely distracted when making a sale, ignored an opportunity to describe the benefits of a shopping basket, and stared blankly as Tom slid sideways through the doorway.

Still fixed on Ben's enormous shadow, Doc handed the lone customer her change, missing the woman's hand completely, and dropping the coins onto the counter. "Thank you," he said, oblivious to the rolling coins, "You have a nice day, now."

The woman collected her coins and her sundries, and moved toward the front door. When she saw Tom, she slapped her palms against her cheeks and her purchases went sliding through her arms to the floor.

Ben pulled Tom out of the way and sat him at the counter.

Doc came around and helped the woman load her things into a shopping basket and escorted her out of the store. Out on the porch, he peeled a hand from the woman's face and curled it round the handle. "No charge for the basket, ma'am," he said, sending her on her way.

Doc hurried back into the store and behind the counter. "What the hell are you doing," he said, pointing from the hip like he was drawing a six-shooter. "Who the hell is that?"

"His name is Tom," said Ben. "He's a musical genius."

Doc gave Tom a once-over.

"Being dat Tom is blind," Tom said, "There is some folks dat say, 'Blind Tom'."

"He prefers, Tom," said Ben, taking a seat at the counter. "Tom's playing at the Clubhouse tomorrow, gonna be the star of the whole shebang."

Tom folded his hands in his lap and rocked his head back and forth, humming, and taking in the sounds and smells of the General Store.

212

"Then what are you doin' bringing him here?" said Doc. "Won't they be missin' him?"

"They don't know we're gone," said Ben. "And he ain't never been out on his own before, do him some good to see how the rest of us live."

Doc waved his hand in front of Tom's face and whispered to Ben, "I don't reckon he'll be seeing anything."

"His employer, this General fella," said Ben, "just totes him around the country padding his own wallet. I had to get him out for some fun of his own."

Tom stopped humming and his mouth drooped. He twiddled his thumbs and swung out his feet, kicking his toes on the counter.

"He don't look like he's havin' much fun," said Doc.

Ben leaned in to Tom. "Hey Tom," he said, slapping the back of his hand against Tom's bicep, "You havin' fun?"

Tom smiled. "I hear da sound of a creakin' rockin' chair." He took a deep breath and went on, "Oh, and da smell of roasted coffee...and a mess of rhubarb pies, too." Tom licked his lips and rubbed circles around his belly. "Tom would love to get his self some of dat coffee and pie."

Ben gave Doc an order in pantomime, and Doc went reluctantly to the restaurant, returning with a cup of coffee and whole pie for Tom, and a single slice for Ben and himself.

"Pour us up one of them Doctor Peppers," said Ben, "and get out that log book with the flavors in it."

Doc rubbed his thumb against his fingers, already out twenty cents for the pie and coffee.

"Tomorrow," Ben said.

Doc popped open a Doctor Pepper and split the drink between two glasses.

"Some for Tom, too," said Ben.

"Coffee and soda?" said Doc, shaking his head while he brought out a third glass.

Tom gulped the coffee then the Doctor Pepper, and a little bit of both ran down his chin.

213

"Havin' fun, now?" said Ben.

Tom nodded as he wiped off his chin with the back of his hand.

Ben took a big bite of pie, smashing it against the roof of his mouth and savoring the flavors. He washed it down with a gulp of Doctor Pepper. "It's rhubarb," he said, pounding his fork-fist on the counter.

Doc went through the same ritual, gently nodding his head as he chewed. "Rhubarb it is," he said, writing the word "rhubarb" next to the number twenty-three.

Tom took a bite of pie. "Mmm, rhubarb...dat is good." After a slurp of soda, he brought his chin to his chest and let out an obnoxious belch.

Doc laughed. "This is your musical genius?"

Ben set his fork on the counter and wiped his mouth with his sleeve. "Let's go next door and I'll show ya. They've got a piano over there, don't they?"

"Sure," said Doc, "But my pa ain't around to watch the store. I ain't leavin' it vacant so you and your burly friend can tinker around on the piano."

Ben twisted round and scanned the room. "You haven't had a customer since we came in."

Doc looked at the two-hundred fifty pound, black, blind man with half a rhubarb pie smeared across his face and said, "Yeah, Ben, I wonder why."

"Come on, Doc," said Ben, "It will be fun, showin' him something he ain't never seen before." Ben set a hand on Tom's shoulder. "You ain't never been to a saloon before, have you, Tom?"

Tom shook his head.

"See," said Ben. "This is just what he needs. Now put up that sign you use in the mornin' after your breakfast and your two cups of coffee... you know, 'back in ten minutes'."

"I don't know," said Doc.

"Ten minutes in the shitter," said Ben, "Or ten minutes in the saloon, what's the difference?"

"Ah, hell," said Doc, "but ten minutes, no more. If my pa decides to come round and finds the store empty, he'll have my hide…and then I'll have yours." Doc grabbed the keys from the cash box and hopped over the counter. "Come on, then," he said, shooing Ben and Tom onto the porch.

Chatter in the dugout stopped, and each old-timer stared silently and scooted back in his seat as Tom passed. The man in the rocking chair rocked so far back, he fell off the end of the porch and into the water trough.

Doc, Ben and Tom stood in front of the saloon's batwing doors, and Doc asked Ben why he'd chosen the saloon, of all places, to take his new friend.

"I told Tom's employer," said Ben, "I'd keep him at the piano, and you said they've got a piano in there. Let's just say I'm keepin' my promise."

Ben straightened his cap and kicked open the shutters. "Always wanted to do that," he said, and walked into the saloon.

29

The saloon where the factory workers wasted time was dark and dank, illuminated by only a few brass wall sconces and a pair of thin gas lamps hanging from the rafters. The room buzzed with the hum of factory stories and tall tales. Flies flew through frozen swirls of cigar smoke, and a musty stench sat in the air, rancid with the smell of spoiled yeast and fermented grain. A dozen round tables crowded with drinkers and gamblers filled the center of the room, and a layer of sawdust for spilt booze and blood covered the floor. The men not playing faro or rolling dice at the tables stood around a mahogany long-bar complete with copper spittoons beneath the foot rail for spitting, and towels hooked to the front of the bar for wiping. Behind the snappy-dressed bartender was a shelf lined with whiskey bottles, and a stained mirror in which Ben could see the hazy reflection of the barroom.

The piano sat against the far wall, tucked underneath the stairway landing by the back door. Ben pointed over a patchwork of tweed caps. "Doc," he said, "why'd they put the piano way over there?"

The General Store's proximity to the saloon was the only reason Doc, who didn't drink or gamble, had spent any time there, and only then it was to let the husband know the wife had finished shopping. "Sometimes the audience here can be a bit unstable," he said, leading Ben and Tom along the wall. "Puttin' it back there makes for a quick getaway."

The three shuffled past a large oval table padded with green baize and surrounded by six men playing faro. Like the rest of the patrons, the men were locals, steel workers either on their day off, or in between shifts. Not one of the punters took their eyes off the cards as they passed, not even to flash a mean, 'go-on…get' glare. Tom, Ben and Doc were flies not worth swatting at.

Ben couldn't figure what would make a crowd like this unstable, but he didn't bother Doc for a further explanation. He was too excited to get Tom to the keys and show the room what real entertainment sounded like.

If the River Fork Club's polished Steinway represented elegance and sophistication, then the saloon's unfinished upright was its opposite. Stained, dented, and chipped from a combination of tobacco spit, flying fists, and whiskey bottles, it sat like a relic, hidden under the dark stairwell, waiting to be discovered by only the most daring of musical explorers.

In a small wall-space between the top of the upright and the stairway landing hung a long, thick-framed mirror with fancy swirls etched in the corners and the word SALOON printed in big frosty letters across the front. Ben could see the entire room reflected in the glass. He sat on the bench and pecked at random notes. Every so often, he would hit a key that stuck from spilt beer and whiskey, or one that wouldn't make a sound at all. He punched at one of the silent keys while he looked over the saloon in the mirror.

Reflected between the double O's was a man dressed in black trousers and a matching black jacket and bowler. He had joined the locals at the long-bar and captured their attention. He twirled his handlebar moustache as the bartender poured out a dozen shots of what Mr. Black referred to as 'coffin varnish'. When he pulled out a folding bill and paid for the whiskey, Ben understood why Mr. Black was so popular.

As Ben watched Mr. Black in the mirror, the double O's began to bounce in a steady rhythm. A door above squeaked opened and slammed shut, and a pair of feet padded across the landing and down the stairs. A woman in a pleated red dress and skimpy black corset, two sizes too small, sauntered across the floor to Mr. Black.

The pink ostrich plume pinned to her bun of black curls fluttered as she leaned in and whispered in his ear.

Mr. Black looked the woman up and down. "Is it that time again, Miss Moonlight?" he said in a volume the entire barroom could hear.

Everyone took notice except the men at the faro table who were too busy debating whether or not the dealer was using a rigged box.

Mr. Black threw another bill at the bartender. "How about another round of drinks, first?" he said, walking off and leaving Miss Moonlight with the freeloaders.

Mr. Black made his way to the piano where Ben sat watching the room in the mirror and pecking at the broken key. "You the entertainment, son?" he said, slapping a fifty-cent piece on the lid of the upright. "How 'bout favoring us with a tune. Somethin' sophisticated."

Ben stared at the shiny coin, the embossed figure of the goddess Liberty in the center, the raised row of stars lined up around the edge.

Mr. Black left as quickly as he came. "None of that nigger ragtime," he said over his shoulder.

Ben waited until Mr. Black returned to the bar and his preoccupation with Miss Moonlight's stockings before giving his seat to Tom. "Play a classical piece," he said, "like the other night, somethin' real impressive."

Tom sat at the broken piano as if he were a monarch assuming the seat of the throne. He reached up and slid his fingers along the lid until his arms were stretched wide, then he ran his palms up and down the sides as if he were caressing a fine woman. He straightened himself on the bench and spread his hands across the ivories, lightly skimming the surface of the keys.

Ben bowed in to Tom. "You ready to bring 'em to their feet?"
Tom nodded.

"Be careful around middle C," said Ben. "There's a few keys that ain't workin' right."

"I know," said Tom. "Tom'll just play around 'em."

And he did, seamlessly adjusting melodies and transposing chord progressions through a difficult Chopin polonaise without missing a note. Then he chopped through a Bach fugue with ease, skipping eighth notes, and doubling up sixteenth notes to maintain the staccato beat.

Ben had spent hours struggling to produce sounds like this on the Club's perfect Steinway, and here Tom was, pulling out impeccable arpeggios and flawless cadenzas from a busted bar piano. For a brief moment, Tom had turned the dingy saloon into a New York City music hall.

Although Tom's selections would have typically gone unnoticed and unappreciated, or even sent the performer dodging whiskey bottles and fleeing for his life out the back door, the man buying the drinks was happy. And as long as he was buying, no one complained.

Mr. Black was enjoying the music, and the fragrance of Miss Moonlight's Jicky perfume, when six men in wide-brimmed Stetsons stumbled through the batwing doors. Straight from Texarkana, they wore long canvas dusters and thick mustaches. Their spurs chinked on the wood-planked floor as they made their way to the bar.

After ordering a round of whiskey, the Texan who paid for the drinks took his glass and wove through the gaming and card tables toward the piano.

"He's comin' this way," said Ben, "what do I do?"

Doc pushed at Ben's back, but Ben stood firm, a stubborn mule.

"Maybe he wants to request a song," said Doc.

The Texan was getting closer. Ben tried to keep a cool face.

The Texan tipped his hat and took a sip of whiskey. "How's about some real music, son," he said, huffing out the stink of booze and bad breath. He took out a dollar bill, waved the fluttering face of George Washington in the air, and slapped the buck on top of Mr. Black's half-dollar. "Y'all know The Yellow Rose of Texas?"

Tom leaned back as he breezed through a Schuman toccata. "Tom knows that one."

"All right, mister," said Ben, refraining from haggling over price, "We'll play it for you."

"And sing it, too," said the Texan. "Loud. Think y'all can do that for a dollar?" The cowboy threw back the rest of his red-eye, slammed the empty shot glass on the dollar bill, and meandered around the tables back to the bar.

"Holy shit," said Doc, "a dollar, for playing a song."

Ben patted his empty pockets, admiring the bonanza accumulating atop the upright. "Now I know why that General keeps such a keen eye on his prodigy."

"You want Tom should play da song for dat man," said Tom, finishing the final run of the toccata.

"And sing it real loud, too," said Ben. "Give him his money's worth."

After an introduction of strong chords that turned the head of every whiskey drinker at the bar, Tom pounded the melody and belted out the words from the diaphragm.

There's a yellow rose of Texas, that I am goin' to see.
No other darky knows her, no darky only me.
She cried so when I left her it like to broke my heart.
And if I ever find her, we nevermore will part.

Ben left Tom at the piano and wandered around the room, soliciting song requests in hopes of adding more coins to the kitty. The men at the tables ignored him, their heads buried in the dice and the cards.

The Texan was at the long-bar, sipping another whiskey. After proclaiming Texas should be recognized as its own independent nation, he moved in between Mr. Black and Miss Moonlight. It was apparent, from his swagger, that this wasn't the first saloon he and his posse had visited that afternoon. He plucked at Miss Moonlight's choker and joined his gang, in full voice, for the chorus.

She's the sweetest rose of color this darky ever knew.
Her eyes are bright as diamonds, they sparkle like the dew.
You may talk about your Dearest May, and sing of Rosa
Lee.
But the Yellow Rose of Texas beats the belles of Tennessee.

The Texan splayed his arms and sloshed a bit of whiskey onto Mr. Black's stiff-pressed jacket.

Mr. Black tapped the Texan on shoulder and protested while dabbing his lapel with a handkerchief.

The Texan reached into his duster and removed a money-roll ten times the size of Ben's lost cigar-box savings. He peeled off a dollar bill and stuck it in Mr. Black's coat pocket. "That ought to be enough to replace those shoddy rags."

"I beg your pardon," said Mr. Black, smoothing his glossy revers, "this suit is fashioned from fine silk thread, handmade at my own factory in Philadelphia."

The Texan posed with arms akimbo. "And this is waxed cotton from El Paso," he said, modeling his duster like an advertisement in the newspaper supplement, "greased and dirtied from my work in oil refinement."

Mr. Black scoffed. "Refinement?" he said, snubbing his nose at the Texan. "Considering your taste in music, you obviously don't know the meaning of the word."

The Texan, a foot taller than Mr. Black even without his high-crown hat, leaned in. "You mean those cradlesongs that nigger was playin'? Hell, they damn near put me to sleep. Maybe you'd do better at that factory of yours if you took to pillow making."

"My business is just fine, thank you," said Mr. Black. "And that man at the piano is a virtuoso. Any fool can hear that. Forcing him to play that trite southern anthem is as embarrassing as it is degrading. No musician should ever have to bend over and stoop so low."

"But a woman should," he said, turning his attention to Miss Moonlight. "Come on darlin', let's find out how flexible you are."

221

Mr. Black grabbed the Texan by the arm.

The Texan spun around, tipping his shot glass onto Mr. Black's jacket and dousing the other lapel. "There," he said, "now they're a match. Gives you a tougher look, too, trotting around in that pansy silk."

Mr. Black socked the Texan in the mouth.

With only a hint of discomfort, the Texan rubbed his jaw, drew his arm back, and let his fist fly. Mr. Black's bowler flew over the bar and onto the neck of a whiskey bottle. Before the derby stopped spinning, the rest of the Texans had thrown their own punches, showering the bartender with tweed caps.

The scuffle quickly spread around the length of the bar, the locals swinging at any Texan within range. The Texans, singing their anthem with Tom, slugged and kicked back. Mr. Black sat unconscious on the floor, sagging between the foot-rail and a spittoon. Miss Moonlight and her fancy feathered hair had already flown upstairs, back into her cage and closed for business.

Ben ran to the piano as Tom sang and played on, 'But the Yellow Rose of Texas beats the belles of Tennessee'.

"Sing somethin' else," said Ben, leaning over the keys. "I don't think they like that Texas song."

Tom kept playing. Conversation seemed to flow easier for him with his fingers moving across the keys. "What do you want Tom should sing?"

"I don't know, but somethin' the complete opposite of what you're singin' now."

The brawl spread to the center of the room when a Texan threw a local into the middle of a dice game, upsetting a shooter who had just made his point.

"Hurry," said Ben, "Play something else."

Without stopping to regroup, Tom belted out exactly what Ben had instructed, the complete opposite of The Yellow Rose of Texas. He banged on the keys, and shouted the melody at the top of his lungs.

Mine eyes have seen the glory of the coming of the Lord
He is trampling out the vintage where the grapes of wrath
  are stored
He hath loosed the fateful lightning of His terrible swift
  sword
His truth is marching on.

Now the entire room was swinging, more eyes seeing stars than the coming of the Lord. Texans with locals, locals with Texans, and because no one had any idea who or what had started the fight, locals with locals. The only areas undisturbed were the piano cave and the faro table, where the players were so engrossed in the turn of the cards there was no time to care about Yellow Roses or Hymns of the Republic.

The sound of crashing tables and smashing whiskey bottles was drowned out when Tom came to the chorus. Every local took up arms, literally, pounding each other in guts and gullets and belting out with native Union loyalty...

Glory! Glory! Hallelujah! Glory! Glory! Hallelujah!
Glory! Glory! Hallelujah! His truth is marching on.

Out of nowhere, one of the locals flew past Ben and slammed into the piano, knocking the upright off kilter. Tom stood up flapping his arms and hollering, "Oh Lordy...Oh Lordy."

Ben tried to calm him, but Tom kept flailing like a chicken headed to the chopping block. "Doc," yelled Ben "what do we do?" He looked left and right, but Doc was gone.

Ben scanned the room in the fancy mirror, searching for Doc while he worked to settle Tom. Out of the corner of his eye he spied the money sliding off the piano lid. He scurried around Tom and swiped it just before it fell over the edge. Windfall in hand he started toward the back door, but Tom grabbed him by the shoulders and spun him round. Ben dodged flying whiskey bottles and errant haymakers as Tom, holding on to Ben like a shield, bobbed up and down behind him. Ben twisted free and squared himself to Tom, soothing him with gentle pats on the chest.

Just as Tom was calming down, another brawler tumbled past and took out what was left of the upright. Tom started shaking and swinging his arms in crazy circles. Ben shuffled back to clear Tom's reach and landed in a two-arm grasp that emptied his lungs.

The big Texan locked Ben in a bear hug, grabbing at the hand that held the money and trying to pry his fingers apart. "Give me my money back, boy," he said, "you ain't getting away that easy."

Unwilling to part with the cash he and Tom had rightfully earned, Ben struggled to break free, twisting and turning in awkward contortions while keeping the money just outside the Texan's reach. But the Texan's hold was strong, and Ben was only able to free up enough space between them to catch a shallow breath. Tom was still flailing away in front him, with punches so close to his face he could feel a slight breeze coming off the knuckles.

The Texan's grip tightened and Ben was lifted off the floor. With his arms pinned at his side, he swung his legs out and kicked his heels into the cowboy's shins. The hold loosened and Ben slipped free, quickly ducking under Tom's whirling punches.

The Texan leaned over to grab his leg and his jaw met with one of Tom's flying fists. He stumbled backward in a cross-eyed stagger and fell to the floor.

Ben looked over the room again, fearing Doc may have been caught up in the skirmish, and saw the Texan's posse eying him from the long-bar. They seemed to have taken an interest in his and Tom's handiwork and were pointing at Ben with fists and fingers. They pushed their way through the fighting and headed straight toward the back of the room.

30

The big Texan was out cold. Ben rifled through his duster and pulled out the roll of cash. He mulled over its many potential uses, and resisting temptation, threw out his hand, scattering the bills across the floor. As the Texan's posse scrambled to retrieve the money, Doc burst through the back door and grabbed Ben by the cuff. "Come on," he said, "time to get."

Ben and Doc shoved Tom out the back door and into the wagon bed and raced up onto the bench seat. As they pulled around the front of the saloon, a tangle of bodies crashed through the batwing doors, kicking and swinging and rolling into the street. The Battle Hymn of the Republic followed them up the hill to the edge of town. By the time they reached the first factory, the faint chorus of 'Glory, Glory Hallelujah' had faded away.

Ben checked on Tom who was flopping around in the bed like a giant black bass out of water. "It's all right, Tom," he said, "We're headed to the Clubhouse." Ben turned to Doc, "I think we've all had enough fun for today."

Doc gave Ben a resentful glare.

"We've got to settle him," said Ben. "Ain't no way we'll be able to control him like this."

Doc smiled and reached between his legs and handed Ben three bottles of Doctor Pepper. "I've got just the ticket," he said, pulling back a red checkered towel and uncovering two fresh rhubarb pies.

When Tom smelled the pies, he sat up like a puppy dog and

225

crawled to the front of the wagon. Ben handed Tom a Doctor Pepper and one of the pies. The trouble at the saloon was now a distant memory, and Tom sat back against the headboard and ate his pie and drank his Doctor Pepper. The three men rode along, enjoying their treats as the wagon bumped past the open ovens toward the dam.

When they reached the bridge, Doc stopped the wagon. "All right," he said, "You'uns can walk from here. I gotta get back to the store, and quick…see if I still have a job."

Ben hopped off with his bottle, and pointed to the half-eaten pie. "You mind if I take the rest of that?" he said.

"Go ahead," said Doc, "and make sure Tom takes his too. I'd like to get rid of the evidence."

"Come on, Tom," said Ben, "This is where we get off."

The sugary pie had given Tom a burst of energy, and he jumped out of the bed with his pie and Doctor Pepper.

Ben reached into his pocket and pulled out the dollar bill and the fifty-cent piece. "Had to make sure we didn't run off without our actual," he said, slapping the coin and the folding money on the bench-seat next to Doc.

"That's a lot of money," said Doc, thumbing the bill. "Enough to get you half way to New York."

Ben took a long hard look at the creased bill, the shiny coin, and the fresh band of rawhide around Doc's wrist. "Take it," he said, "for your wedding. Use it to buy that gal of yours something real nice."

Doc clicked his cheek, reined the horse around, and headed off toward town. "Ten minutes," he grumbled as he rode away, "Can't imagine the trouble you'd get me into in twenty."

Ben and Tom made their way across the dam, steering clear of a broken pickaxe lying in their path, and sat on the edge of the bridge about a hundred feet from the spillway. The sun was dropping into the western void behind them, drawing with it the last bit of cloud-filtered daylight. Ben looked out at the Clubhouse, the cottages, the lake. A blue heron pounded off the roof of the boathouse and glided freely over the choppy waves into the violet glow above the water.

Ben swigged down the rest of his soda and pitched the empty bottle into the lake. He got up and followed it toward the rushing water of the spillway. The lake was almost to the top of the dam, and he could easily see the bottle as it picked up speed, racing with the current along the rock ledge and heading straight for the waterfall. When it disappeared under the bridge, he ran to the other side just in time to watch it fall over the edge of the dam and shatter against the boulders below. If Doc were with him, he would have yelled out with excitement, "Did you see that?" He knew Tom had not, and he returned quietly to the edge of the bridge.

Tom was humming, his mouth stuffed with pie. Ben sat next to him and stared at the folds of skin covering his eyes. "When did you lose your sight?" he asked.

Tom dropped another pinch of pie into his mouth. "I ain't never lost it."

"But you're blind, ain't ya?"

"Yessir," said Tom, "but da way I figure, you can't lose somethin' you never had."

Ben recalled the night on the porch, when Percival had told him about his mother, and sighed softly. "Yeah, I suppose you're right."

A cool breeze blew off the water, dragging with it a soft rain and the faint smell of woodfire. Ben looked up and felt the drops against his face. "What do you like to do for fun, Tom?" he said, realizing only now he should have asked this question before taking Tom to the saloon and starting a riot.

Tom scooped around the sides of the pie tin and licked his fingers. "Tom loves playing da piano."

"Besides that. What do you like to do when you ain't playing the piano."

Tom handed Ben the pie tin, picked and licked clean. Ben stacked it with his and set them on the bridge.

"Listen," said Tom.

"That's what you like to do," said Ben, "listen?"

Tom sat on his hands and leaned out and back, swinging his feet over the edge of the bridge and swaying his head as if in a trance. "Listen," he said, "and tell Tom what you hear."

Ben looked at the spillway. "I hear the waterfall," he said.

"Dat's good, dat's good. What else."

Ben strained to hear, but nothing came through except the rush of water over the falls.

"Close yer eyes," said Tom.

Ben shut his eyes.

"Now relax, and let da waterfall fade away. Then listen...listen real good."

Right next to him, Ben heard the sound of a timber rattler. He opened his eyes and pushed himself away. "Look out, Tom," he shouted, "I think it's gonna strike."

Tom rolled his head and laughed out loud. He ground his teeth and made the sound of the snake again. Then he fell onto his back and laughed some more.

"Jesus, Tom, you scared the daylights out of me. How'd you make a sound like that."

"Oh...dat's da other thing Tom do for fun. Tom loves to imm-i-tate da sounds. Now you listen, maybe you can do da same. You just let da sounds come to you."

Ben let go the tightness in his shoulders. He took a deep breath, closed his eyes, and listened. One by one, the sounds of the valley came to him. He heard a train whistle blow in the distance, and he pictured the Day Express rolling along the rails against a background of blurry pines. He heard the rustling branches of the sugar maples along the water's edge, and the call of an eagle, and in his mind he saw the free-bird floating on the wind high above the trees, searching for a meal. Behind him, the steady drone of the factory engines; in front, the patter of the rain off the water, and the clinking of wine glasses from the cottages.

Then Ben heard a noise that reminded him of the General's hacking bronchial cough. It must be the men, he thought, returning

228

from their tour on the Wind Tamer and coming down from the boathouse.

Ben opened his eyes. He grabbed Tom by the arm and pulled him to his feet. "Come on, Tom," he said, "we gotta get."

He turned to Slug and his two sidekicks standing in the middle of the bridge.

Slug had his nose stuck into a can of turpentine. He took a big whiff, let out a wheezing cough, and threw the tin can into the lake. He folded his arms across his chest and stared at Ben. "I remember tellin' you not to come round here."

Red and Skinny ditched their cans and moved behind Ben, snickering like two drunken hyenas.

Ben stepped in front of Tom and stretched out his arms, as if to indicate Tom was off limits. "I ain't looking for no more trouble with you."

Slug stumbled forward, pounding his fist into his palm. "That's what you keep sayin'," he said. "Too bad, though, you keep finding it. And now you went and found some trouble for your big, blind, dumb, nigger friend too." Slug lifted his head, nodding at Skinny and Red. "Guess we'll have to do somethin' 'bout him, eh boys."

Red and Skinny snuck up on Tom and wrenched his hands behind his back. Tom cowered like a frightened animal, and they forced him across the bridge toward the lip of the dam.

"Throw him over," said Slug, walking up calmly to Ben.

Ben ran toward Tom, but Slug beat him off the line, catching him by the shoulder and shoving a fist deep into his stomach. Ben grabbed his gut and fell to his knees.

Red and Skinny moved Tom closer to the edge.

Tom, who was twice the combined size of his attackers, offered no resistance, his hands still pinned behind his back, his head twitching at the shoulder.

Ben looked up and saw Slug's foot coming straight for his head. He rolled over just as Slug's shoe went whizzing by his ear.

The missed kick forced Slug off balance, and he fell onto his back.

As Slug gasped for air, Ben grabbed the pie tins and banged them together like cymbals. "Fight 'em off of you, Tom," he yelled. "Fight 'em off."

The crash of the pie tins sent Tom into a fury, running in place and swinging his arms like a broken windmill. One of Tom's hands found Skinny's neck and locked around it like a vise. Tom threw Red to the ground and brought his arm high above his head and pounded at Skinny's skull like he was hammering a rail spike. The bones in the boy's face cracked, and blood streamed from his swollen nose.

Red got up and pried Tom's hand from Skinny's neck, and the two fled, leaving a trail of blood behind them as they ran off down the bridge and into the trees.

Slug was back on his feet and pulling Ben up by the collar. "Now you're really gonna get it," he said, cocking back his arm.

Before Slug could throw his punch, Ben gathered all the strength he could muster and let loose an uppercut that found Slug's chin. Slug's head snapped, and he staggered backward, his head wobbling atop his neck like a broken candle. He fell over the edge of the bridge, bounced once on the rock ledge, and splashed into the lake.

"Holy shit," said Ben, "I killed him."

Ben ran to the edge of the bridge, but there was no sign of Slug.

"Tom...Tom," Ben called, "I'm gonna need your help."

Tom was rubbing his hands on his legs and twitching. "What do I do. What do I do?"

"Calm down. Calm down and stay there till I come get you."

Ben climbed onto the rock ledge. He had only a foot of jagged rock to stand on, and he held on to the side of the bridge for balance, looking up and down the edge of the dam where Slug had fallen over.

Slug popped up, gasping for air and slapping his arms against the surface of the water. "Help, help. I can't swim."

Ben inched along the rock ledge as the current pulled Slug closer to the spillway. "Keep your head up," Ben shouted. "Try to grab on to the rocks."

Slug dipped under again, gurgling, "I can't...I... I can't reach it."

Ben hurried to get ahead of Slug before he reached the spillway, leaping over the riprap with giant steps and nearly losing his footing between the cracks in the rocks. Lake water poured over the dam with a thunderous roar, and the suction from the waterfall was dragging Slug along the rock ledge faster and faster. Ben was now even with him and almost to the spillway. An undercurrent got hold of Slug's legs and swung his feet to the surface and drew him under the bridge.

Slug's head disappeared, and Ben reached down and caught hold of his arm. Ben's cap fell off and was quickly swept under the bridge and over the edge. The rushing water was pulling hard, and Ben didn't know how much longer he could hold on. "Tom," he shouted. "Tom, I need you."

Ben had no idea if Tom could even hear him over the noise of the waterfall, much less be able follow his voice to the edge of the dam, but he kept calling. "Tom, Tom, Tom. Over here, Tom, Tom."

The current was too strong, and Ben's grip on the rocks, and on Slug's arm, was slipping. He couldn't hold on any longer. He let go of the rocks and fell into the water. As he went under, he felt a strong hand grab him tight around the ankle. In one swift motion, Tom pulled Ben and Slug over the rock ledge and onto the bridge.

Slug sat up coughing and gagging. He leaned onto his side and retched. When he'd regained enough strength to stand, he got up and limped away.

Ben was still gasping for air, staring back and forth between the spillway and the spot on the bridge where Tom had been. "How the hell did you know where I was? How...how the hell did you find me... how the hell did you get hold of me?"

Tom lifted his head and smiled. "Tom was listenin' real good."

31

Ben knew the quickest way into the dining room was lakeside and through the patio door. He led Tom alongside the water's edge to where the boardwalk met the patio deck and the shoreline slanted up toward the Clubhouse. They stopped beneath the plank walkway, and Ben spotted the faint glow of a lantern coming down from the boathouse. With Tom at his side, he hid behind one of the support pillars until the figure reached the patio deck. He peered around the column for a good look at the man.

Parke hooked the lantern over his arm, retrieved a jingling ring from his coat pocket, and slid one of the keys into the door handle. He wiped his feet and removed his hat and went inside, closing the patio door behind him.

"Hold on to me," said Ben, placing Tom's hand on the back of his shirt. "We're gonna head up this hill."

Tom tugged hard on Ben's shirt as they scaled the steep embankment. Just shy of the top, Tom slipped and they slid down the hill. Ben dug his feet deep into the mud, slowing their descent and allowing Tom to regain his footing. When Tom signaled he was ready to try again, they climbed back up the hill to the edge of the patio deck. The big windows gave Ben a clear view inside the Clubhouse. He watched Parke walk across the dining room floor and into the foyer. "That's good, Tom," he said, "He's headed into the lounge. We'll get over to the piano, and they'll never know we were gone."

Ben hoisted himself onto the wet wood and turned to Tom still crouched behind the edge of the deck. "Stay down till I tell you to come up. We've already found out that hiding behind me is a bad idea."

Ben crawled to the door and reached for the handle. He twisted and pulled, but the door was locked. He quickly dismissed the idea of having Tom bust it open, and crept back to edge of the deck. "We'll find another way," he said, "Come on."

Ben pulled Tom around the Clubhouse to the employee entrance. A wet chill seeped through his clothes sending a shiver down his back. He found some semi-clean, semi-dry towels inside a laundry bag and pat dry his shirt and trousers. Tom stood at his side like a trained soldier awaiting orders. The back door was locked, and Ben searched his pockets for the skeleton key. He found nothing except the folded picture of his mother, still tucked away in his hip pocket. The key must have fallen out when he went into the water, and was either at the bottom of the lake, or half way to Johnstown by now.

The only other way into the Clubhouse was through the front door, not a very safe route if he wanted to keep their re-entry a secret. The front porch entrance would take them straight through the foyer and right past the open doorway of the billiard lounge.

"Damn it," said Ben, taking Tom's hand and leading him down the side of the Clubhouse. "I can't figure why anyone would want to be a burglar. Far too much trouble this business of sneakin' around."

Orange flames flickered inside the curved glass bowls along the Clubhouse wall, and an open window let out the idle conversation from the men inside the lounge. A street lamp lit the front porch where a lone doorman sat rocking inside a cloud of cigarette smoke. He was whistling an improvised tune and staring vacantly at the General's black Victoria parked in the drive.

Ben pushed Tom back, and they retreated to the corner of the Clubhouse. He squatted behind the old buckboard wagon and yanked Tom down to one knee. "All right, Tom," he said, "you've gotta walk behind me real quiet...quiet as a mouse, you hear?"

"Yessir."

"Good," he said, patting Tom on the shoulder. "Now, pretty soon I'm gonna give you a poke in the side. When I do, you make that rattler sound, just like you did at the dam. Can you do that?"

"Yessir, Ben. Tom can do that."

The white pines and sugar maples blocked the moonlight, and outside the glow of the streetlamp, the area in front of the Clubhouse was pitch-dark. Ben and Tom left the cover of the buckboard and made it to a thicket across the drive, directly opposite the doorman still puffing and whistling in his rocking chair.

The enormous black Shire hitched to the Victoria slept standing, its eyes shut tight. One of its front legs kicked irregularly at the ground, and its head twitched as if it were dreaming. Ben pulled Tom behind the brush and jabbed a finger between his ribs. Tom snickered, and made the uncanny sound of a timber rattler ready to strike.

With a sudden jerk, the stallion opened its eyes and raised itself in the air, swinging and punching its front legs like a prize fighter. It shot down the drive with the black Victoria in tow. The doorman sprang from his chair and gave chase as the runaway carriage bumped over the cobblestone road toward the dam.

Ben watched for a reaction from the men inside the lounge.

Crick popped his head out the window. "Just a little trouble with your horse, General," he said over his shoulder. "Not to worry though, the doorman is seeing after it."

A crackling cough came from the General. "Shut that god damn window. It's that cold air that's giving me the pneumonia."

Crick closed the window and pulled the curtains shut.

Ben came out of the brush. "Come on, Tom, let's go."

Tom stayed right on Ben's tail as they ran across the driveway, up the front porch stairs, and into the Clubhouse.

Inside the foyer, they crouched beside one of the fancy étagères that lined the perimeter of the dimly lit room. Oil paintings of some of the club members hung on the walls, and their stiff faces glared down at Ben with disappointed frowns. On the opposite wall, between the portraits of Andrews and Crick, a large gold-framed mirror gave Ben a reversed view of the men inside the lounge.

Crick, Addison, the General, and Parke were smoking around an oval table set with a familiar green bottle and a pitcher of water. Crick, Addison and Parke drank the pernod in beveled glasses while the General, complaining the smell reminded him of his physician's medicine bag, drank scotch from a snifter. Addison topped off his glass, and the herbal fragrance of the absinthe drifted into the foyer. Ben caught a good whiff, and stuck his finger under his nose to keep from sneezing.

Parke had never been known for his excessive drinking, and Ben was surprised when he saw him tip back his head and gulp a full glass. Parke winced. After a bit of ribbing from the others, he reached for the green bottle and refilled his glass.

Behind the men, through the hovering rings of tobacco smoke, was a small, open doorway that led to the billiard room. When Ben heard Parke challenge Crick to a game, he saw their opportunity to sneak past. He turned and put his hand on Tom's shoulder. "Straight for the piano," he said, "and keep your head down."

32

Crick found an ashtray on the mantle and exchanged his cigar for a snifter of scotch. "Are you certain you'd like to do this now, Mr. Parke?" he said, "Perhaps another time, when you have more of your wits about you."

"Very certain," said Parke, chalking his cue.

Crick set down his glass and went to the cue rack and thumbed through the sticks as if he were choosing a sword for battle. The two men had dueled at the billiard table before, but with Crick always bowing out claiming, "Trouble at the foundry" or "arthritic flare-up." With Addison and the General as spectators, though, Parke hoped Crick's pride would keep him from quitting.

"And the wager?" asked Crick, still searching for his weapon.

"Just a simple answer to a simple question, Mr. Crick, that's all."

"Well if that's all, then why not ask your question now and get it over with. It would save you the embarrassment of losing, and me the trouble finding a decent shaft."

Parke watched Crick struggle with the cues. "Hardly as satisfying," he said, retrieving a horsehair brush from under the table and sweeping the felt. "Though I do hope you'll have the decency to find your own stick, and allow me the pleasure to enjoy mine."

Addison and the General sat in high-backed cushioned chairs separated by a small tea-table. As Crick and Parke prepared for battle, Addison prepared for spectating with a glass of absinthe.

Addison used the Bohemian method, igniting the drink with a flaming cube of absinthe-soaked sugar, and dousing the burning beverage with the chilled water.

The General took out a fresh grip of plug tobacco and stuffed his pipe. "Hurry it up, Mr. Crick," he said, "we haven't got all night."

Crick had hold of two sticks. "And the game?" he said, "pocket, carom, strait-rail, balk-line?"

Parke held his own cue to his lips and blew a cloud of chalk-dust from the tip. "Snooker," he said.

"Very well then," said Crick, putting back the short stick and drawing the long cue from the rack. He gave the General an apologetic bow. "Needed to make sure I chose the appropriate shaft for the appropriate game."

Crick leaned his weapon against a corner pocket, took the triangle off the pendant lamp, and racked the red balls. Parke fetched the colored balls from one of the pockets and set them in their position on the table. As Parke placed the black ball, the sound of rattling glass came from the dining room.

"What was that?" Parke said.

"What was what," said Crick.

The General shrugged.

"I heard it, too," said Addison, "It came from the dining room... the chandeliers."

The General puffed his pipe and sipped his scotch. "It's just the boy and my prodigy," he said, "They've been at that piano all day. Tom must be bored, and seeing how high he can toss that boy into the air."

"I've just come from the dining room," said Parke. "There's no one there."

"I told them two to stay at that piano," the General said. "You trying to tell me my employees aren't followin' orders?"

"All I'm telling you," said Parke, "is that I was in the dining room not twenty minutes ago, and no one was there."

"Come to think of it," said Addison, "I haven't heard any music since we came in."

The General looked around, waiting for someone to nullify any further interest in the matter, but when the rest of the men simply stared back, the General pushed himself up from his chair. "Ah, hell," he said, "let's have a look, then, I'll show you."

When the men came into the dining room, Ben was perched on Tom's shoulders, looping a long red streamer over the arm of a chandelier. Ben kicked his heels and spun Tom around like he was turning a horse. "Oh, terribly sorry to disturb you, gentlemen," he said, reaching up and tying off the streamer. "The chambermaids must not have hung these properly. We've spent the better part of the evening re-tying them."

"You see, Parke," said Crick, shaking his head, "Just the boy and the nigger. Jesus, I reckon you must be blind, too."

"Well hurry it up then," the General said, "And get Tom back on that piano. Tomorrow is the big show."

"Yes, sir," said Ben, "Almost finished. We'll get right back at it. So terribly sorry."

The men retreated to the lounge with Parke in the rear. When he came to the doorway, he noticed two sets of muddy footprints coming from the front door. He traced the tracks across the foyer and into the dining room where Ben sat balanced atop Tom like a circus performer. Parke's eyes tracked up until they met Ben's guilty smile.

Parke returned to the billiard room and felt the effects of the absinthe setting in. No more, he told himself. Liquor had always been Parke's demise when it came to sport. Crick, on the other hand, excelled under the influence. The more Crick drank, the better Crick played. A snooker match of nine frames generally lasted over an hour, but Parke, knowing the General wouldn't last ten minutes, convinced Crick to settle their wager with only one frame.

"One frame it is," said Crick, "No need to prolong the agony, eh Parke."

Crick won the coin toss and took his first visit to the table. Parke stood by the tea-table while Addison gave the General a quick run-down of the game. "Pot a red ball, one point," he said, "then pot a colored ball for its respective point value. Once all the reds are potted, pot the colored balls in order: yellow, green, brown, blue, pink, then black. If the opponent 'snookers' you, and you can't strike your object ball, that's a foul, up to seven points if the black ball is involved. The player with the most points at the end of the frame, wins."

The General shook his head. "Too god damn complicated. Why not just give 'em each a Colt and count to ten, much easier that way."

After running up a dozen points, Crick left Parke with a nice cluster of colored balls near the corner pocket. Parke leaned deep over the table, lining up the cue ball and drawing his stick back and forth the way a cellist draws a bow across the strings.

"If I'm not mistaken," said Addison, "Snooker has its roots in India."

"It does," said Parke, potting a red then the brown, "And a strange group of men, the Hindus."

"Indeed," said Crick, "The things they do with their swords and snakes."

Parke continued his run of the table, heavily chalking his cue after each shot. He ran a break of twenty-four points before fouling and giving two points back to Crick.

"Very impressive, Mr. Parke," said Addison, following the game intently. The General, however, had nodded off.

Crick set down his glass, took his cigar from the onyx tray, and played the rest of the game with the smoldering nub clamped tightly in the corner of his mouth.

Crick lined up to pot a red ball in the side pocket, and Parke backed away for a broader look at the table. "It's not the antics of the Hindu men I find strange," he said, "but their fondness for polygamy."

"Yes," said Addison, "I recently read of a Hindu that has just taken his fiftieth wife."

Crick broke up a grouping of red balls, and the sound of the cracking ivory woke the General. "Fifty wives," he shouted, juggling his burning pipe. "That's fascinating. I've never been able to handle just one." The General yawned and went back to snoozing.

Addison slid the pipe from the General's loose fingers and set it, chimney side up, on the tea-table. "Speaking of wives, Mr. Crick," said Addison, "I haven't seen your lovely Ada, today. Has she taken ill?"

"You could say that," said Crick, relinquishing control of the table to Parke. "It appears her hallucinations were not simply associated with an over-indulgence in liquor. I sent her for a stint of relaxation and recuperation at a lovely hospital in Virginia."

Parke and Crick continued taking turns at the billiard table until after a seventeen point break by Crick, only one red ball remained. Parke potted the last red, and stepped back to plan out his run at the colors. "And what do you say, Mr. Crick, to a man with a fondness for so many women?" said Parke, potting the yellow ball with a nice two-carom bank, but fouling after a cut-shot attempt at the green.

Crick potted the green straight into the side pocket, leaving a clear shot for the brown in the corner. "I'd say, what a dandy situation for the man."

"And what if the woman is attached to another man?" said Parke.

Crick potted the brown ball in the corner pocket, and with some reverse English, potted the blue, drawing the cue ball back to the dead center of the table. "A satisfied woman never strays, Parke," he said.

"And what if she does? Does the husband have a right to know?"

Crick kept his gaze on the remaining balls. The black and the pink were pinned against the end-rail, their curved surfaces barely touching. He came around the front of the table and lined up what would turn out be the last shot of the game. Even if Crick fouled, the only way for Parke to win was to pot both the pink and the black on his next visit. With careful English, Crick sent the cue ball slowly toward the two balls against the rail, stopping it in fused contact with the black, impossible for Parke to pot the pink without fouling.

Crick returned his cue to the rack and reclaimed his beverage from the mantle. "Ignorance is a blissful state for the fool, Parke," he said, raising his snifter and tipping back the rest of his scotch. "And it appears that I've snookered you."

Parke stared at the trio of touching balls, the black resting perfectly between the pink and the white. He tossed his stick on the table and walked away. "That, Mr. Crick, you most certainly have."

33

The uncomfortable stiffness Tom had been carrying with him since the fight on the dam was gone, and a peaceful smile returned to his face. He took a deep breath, exhaled slowly, and began to play.

Ben stretched out on the floor next to the windows and stared up at the chandeliers. As Tom played an unfamiliar melody, Ben pictured the glass tears dripping from the chandeliers onto the tablecloths, splashing up tiny bouquets of red, white, and blue.

"What's that tune?" Ben said.

Tom went into a series of arpeggios that descended from the highest notes on the piano and mimicked the sound of trickling water. "Dat's a song Tom made up his self when he was five years old. Tom calls it Falling Rain."

"You gonna play that tomorrow at the show?"

"Maybe. Never know what Tom will play till he gets out there."

Ben sat up Indian style and squirmed around, adjusting himself in his wet clothes. "Ain't you got a list, or a program, or somethin' that tells you what to play? I believe I'd freeze right up if I didn't have a song list, and my sheet music." Ben laughed, remembering Tom's blindness, "Sheet music, heck, that wouldn't do you any good."

Tom played another drizzle of rain drops. "Tom just plays what comes to him, or what da folks call out. Sometimes one fella will holler 'play Yankee Doodle'. Then somebody else will say 'play da Brahms lullaby'. So Tom stands up and says to both dem fellas, and to da rest of da folks, 'Tom will now play Yankee Doodle and da Brahms lullaby at da same time'." Tom laughed, his fingers bouncing across the keys. "The way I reckon, if God gave me da talent, it's all in his hands anyhow."

Ben went to the window and pressed his face against the glass. A combination of filtered moonlight and factory fire reflected off the scattered clouds and onto the lake. The water was at the top of the rock ledge, and at the spillway there was a disturbance in the water. A school of black bass thrashed about, trapped against the fish screen. The heavier fish were helpless, but the smaller ones were jumping out of the water and riding the waterfall over the edge.

Ben returned to his seat on the stage. "And where will you go, Tom, after tomorrow's show?"

"Da General says we's headed south. Says dare's a heap of folks in Tennessee and Alabama can't wait to hear Blind Tom. Says we gonna play da halls in Georgia, Louisiana, and Miss-i-sip-ee. Tom loves travelin' da south...get his self some of dat fine southern cookin'."

"What's it like, Tom?"

"Well," he said, "Dare's da fried hot chicken, da collard greens and grits, da sweet potato pie and a mess'o biscuits to clean da plate. And dare's da sweet tea and da..."

"I mean the travelin' around. This place and that. You ain't never wish you could just settle down, with your family and all?"

"Tom's family is da General."

"How about the rest of your family, you ain't never miss 'em?"

Tom sat quiet. Ben hadn't seen him give this much thought to one of his questions before. Slowly, Tom's expression tightened, and he struggled to get his words out. "Sometimes," he said, "when it rains real hard, Tom misses his mammy and his pappy. But da General, he say we'll see dem again someday, when we get to Heaven. Maybe we'll stop dare on da way to Alabama. You think we might stop in Heaven, Ben, on da way to Alabama?"

Ben lay flat and stared up at the streamers and the flags and the chandeliers. "I don't know, Tom," he said, "maybe."

Tom went to the keys and played a curious melody, similar to the previous tune, but much lower in pitch and harder in tone, driving, impatient, restless. He played a repetitive rhythm of rumbling bass notes against a syncopated melody of falling octaves in the right hand.

"Rain again?" said Ben.

"No more rain," said Tom, his eyelids shut tight, his jaw clenched. "Tom played da happy and da sad." He pounded his left hand hard and picked up the tempo. "Dis is da angry. Dis is da thunder storm."

Ben fixed on the shimmering chandeliers as the pounding roar and the howling wind of Tom's thunder storm filled the room. He shut his eyes, fearing the entire Clubhouse might suddenly come crashing down around him.

Parke took the news of his wife's infidelity rather well. In fact, he was relieved. Now that there was no doubt, he could focus on more important tasks like fixing a neglected dam, rather than his desire to throw Crick over the edge of it. Though it would be rather satisfying, he thought, to reveal his knowledge over dinner, perhaps. He could follow up one of Crick and Andrews's theoretical debates on integrity with a hypothetical doozy of his own.

He set aside plans for revenge and went to his bedroom window. He pulled the curtains aside and opened the window and stuck out his head, looking up to the mountains and back down into the valley.

Patchy clouds moved across the sky, and the glasslike surface of the lake was eerily still. Tomorrow he would get an early start on the spillway, before the parade arrived. After the festivities, he would work through the night and have the waterway cut by daybreak Monday morning. A peaceful calmness lingered in the air, and he closed the window and climbed into bed, scooting up next to the burning nub of his bedside candle. The candle flame vanished into a pool of melted wax, and he gazed through a stream of smoke and out the window, comforted by the break in the clouds and the curious smile of a crescent moon.

34

The Decoration Day parade scheduled to pass by Clem's house never came. Instead of a patriotic procession, Percival found the river overflowing its banks, and a swift current marching through the streets. The rain came down in heavy drops, like pebbles, pounding his shirt and thumping the top of his head. He looked down the hill where the river had swollen up over the road and washed into the homes. Children peered out of second-floor windows, pointing and staring upriver, seemingly unconcerned that their basements were underwater. He ran to the end of Clem's property for a better look at the town proper. A good thing for the children it was Sunday, he thought, for the schoolhouse that sat in the gully on Cinder Street was flooded past the windows. He saw the shop owners on Main Street, frantically moving displayed goods off the porches and into their stores. Henry Howell had a big push broom and was sweeping the water off the vacant dugout. The lower half of the town was under water. Percival had seen the river rise before, but never so high and so quickly.

The road behind Clem's property ran next to the tree line on high ground, and Percival made his way to where the muddy path fell off toward the west side of Main Street. The roads on that end of town were also underwater, and the shanties closer to the river had taken in the flooding half-way up the walls. Some of the townsfolk were wading through the streets carrying household goods. Others sought refuge on the roofs. Those with umbrellas huddled close together, those without pulled their coats tightly over their heads. On one of the rooftops, a man with a rifle was passing time leaning against a chimney and taking potshots at roof rats. In an instant, the thick mist turned into a heavy downpour, and Percival fled back to the house.

He expected to see his son asleep upstairs, but when he came into Ben's room he found it empty, the bedding undisturbed. He raced downstairs for a thick wool overcoat, grabbed a wide brimmed hat from the kitchen table, and ran to Clem's place. When he came in, Clem had a pot of coffee boiling on the stovetop.

"Reckon we won't be firin' up that oil barrel today," Clem said, "Looks like she decided to open up on us after all."

Percival looked around the room, darting back and forth from one wall to the other. "Have you seen Ben?"

Clem shook his head. "I haven't."

Percival went to the door and closed the screen. "It's coming down hard," he said. "Harder than I've ever seen before. Most of the streets in town are already flooded. It must have rained in sheets through the night."

"We've got a good spot here," said Clem. "Have some coffee while we ride it out."

Percival feared Ben may still be at the Clubhouse, and if it was raining as hard as it was in town, the flooding must be worse at the dam. He clasped his hands behind his head and twitched nervously. "I can't sit here while Ben's missin'. What if he's caught in the water tryin' to make his way down the hill? What if he's stuck near that dam? You said yourself not to trust it." He pressed his nose against the screen door and peered outside. "I can't stay here drinkin' coffee with you while my son's out in this storm. I gotta go to him, I gotta."

"Ben's a grown man," said Clem. "You can't keep protectin' him from every bit of trouble. He's got gumption. He'll be all right. Besides, he's probably held up inside that castle on the hill. Fact is, I'd be more inclined to trade places with him."

247

Percival knew his son. Ben would never sit inside that Clubhouse and watch the valley wash away. Percival buttoned his coat and pulled his hat tightly over his head. "I told him I'd meet him at the dam, and that's what I'm goin' to do. I'd be lettin' him down if I didn't."

"Damn it," Clem said, grabbing his hat and coat, "I'm going with you." He went to the back of the house and returned with his coat on and a length of rope hooked over his shoulder. "Come on, let's get up to the dam before that river rises any further, less you want to swim there."

As they came down the porch, Clem's knees buckled, and he grabbed Percival by the shoulder to keep from falling. He wheezed and reached for his chest.

Percival grabbed Clem around the waist. The strong body that once lifted heavy oak tables and solid maple cabinets without breaking a sweat felt frail and weak. Percival slid his arm around Clem's bony ribs, and it seemed as if his fingers had gone straight through his side. "Come on Clem," said Percival, guiding him back up the porch, "Let's get you inside."

Percival helped Clem into bed and went downstairs and returned with a damp cloth and a cup of water. He tilted Clem's head back, set the cloth on his forehead, and held the cup to his mouth.

"What are you doin'," said Clem, pushing Percival's hand away, "Let me up."

"You ain't goin' nowhere," said Percival. "You lie here and rest, and I'll heat up some tea. I told you all that coffee's gonna do you in."

Clem lay on the bed and breathed deeply until the color came back to his face. "Tea?" he said, "No tea, no nothin', just let me rest, I'll be all right."

"That's what you said the last time, yet here we are again."

"I'm alive, ain't I."

"Barely. Now let me fix you up somethin' to calm your nerves, a good hot tea will do the trick."

Clem pushed himself up against the headboard and rubbed the back of his neck. "You ain't got time to fix me no tea. Now get out there and find your son." He slid the rope off his shoulder. "Take this. I reckon it may come in handy."

Percival knew Clem would refuse caretaking, and headed down the stairs. "You sit tight, you hear. I'll be back with Ben, and then we'll get that heart of yours looked at."

"Go on, get to your boy," shouted Clem as Percival flew out the front door.

Percival jogged at a steady pace through spurts of heavy rain. The bluegrass grew thick alongside the road, and kept his feet from sinking into the muddied earth. He wove through a grove of pines to a clearing near the banks and an entire neighborhood taking in water like a sinking ship. The middle of the river was moving fast, but at the banks, the water swirled in eddies, trapping the floating debris near the shoreline.

As Percival passed, a man with a gimp came up the hill, waving his arms and shouting in German. He was short and round, and his belly bounced over his belt as he ran toward the road. Percival kept his head down and picked up his pace, but the man, despite his limp, cut him off.

The immigrant shook Percival by the lapels, pointing to one of the homes that had slipped off its foundation and was being pulled toward the fast flow of the river. Percival struggled to break free, but the look in the man's eyes made him stop. The man kept shouting and pointing to the home, rain and tears washing down his face. Percival didn't speak a word of German, but the universal language of a father in distress was clear.

Percival ran with the man to the water line where a short woman stood holding an infant, both were soaking wet, blue-faced and shivering. Behind them, their two-story home bobbed like a buoy, saved from the pull of the river by a bushy sugar maple wedged between the home and a small island of rock and mud.

The immigrant grabbed Percival by the shoulder, "Gitta, Gitta," he shouted, pointing to a figure in the fogged dormer window clutching a rag doll. Percival led the family away from the water and signaled them to 'wait here'.

Percival let out a deep breath and waded into the water, carefully dodging the drift of housewares, clothing, and furniture swirling past him. Half-way to the house, he came to a sudden drop-off and lost his hat as the undercurrent swept him off his feet. The water was frigid, the current strong. He pounded against it and grabbed on to the crossbar of a telegraph pole. The river tugged at his feet, and he hooked his legs around the pole and slowly peeled the rope from his shoulder. He tied one end of the rope to the top of the pole and the other around his waist. The floating house was moving, and he didn't have much time before the flood carried it away.

As he secured the rope, he heard a series of loud cracks, the sound of timber snapping. He looked upriver and saw the neighboring house breaking apart. Suddenly the home split in two, and the family of four huddled around the chimney tumbled off the roof, screaming and flailing. Percival watched helplessly as they fell into the river and were swept away.

Still short of the house by twenty feet, he waited for a large dresser to float past, pushed off the pole, and swam hard to the edge of the roof. The rushing water punched at his face and pounded in his ears, and he could no longer hear the screams of the German couple waiting on the shore.

The rain made the wood shingled rooftop difficult to grip, and Percival strained to hang on between cloudbursts as he traversed along the edge to the dormer. He shook his coat sleeve over his hand, grabbed the cuff to pad his fist, and smashed out the window. Thick shards fell into the water and the girl jumped back, crying and still clutching her rag doll.

As Percival cleared away the jagged remains of the window, the house jolted. He grabbed hold of the roof with both hands and pulled himself onto the small slope next to the window. "What's your name?" he said to the girl.

"Gitta," her voice no more than a whimper.

"All right, Gitta," he said, extending a hand toward her, "I need you to come out onto the roof. Can you do that for me?"

Gitta nodded. She stepped out the window, reaching for Percival, and the rag doll slipped out of her hand. She lunged for it and fell. Percival caught her by the arm as she hit the water. A strong pull came from below, and Percival was thrown into the water as the maple tree snapped and the house floated off into the river. The slack in the rope let out, and Percival wrapped his arms around Gitta, the current tugging them further from shore.

Percival looked at the bank and saw a group of men scrambling to form a human chain and retrieve the rope from the telegraph pole. "Hang on," the men shouted, pulling on the rope. A thick piece of deadwood floated by, and the men timed their pulls to avoid running Percival and Gitta into the debris.

Percival held Gitta tight against his chest, treading hard and using his free hand to keep the girl's head above water. She wrapped her arms around him and pressed her cheek against his. Percival's thoughts shifted to Ben, hoping he would soon have the chance to hold his son the same way. At the shoreline, the German man was crying and reaching out with both arms. The bond between father and child was strong, and Gitta twisted out of Percival's grasp and stretched toward the shore. The current pulled them apart and Gitta slipped, but Percival held on and powered against the tug of the river. Slowly, the men pulled them onto the bank. When they were clear of the river, Percival handed Gitta to her father. The reunited family embraced, and Percival continued up the hill on his search for Ben.

He followed a path outside a thick cover of evergreens uphill toward the factories. Fire and chimney smoke stained the grey clouds with streaks of crimson like smeared blood. Even in the pouring rain, the haze over the valley was thick, and it was difficult to tell where the smoke from the chimneys ended, and the bleeding clouds began.

The sidings next to the factories were cluttered with abandoned backpacks and haversacks, some hanging on the signal arms and switches, some floating in the water pooled between the uneven mounds of ballast rock. Percival came up to a group of laborers who had found shelter inside an empty boxcar. They were huddled close together, warming their hands around a small fire. One of the men reached out and Percival took his hand and lifted himself into the car.

"You'uns hear anything about the reservoir?" said Percival, "Is she gonna hold?"

"Can't say," said one of the men, "We sent a man to the telegraph tower at the Number Six Bridge over an hour ago. Haven't heard hide nor hair from him since. The foundry up the hill's already takin' in water, and we're gonna hold out here. I'd suggest you do the same."

The fire that warmed Percival's face filled the boxcar with a choking smoke. He ignored the man's advice and went out into the rain. At the far end of the boxcar, the rails turned sharply toward the river, guiding him straight to the Number Six Bridge.

He came down the hill and saw two trains held up alongside the river. The Number Eight was on the near siding, the Limited across the river. A large section of track had washed out in front of the Number Eight, and the engineer was milling about, surveying the damage. Percival hopped over the track behind the engine and hurried past.

Behind the swollen lattice of the telegraph tower, he saw another train held up across the entire span of the bridge. A painted banner was attached to the rear car, and although the rain had washed away most of the writing, he could still make out the hand-drawn masks of a happy and a sad face, and the blurred words, Night Off Company Troupe in fancy cursive letters. The conductor and the engineer were coming down the bridge toward the telegraph office. Percival followed them up the stairs and waited outside while the two men talked to the operator.

From the tower, Percival could see the blurred image of the dam. What had once been a peaceful backdrop for summer picnics was now a five-hundred foot wide curtain of water pouring over the face of the dam. The dam was more than a mile away, but the sound of the crashing waterfall was so loud, he felt as if he were standing right next to it.

Beneath him, the six coaches of the troupe train stretched across the deck bridge from the telegraph tower to just shy of the coal tipple at the other end. Percival shivered, watching the water rise. One of the men came out and pulled him into the office. A woman behind a desk worked the telegraph while the two men hovered over her shoulder.

One of the men turned to Percival. "I'm Walkinshaw," he said, "the engineer of that stranded troupe train, and this here is conductor Warthen."

Percival shook their hands and thanked them for the temporary shelter. "I've come up from town," he said, "my boy's up at the Clubhouse. Any news on the state of the reservoir?"

"Jesus," said Warthen, "You're soakin' wet. Have you been in the river?"

Percival took off his coat and hung it on the rack next to the doorway. "A lot of flooding in town. Lots of folks and homes spillin' into the river. How is it up here?"

Walkinshaw pointed at the woman. "Trying to find out. Came in here to get our orders from Emma, here, like everyone else, but it seems there's trouble with the wires."

Emma pushed herself away from the desk and looked up at the men. "Nothing," she said, "Except for the line to Mineral Point, all the wires are down."

"What about that speaking telegraph," said Walkinshaw, "Same trouble with it?"

"All down but the line to the Clubhouse. I've been trying for the past hour, no response."

"So what, then," said Warthen.

Emma read the last message that had come through. "Says here for all trains with red lights to hold where they are."

Percival looked out the window at the dam. The lake water was now flowing over the entire width of the embankment. "You ain't thinkin' 'bout keepin' that train above the river, are you? Hell, even I know that's a bad idea."

Walkinshaw joined Percival at the window. "I think he's right. We gotta get her off the bridge."

"I agree," said Emma.

Walkinshaw went on. "Warthen, you get on up to the Limited. Tell Hess to back up so we can clear the tipple while I get our train ready to move." Walkinshaw looked at Percival. "Sure could use some help settling the passengers. How 'bout it fella, you with us on this?"

Percival knew Ben was up there somewhere. Any more delay and all the access roads would be washed out. He was running out of time. "I don't think so," he said, "I've gotta get to that Clubhouse, quick. I gotta get to my boy."

"South side's the fastest way," said Emma.

"She's right," said Walkinshaw, "Get across with us on the train, and when we back her up the hill, you'll be almost there. Besides," Walkinshaw pointed out the window, "It don't look like anyone's crossing over that dam, now."

Percival looked out the window and squinted to bring the top of the dam into focus. A large chunk of earth and rock at the center of the dam suddenly gave way, and the lake burst through, taking a section of the carriage road along with it. He was too far away to tell if anyone had fallen into the water, and for the moment chose not to think about it.

The men put on their coats and hats and Warthen turned to Walkinshaw. "Anything you want me to tell Hess when I get up there? Besides moving the Limited up the hill."

Just then a call came into the office over the speaking line, and the group went silent. Emma lifted the receiver to a shouting, loud enough for everyone in the room to hear. "Head for the hills," the voice said, "The reservoir at River Fork is coming out."

Walkinshaw pulled his head up and said to Warthen, "Tell Hess to do it fast."

Percival grabbed the receiver from Emma's hand and shouted into it, "Ben…Ben…can you hear me, I'm at the Number Six Bridge…can you hear me." There was a muffled sound on the other end, some static on the line, but that was all.

"Come on," called Walkinshaw, "No time to spare."

Percival dropped the receiver and rushed down the stairs. "That was my son," he yelled, "That was Ben."

Warthen went to the Limited while Walkinshaw climbed into the troupe train and gave the order to feed the fire box.

Percival pulled himself into the passenger car with the fancy banner. The theater performers, mostly women and children, sat shivering in their seats, scared and confused. A man with a cane got up from his seat. At first glance, Percival took the cane for a theater prop, but as the man hobbled down the aisle, Percival saw he was a cripple.

"What news about the dam?" the man said. "Is it going to hold?"

Percival studied the faces of the women and children desperate for good news. For a moment, he considered saying something to placate them while the men moved the train off the bridge. But the desire in their eyes to know the truth overcame him. The women pulled their children close and stared silently at Percival. "We've just received word from the Clubhouse," he said, "The reservoir at River Fork is coming out."

The man with the cane dropped clumsily into an open seat. Without a word, the women pinned up their clothes and buttoned up their coats. Some of them closed their eyes, and Percival could see their lips moving with the cadence of silent prayer.

35

Parke woke to the sound of drumming rain. The wind rattling the window had whipped up the lake into a scattering of white peaks. He stared into the fog, brought his focus to the windowpane, and followed a droplet as it zigzagged its way through the condensation to the puddle at the bottom of the casement. He struck a match, using it first to ignite the mantle of a gas lamp, then to light a cigarette. After a long draw, he dressed, and went to the adjoining room to wake his wife.

The sheets and pillows were clumped together in a pile at the foot of the bed, and bottles of hair treatment and perfume were strewn about the floor. The hat trunk he had bought her for their honeymoon was gone, and so was Lily. Except for a crumpled dress and a crushed bonnet, the wardrobe was empty. Only the pungent blend of citrus and alcohol remained in the room.

Out in the hallway, he found the guestroom doors opened wide and all of the rooms vacant. He hurried downstairs, through the dining room, and into the foyer where he heard the splashing of hooves in the drive.

He came onto the front porch and saw Crick standing in the rain beside a faded black Victoria, holding a wide, black umbrella and directing the members to the cabs lined up alongside the Clubhouse. The members, shielding themselves with borrowed umbrellas, rushed in pairs to the awaiting coaches, the big Belgian draft horses huffing steam and kicking impatiently at the mud while the coachmen, shrouded in woolen overcoats, sat perched atop their box seats ready to depart.

Crick trotted up and down the drive making broad sweeping motions with his free hand as if he were shooing cattle from a stockyard, and one by one the carriages rode off. The last carriage pulled up and stopped next to Crick. Mr. Addison popped his head out the side window. "Thank you, Mr. Crick," he shouted, "for alerting us to the severity of the storm, and for taking such a sincere interest in the safety of your guests."

Addison's coach continued on, and Parke stepped off the porch and onto the driveway. The smell of wet cobblestone hung in the air, and he marched through the puddles toward Crick and the Victoria.

Crick glanced over his shoulder. "I guess you were right, Parke. Looks like that storm's gonna hit us after all. And pardon the pun... but as far as that Decoration Day shindig you were plannin'... looks like it's gonna be a wash."

Parke wiped the rain from his brow and stared into Crick's sunken eyes. "Everyone gone?" he said, monotone.

"Everyone," said Crick, tilting his umbrella to shield himself from the wind. "And a telegraph was sent early this morning, telling those scheduled to arrive to stay away from River Fork."

The rain was falling in spurts, and Parke flipped up his collar and covered his ears. "The General, and the blind Negro?"

"First to leave. And with my two hundred dollars, to boot...the old crook."

"The Italians?"

"Down at the sporting field, dismantling that stage of yours before the wind rips it apart."

"And you?" said Parke, stepping in front of Crick and blocking his way into the cab. "Hurrying off as well, I see."

Crick eyes wandered. "Big trouble brewing in Homestead. I've gotta get there quick. Operator at Union Station says they're about to close all westbound tracks."

Parke propped himself against the carriage door. A hint of citrus

257

seeped through a crack in the window. He turned and stared into the darkened cab. "Is that so?"

Crick sidestepped Parke in an attempt to enter the cab, and Parke stopped him with a palm to the chest.

Crick backed away and teetered on his heels, fidgeting with his coat and shifting glances between Parke, the Victoria, and the other carriages heading off toward the dam. "I'm in a terrible rush, Parke, so if there's nothing else."

Parke stood silent, and slowly reached into his coat pocket.

Crick eyes followed Parke's hand.

In a swift move, Parke drew out a flash of silver steel.

Crick winced and turned away.

Parke opened his cigarette case and took out a cigarette. He stepped under the cover of Crick's umbrella and struck a match and lit the cigarette, drawing deeply on it and blowing a stream of smoke in Crick's face. Parke turned to the cab window and stared at the shadowy figure inside. "Is this what you want?"

There was no answer from inside the cab. He waited a moment and backed away, the end of his cigarette quickly snuffed by the rain.

Crick hurried past and climbed into the carriage. "If you ever happen to see that 'General' fella again," he said, slamming the door shut, "tell him he owes me two hundred dollars."

Crick's cab rode off down the driveway.

Parke stood alone in the rain, watching the wagon train until the carriages reached the far side of the bridge and vanished into the woods.

He ran down the hill to the sporting field where he found a small group of Italians collapsing the stage tent and loading the wooden chairs onto a flatbed wagon.

Damato appeared from behind the draft horse. "I'm sorry, Mr. Parke," he said, "Mr. Crick told us to take it down."

"It's all right," said Parke, now drenched from head to toe. "But taking down the stage will have to wait. I have a more important job for you."

Parke told Damato to find as many laborers as possible: Italians, Germans, locals, farmers, anyone with a strong back. "And tell them to bring shovels...pickaxes, too," he said, "anything they can find to cut into the face of that dam." He brought Damato closer to the water and pointed out the areas where he wanted them to dig. "Pockets carved out along crest with levees built up in between, and deep trenches around the edge of the dam on both sides. I'm going to check on the feeder streams upriver. Depending on how much water's coming off the mountain, we still may have time to get that spillway cut before the lake overflows."

Parke sent Damato on his way and hurried across the lawn onto the boardwalk. When he reached the patio deck, he saw the entire lake churning with foamy whitecaps like soapsuds in a giant washbasin. A collection of logs and planks floated toward the dam, the smaller pieces drifting to the sides and swirling in eddies near the banks.

The rain had backed off, and he sprinted to the boathouse. He found an oar, grabbed a tin pail off a rusted hook, and climbed into a small dinghy. He untied the boat from the dock and pushed out onto the lake.

He paddled between the swells as the rain thumped against the wooden hull, nothing on his mind but the condition of the feeder streams. Normal levels and slow moving currents meant Damato's men had a good six hours of digging, flooded banks and rapid torrents meant less than two. He had to get the water out of the lake and release the pressure accumulating behind the dam. Too much water from the feeders would fill the lake quickly, and he knew once the lip of the dam was breached, the water would soak through the rock face and disintegrate the entire embankment.

Moving against the current was slow going, and after an hour of laborious rowing, he approached the end of the reservoir. It wasn't until the keel scraped over the top of a barbed wire fence that he realized he was moving off the lake and into a cow pasture. He paddled to the end of the flooded field and pulled the boat ashore.

It was raining again, and Parke took shelter in the woods.

Heavy drops fell from the swollen branches. The air itself was wet, and the ground boiled with water. Even under the cover of the trees, the earth could hold no more. He tried his best to follow a solid path, but by the time he reached Laurel Creek, his shoes and trouser cuffs were caked with mud.

He came out of the woods and a rush of water nearly swept him off his feet. Laurel Creek, which usually ran at a depth of less than a foot, had swollen up with freshets out twenty feet past its normal banks on both sides. The spot where locals came to fly-fish now ran even too deep and too fast for a horse to cross. Beyond the flooded creek, Elias Crain and his hired hand were moving their cattle to higher ground. Parke retreated into the trees and continued on to Bear Creek and the Reynalds's lumber mill. Yellow Run, which fed Laurel Creek and Bear Creek, had washed out the Reynalds's property, grabbing logs and mill-planks from the shoreline and taking them into the creek now flowing at the speed of a raging river. A large amount of debris was being fed downstream, and the rain showed no signs of letting up.

Parke hurried back to the dinghy, mindful not to lose his shoes in the mud, but when he came out of the woods, the boat was gone. He looked down the shoreline and found it floating off toward the lake. In less than ten minutes, the water level had risen two feet and set the small boat adrift.

He waded out, retrieved the dinghy, and brought it to shore, bailing the water out of the hull. With the help of the current, he rowed with quick strokes back to the boathouse. At the bend, he found that the condition of the lake and the shoreline had worsened. The debris carried by the feeder streams now covered most of the reservoir, and a mass of driftwood was piled up at the dam. The blockage had pushed the lake water up past the sloping embankment in front of the Clubhouse and washed away the lower half of the boardwalk.

Parke tied off the dinghy inside the boathouse and ran to the stables. Now that the boardwalk was out, the fastest way to the dam was on horseback. He saddled a mare and set off, racing past

Bear Run where the culverts beneath the small bridge there were about to collapse. It would only be a matter of minutes before the feeder strayed down toward the Clubhouse. He prayed Damato and his men had made progress, but either way, they were running out of time.

Parke rode down the hill, digging his heels into the horse's ribs until he reached the dam. Damato was on the near side of the bridge resting his pickaxes on his shoulders like a pair of hunting rifles. In front of him, spread out across the bridge and along the rock ledge, were over fifty men, many of them curious onlookers who had come down from their properties to investigate the condition of the dam. The mill owners and farmers were now working alongside the Italians, cutting and picking away at the tough shale. Some had shoveled up mounds of earth at the center of the dam to hold back the water. One man, off the far side of the bridge, was cutting a trench in the mud with a horse and plow.

Parke rode across the dam like a mounted soldier, jumping over the open spaces where the men had removed the planks to better swing their axes. He shouted as he rode back and forth, commanding them to dig harder and dig faster.

The rain and the feeder streams had fed the lake to its limit, and at the spillway, the fish screens were clogged with dead black bass and debris and were ready to give. Parke peered over the face of the dam as he rode back toward Damato. Jets of water were shooting out through holes in the riprap as if the entire mountain had sprung a leak.

He stopped his horse at the end of the bridge, dismounted, and turned to Damato. In two hours of digging, the strong Italian and ten of his men had only managed to cut a channel four feet wide and two feet deep. Parke demanded they keep digging. "Put half the men at the trench," he shouted. "Tell them to dig as deep and as wide as they can."

Parke grabbed an axe and ran to the spillway, staring with eyes aghast at the voluminous black clouds rolling over the mountain, the rain tracing down from the thunderheads in striated grey

261

columns. He screamed above the roar of the waterfall. "And bring a group over here."

Damato's men had given up. They stood motionless at the sewer that now had but a trickle of water running through it.

"Bring your axes, and hook them onto the fish screens," Parke yelled, wheeling his axe above his head and driving it into the dam. "Cut away the edges, and rip it out."

Damato's men clambered up the lawn toward the tree line, but Damato picked up an axe and joined Parke at the spillway. The two men chopped away at the earth around the metal grates, spearing some of the black bass still trying to jump over.

On a downswing, Parke caught a glimpse of the Clubhouse. He left the axe stuck between the rocks and looked up. The lakeside of the building was swelling as if someone had pumped it full of hot air. With a deafening shatter, the dining room windows blew out. In almost comical disbelief, Parke watched as the entire contents of the River Fork Clubhouse, including the shiny black Steinway, spilled into the lake.

Behind him, the center of the dam began to crumble. He swung around and screamed at the men to run, but it was too late. Before they could react, a channel in the shape of a giant V opened up in the rock, dragging the middle of the bridge and three of the men over the edge.

Parke felt the bridge shaking beneath him as the lake found its way over the crest. Water now poured over the full face of the dam, with a heavy stream flowing through the middle, eating away the soil and unearthing boulders the size of cattle. The men trapped opposite the spout dropped their axes and fled to the far side of the bridge, and Parke shouted at them to head for the hills.

Parke turned to the spillway and pried his axe from the rocks and began swinging it into the dam in a whirling frenzy, cursing and screaming and chanting, "No, no, no."

Damato caught the axe in mid-swing and pulled it from Parke's hands. "Enough, John," he said, "time to go."

Parke stood for a moment in a silent daze, regarding the lake, the clouds, the Clubhouse. He turned and looked at Damato then ran to the end of the bridge and mounted his horse, calling back over his shoulder. "Giulio, my friend," he said, "get yourself to the tree line, tell everyone to move to higher ground, as far away from the dam as possible."

Damato dropped the axe. "And you," he said, "where are you going?"

Parke stared out over the valley at the rows of utility poles still chained together with telegraph and speaking wire. He kicked his horse into a strong gallop toward the Clubhouse and shouted, "To warn them."

"River Fork, Mineral Point, Moxham," Parke shouted as he raced up the hill, his horse nodding assent with each stride. "Morrellville, Millvale, Johnstown."

He would call to the major towns and towers first. Once they were notified, the warning could be spread on foot, horseback, even shouts from the rooftops if nothing else. Parke said a quick prayer, praising Andrews's showy speaking device, and reciting the names of the towns aloud. When he came out of the clearing and onto the Clubhouse drive, he reined the horse to a stop. He sank into the saddle in disbelief, and slumped over as if he were about to be sick. An enormous hemlock was blocking the entrance to the Clubhouse. Its thick trunk ripped out by the roots straddled the drive, its bushy peak jammed through the front door. He goaded the horse to the front porch, hitched it to a pillar, and went to the doorway now barricaded with pine needles and waterlogged boughs bent back on themselves like the ribs of a collapsed umbrella. He struggled to force his way through, but the tree was wedged in tight, and any attempt to bend or break the branches was useless.

He paced in a tight circle, thinking of the fastest way into the Clubhouse, and hurried around lakeside where the dismantled boardwalk floated in the expanding swells below. The steep hillside

263

that once surrounded the Clubhouse was almost completely eaten away, and what was left was soaking up the flooding like a muddy sponge. Parke scooted carefully along the wall of the Clubhouse, and a rift opened up before him, carving away a large chuck of earth. He pressed himself against the wall and retreated as the hillside sloughed off into the water.

With no chance of reaching the patio deck, he circled back to the drive, splashing through the puddles and hurdling over the soggy, stringy roots of the hemlock reaching out from the base of the tree like tentacles. Along the length of the Clubhouse, a mound of mud and twigs was piled up against the wall, smothering the kitchen door and the small windows of the lounge. Further down, the mud mound grew higher and wider, climbing up over the gas sconces and covering the office window just shy of the top.

Parke climbed up the mud mound to the thin line of exposed glass and saw the telephone on the pedestal stand behind the desk. It was a long stretch, he thought, but if he broke out enough of the window, he could reach it.

Hoping to find something to smash out the window, he went to the old buckboard wagon and climbed into the bed and threw back the canvas tarp. A startled drove of wood rats scurried off into the corners and disappeared through the holes in the rotted boards. He sprung back, landing on the soggy planks with a thud and shaking loose the axle. The back end of the wagon dropped, pitching him to the ground.

Dazed from the fall, he rushed to the mud mound and the small strip of window. He cocked his arm and smashed his fist straight through the plate glass. He recoiled with a jerk, and the jagged edges ripped open his sleeve and sliced his forearm elbow to wrist. He clasped his arm tight against his chest and cursed. When his arm had gone numb from the pain, he reached through the broken window and pushed his body as hard as he could against the mud mound, reaching and stretching until his fingertips touched the smooth, curved wood of the bell. He flicked at the telephone in an attempt to move it closer, but his fingers, slick with blood, only pushed it further away. Even with his arm fully extended, and his face pressed willfully against the razored jaw of the shattered window, he could not grab hold. With a thrust onto his toes, he strained forward with one last reach and lost his footing, sliding down the mud mound and rolling over onto his back.

A whistling wind blew through the driveway, carrying with it a weak, desperate shout for help that brought Parke to his feet. He went to the front porch and found the plea coming from behind the immovable branches of the hemlock that had sealed off the Clubhouse. Someone was still inside.

36

A chill lapped against Ben's cheek, taking him away from a Brahms sonata. He rose quickly and hit his head on the curved edge of the Steinway. He rubbed at the knot to dull the pain and scooted back toward the fireplace into a pile of muddy ashes. The piano bench where Tom had sat lulling him to sleep the night before was empty. The General must have come sometime after Ben had drifted off, and in his drunken state had overlooked him snoozing beneath the piano.

Ben called out, but there was no answer. The ground floor was abandoned. Above him, he heard the muffled beating of footsteps across the second-floor hallway. They clomped about and met at the top of the staircase. Four chambermaids came down singlefile carrying baskets filled with clothing and fancy feathered headwear. One of the women was holding a cut-glass perfume sprayer and misting herself behind the ears. As she sped through the dining room, she lifted a candelabrum from one of the tables and stuck it impulsively into her basket as if she were shopping at the grocery and crockery.

After the maids disappeared into the foyer and out the front door, Ben stepped off the stage and splashed across the flooded dining room, navigating around the red, white, and blue tables to the big windows. It was raining hard, and the lake was barely visible through the fogged glass. Shadowy rows of driftwood and debris moved across the white caps, and at the crest of the dam, a

266

mound of dead wood, brush, and small trees was piled up at the fish screen. The reservoir was full, and scheming a way out.

When Ben pulled open the patio door, the pooled water rushed past his feet and followed him out onto the deck. He stood under the small awning and saw the lake had found its way up the shoreline, uprooting the wooden pillars of the boardwalk. Except for a small section near the boathouse, the plank walkway where valley gazers and young lovers once strolled had been washed away. With the boardwalk gone, and the sloped earth alongside the Clubhouse sloughing off into the lake, there was now a twenty foot drop from the patio deck to the newly-cut shoreline. The storm raged all around him, the wind and the water peeling the valley apart. He thought about what Clem had said, and what everyone else had feared. Now he was watching it happen.

Ben left the cover of the awning and let the rain descend upon him. He stroked his hair, and the cool water ran down the back of his neck and under his shirt. He scanned the length of the bridge, but there was no sign of his father, only a group of laborers hacking at the center of the dam with pickaxes. He waved his arms high over his head and shouted to the men at the dam.

A tall man in heavy brown overalls set down his axe, brought a hand to his forehead in salute, and looked up toward the Clubhouse. After a moment, he ran his sleeve across his brow, grabbed his axe, and continued swinging it into the rock. With no way to get down from the deck, Ben retreated to the shelter of the Clubhouse.

The gas lamps and the chandeliers had not been lit that morning, and the faint light filtering through the hazed windows gave little clarity to the darkened room. It was very clear, however, that the entire ground floor of the Clubhouse had taken in over two feet of water, and that the ritzy River Fork bragging-hall was now nothing more than a decorative wading pool with pots, pans, dinner plates, and toppled furniture floating around it like flotsam and jetsam. Ben looked at all the banners, flags, and patriotic streamers that would unfortunately go unappreciated this year and thought how strange, so many people had hoped to get into this place, and now he was so desperately trying to get out.

A loud thump came from the front porch, and Ben slogged through the slackwater into to the foyer. Something large and heavy was blocking the front door. He lowered his shoulder and shoved, but it wouldn't budge. His pushing and shoving soon turned to fist-pounding and calls for help, shouting until his throat was sore. He stepped back, raised a foot, and set it next to the brass handle. The floor was slippery, and he didn't have enough strength to kick open the door. He pounded and shouted and rammed it again with his shoulder, and finally gave up.

With big steps, he made his way into the kitchen. Pots, pans, vegetables, even Jean Pierre's famous escargots were swimming between the legs of the work table. On the wall next to the stove, Ben found the source of the flooding. A hole the size of a stock pot was letting in a constant flow that had knocked over the corner table, spilling the flour, sugar, and vinegar, and turning the stagnant water into a soupy paste that smelled of pickles.

Ben labored through the sludge into the utility room and was overcome by the foul smell of urine and feces. The flush toilet was gurgling from deep inside the pipes and churning up a mess of dismembered sewer rats and soggy brown excrement that spilled over the rim of the bowl and floated around the room in coagulated lumps. He took two steps toward the back door and the overwhelming stench spun him around. The taste of a greasy ham hock came up through his throat, and he spat a chunk of half-digested pork fat into the cesspool and fled the room.

Back in the dining room, he lifted his head and filled his lungs with fresh air, and noticed the long, thick streamers of colored canvas still hanging from the chandeliers. He searched for a melody, something to comfort him inside the safety of the Clubhouse, but the only tune that came to him was Blind Tom's Thunder Storm. The drop to the shoreline wasn't that far, he thought, and a few strands of canvas tied together would give him plenty of length.

He told himself he should stay in the Clubhouse. It was safe on the hill. But what about his father? They were supposed to meet at the dam. What if his father was caught in the storm? What if the dam didn't hold?

Ben made his way to the stage. He climbed atop the Steinway and untied three canvas strands from the chandelier and went outside to the patio deck.

It was raining hard, and Ben wasted no time tying the streamers together for a makeshift rope. He shouted at the men on the dam, but as before, his scratchy calls went unanswered. Praying for a break in the storm, he tied one end of the rope to the patio door and dropped the other over the deck. The rain fell harder, and the wind blew stronger, as if the elements had no intention of making his escape any easier. Below, the black water sloshed over the splintered boards of the broken boardwalk, lapping up at the frayed ends of the canvas rope, as if daring him to climb down.

He sat at the edge of the deck and swung his feet over the side, dangling them above the swirling water. With a deep breath, he grabbed hold of the rope and dropped over the edge, his clothes sticking to his skin like a heavy moss, and the weight of his waterlogged shoes pulling hard as if someone were hanging from his feet. He reached the first splice in the rope, and a spray of icy pellets hit the side of his face like frozen buckshot. A gust of wind spun him round and he started to sway. Suddenly, a wave crashed beneath him and jarred loose one of the thin support pillars. The deck dropped, and Ben with it, and the canvas strands began to tear apart. He wrapped himself around the rope and held on.

The patio deck was collapsing, the canvas rope weakening. He couldn't risk climbing down, and the drop was too far to let go. He stretched his foot to the closest rigid pillar and pushed and pulled himself back onto the deck. He rolled onto his back and heard a loud crash from the front of the Clubhouse.

The dining room was filling quickly, and the weight of the water slammed the patio door shut behind him. He trudged in waist-high water to the piano and looked into the foyer. An evergreen had smashed through the front door. The tapered peak was wedged into the entranceway and releasing the pungent smell of hemlock into the air.

The freezing water was now up to Ben's chin, and his feet lost the floor. The Steinway lifted free of the stage and drifted up behind him. He treaded water, inching his way into the foyer as bare table-tops floated around him like giant, brown lily pads. He grabbed a thin branch and pulled himself toward the doorway until he could see the drive through an opening between a cluster of pine cones. A river was running past the front of the Clubhouse, and tree limbs and branches tumbled in the whitewater as it rushed over the cobblestone drive like rapids through a riverbed. Most of the water was feeding toward the lake, but a small finger had cut its way across the front porch and into the Clubhouse.

The ebony wing of the piano bumped Ben on the back, encouraging him to pull his way through the prickly branches. He was working his way toward the doorway when a limb under the surface snapped, and a surge of water rushed into the room.

He lost his grip on the branch, and the swell tossed him atop the Steinway, sending him to the far end of the foyer. Using his hands as oars, he paddled the piano like a rowboat back toward the front door. Behind him, he heard the sound of bending wood, the creaking and cracking of timber just before it splinters in two.

Ben spun around and faced the dining room as another swell passed under him and moved through the water like a serpent. The wave rippled across the dining room and struck hard against the big windows. The pressure was too great for the thin wooden frames and the fragile panes to handle, and after bowing out as far as they could, the windows exploded as if blasted by dynamite.

Ben covered his head, the crash of shattering glass pounding in his ears. The flooded room emptied, and a rush of murky, foamy, debris-cluttered water drained out of the dining room and cascaded over the sagging patio deck as if someone had pulled the bung from a giant beer barrel.

Fancy cushioned chairs, tea-tables, billiard sticks, even Mr. Addison's empty bottle of absinthe rushed passed him as he

270

grabbed hold of the piano. He was prepared to go over the edge, and he held his breath on the next swell. Like an ocean wave, the surge lifted the back end of the piano and sent Ben and his black raft racing toward the wide, gaping hole in the wall.

He had ridden the wave half-way through the room when an idea to avoid a deadly plunge struck him. He pushed himself onto his knees, and with the balance of a tightrope walker, stood up on the piano. He was getting close to the end of the room, and he threw up his arms and hooked onto one of the chandeliers. The Steinway floated on as the chandelier swung him out and back. He turned his head and watched the piano as it fell over the edge of the porch and into the lake.

Ben held on tight, dangling from the chandelier as the dining room emptied beneath him. When the torrent stopped, he tugged on one of the streamers, slid down, and dropped to the floor. A trickling brook flowed through the Clubhouse, but the river that had flooded the drive had changed course.

When Ben came into the foyer, he found the hemlock still blocking the doorway. Some of the smaller limbs had snapped in half, and he figured with enough strength, he could pull or twist them apart. He stripped away an obstruction of the thin branches, only to reveal another barrier of cones and needles behind it.

While searching around the sides of the doorway for another gap, he heard the chime of glass breaking, precise and purposeful as if by deliberate force. Someone was outside, trying to get in.

Ben pushed his face into the needles. "In here," he shouted, "I'm in here."

37

"Who's there?' Parke said, "Who's in there?"

"It's me, Ben."

Parke peeled away the branches to see Ben's face, but there wasn't enough room for anyone to pass through. "Ben," he said, "Go to the office and see if the speaking telegraph is still connected. Hurry."

Splattering footsteps trailed off toward the back of the Clubhouse. A minute passed, and Ben called back faintly, his voice hollow in a watery echo. "I think it's working."

"Good," Parke yelled, "Now pick up the bell and speak into the mouthpiece."

"How does it work?"

Parke stuck his head through the branches and yelled. "Lift the bell off the cradle and speak to them. Tell them the reservoir at River Fork is coming out. Tell them to run for their lives."

Parke backed away and studied the hemlock, the bristly peak blocking the doorway, the stripped trunk spanning the drive. He stared up beyond the Clubhouse to the tree line, where the utility pole still stood firm in the hardened cement. He pictured Ben's voice flowing through the wires, down to the people of the valley, and prayed they would all heed his words.

Then he saw a wave of water crashing through the trees, flowing around the utility pole, over the Hemlock, and flooding the drive. He went to steady his horse, and the mare reared up and yanked him off the porch into the mud. A sudden flash lit up the sky, and a deafening crack of thunder exploded in the air.

Parke sat up and saw the splintered utility pole tumbling end over end directly toward him. He scurried to the edge of the wall as the pole speared the end of the Hemlock, ripping the pine from the doorway and spinning it round in the drive like a propeller. After removing the evergreen, the utility pole continued down the hill toward the lake, the severed wire thrashing about like a cracking whip. Miraculously, the pole, the tree, and the rapids had missed Parke and his mare, and as he recovered, Ben came storming out the front of the Clubhouse.

Parke jumped up and ran to him. "Did you tell them? Did you tell them about the dam?"

Ben nodded.

"Thank you, Ben," said Parke. "Thank you." Parke hugged Ben and pulled him into the Clubhouse. Ben broke free and ran outside.

"What are you doing?" said Parke, "Where are you going?"

"I have to get to the Number Six Bridge."

Parke shook his head. "It's too dangerous. The dam is going to come out at any minute."

"My father is there," said Ben. "I have to go to him."

Parke saw the determination in Ben's eyes. "Take my horse," he said. "There's no way you'll make it on foot." He brought the mare to the edge of the porch and lifted Ben onto the saddle. Without a word, Ben raced off down the mountain.

Parke went inside and straight to the office. The flashflood that had washed away the utility pole had also removed the mud mound from the window. The telephone had been ripped through the wall, the chairs and the settee were gone, and the fancy artwork, including the self-indulging portrait of Crick and his string of black bass had been stripped from the wall. He opened the safe, and a stack of soggy papers spilled out onto the ground. He picked up the papers and carefully peeled them apart in hopes they could be salvaged as evidence of Crick's liability, but the ink had smeared and bled through all the pages. Every one of the documents was now illegible. On the floor beneath the desk, the stack of work orders signed by Crick floated in the water, washed out and totally destroyed. He picked up the papers and ripped them apart, cursing and sobbing.

He wandered through the debris, out the opened wall where the windows had been, and onto what was left of the patio deck. At the dam, the channel of water pouring through the center had cut away a good amount of rock and earth, and the void now descended all the way to the center of the embankment. There was very little debris left in the lake. Most of it had washed through the giant spout and into the river.

Parke stood alone at the edge of the sagging deck, and for a moment, the wind and the rain stopped. Even the rush of water over the dam froze in mid-air. Then a terrifying sound came from the mouth of the reservoir, the screech of rock grinding against rock, the roar of an entire mountain being moved by a Greater power.

The dam crumbled, and the lake pushed its way through, taking the entire earthen embankment with it. It tore apart the land on both sides and ripped open a gaping hole a thousand feet wide.

Parke trembled with fright as he watched the lake empty into the valley. "Don't take them all," he said. "Please Lord, don't take them all."

Then the pillars beneath the porch washed away, and the patio deck at the River Fork Clubhouse fell into the water.

38

Ben's horse gave out on a steep slope that shot straight down to the river about a hundred yards short of the Number Six Bridge. The mare exhaled a heavy mist from its nostrils, and its shaking legs sank deep into the mud. From the hillside, Ben saw the troupe train stretched across the tracks above the river. Flames spat from beneath the engine and clouds of steam shot through the funnel as it chugged toward the end of the bridge. On the near siding, coupled with six box cars, The Limited was backing up the hill toward the roundhouse.

Ben left the mare and side-stepped down the slope to the edge of the river. A mound of rock and debris, pieces of the dam, he figured, rushed by in the water below. The mangled clump passed under the bridge and raked against the shoreline, striking the rickety base of the coal tipple. The heavy bucket atop the tower swayed, listing out over the bridge until the entire tipple fell forward, crashing onto the tracks in front of the troupe train. Coal sprayed out of the bucket and onto the water like buckshot, and the split wood of the tower wedged under the engine's front wheels, bumping it off the track.

The engine jolted to a stop, and Ben saw a man jump out of the rear car, ushering the passengers onto the track and directing them toward the near side of the bridge. One of the passengers appeared to be injured, and the man dragged him along with one arm while shouting at the rest of the people to run. When the man reached the wreckage by the engine, Ben realized it was his father.

Ben ran down the hill shouting and waving his arms.

Percival looked up and acknowledged Ben with a nod, ignoring the joy of their reunion and simply yelling, "Run...run."

Ben scrambled to the bridge and found a solid patch of ground in front of the fallen tipple and the cage of wood separating him from his father. Women and children, some still clutching their grips and valises, filed through the crisscross of broken lumber, and Ben helped the engineer move them off the bridge. The lame man came through, and the engineer guided him up the hill with the others.

"Go," shouted Percival. "Get up the hill."

The engineer of the Limited had stopped his train on the siding and was helping the people up the hillside. Ben pounded toward them as the roar of grinding granite came from the dam. Following the eyes of everyone on the hill, he turned to see the entire face of the mountain moving forward, freeing itself from the crumbling earth around it.

The embankment was spitting the trees out by the roots, and a giant waterspout poured through the center, plucking off boulders and throwing them into the river like skipping stones.

The sky rumbled, and a downpour washed out the layer of mud under Ben's feet and he fell onto his hands and knees. He turned to the bridge and saw his father still climbing through the tangled wood.

As Percival stepped through an opening in the mess of lumber, a rail tie beneath him split and his leg shot through the bridge. His body jerked forward, and he braced himself on the rails. He struggled to free himself, but his leg was stuck.

Ben got up and slid down the hill to the siding.

The engineer of The Limited jumped into his cab and waved Ben off the tracks, sounding the warning whistle in short quick bursts as he raced down the valley.

After the last car passed, Ben ran to his father. "Hold on, pa."

Percival shouted back, his body slipping further through the bridge. "Forget about me," he yelled, "get back up the hill...now."

"I'm not leaving you," said Ben, stepping down to where the bridge met the bank.

Ben wrapped one arm around a wooden beam and reached for his father with the other. He turned himself sideways until he couldn't stretch any further. "Take my hand," he said, twisting his head toward the dam.

Until now, Ben had ignored the freezing wind and rain, but his whole body convulsed in a shiver that chilled him to the bone when he saw the lake curl over the dam like a tidal wave, crashing against the rocks and churning up a watery mess of black earth and clay headed straight toward him.

Ben felt his father grip his hand as he watched the reservoir pick up speed, fanning out along the hillsides and gathering mud and debris of all sorts. A strong, blue pocket of air traveled in front of the wave and blew over him, throwing a spray off the surface of the water and tearing away the loose planks of the shredded tipple. Across the river, the telegraph tower crumbled, and the operator's office dropped into the floodwater and floated away. Ben hunkered down as pieces of the bridge flew through the air in a cyclone of wind and water dismantling everything around him.

Ben felt as if he were in the midst of a hurricane. His feet sank deeper into the mud, and he grabbed hold of his father with both arms and pulled with all his might. Percival fell forward, and they dived onto the bank just as the floodwater rushed over the bridge.

They raced up the hill, the full force of the torrent now raging toward them. They stopped at the tree line and turned to face the river. The wall of water slammed into the troupe train and lifted it into the air as if it were a child's toy. Ben cringed as the train flipped over, and the rush of the river plucked the cars away, one by one, like beads on a string.

The water climbed up the bank, and soon it reached Percival and Ben at the trees. Men, women, and children were swimming near them, and when the water rose past their chins, Percival shouted at them to grab hold of the tree branches and the brush.

"Hold on as tight as you can, Ben," said Percival, "and let the water pass."

Ben nodded, watching a series of tree trunks sail by while the undercurrent tugged at his feet. A young boy floated by behind one of the logs, his swollen body bobbing face down in the water. The side of his head was crushed in, and one of his arms was twisted the wrong way. Ben looked through the dripping pine needles at his father. "Are we gonna die?"

"Just hold on, Ben. Hold on, and we'll ride it out together."

Suddenly one of the floating logs veered off course and struck the pine and shook Ben so hard he didn't realize he'd been thrown into the water until he heard his father screaming for him in the distance. He spun round and round as he floated away. Swells of black water blocked his view of the pines, and anyone at the tree line. "Pa," he shouted, drifting further into open water.

Ben let the current take him, and once again he heard his name, this time from somewhere downriver. He pushed his head as far as he could above the water, and a brief moment of bittersweet joy came over him. He hadn't lost his father. His father was in the water with him.

39

With a churning mass of rock and earth before it, the reservoir poured through the hole in the mountain and raced into the valley. It spilled into the Lower Stone River, overflowing the banks and fanning out wide on both sides. In deep channels, it climbed up the hillsides to the white pines and the sugar maples and ate away the soil beneath their roots until they fell over. Then the water tracked through the thick forest like a crafty hunter, and the deer and the wild turkeys were overcome by the flood and drowned. And the flood took the dead animals and the fallen trees and carried them along. And the trees that didn't fall made the water swell and rise, and the birds and the squirrels hiding in the branches were washed away. Thunder shook the sky, the wind blew in gusts, and rain fell in downpours as the flood traveled down the mountain, moving through the groves and the clearings and into the farmlands. And it drove the people from their homes, and carved deep gauges in the fields, flooding the soil in giant rivulets and uprooting the crops and the grass.

At the properties, a potato farmer and a miller had moved their families up the hill after the rising water flooded their farmhouses. The farmer was coming down to unlatch the corral gate and move the cattle to high ground when the flood broke through the trees and into the field. He left the livestock caged beside the barn and ran up the hill, and the flood rushed through the corral, drowning the cattle and the pigs and the chickens. The water lifted his work wagon off the ground and carried it into the miller's waterwheel, ramming it off its cradle and slamming it into a woodshed. The planks alongside the shed fell into the flood, and right behind it, the woodshed itself. The farmer slopped to the tree line where his and the miller's family stood shivering between the sodden pines. The flood washed over the properties, leveling the barn and farmhouses, and plowing through the lumber sheds and the cutting house, sweeping away the labor and livelihood that had lasted the two families more than four decades.

Past the farm and sawmill, the water broke through Hopper's dam at Portage creek and decimated two other acreages before falling off the hillside and onto the tracks in front of the factories. A group of laborers seeking cover from the rain scurried out from beneath the railcars like ants as the flood raced over the stocking rails. The water tore through the ballast and picked up the gondolas on finger-like peaks and flipped them over, spilling loads of coke and scrap iron onto the men and crushing them. Then the water rushed over the bodies and lifted one of the smokers off the tracks and shot it into the side of the rolling mill like a cannon ball.

Further downriver, the casters and wire pullers were busy working when the floodwater found its way inside the foundry and spread out across the factory floor. The cradles beneath the Bessemer hearths teetered as the flood rolled through, and one by one, the giant cauldrons tipped over. The men cried out as the molten metal poured over them, burning away their hair and clothes and peeling the flesh from their bones. A cloud of steam shot to the ceiling and filled the room, and the floodwater rose and drowned the rest of the men inside.

The water left the foundry and washed over a double flatbed loaded end to end with stacks of coiled razor-wire and continued on toward the center of River Fork. Even if the communication wires hadn't failed, and news of the reservoir coming out had made it to the town, no one would have been prepared for the destruction that was headed their way.

When the wall of water came, it was as if a warship had opened fire on the town with torpedoes of telegraph poles and tree trunks, and an artillery barrage of train cars, farm machinery, and water towers. The wave shelled the town, and the people screamed in horror, writhing helplessly in the water as they were thrown against the floating debris and captured by the flood. Black clouds pounded the townsfolk in bursts, and those not yet in the water didn't see the attack coming until it was too late. Once the flood hit Main Street, it spread out and absorbed every business and home in town.

Away from the river-channel, the water moved slowly through the streets. Spectators gawked from second and third-floor balconies. Just when it seemed trouble had passed them by, a boulder, or a wagon, or a train car rammed the side of the building, collapsing it like an accordion and dropping the unsuspecting onlookers into the water.

At the First Baptist Church on Cinder Street, Reverend Beale had gathered a dozen parishioners and moved their prayer circle from the sacristy to the rooftop. The group was holding hands around the steeple and praying when a mound of mud and silt, pushed from behind by the trunk of an enormous pine, swept over the roof and knocked the believers and the crucifix-crowned spire into the water.

The men and women slid off the roof and into a soggy clutter of debris. They floated in the icy water and were pulled by the current into the open river. Just ahead of them was a muddy knoll, and coming up rapidly from behind was a silver serpent, fifty feet long. The mesh of razor-wire closed in and wrapped itself around the group, ensnaring them like fish in a net, creeping up their legs and twisting around their arms like vines until they could no longer swim. The more they thrashed about, the further the sharpened barbs cut into their frozen skin. With legs tangled, and shredded flesh seeping blood, the followers from The First Baptist went under. They fought to free themselves from the twisted metal, and the murky brown water turned a deep, dark red. When they came to the knoll, their limp bodies rose to the surface and washed lifelessly onto the shore.

The people late in retreating to higher ground ran for their lives, but the mighty mountain of water eventually overcame them and pulled them in with the soggy rubbish. The ones struck by logs, trees, or metal beams were killed instantly. Others, mostly children and the elderly were simply consumed by the raging water and drowned.

The fortunate ones, who had found themselves drifting in open water, latched on to passing logs or tree branches and rode the navigable current to the banks or to the small islands poking up between the bends in the river. When they came out of the water, they paced aimlessly, dazed, naked, shivering.

Owen Ahl, the day laborer, knew he and his family wouldn't be parading to the dam that morning, but he let his two girls put on their Decoration Day dresses just the same. The family had eaten supper and was watching the flood from a second floor window when a tumbling pine crashed through their dining room and ripped their home apart. Owen had been thrown next to the remnants of a wagon bed and out of the reach of the river, but his wife and twins had been pulled in.

After searching the banks with no success, he grabbed a section of the splintered wagon bed, and with the flat planks pressed tight against his belly, he launched himself into the river, calling out for his wife and daughters as he rode the current downstream.

At the end of town, the movement of the water stopped. A mass of train cars, shredded steel, and split houses was piled up and clogging the single-arch viaduct at Smith's Crossing. The river suddenly made an about face, and the backwash overturned Owen's raft and dragged him under. Caught in a whirlpool, he struggled for air. As he went down, for what he thought would be the last time, a strong hand grabbed him by the collar and pulled his head above water. Owen gasped and looked gratefully into the eyes of Bennett Marsh.

40

Though the flood had bombarded the viaduct with a great deal of ammunition, the first attack wasn't strong enough to take out the heavy masonry bridge at Smith's Crossing. The water had literally hit a brick wall. Ben steered Owen to the bridge and Percival pulled him up. Ben took his father's hand and fished for something to stand on. It wasn't until after his father had hoisted him onto the flat surface of an overturned boxcar that he realized the soggy stepping stone was a dead body.

The boxcar sat angled against the bridge among the pile of twisted metal, trees, and brush, the low end underwater, the high end sloping upward toward the bank, making a perfect ramp for a run-and-jump to shore.

Ben sat slumped over with arms on knees, wiping the mud from his face and spitting out bits of silt and rock while Owen paced the length of the boxcar, searching the slackwater for his wife and children. More people floated to the bridge, and on the far side, two half-naked men scampered out of the water and crawled onto the broken stones like sewer rats. Owen staggered back and forth for several minutes, studying the people as they came onto the bridge, but there was no sign of his family.

"Maybe they've already passed," said Ben.

"You think so?" said Owen. "You think they're all right?"

"The current slows down at the oxbow," Percival said. "Then it's a straight shot to Johnstown. If they've made it past here, they'll be all right. We'll head down by land and meet them at the Stone Bridge."

Percival's words calmed Owen, and for the next few minutes the mood at the bridge turned to one of relief.

The reprieve was short lived when Ben grabbed Percival by the arm and pointed upriver. "It's comin' back," he said, tracing the wave as it raced toward the viaduct moving faster and stronger than before, armed with more water and a more abundant collection of munitions.

Percival pulled Owen and Ben to the low end of the boxcar. "Get a good run at it," he said, "Then push off the edge and jump for the bank."

Percival went first, making it onto the shore with an exceptional leap. Ben followed with a run and a push off the edge of the boxcar, floating through the air and landing on all fours like a flying squirrel. When he got to his feet, he looked upriver at the oncoming wave. The surge was flattening the landscape like a steamroller, the draft of air in front knocking down people and objects even before the water had hit them.

In an awkward trot, Owen hobbled to the end of the boxcar. He prepared to make the jump and the viaduct jolted, pulling the boxcar away from the shore. The movement threw Owen off balance and his feet slipped out from under him. He landed hard on his side, and Ben heard the crack of bone against metal. Owen hung over the boxcar's steel edge, his face pressed flat against the wooden slats, the undercurrent pulling at his feet and dragging him into the water.

Ben saw the tidal wave closing in. "Hold on, Owen," he shouted, preparing to leap back to the boxcar. He crunched down, ready to start a sprint, and a strong hand grabbed him by the shoulder and moved him aside.

With the youthfulness of a teenager, Clem ran to the eroding lip of the bank and jumped, clearing the ten foot gap and landing on the floating boxcar. Without a word, he lifted Owen from the water and dragged him to the far end. Then, with one hand on

Owen's collar, the other hooked onto the seat of his pants, he ran Owen down the length of the boxcar, and with a strength greater than any man Ben had ever seen, threw Owen into the air and onto the shore. The boxcar drifted away, and Clem waved his arms toward the hillside. "Get to the hill," he said, "Get to the hill."

The utility pole split by lighting at the Clubhouse tumbled end over end at the front of the wave. Ben shouted at Clem to move out of the way, but Clem stood motionless, facing the wave and the pole with eyes closed and arms outstretched. Ben ran for the river, but Percival grabbed hold of his arm and dragged him up the hillside. Ben pulled away and looked back just as the top of the pole tilted up and struck Clem flat against his arms and body. Clem flopped back into the water and drifted down the river and out of sight.

Like the spade of an immense plow, the debris-cluttered water washed over the channel and cut its way through the viaduct. The front of the flood was tilling the soil, preparing it for the free flowing water behind to come along and wash the valley away.

Percival left Owen at the tree line and came down, shaking Ben out of a frozen daze. Ben stumbled up the hill, and the earth beneath his feet suddenly vanished. He fell into the water, pulling his father in with him. The tug of the current rushed them downriver as Owen hugged a small pine at the tree line and watched helplessly.

Percival and Ben were riding the current when a wide, low-pitched rooftop floated by crowded with over twenty survivors. They swam to the edge where two men pulled them onto the wood-shingled raft.

The grave situation made introductions irrelevant, and the half-naked men and women, too frightened to be embarrassed, sat hugging themselves as the swirling water spun the shake roof round in circles. Dizzy and disoriented, some of the passengers gagged into cupped hands, others vomited into their laps.

At the oxbow, the rushing river subsided, and the moans of the dying echoing through the canyon faded away. The roof stopped spinning and righted itself with the slower moving current. Still fully clothed, except for his shoes, Ben copied his father, pushing himself up the sloping roof and gazing at the passing countryside with a strange feeling of peacefulness, almost as if he were sailing on a steamboat down the Mississippi.

The strangers held each other, huddled at the peak of the roof. The sick ones remained silent while the others prayed quietly to themselves and sobbed. Ben shuddered, knowing the river would soon turn violent again when they came to the rapids at Mineral Point. He drew his knees to his chest, hung his head, and cried.

Percival put his arm around Ben and leaned in. "Tell me about that music school."

Ben rolled his head against his knees, whimpering softly, almost laughing. "It doesn't matter now, pa," he said, sniffling. "I ain't goin'. No use in talking about it."

"Don't be saying that," said Percival. "You were right. Your place ain't in this town."

"Pa," said Ben, "there ain't no town no more. No town, no home, no money, no train ticket, no music, nothin'."

"Don't give up hope, Ben. We're gonna get out of this, you'll see. And when we do, I'm gonna put things in order, put us back on our feet." He bent in and looked Ben straight in the eye. "Whatever it takes, we're gonna make it, together, you hear me."

Ben drew a palm across his face and wiped away the water and looked up into the grey sky. A frayed strand of lightning flashed over the mountains, scattering in all directions and trailing off into the distance, and for the first time in his life, he believed in his father, trusted him. He swung his head around and smiled. "It's gonna be the finest school in the country," he said, "maybe even the world."

Crackling thunder rolled over the hills, and Percival pulled Ben close. "Tell me more," he said, "I want to know."

Ben felt the cool rain wash over him. He had seen the sincerity in his father's eyes, and in a shivering stutter, he went on about the academy, the enrollment letter, the music pin, the dinner at the Clubhouse, Mr. Damrosch, and the perfect Steinway. He shared his trip to the saloon, and the time he'd spent with Blind Tom. He even described one of his favorite Beethoven sonatas, humming a few bars of the third movement for effect.

The roof spun around in a smooth circle and floated through the last curve in the oxbow.

"And this is what you truly want?" said Percival.

Ben nodded. "More than anything."

Percival sighed. "Then I say you do it. Nothing would make me prouder. And I'm sure your mother would be proud too."

Ben suddenly remembered the only thing he still carried with him. He reached into his hip pocket and took out the photograph of his mother, now pasted together in a small square and washed out from the water. He unfolded it and gave it to his father and it melted away in Percival's hands.

"I should have given it to you sooner," Ben said. "I'm sorry."

Percival tapped at the center of his chest. "A picture will never replace what's in here."

The roof-raft moved out of the oxbow and headed toward Mineral Point, running through a tapered pocket in the canyon shadowed by sloping hills on either side. A half mile ahead, whitewater roared from the mouth of the rapids, and the roof picked up speed. Two men and an elderly woman stood up, and a sudden drop jostled the raft and threw them into the water. Their bodies raced toward the constriction in the canyon where the river narrowed to a small chute and flushed out wide on the other side.

Screams from injured townsfolk along the banks grew louder as the roof-raft passed the lone street of the small milling town. Most of the buildings had been washed away, and crowds of survivors were sitting amidst the piles of bricks and broken wood, and atop the embankments alongside the river.

There was a commotion up ahead at a notch in the bank, and Ben saw a throng of people standing on a knoll pointing upriver. A young girl was riding the current atop a mud-soaked mattress. She was no more than eight years old, and though her clothes were smeared with mud, Ben saw the outline of a red, white, and blue dress. He got up to his knees. "Look, pa," he shouted, "One of Owen's girls."

Ben looked back at the men on the knoll holding ropes and poles at the ready. "They're going to fish her out," he said, pointing to the men waiting to capture the girl as she drifted by.

The mattress was drifting away from shore, and Ben realized the girl would be too far away for the men to grab her when she passed the knoll. She flopped about as her raft dropped over the rocks between the rubbish. Ben crawled to the back of the roof and stood, ready to push off into the water.

"No," shouted Percival. "Let her go. You'll be drowned too."

Percival got to his feet, but something big hit the roof and knocked him down. The roof pitched upward, and Ben leaped into the water.

The girl rolled off the mattress and splashed toward him.

Ben's head dipped under. He came up, then went under again. He came up again, but this time, he'd lost sight of the girl.

Owen's girl screamed, "Help...help."

Ben listened for the girl's screams and swam toward the sound of her voice. The muddy mattress floated by, then the girl behind it. Ben grabbed her about the waist and flipped around to face the knoll. Owen's girl clutched his throat, almost choking him. He searched over the rolling waves, but the roof-raft had drifted out of sight. His only direction to safety was the notch at the bank.

The knoll was only a short distance away, and the men shouted at him to throw the girl. Ben churned his legs, pedaling through the water until he found footing in a small eddy, and some of the men threw in their ropes and held out their poles. Still, he couldn't reach them without letting go of the girl.

Exhausted, he gathered his last bit of strength, peeled the girl from his neck, and with a deep bend in the knees, threw her into the arms of one of the men. Ben caught a quick glimpse of her as she was carried to safety, and the sound of rolling thunder snapped his head upriver.

A giant, disfigured barrel, black as night, that seemed to span the breadth of the channel was spinning through the water straight toward him like a runaway paddlewheel. The solid iron wheels threw up a wave of whitewater after each whirling revolution until the riveted drum was no more than ten feet away. Ben froze, his eyes clenched in a tight squint and locked on the engine. It spun over once more, clipping a half-submerged boulder and launching into the air. The side of the smokebox was right in front of Ben's face. He stared at the marking as if he were holding a chalkboard at arm's length. It read, "No. 8".

41

Ben tried to duck, dive away, shield his face in defense, but every muscle in his body tensed and tightened, and he was unable to move. The air went strangely still, and the engine stopped spinning and hovered above the water as a shadowy blur. The constant hiss of the rain off the water slowed to a sluggish beat, and the jumble of shrieking voices changed to separate, low-pitched moans and calls for help. Ben stood stiff, chest-high in the water, waiting, staring at the blurred image of the engine.

Suddenly the muffled drone resonating in his ears grew to a booming shrill, and a powerful gust blew over him. The rain pounded, the moans turned to screams, and the engine came into focus and raced forward. Ben took a deep breath, curled into a ball, and dropped underwater.

The engine whooshed overhead and landed with a concussion that shook the ground and lifted the water into an exploding upsurge. Ben rose with the swell and was launched into the air, hitting the water with a hard splash and instantly smothered by the thick, floating debris of foliage, fur, and flesh. The current swirled and pulled him under and he sank fast, tumbling end over end until he landed on his back with a thud, forcing the last bit of air from his lungs. He looked up to the surface and the cloudy water rushed into his eyes, filling them with the sting of sand and silt. He stifled a breath and pushed off the bottom and his body jerked back. He reached down to find his leg lodged between a pair of boulders, the jagged edges digging deep into his foot and ankle. No air, a thumping pressure building inside his head, writhing in pain, he panicked and swallowed a gulp of chalky siltwater. The tiny rocks scraped the back of his throat as he struggled for the surface, and a biting pain shot through his leg. He grabbed his leg with both hands and pulled, but the rocks collapsed around his leg, trapping him below the knee.

He forced open his eyes and through the murky water saw a blurred light. He stretched his arm toward it as a strange heat began to warm him from the inside out, spreading from his chest, through his legs to his toes, through his arms to his fingertips, until his whole body tingled with a prickling pulse. He closed his eyes to the darkness and drifted away into a calm serenity, ready to accept his watery grave. The blackness inside his head turned brilliant white. He thought of his life, the things he'd done, the things he'd left undone. The melodies of every song he'd ever played glided over a green meadow and joined together as if all the days of his life had been reduced to this second in time. He floated, suspended in the water, and waited.

Then the water began to flow around him, under his clothes, into his mouth, nose, and eyes, and his body grew cold again. He felt a strong pressure grip his hand, tugging and pulling and stretching him taut. With a quick jolt, his ankle popped, and a sharp cracking sound traveled through the water in a hollow echo. His foot wriggled between the stones and he felt the flesh peeling off his leg. Pain set time in motion, and now he was moving free of the stones and being pulled from the water.

His first breath was short, no more than a hurried reflex, drawing in only enough air to cough and expel the taste of the river. His second breath was long and deep, filling his lungs until he gagged and spat out a mouthful of lake water. On the bank, he coughed violently and vomited over and over again. Spitting and panting and hacking up loose gravel from the back of his throat, he sucked in big gasps of air until his body stopped shaking and his breathing returned to normal. He scraped away the blinding silt and mud from his eyes, wiped his face with the underside of his shirt and rolled onto his side, preparing to give thanks to both of his Saviors, first with a glorious, then a grateful, "hallelujah." He looked up the bank, along the shore, back at the river. There was no one there. The knoll where the men had stood with their ropes and poles was gone and so was the roof-raft. Further downriver, the black engine spun over one last time and disappeared.

Ben collapsed onto his back. The mud was soft and cool, and he wanted to stay there and rest, even sleep. His body had ached steadily since he was pulled from the river, and slowly the tense pressure that stiffened his muscles released and he regained his strength. With a push from his good leg, he staggered up the hill to the tree line, popping his ears and squeezing his eyes shut to flush out the brackish siltwater.

He found a path and hobbled over the sodden pine needles, stopping to urinate at a low tree branch still attached to its trunk by a few strands of soggy bark. He looked down at his leg. The rainwater flowed clear and clean through the holes in his pants and came out over his swollen ankle tinted bright red and clotted with folded chunks of loose skin. He cupped his hands and caught some of rain as it fell through the trees. Even after swallowing mouthfuls of lake water, his body ached with thirst.

He limped on, his injured leg too weak to bear his weight, and came to a ridge overlooking Johnstown with a bird's eye view of the constriction in the river. Below, the speckled stones jutted from the rapids like gravestones, churning up froths of dirty yellow foam like the spit of a rabid dog. He peered over the crags at the splintered pieces of the roof-raft rapping between the rocks.

Past the chute, the river fanned out again, and he found what was left of the shake roof floating toward the Stone Bridge, its lone passenger balanced triumphantly at the center. His heart pounded as he called to his father, but his weak, abbreviated cries were lost amidst the screams of the injured on the banks, and the shouts of those attending to them, and soon the roof-raft and his father drifted out of sight.

Ben's leg was throbbing, his foot bleeding heavily, but the excitement flowing through him numbed the pain. He slid down the hill and made his way toward Johnstown favoring his injured leg as best he could and still keep a good pace.

Even within the path of the flood, there were parts of the landscape left untouched, where the water had channeled around a low bluff or a row of pines and carved out small escarpments. Ben followed a path atop a narrow plateau held together by thick brush and trees.

He trudged on, and the sky grew dark, pale, and grey, shadowing the narrow path littered with forest animals, dead and dying. Midday turned to dusk, and soon the plateau fell off into the flooding and he came upon the center of Johnstown and what was left of the brick-laid, three-storied Main Street. Except for a group of stone buildings at the far end, every structure along the riverfront lay toppled, reduced to a haphazard mixture of crumbled mortar, tangled steel, and splintered lumber.

Ben looked back toward Mineral Point, tracing the direction the roof-raft was headed, and set off for the Stone Bridge still standing defiantly at the end of the valley. When a clear path took him too far off course, he climbed atop the rubble and pulled himself along until he found a solid stretch of earth closer to the river. Screams of profane agony rang through the streets, now all visible since there were no buildings rising up between them. Disfigured mounds of hair and legs and arms lay half-buried in the rubble, and Ben had to remind himself they were people. Flattened horses, some still attached to their shredded wagons, gasped through bloody nostrils and stared up with glossy eyes, as if wishing for a shotgun to end their misery.

At the bridge, the valley leveled out. Gravity was no longer the racing river's ally. The flood, like a train with an empty engine furnace, had run out of steam. The destruction was over. People who had survived the ride down the mountain were milling about the wreckage at the bridge, hugging each other and raising their hands toward the heavens, giving gratitude to God.

Ben limped past the townsfolk sifting through rubbish searching for their possessions and loved ones. A heap of lumber capped with a flat plank held the remnants of a telegraph tower, and Ben climbed up. Darkness was settling upon the valley, but a narrow streak of sunlight broke through the clouds, and the surface of the water glistened with a shimmering, multicolored iridescence.

From his roost atop the fallen tower, Ben scanned the bridge and saw the roof-raft lapping against the solid stones. Many people were staggering back and forth across the bridge, and he shouted, hoping one of them was his father.

A tall man stepped through the crowd and onto an overturned tank car. He paced the length of the car along the rim, bending over at the waist and studying the slackwater. Slowly, the man rose and lifted his head.

Relief and joy overpowered the pain in Ben's foot and leg. "Pa, pa," he shouted, waving his arms in big circles. He stumbled off the broken tower, half-running to the bridge, "Over here."

As Ben came closer, he saw the panic that surrounded the bridge, a hysterical madness, mobs of people running, staggering, collapsing. Shrill screams swallowed Ben's calls, and he realized his father had not heard him.

Percival turned away, his gaze fixed on a group of survivors who had just washed onto the bridge in front of the tank car. He rushed to them and climbed down and dropped into the water.

Ben lost his father amidst a frenzy of flailing arms splashing wildly and reaching out for rescue. Behind the struggle, a gaping hole in the side of the tank car was emptying gallon after gallon of diesel fuel into the water, and on the far side of the bridge, two more tankers had sprung leaks, dumping thick glops of oil from their bellies.

A dark cloud rolled over the mountain, blocking the last bit of daylight and hovering solid over the bridge until the sun dipped behind the horizon. Night fell, and the air turned moist and frigid.

As Ben looked out over the bridge, a somber cortege of men carrying victims by the hands and feet passed before him headed toward a small church still standing near the end of town. Out of nowhere, a swarm of people, robbed of their clothing by the flood, scurried out of the rubble and descended upon the dead like vultures and ripped the coats and clothes from their backs. They covered themselves and hurried away, and the men picked up the naked bodies and marched on toward the church.

Ben shivered, only in part from the drop in temperature, and moved closer to the bridge. His father had left the people at the tank car and was racing to the opposite side of the river. Ben called out again, but Percival had moved out of ear shot and disappeared into the dark.

Ben went to the water and waded out, ready to swim across when he was blinded by a sudden flash of light. The sky shook, and a powerful blast of thunder rattled his head. He opened his eyes to find the bridge consumed with fire, blazing in a bluish-yellow glow, the fingerlike flames casting off bits of splintered timber, hair and flesh still aflame, and releasing an intense heat that scorched his face.

Bodies dripped from the burning bridge like candle wax, igniting the oily surface of the water. Wiry screams sounded across the river, and the thrashing of arms and legs started a movement of small waves that carried the burning oil to the banks and set fire to the debris along the shoreline.

Ben cried out, calling his father by name, praying for his safety as he hurried out of the water. He splashed along the bank, screaming for his father while a group of men picked away at the base of the bridge attempting to free a woman pinned under the wreckage. A large stone had crushed her from the waist down, and one of the men hollered for a hacksaw and began sawing off the woman's leg.

Ben came on to the abutment at the end of the bridge and peered into the flames, batting the falling cinders from his face. Behind a wall of black smoke he saw a man emerge from the fire. Ben broke into tears and stumbled forward toward the singed and soot covered Percival. He smiled broadly as his father gripped him hard and lifted him up, squeezing into him the love he'd feared lost.

"Thank God you're all right," said Percival, setting Ben down and running his hands over Ben's head.

"I'm all right," said Ben.

Father and son fled the apocalypse at the Stone Bridge and hobbled up the hill to the church. Men, women and children lay dead and dying all around them, and as much as Ben and Percival would have wanted, they did not stop to help. Shelter and rest were the only things on their mind, and the church up the hill was the only place they knew of to find it.

Spared from the flood's wrath was the white, wooden church on Olive Street. The chapel was built in-the-round, capped with a sloped roof of rectangular beams and anointed at the top with a hammered-iron crucifix. Percival and Ben staggered up the stairs and onto the porch.

A man in a black cassock came rushing out the open door. He held a small lantern in one hand and introduced himself as Father Lichtenberg. "Come in...come in," he said, guiding them into the chapel with his free hand.

The reverend led Ben and Percival through the candlelit nave to an empty spot on the floor. He sat them against the wall and hurried off, returning with a handful of torn cloth strips and a small bowl of water. He held up the bandages, "For your leg," he said. "Start at the ankle and wrap up to the knee. Use the water to wash only; it's not safe to drink. After you've had a rest, you need to get yourselves up the road. We've arranged a temporary hospital at the library." He glanced around the room, at the lumpy mounds stacked on the pews and covered with white sheets. "This place is not for you."

A group of men came in to the chapel, each one dragging a body behind him. Father Lichtenberg went to the door and showed them to an open area at the back of the room.

Ben shuddered, trapped inside the makeshift morgue. Still, the sanctuary was the warmest, most pleasant place he'd been all day. He lay back, and Percival wrapped the cloth bandages around his leg. "Do we really have to leave, pa?"

Percival offered Ben a comforting smile. "We'll be all right here for the night," he said, helping Ben to a seated pose. "I don't believe the good Father will throw us out. We'll get some rest, and head off for that library in the morning."

Percival gave Ben a one-armed hug and pushed himself against the wall. He shut his eyes, folded his arms neatly against his chest, and slept.

Ben's foot burned with a strange heat, what he imagined it might have felt like had it been dipped in the molten metal of a foundry hearth. Somehow, he'd managed to race along the river without so much as a twinge, but in the shelter of the church, the pain crept up out of nowhere. He rubbed his leg above the ankle and lay down next to his father and stared up at the dimly lit rafters. He was hungry and thirsty, but there was no food or water; he was tired, but he could not sleep. His thoughts raced through the day's events, trying to make sense of it all. Why did this happen, the devastation, the ruin, the suffering? Why had so many died, and why had he survived? Like the crackling fire raging out of control at the bridge, Ben's mind burned with questions. He hoped that in this holy place, God would reveal his purpose for unleashing such destruction upon the valley. He prayed in the dark and listened, but no answers came. He wondered if they ever would.

42

The shoes Father Lichtenberg had given him were too small, and Ben's foot throbbed as he walked past the pews lined up against the wall of the chapel. Gas lamps under stained-glass windows illuminated mosaics of the apostles who looked down upon the lumpy shrouds as if they were administering the last rites to the bodies underneath. Inside the church, the musky air was hot and humid, perfect conditions for the rapid decay of human flesh. Blowflies swarmed in little black clouds over the rotting corpses, and the smell of death filled the room.

Men with handkerchiefs covering their mouths and noses kept filing into the church with more bodies, and when the thin legs of the benches could support no more, they stacked the dead on the floor. Ben wondered if his friend Tom was one of them. He searched the pews and the puzzle of bodies lying motionless under the blankets, lifting back the sheets only to find swollen limbs of pale white skin.

"Have they brought in any Negros?"

The reverend shook his head. "No, but they may have put some out back."

Ben walked through the small sacristy and out the back door. Piled up next to a work shed were a dozen Negros, splayed and stacked one on top of the other like gunny sacks. Clothing draped from the bodies in torn rags, uncovering a tangle of engorged limbs that meshed into a communal bruising of deep purples and greys. Ben turned away and took two deeps breaths. He returned his gaze to the pile and studied the faces, black and bloated, eyeballs bulging and glassed over in a milky haze like fish eyes, opened wide and staring, but none of the corpses resembled his heavy-set friend. He continued around the chapel to the front porch, his ankle throbbing, the sole of his foot stinging in sharp pricks as if he were stepping on shattered glass.

He found his father on the porch stairs and sat next to him. The air was crisp and cold, the complete opposite of the muggy chapel. There was no rain, no wind, save an arid breeze stirred up by the fires at the bridge. The once rising buildings now lay bent and broken, strewn about in random, shapeless mounds. From the church porch, Johnstown resembled more a battlefield than a bustling city, with the sky streaked in a reddish-brown glow from timber and diesel smoke, and the earth littered with the casualties of the flood.

The water had strangely subsided, leaving the streets the consistency of a beef stew left simmering too long on the stove. Townspeople wandered through the muddy streets, some moving bodies to the roads for the ambulance wagons to reach them, others removing debris from the rails and propping up the broken tracks with rudimentary cribs. Still others simply roamed about the destruction, sobbing, crying out for their family and friends.

Ben took in the devastation. "How long until help arrives?"

"It's an awful mess," Percival said. "At least two or three days, maybe sooner if they've already sent someone."

"We have," said Father Lichtenberg, coming out onto the porch. "He left early this morning for Somerset. If all goes well, we should have a relief train here with medicine and supplies, food and fresh water by sundown. And the two of you should be headin' to the library." He pointed at Ben's leg, "You need to get that looked at right away, son."

Ben looked at his foot. His borrowed shoe was soaked with blood, his ankle swollen up over the laces and bruised a deep black and blue. He grabbed at his shin, and a sharp sting shot up through his leg and into his hip.

"Another wagon will be by shortly," said Father Lichtenberg, "It'll take you up to the library."

Father Lichtenberg went inside, and Ben and Percival waited on the porch for the wagon. Except for the sound of dogs howling in the distance, there was a strange quiet in the air, no humming or clanking from the factories, no blasting of train horns, just a confused silence as the people of the valley struggled to put what life they had left back together.

Ben's clothes were still damp, even after twelve hours out of the water, and the cold air cut through him and bit at his ears and fingers. He copied his father, rubbing his palms together and huffing into cupped hands to warm his face. After an hour of watching body after body being hauled into the church, he heard the sound of hooves thumping up the muddy road.

A man in dry clothes stopped a flatbed wagon in front of the church. A lone passenger lay unmoving in the bed, set atop a stretcher of canvas and covered with a wrinkled brown tarpaulin. Father Lichtenberg came out to help the driver, motioning first to Percival and Ben. "I need to get these two to the library," he told the driver.

The driver nodded. "But if I fill up along the way," he said, "those who can, will have to walk."

"That'll be fine," said Ben, "We're awfully grateful for the lift."

Percival and Ben made their way to the wagon, and Father Lichtenberg and the driver pulled the unfortunate from bed. As they slid the body off the wagon, a limp arm fell out from under the tarp. A frayed leather band encircled the dead man's wrist, the name 'Jennie' burned into it along the side.

Ben stumbled and fell against the wagon wheel.

Percival grabbed him by the arm.

Ben watched the men take Doc's body into the church. "That was my friend, pa," he said, "My best friend."

Ben sobbed on his father's shoulder and asked him why his friend had to die. Percival held him tight, consoling him with gentle strokes up and down his back. "I don't know, Ben," he said, "I don't know. And I don't believe there's a soul down here that does."

Ben climbed into the wagon, his father's arms still wrapped around him, and the driver pulled away from the church. They bounced along the pitted road to the library, and Ben grew angry. Angry at the rain for flooding the lake, angry at the dam for not holding it back, angry at Tom for leaving, angry at Clem and Doc for dying, and angry at himself, for surviving.

Up ahead, the driver stopped at a fallen telegraph pole and jumped off. He ran to a group of men lifting the crossbar end off the ground. They dragged an injured man out from under the pole and carried him to the back of the wagon and dropped him next to Ben. The injured man lay still, moaning, holding his chest, blood oozing through his coat and over his fingers. Not a minute later, the driver stopped again, and he and another group of men uncovered a woman pinned beneath a drowned horse. She was gasping for air and screaming. The men carried her to the wagon and set her in the bed and leaned her against the sideboard. After a half-mile, she stopped whimpering and slumped over into her lap. The library was just up ahead, but the woman was already dead.

When the ambulance wagon reached the brick building on Locust Street, Ben could see the people coming down from the hills in droves, lugging clothing, water jugs, and other supplies into the makeshift hospital. The wagon stopped next to a toppled replica of the Liberty Bell, and Ben and the rest of the wounded were hurried inside under the direction of a short, stout woman officially dressed in army blue.

The woman directed the injured to different areas of the room, commanding with an authority and a confidence usually saved for the battlefield. She took the most critical to a row of toppled bookcases with sheets of plywood set over the shelving, transforming the cabinets into crude hospital beds. After a brief consult with one of the nurses, the stout woman left, and her

301

assistant came over to Percival and Ben and sat them opposite the librarian's desk. "Miss Barton will be right with you just as soon as she finishes with the others," the nurse said.

"I'm fine," said Percival, grasping Ben by the shoulders. "It's my boy here I'm worried about."

Ben grimaced and grabbed his leg. "I can't feel my foot," he said, "My leg's goin' numb, too."

The nurse looked at Ben's leg. "She'll be with you soon," she said, and went quickly to the woman sitting behind the desk. The pencils, papers, and reference books that normally occupied the librarian's desk had been replaced by a small apothecary of bandages, camphor bottles, balsam, and lint.

"You think this woman's gonna help me, pa?"

Percival stroked Ben's arms and looked around the room. "Right now, this Miss Barton woman is your best chance until we get to the factory hospital in River Fork."

While they were waiting, a man came up and dropped a large wooden crate at Percival's feet. "Don't be too picky," he said, pointing to the box full of shoes and heavy coats. "One size fits all...dry."

The man left before receiving thanks for the gifts, and Percival and Ben put on the dry clothes right there on the floor of the Library. Men and women, naked and clothed, none of these things mattered now to anyone. Ben was pulling up his pants when Miss Barton entered the room. She helped him to his feet and took him to one of the overturned bookcases. She unfolded a patchwork quilt and spread it over the plywood and sat Ben down.

"I'm Clara," she said.

Ben introduced himself.

"All right, Ben, let's have a look."

Clara folded back Ben's pant leg and peeled off Father Lichtenberg's cloths in saturated strips, using her finger to hold down the flaps of loose skin that had stuck to the bandage. A long gash ran from the top of Ben's shin to his mangled foot. Clara scrubbed the wound with a handful of camphor soaked lint, and Ben cringed each time she took the bottle and doused the cut with more medicine. When she finished, she dried his leg and applied a tight dressing of clean cloth that spiraled from his toes up to his knee.

She slipped a dry shoe on Ben's good foot. "Find something to help support your weight," she said. "A thick walking stick would be fine. Now go see the man outside for some drinking water."

Clara moved to the next patient, and an older nurse traded places with her. "Try to get some rest," the new nurse said, "I'll be back in a moment."

Just as Ben dozed off, the new nurse returned and shook him gently about the shoulders. "I'm sorry to wake you, son," she whispered. "We're going to need this bed."

Ben struggled to push himself up. He looked around the room, and, for a moment, had forgotten where he was.

The nurse caught hold of his arm. "Here," she said, helping Ben to his feet, "Is anyone with you?"

Ben looked around to get his bearings and pointed to the librarian's desk, and the nurse escorted him to his father.

"This boy needs to rest," the nurse said to Percival. "Do you live close by?"

"No, ma'am. I was hoping we could find a wagon to take us up to River Fork."

The nurse surveyed the crowded room, and the wounded waiting outside in the street. "Most of the wagons are being used to bring in the injured and carry away the deceased," she said. "You might be able to catch a ride to the end of town, but I doubt you'll get much further than that."

Percival took one of the jackets from the clothing box for himself and gave one to Ben. "Bless you, ma'am," he said.

"Thank you," said Ben, putting on the coat, "And thank Miss Clara for me, too."

"I will," the nurse said. "And you get that leg looked at by a doctor as soon as you get to River Fork. A wound like that, left unattended, is likely to get much worse."

Percival and Ben went outside, and the man doling out the

303

fresh water gave them each a ration. They sat on the crumbled reproduction of the Liberty Bell with their tin cups and waited. Thirty minutes passed, and a wagon pulled up to the library. The nurses came out and rushed the injured inside while a group of able men quickly refilled the wagon with dead bodies. Percival got up and went to the driver. They talked for a minute, and Percival returned shaking his head, and the wagon rode away. For the next two hours, more wagons pulled up, and each time Percival came back to Ben with the same news, the wagons were either dropping off, picking up, or headed in the opposite direction. Soon the wagons stopped coming.

"How's your leg?" Percival said.

"Hurts, bad, pa."

Percival looked up and down the road. "We can wait a bit longer, if you want."

Ben shook his head. "If we take it slow, I'll be all right."

Percival got up and sifted through a pile of debris next to the broken bell and found a crooked tree branch. He measured it against his hip and handed it to Ben. "Here," he said, "use it to keep your weight off that leg."

Ben took the soggy walking stick and peeled off the sprigs. He thought of the General and laughed. "You wouldn't happen to have a pipe and a plug of tobacco, would you?"

Percival gave Ben a puzzled look.

"Just never thought I'd be usin' one of these until much later in life," said Ben. "It won't make my hair turn grey, or give me the pneumonia, will it?"

"I'm fairly certain it won't," said Percival, helping Ben off the broken bell, "but we can ask the doctor when we see him to make sure. Now let's go find a wagon."

The rain and the cold of yesterday was gone, and now the sun beat down over the valley, drying up the puddles in the road and cracking the topsoil into tiny squares like honeycombs. Across the open sky, threads of grey smoke rose in stalks where the towns used to be, climbing up into puffs like mushroom caps and feathering out over the landscape. Ben pointed to a thin grey strand at the top of the valley, barely visible above the horizon. "Is that River Fork, pa?"

Percival squinted, covering his eyes to shield the midday sun. "About fourteen miles away."

They headed up the road, and Ben recalled the wagon ride he and Doc had taken to Johnstown, and how a strong horse traveling downhill on clear roads took nearly half a day. He sighed, dragging his injured leg behind him, plagued with the thought of limping uphill over fourteen miles of muddied trails.

Percival cradled his arm under Ben's. "I was wonderin', Bennett," he said. "How's about telling me more about that music school. What was the name of that fella…Baton, Brethren?

"Beethoven?" said Ben.

"Beethoven, that's the one…tell me more about that fella."

Ben smiled, and they plodded on, still not a wagon in sight.

The sun had slipped well behind the hills, and night fell upon the valley, cold and empty. Ben stumbled through the pine-needled mire trying to keep up with his father, and was ready for another rest when up ahead he spotted a glint of light shimmering in the darkness like a beacon. He pointed toward the fire. "Look, pa."

"I see it," said Percival, picking up his pace.

Ben limped after him, his slackleg dragging a half-step behind.

They came onto a stretch of level ground, and Ben saw a group of men circled around a bonfire, each one resting a longrifle across his lap. The blaze cast light onto a large masonry building flanked by mounds of debris. Some of the lettering attached to the side of the building had fallen off, but Ben could still read the words highlighted against the faded bricks, Moxham Middle School.

There was a murmur of voices in the air, and the smell of burning pinewood.

Ben and Percival moved closer to the fire, and one of the men got up hugging a shotgun against his chest. "Hold up," he said. "Where are you comin' from?"

Percival stepped in front of Ben and stopped. "Johnstown," he said.

"Where you headed?"

"River Fork."

The bearded, burly man looked Percival and Ben over. He raised the shotgun and walked around behind them and peeked into the darkness.

"My boy's injured," said Percival. "We were hoping to find shelter for the night."

The man came back around and leaned over and looked at Ben's leg. He went back to the fire and lowered the shotgun to his side. "My apologies," he said. "Just that we've had some thieves comin' round, stealing food, water, belongings off the dead. Had to make sure you'uns ain't one of them. Name's Everett. I'm in charge of this shelter. And these men here are my deputies."

Ben and Percival followed Everett across the yard and through the open doors of the middle school. The large room was lit by candles and gas lanterns and heated by more than a hundred men, women, and children crowded on adolescent-sized benches and sprawled out on the floor. "Blankets are over there," Everett said, using the barrel of the shotgun to point around the room. "Benches are for women, children, and the elderly. Gravely ill and injured over there. The rest, anywhere you can find a spot. Food and water distribution is along that wall."

Another gunman came up and whispered in Everett's ear. "And one more thing," Everett said, walking away with the deputy, "if you see someone expire, drag 'em out back with the others. Can't have no diseases spreadin' round this place."

When Everett and the deputy had left, Ben took one step toward the food line and collapsed.

306

Percival bent down and picked him up and took him to a spot against the wall and set him down.

"I'm thirsty, pa."

"Rest here. I'll get us some food and water."

"And a blanket, Pa?"

"A big thick one."

Ben pushed himself against the wall, his leg throbbing steadily, a sour smell like spoiled milk seeping through the holes in his pants. He looked around. Along the back wall, men were handing out bread and water to a long line of people. At the front of the room, Everett and his deputy were back inside walking up and down between the benches, looking left and right with serious stares. When they came to the food line, a boy of about fourteen shot out from the crowd and darted toward the back door. Everett and the deputy gave chase and caught him before he could escape. They pinned the kid against the wall, opened his coat, and pulled out a woman's handbag, two loaves of bread, and a large canteen. Everett raised the butt of his shotgun and drove it into the boy's forehead, dropping him to the ground. The deputy grabbed the boy by the ankle and dragged him out the back door. Ben heard a loud thud, then another, and the two gunmen came back inside wiping off their rifle stocks on their coats.

Percival returned with a cup of water and a small piece of bread.

The bread was stale, but the water felt cool in Ben's mouth. He swished it round and savored it all the way down to his belly. "I sure hope we find a wagon," he said.

Percival sat next to Ben, leaning in and speaking in a whisper. "I met a man in line," he said. "I told him about you and your leg. Says he's got a wagon headin' up to River Fork early tomorrow morning." Percival sat back and pulled Ben's head onto his shoulder. "We'll be home by ten and have you at the hospital before noon."

"Will they fix my leg, pa?"

"You bet they will. Better than new."

Ben sagged against his father and closed his eyes. "Wake me up, pa, when it's time to go."

"Bennett. Bennett."

Ben rubbed the crust from the corners of his eyes and looked up at his father. "Pa?"

Percival pulled him up. "Come on, time to go."

Ben grabbed his walking stick and wrapped his free arm around his father's waist and hobbled outside into the morning sun. A rickety wagon was parked next to the smoldering bonfire. Several people were seated in the bed, and more were lined up alongside waiting to get on.

"Stay here, Ben," said Percival, walking up to the driver.

Percival and the driver talked for a moment then the driver turned away and went to the horse.

Percival threw his hands in the air. "You said there was room for us," he said. "My boy is injured. We need this ride."

"I don't know what to tell you mister," the driver said, tightening the bridle. "We're all full."

Percival pointed at the wagon bed. "There's still plenty of seats in there."

"Already taken," the driver said, returning to the back of the wagon.

A fat man in clean clothes came up to the bed. Ben saw him slip the driver a folded bill. The driver put the money in his pocket and guided the fat man onto the wagon. "All full."

Percival grabbed the driver by the neck and shoved him against the wagon.

From nowhere, Everett appeared and separated the two men with the barrel of his shotgun. "Is there a problem?"

Percival let go of the driver. "This man said there'd be space for us on his wagon, now he's reneging."

"It's his wagon," said Everett, leveling the shotgun at Percival. "He can load it with whatever or whoever he wants. Now I suggest you back away."

"It ain't fair," shouted Percival, grabbing hold of the driver and raising his fist.

Everett flipped the shotgun around and drew it above his shoulder.

"Don't," Ben shouted.

The men turned.

"We'll find another way, pa," said Ben. "Please Mister Everett, don't hurt him."

Everett lowered his gun, and the driver hurried to the front of the wagon and drove away.

They plodded up the mountain, passing through Franklin, Woodvale, Prospect and Millville, each town more devastated than the one before it. The pain in Ben's leg had spread into his hip, and he had lost all feeling in his foot. With each mile, he grew weaker, and when they came into Morrellville, and a saloon turned food-distribution center, he had to be carried inside. They spent the night at a church up the road, sharing the fellowship hall with a hundred and fifty others left homeless by the flood. After a breakfast of stale bread and coffee, they left Morrellville and came upon the devastation at River Fork. If Ben hadn't known better, he would never have had taken it for a town, much less the thriving steel producing giant it once was.

Except for some of the large masonry structures, every building had been crushed to the ground, every business leveled, and every factory chimney toppled and stomped into the mud like a boot to a cigarette. Townsfolk roamed solitary through the streets, picking at the rubble and assembling the salvage into small piles. Some took their treasures to the folding tables set up along the street corners where people were trading one needed item for another. Men in pairs carried limbless bodies on stretchers made from canvas sheets, wooden planks, doors, to a level bluff where a stone church sat cockeyed in the dried mud, and laid them out face up in rows before the priest to be counted and recorded. Black smoke trailed up from the pyres burning alongside the road, fueled by the stiff carcasses of drowned horses, cows, and dogs that still lay rotting in the streets.

On Main Street, the sins of the saloon had been washed away, the wrath of God unleashed upon it as it was with Sodom and Gomorra. The only memory of Howell's General Store was the big display table, now wiped clean of its contemporary cookware and fashion. Atop the rubble, Ben saw a long sheet of wood, and realized it was the solid oak counter where he and Doc had laughed together and drank their Doctor Peppers. He tried to picture the store the way it was, the wood plank floor, the smell of fresh Chase and Sanborn's, the old-timers batting the breeze on the front porch.

With one hand on his walking stick and the other around his father's waist, he limped up the hill to the end of Main Street. All the homes had been swept away, except for two. Two homes on a knoll, with high shake roofs and covered porches, set behind a simple wooden garage and spaced evenly between two grand sugar maples.

Three days after the lake at River Fork emptied into the valley, Ben was finally home. The big barn doors dangled from the hinges, and the small door next to them had been ripped completely off. He stepped into the shop and across the floor still covered with a thick mixture of mud and soggy sawdust. The sandbags Percival had piled up along the walls were gone, but somehow, they had stayed in place long enough to keep the water from toppling some of the stacks of unfinished furniture inside.

Percival walked around the room surveying the damage and Ben continued out into the yard. The tables and benches the day laborers had sat upon at the bountiful turkey feast were gone, as was the oil drum. In its place lay a cluster of broken pieces of wood.

At first glance, it looked like an unrecognizable mound. But as Ben came closer, he noticed small black and white strips, like licorice candies, strewn about the ground. A tangle of wires, thick and thin, were bent and twisted around the top of the stack, and a large sheet of curved wood, polished-black on one side, roasted burnt-umber on the other, held the pile together. After a moment of intense scrutiny, he realized he was staring at the River Fork

Clubhouse Steinway. He picked at the rubble with his stick and fell to his knees.

The next thing he knew, he was being carried into the house and dropped onto the floor. He head was spinning, his stomach convulsing in short spasms. He looked up at his father. A blast of heat flowed through him, and streams of sweat ran down his forehead. "Are we home?" he said.

Percival squeezed his hand. "We're home."

Ben could no longer feel the ground beneath him. "Pa?" he said, "I'm scared."

"I'm right here, Bennett. I won't leave you."

Ben's head pounded and his throat tightened. He reached for his chest and felt around. "My pin," he said, "where's my pin." He closed his eyes, and his father was gone.

EPILOGUE

Opening up the shop had become routine for Percival, one of those good habits parents always wish upon their children, like saying please and thank you, or washing up before supper. After organizing his projects for the day, he opened wide the street-facing barn doors, fastened them to the side of the garage, and brought out a few of his best finished pieces for display, hoping to attract the attention of potential customers.

Satisfied with the arrangement of his merchandise, he went inside, swept the floor, twice, and set up his work bench with an array of wood finishing products: sandpaper, steel wool, wood-stain, lacquer, and shellac. Finally, he loaded his overalls with all the necessary implements a fine cabinetmaker required at the ready.

The final coat of shellac he'd brushed on the day before had set-up nicely, and Percival pulled the dining table away from the work bench and covered it with a canvas tarp. Four more orders needed to be delivered by the end of the week, and he was excited to have the first and most important one finished. He reviewed his work orders and went straight to a bookcase that needed refurbishing. He had finished sanding and staining the side panels, and was working on the face frame when a woman's voice drifted across the shop floor.

"Is anyone here?"

Percival peeked around the bookcase, then hurried to the work bench and emptied his pockets. He grabbed a rag, dipped it into a tin of turpentine, scrubbed his hands, and came out to the shop floor.

"Well, Miss Claire," he said, rubbing his hands on his pants to remove any bits of wood stain the turpentine might have missed. "You didn't need to come all the way down here. I was making plans to bring the table up to you."

Percival enjoyed Claire's unexpected and often unnecessary visits, and usually spent the first moment of each encounter pretending to clean his hands while he looked her over. He thought of her as the prettiest water widow in River Fork, and hated it when others referred to her as just another flood relic. He believed her to be an honorable woman. After putting her things in order, she had moved back home to work the lumber mill with her father and three brothers. She was tough, a hard worker, and could keep up with any of the men at the mill. This morning she came dressed in work pants and a heavy flannel, her hair pulled back into a tight, lumpy knot. But in an evening dress, no one would ever take her for a logger.

Claire put her hands on her hips and smiled. "I'm a woman who likes to inspect my merchandise before it's delivered."

Percival threw back the canvas like a magician pulling the cloth from a perfectly set table. He waited for Claire's approval.

Claire ran her fingertips over the smooth surface of the table top. "Reckon now I'm the proud owner of a beautiful dining table from the most respected cabinetmaker in town. And I'm not just saying that because you're the only cabinetmaker in town, either."

Percival laughed. "So you like it?"

"Very much." Claire looked around the room. "You've done such a fine job taking over this shop. Mr. Clement would have been proud. You keep making furniture like this, and you'll never get a day's rest."

"While it lasts," said Percival, "Soon, one of Clem's kin will come with an upper-crust lawyer and claim it for his own. But until that happens, I'm gonna keep at it."

"I know you will," said Claire, moving away from the table and walking up to Percival. She bit at her lower lip, her eyes on his, and slowly moved her hand to Percival's face.

Percival blushed and closed his eyes.

313

Claire thumbed away a thick smudge of wood stain from his cheek. "You know," she said, "you could save a lot of money if more of that wood stain ended up on the wood instead of on your face."

Percival laughed.

"Now, contrary to what you might think," she said, "I did come down here for another reason." She reached into her waistband and pulled out a copy of that morning's Tribune and handed it to Percival. "I thought you might like to see it."

Percival caught the headline right away.

On the Anniversary Of The Great Flood
The Loved Lost, But Not Forgotten

On the front page, there was a feature article recounting the events of that fateful day. Opposite the story was a map outlining the path of the flood. Underneath, there were a few more stories, one about a housing development north of Main Street near completion. Another about scratching plans to rebuild the River Fork Clubhouse, and another, more uplifting piece about a new schoolhouse and library to be erected with the help of a generous grant from one of the Club's former members, Mr. Charles Andrews.

On the second page was a list of names, an alphabetical registry of those who had lost their lives in the Great Flood, exactly one year ago. Page after page, the names kept going on and on, 2,209 in all. Percival folded up the paper and gave it back to Claire.

"They forgot one," he said.

"I know," said Claire, "I'm sorry."

Before he showed Claire an emotion he wasn't quite ready to bare, Percival returned the discussion to the dining table. "So," he said, holding back his tears, "everything meets your approval?"

"It does, handsomely."

Percival covered the table with the canvas. "I'll have it up to you right after lunch."

Claire folded her arms against her chest and stared at the

floor. "Actually," she said, "I was hoping you could bring it by later." Now it was Claire who was blushing. "Perhaps, closer to suppertime?"

Percival tilted his head and gave Claire a curious smile.

"With all the heavy plates and dishes I plan to put on it," Claire said, "I think it would be best if we had an expert there...you know, to confirm the table's stability. Wouldn't you agree?"

Percival let Claire know he'd be delighted to help. "Usually," he said, "my work is confined to the shop. But for you, Miss Claire," he gave her a majestic bow, "for you, I'd be glad to make an exception."

Claire smiled.

Percival kept his eyes fixed on Claire, admiring her confident stride as she waltzed across the shop floor and out the door. He hoped that for supper, she'd wear her hair down.

Percival hurried into the house to change. Before calling upon Miss Clair later that evening, he had one more important thing to do that day, and he wanted to wear something nice, something respectful, something that said being there was truly important.

He picked through his armoire and found a pair of freshly pressed pinstriped slacks, a clean white undershirt with brown braces, a fitted double-breasted waistcoat, and a matching jacket. With a crisp bowler to complete the ensemble, and a detailed wiping about the face and neck, Percival looked handsome enough for Sunday service.

He walked down the hall and into Ben's room. The small bedroom, now absent of Ben's personal effects, was clean and orderly. The bedding was tucked neatly under the mattress, and the pillows were tilted purposefully against the headboard, layered and fluffed evenly. Atop the chest of drawers sat an ornate tool box, the one Clem had shown him when he was still too thick-headed to understand why, with the domed lid, the dovetail joinery, and the smooth, rich finish. Percival unlatched the iron clasp and opened the lid. Inside was Ben's music pin. The black music note in the center and the inscription around the edge had faded, but specks of gold still clung to the surface. After six months of searching, he had finally found it in a memory jar at a small church in Millville. He pinched it off the bottom of the tool box and tucked it securely in his pocket.

Percival was leaving through the shop floor when he heard the thud of heavy hooves clomping up the road. Claire must have remembered she hadn't given him a time, and he raced out to meet her.

Instead of his most cherished customer, two men in frock coats and top hats stepped out of a fancy black Victoria, stern and stoic and meaning business. In their stout frames, they came from the coach and approached Percival. The taller man spoke first.

"Good day, sir," he said, straightening his coat and motioning with a head nod to the property before him, "Would this be the estate of the late Mr. James Clement?"

Confused, Percival answered the man's simple question. "It would."

The tall man looked at the papers in his hand. "And would you be one, Percival Marsh?"

Again, it took Percival a moment to confirm. "I would."

Without offering their hands, the men introduced themselves as Casper Stork from the First National Bank and Trust of Philadelphia, and Harrison Golde, a lawyer from somewhere in Wisconsin. Percival was only slightly less confused now. He said nothing, rocking on his heels as he waited for the men to continue.

"Well," said the lawyer, reaching into his coat, "we've come to execute…"

"Hold on," Percival exclaimed, fending the men off with open palms, "I'll be happy to vacate. No need to go and do anything drastic, now."

The lawyer reassured him they weren't there to eliminate him, and removed another document from his coat. "We've come to fulfill the last will and testament of Mr. James H. Clement." He gave a quick look of amusement to the banker and handed Percival a large sheet of parchment. "As you can see," he said, pointing to a section that began with a lengthy paragraph of legal jargon, "it appears that you are the sole beneficiary of Mr. Clement's estate, and all the property contained therein."

Percival's knees buckled, and he stepped back to keep from falling over. "Me?" he said, "the sole beneficiary? What about Clem's family? Surely there must be someone else in line before me."

"Mr. Clement had no family," said the man from the bank. "When the note on the property was paid off last year, we searched high and low for relatives, from Connecticut to California, nary a one to be found. Isn't that right, Mr. Golde."

"That's right," said the lawyer, "It wasn't until Mr. Stork, here, contacted me that we found the legal inheritor, you, Mr. Marsh."

Percival stood speechless in front of the two businessmen.

The banker used a fancy Waterman to point to a dotted line at the bottom of the page then handed the pen to Percival. "If you would just sign here, please," he said.

Percival looked at the banker.

"It's the deed," said the lawyer.

Percival set the paper atop a raised knee and signed the deed against his thigh.

It was the bankers turn again. "Now this one..." The banker handed Percival yet another sheet, "bank copy," he said.

This time Percival signed with confidence, the fact that he'd just inherited Clem's estate finally sinking in.

Mr. Stork took back the bank's copy. "It was my pleasure, Mr. Marsh. Now, we must be on our way if we're to catch the ten o'clock back to New York."

Percival remained frozen as the men returned to the cab, and his mind floated back to the reason he'd put on his Sunday best. He ran up alongside the coach as it drove away. "Wait, wait," he hollered, rapping on the door.

The coachman pulled back on the reins and the carriage jolted to a stop. The banker threw open the door.

"Would it be too much trouble," Percival said, "to give me a lift up the hill?"

The two men obliged and scooted over to make room.

Percival nodded respectfully and stepped inside.

Right off the main road to the depot, Percival instructed the driver to stop at the entrance to the cemetery. "If you don't mind," he said, "I won't be long, only a few minutes."

Again, the men gave Percival a stoic nod and waited as he walked across the lawn through the open gate.

Thick clumps of grass cradled the granite headstones that filled the River Fork cemetery in long narrow rows like shallow grey cornfields. Even after a year, the rows kept growing longer. Many families had just now saved enough money to honor their loved ones with an official marker.

Percival walked to one of the headstones at the far end of the cemetery. The curved stone wasn't fancy or decorative, just simple and strong like the man it honored. He came around the front, and just as he had done the day he'd placed it in the ground, read the epitaph out loud. "1815 – 1889, Here lies James H. Clement, a true savior, taken from this world, but in our hearts forever." Percival took out the deed, held it up to the stone, and mouthed the words, "thank you."

Back in the coach, Percival sat silently until the driver pulled into to the station. From the depot, the valley looked reborn. Green grass and flowing meadows of red and gold had returned to the rolling hills, and new homes sprung up between the bends in the river that now flowed through River Fork at the pace of a gentle stream. Solid bridges, towers, tipples, and scaffolds had been rebuilt, and new railroad track had been laid. The lake and the Clubhouse were gone, and now, an enormous crater sat at the top of the valley. Below, the landscape had almost completely returned to normal. Percival thanked the men for the lift, and, pressured by the hands of the depot clock, ran as quickly as his fitted attire would allow to the landing where he found the eastbound train still waiting at the station.

With the help of a wooden cane, Ben stood tall and pressed his shoulders back. "Over here, pa," he shouted.

Percival hurried across the landing, almost knocking over a young couple saying their goodbyes locked at the mouth. He came up to Ben and wrapped his arms around him.

Ben smiled as he shared a quick embrace with his father. "You made it," he said.

"Of course," said Percival, "Not a chance I'd miss seeing my son off to the big city of New York. In fact, I have to say, I'm a bit jealous."

"I'm sure you have plenty to do here, pa," said Ben, lifting a brand new knapsack onto his shoulder and straightening his posture with the custom-crafted cane of smooth-sanded sugar maple.

Percival patted his shirt pocket. "I do, Ben, plenty."

Ben listened as Percival shared his dinner plans with Claire later that evening, and the news of his recent inheritance.

"I knew you belonged in that woodshop," said Ben. "Clem knew it too."

After Ben acknowledged his father's brief review of 'watch out for's' and 'be careful of's', the conductor shouted for all to board.

"Nervous?" Percival asked, walking alongside Ben to the train.

Ben wagged his head. "A little. I won't know a soul."

"I wouldn't worry about that," said Percival, "I don't reckon you'll have much trouble meeting people, an outgoing, jovial fella like yourself. Especially with so many schools and institutions there, engineering, architecture...."

"And art?" said Ben.

"Lots of art schools too," said Percival. "Maybe you'll meet someone there."

Ben smiled. "Yeah, pa, maybe I will."

Percival helped Ben up the stairs. "Oh," he said, reaching into his pant pocket, "I almost forgot. I found somethin' I thought you might like to take with you." Percival took out the music pin and handed it to Ben.

Ben's eyes widened, and a smile stretched across his face, ear to ear. He reached out and took the pin. The flecks of gold sparkled in the sunlight as he turned it round. "I don't believe it," he said, stammering. "How? Where did you find it?"

"The day I brought you home from the hospital a woman came by the house. Said she was from a group call the Red Cross and checkin' in to see who'd survived and who was still missin'. She told me about the recovery centers they'd set up all over the valley at the schools, libraries, churches. Mostly to help bring closure to those who'd lost loved ones in the flood. While you were recovering, I went to every one of them centers from here to Johnstown lookin' for that pin. You wouldn't believe the things people found in the rubble: watches, earrings, jewelry, a baby's quilt they used to pull people out of the flood, you name it. I was about to give up when I stumbled upon a mason jar filled with bracelets and wedding rings at an old church in Millville. I turned it over, and there it was, just slid out into my hand."

Ben leaned on the cane to brace himself. He gave the pin a good look and attached it to his shirt right above his heart. "Thank you, pa."

"Wear it well."

Ben reached down and gave his father a farewell hug around the neck. "I will."

Percival patted Ben strongly on the back the way men do and said, "Take care son, I'll see you around Christmas time."

"All right, pa, you too," Ben said, and boarded the train.

Unlike the stuffy, dank passenger car Ben remembered from when he and his father had first come to River Fork, the fancy Pullman was steeped in the rich, luxurious smell of velour, with red-cushioned sitting chairs and mahogany tea tables along the depot side, and smooth, matching bench seats on the other. Ben showed his ticket to the conductor, and asked him if he was in the right car. The conductor nodded and escorted him to his seat, passing by a handsomely dressed group celebrating a birthday over a toast of champagne.

Across the aisle at one of the tea tables, a man in a pressed suit was blowing kisses out the window to his sweetheart. Next to the woman, Ben saw his father waiting patiently on the landing. Ben raised his hand for one last wave goodbye, and as he took his seat, a funnel blast from the engine moved the train out of the station. He was fumbling for a place to set his cane when the conductor returned.

"I'd be more than happy to stow that for you, sir," the conductor said.

Ben handed the man his cane.

"And the valise?"

Ben clutched his knapsack tightly against his chest, measuring the weight of the sheet music inside. "No thank you," he said, "I'd like to keep it with me."

The conductor left, and Ben sat back against the soft velvet and stretched out his leg, permanently stiff and straight, a memento from the flood he now carries with him, a constant reminder with every step, of what he'd gone through, and what he'd overcome.

What he had told his father on the landing wasn't entirely true. Of course it would take getting used to, new people, new places, a new lifestyle, but he was by no means nervous. He wasn't scared of anything, not afraid of anyone. He was no longer the innocent boy being prodded at by a precocious girl in the back of a wagon, or the hired help being bossed around by the high society businessmen at a fancy clubhouse. Now, he saw things for what they were, merely things, and people for who they were, merely people, all the same, one no better than the other. At the bottom of a river, we all are, when the air is sucked from our lungs, when the earth grabs us and rips us apart, we all are, only people, torn down by tragedy, and if not destroyed, built up stronger because of it. He had faced God's wrath, battled back, and won. He had fought off pain and infection, and though the flood had left him wounded, he was by no means lame. He had gone into the troubled water, and come out healed.

Often, when he was alone, he thought of the friends he'd lost, Parke, Clem, Doc, and he wondered what had happened to those he never saw again after the flood, Andrews, Crick, The General, and especially, Tom. He could still hear Tom talking about himself in that deep, southern drawl, still see him sitting poised at the piano, playing his effortless melodies that floated through the air on angel's wings. He recalled the time Tom had made the sound of the timber rattler, and what he'd asked him to do that night on the bridge.

Ben rested his head against the opened window, closed his eyes, and listened.

The iron wheels thumped in a steady rhythm over the track, and Ben mused at the thought of his fellow passenger's heads bobbing up and down in perfect time with the beat. He let go of the rumbling and the commotion inside the coach, and in his mind's eye, he drifted outside the train. A group of wild turkeys purred in the tall grass near the rails, and he saw the soot-covered millworker Owen Ahl, smiling his big smile and holding his two girls in his arms. Above, he heard the call of a golden eagle, its cry yawning across the sky. It was a clear day, not a cloud for miles. Ben rose up and soared with the eagle, riding high on the wind and dreaming of what lay ahead, as the train, bound for New York City, rolled slowly over the mountain and disappeared.

AFTERWORD AND ACKNOWLEDGEMENTS

On a Saturday afternoon in 1989, I was turning the dial of our living room TV (yes, there were actually knobs on the front of televisions), flipping through the nine channels our flimsy rabbit ears could receive, when I stumbled upon an interesting PBS documentary. At the time more interested in sports than history, I stopped searching for a baseball game and sat silently on the floor for two hours, watching in amazement as the narrator described one of the most horrific natural disasters in American history.

Spring of 1889 and American's were enjoying the spoils of an industrial revolution, but in the small town of Johnstown, Pennsylvania, the wheels of industry had come to a grinding halt. At the edge of a great lake, in front of a fancy fishing and hunting club, a dam had failed, spilling twenty million tons of water into the Allegheny valley and literally uprooting the lives of the 30,000 people living below it. The flood began as a towering wave of whitewater, but water, by itself, could not have caused the devastation in the still photos of overturned boxcars, crumbled buildings, pine-tree-impaled homes, and smoldering steel mills I was seeing flash across the screen. The narrator went on, explaining that the destruction had not been caused by the water alone, but by all the terrible debris the flood had picked up on its way down the mountain.

Picture a fifty foot high wall of water racing along at forty miles per hour, washing over broad swales, funneling through narrow channels, in places less than thirty feet wide. Now, pile up in front of it a giant, turbulent mass of boulders, trees, telegraph poles, coal tipples, water towers, railway track, foundry cauldrons, factory engines, steel ingots, barbed wire, razor ribbon, rolled steel, scrap iron, coal, coke, train cars, train engines, homes, buildings, people, wagons, livestock and bridges, and imagine all these things rolling end over end in a muddy, unrecognizable heap, plowing away the earth and mercilessly leveling everything before it. And when the mayhem stops, and the flood reaches level ground at end of the valley, the nightmare isn't over. The twisted mess piles up at the Stone Bridge in Johnstown, and the upended diesel locomotives, bent and cracked by the flood, spill their fuel into the frigid water, igniting the entire commune of flailing bodies and splintered timber into a violent inferno, incinerating all those fortunate survivors who had miraculously ridden the floodwater safely down the mountain.

How unfortunate, and terribly ironic, I thought, that the flood didn't happen in a farming town filled with tobacco fields, orange groves or cotton crops, but in a steel producing mecca stockpiled with rail cars and razor-wire. Damage to person and property in Johnstown and its neighboring boroughs was immense. In comparison, the Galveston Hurricane of 1900 took over 6,000 lives; the San Francisco earthquake of 1906, over 3,000; the Okeechobee Hurricane of 1928, 3,000. The Johnstown flood of 1889 was the fourth most devastating natural disaster in American history, claiming 2,209 lives, just shy of the terrorist attacks of 9/11 (2,973), but more than Hurricane Katrina (1,836).

Learning about this horrific disaster was sobering, but what was most surprising to me was almost everyone on the west coast I talked to about the flood while writing this book had never heard of it. In reflection, I was also disappointed that in my entire educational experience, not once had the catastrophe at Johnstown been included in any of my American history books. The enormity of the Johnstown story had gripped me, and I wanted everyone else to know about the terrible events of that fateful day in 1889.

Let me now take a moment to apologize to all historians that cringe at historical inaccuracies. The date of the Johnstown flood was May 31st, 1889, not May 30th. I used May 30th because it aided in the narration of the story. So to all the purists who may have been offended by that, I apologize. Also, the name of the town where the story takes place, River Fork, was varied slightly from the actual town where the clubhouse and the dam was located, South Fork, which, by the way, still sits peacefully in the Allegheny valley, seventy-five miles east of Pittsburgh.

The characters Percival Marsh and James Clement are purely fictional, but many others were based on real people (with a little literary freedom taken here as well). Emma Ehrenfeld, for example, worked as an operator at a telegraph tower in South Fork at the time of the flood, and was interviewed, along with many other survivors, shortly thereafter by John H. Hampton of the Pennsylvania Railroad Company. John Parke was the actual resident engineer of the South Fork Fishing and Hunting Club (called the River Fork Fishing and Hunting Club in the story), and contrary to the story, he did not perish in the flood. Charles Andrews was based on the steel magnate, industrialist, and philanthropist Andrew Carnegie. Morton Crick was loosely based on Carnegie's rival and intermittent business associate Henry Clay Frick. Both Carnegie and Frick were members of the South Fork Fishing and Hunting Club. Frank Damrosch, the godson of Franz Liszt, did in fact establish a music academy in New York City that would later become the Julliard School of Music, honorably named after Augustus Julliard who posthumously bequeathed a large portion of his wealth to the proliferation of the arts. Blind Tom was based on the blind musical savant Blind Tom Wiggins, said to have been present in the valley at or about the time of the flood. Bennett Marsh, the underdog with the big heart and the big dreams, is also fictional; however, I'd like to think that somewhere in him, there is a little bit of myself.

I would like to extend my gratitude to those that have helped me in the process of writing this book. To Richard Burkert, Patty

Carnevali, Shelley Johansson, Kim Baxter, Phil Solomon, and the rest of the staff at the Johnstown Area Heritage Association for kindly welcoming me into their museum, and for visiting with me during my stay in Johnstown. To Mike Sr. and Elizabeth Oates, Megan Oates, Jackson and Trevor Oates, Barbara and Art Lammens, Shannon Martinez, Matt and Staci Shackelford, Dena David, my fellow black belt instructors Steve Hopple and Debra Holland, and all the readers who anonymously provided such helpful feedback. To my son, Jameson, who while reading Tom Sawyer together reminded me Mark Twain once said, "When you catch an adjective, kill it." To my son Riley, who because of his drive to never give up, will one day appreciate the painstaking time that went into this novel's creation. To my brother, John, perhaps the second most intelligent person I know, whose skillful eye and keen insight not only helped improve the story, but kept my grammar and misspellings in check. To my editor in Los Angeles, Barbara DeSantis, for pushing what limited talent I have as a writer to new heights. And especially to my wife, Liza, my toughest critic, for her honest opinions, helpful suggestions, the prologue, and for always supporting me in each of my crazy endeavors, but most of all, because she told me to.

ABOUT THE AUTHOR

Michael Stephan Oates was born in Dallas, Texas, and moved to California in 1973. He graduated from the California State University in Fullerton in 1992 with a Masters degree in Business Administration and a Minor in Music. Over the past sixteen years, he has grown his southwestern style restaurant into a thriving fixture in his home town of Fullerton, and has been recognized for his achievements in the industry by California State Senator Mimi Walters and U.S. Congressman Ed Royce. He lives in Southern California with his wife Liza, and sons Jameson and Riley.

SOUTHERN SON
THE SAGA OF DOC HOLLIDAY

GONE WEST
Book Two

Victoria Wilcox

KNOX ROBINSON
PUBLISHING
London • New York

Praise For Victoria Wilcox

"This wonderfully written novel brings together one of the great stories of the American Frontier. Author Wilcox has done a superb job through fiction of creating a sense of time and place and giving us an intriguing look at one of the most controversial figures in the West—Dr. John Henry Holliday."
Casey Tefertiller, Pulitzer Prize nominated author of *Wyatt Earp: The Life Behind the Legend*

"Wilcox pursues the truth in a powerful and moving novel that is not tainted by the legend of its central character, trapped by the documentary evidence of his life, or tempted to ignore history. She tells his story with an intimate voice that is surprisingly fresh and compelling."
Dr. Gary Roberts, bestselling author of *Doc Holliday: The Life and Legend*

"Through her intimate, firsthand knowledge of Doc Holliday, his youthful environs and his living relatives, Victoria Wilcox has discovered and distilled much of Doc's actual history, weaving it in with passeddown family folklore. This firsthand account of Doc's travels and acquaintances rivals other historical novels like Gettysburg and Killing Lincoln.
Don Weber, "New York Times" Bestselling author of *Silent Witness*

Books in the Southern Son Saga
Inheritance
Gone West
The Last Decision

Chapter One

Texas, 1873

The last thing on his mind was a train robbery. Although he knew about the $100,000 in gold rumored to be aboard, enough to make any outlaw eager, no one had ever robbed a moving train west of the Mississippi before. As long as the Rock Island Line's passenger train No. 2, bound from Council Bluffs to Des Moines, kept up its dizzying speed of forty-miles an hour, horsed bandits would have a hard time catching up with her.

But as the train neared Adair, Iowa, it slowed for a grade and a curve, and the engineer hollered out that something was slung across the tracks. He slammed the engine into reverse and the train shuddered and groaned, then jumped the rails. The locomotive thundered down the muddy bank of Turkey Creek spewing smoke and cinders from the chimney and lolling to one side, twisting the couplers and throwing the passenger cars skyward. The ground shook with the impact as steam rose from the troubled creek bed. And waiting alongside the bridge to greet the terrified passengers as they struggled from the wreckage was a white-robed gang of train robbers brandishing pistols and rifles and shouting the Rebel yell...

"You gonna buy that paper, Mister, or just stand there readin' all day?" the newsboy on the Galveston Strand complained as John Henry lost himself in the details of the West's most daring train robbery. The engineer had been killed, thrown from the locomotive then crushed to death as it rolled over him. But the conductor had lived to testify against the James gang that had derailed the Rock Island Line and held up its passengers.

Until that summer, the gang had kept their outlawry to holding up banks in the Missouri back country. This enterprise with the railroads was a whole new kind of crime, and newspaper sales soared whenever there was a report on the search for the elusive Jesse James. Aside from the gruesome death of the train's engineer, it would have been a perfect robbery had the money actually been on board and not delayed until later, leaving the gang only $6,000 in cash and jewelry taken from the express messenger and the passengers. But it was a thrilling attempt, even so, and folks took to the story like a dime novel come to life. Not since the long-ago legends of Robin Hood had there been such a popular out-law, and ladies openly hoped that Jesse might show up in their own quiet towns, bringing adventure and his handsome gang with him. But that was the tenor of the times in 1873: the War was over and the new West was wild, and the country was ready for some entertainment.

But to John Henry Holliday, late of Georgia by way of a fast ride across Florida and a sailing ship to Galveston, the story of Jesse James was more of a relief than anything else. For with the newspapers filled with tales of the dashing outlaw, there was little chance that a shooting on a river in South Georgia would be reported. Not that there was all that much to report about such a commonplace crime: a young black man gunned down by a young white man. But it was John Henry's crime, and though he had run from Lowndes County before the law could catch him, then spent a long night in anguished prayer repenting of his sin and begging for God's forgiveness, he knew that repentance alone would not satisfy the State of Georgia. If the law decided to come after him, he could still hang for murder. So he anxiously read every newspaper he could get his hands on searching for any mention of violence on the Withlacoochee River, and was relieved to see the name of Jesse James, not John Henry Holliday, spelled out across the front page. Let the James Gang get the fame; he'd be happy if his own name never made the headlines.

There was certainly nothing else about him that would draw attention. He was of average height and average build, although a little on the lean side on account of a bout of pneumonia he'd had while spending two cold winters in dental school in Philadelphia. His coloring was fair, his eyes china blue, or so said the girls back home who'd called him hand-some, though mostly it was his cousin Mattie Holliday calling him hand-some that had meant something to him. And though there were other, less pleasing, things that Mattie had called him, as well – stubborn, selfish, arrogant – if those had been his only sins, he wouldn't be in Texas now, reading the paper and watching for any mention of his name or what had happened on the Withlacoochee.

Truth was, he was running from more than just the law. His father had thrown him out of the house and ordered him never to return, the result of a disagreement over his plan to marry his cousin Mattie, though Mattie had already wrecked those plans herself by telling him through her tears that her Catholic faith would not allow first cousins to marry. She loved him but she could not be with him, not ever. And the pain of those two denials, his sweetheart's love and his father's affections, had driven him into a drunken stupor and an unthinking shooting that sent him west fleeing for his life.

Yet other than a few bad dreams, a haunting worry over the long reach of the law, and a still-healing heart, he was in hopeful spirits, having stepped off the ship at Galveston Island sunburned and wind-blown from the sea voyage, and feeling amazingly well. While most of the other passengers had spent their time onboard the tall ship Golden Dream leaning over the rails and vomiting into the turquoise waters of the Gulf of Mexico, the sailing had actually seemed to agree with him. The fresh sea air had cleared his lungs and the prospect of starting a new life in Texas enlivened his mind. And though he had only the vaguest of plans for his immediate future, his long-term goal was set: he would find his way to his Uncle Jonathan McKey's plantation on the Brazos River and beg the family favor of a place in his Uncle's household. For surely his mother's eldest brother, a wealthy cotton planter, would welcome a long-lost nephew from back home in Georgia and be happy to offer him a home in Texas. And once he was settled, he would open his trunk-full of dental equipment and set up a profitable practice in some nearby town, and prove to his father and Mattie both that he was still a fine professional man and not someone to be sent away.

That was the plan anyhow, but first he had some obstacles to overcome.

He had little money to pay for room and board in Galveston, having spent nearly all he had on the ocean voyage from Florida to Texas. He had no trunk-full of dental tools with which to practice his paying profession, having left Georgia in too much of a hurry to arrange for its shipment. And he had no idea of where his Uncle Jonathan McKey lived, other than the recollection that his property was somewhere in Washington County. Still he was glad to be in Texas at last, the place he had heard about and dreamed of since he was a child – though Galveston looked little like the rough and wild Texas of his childhood imaginings.

Galveston glittered at the edge of the ocean like some fancy-dressed lady decked out in jewels. This was no frontier town where cavalry soldiers fought wild Indians, but the richest city on the Gulf of Mexico and the second richest port in the whole United States. The streets were paved with crushed oyster shells that sparkled in the summer sun and gleamed at night under the glow of gaslights. The mansions of the leading men of Texas society lined Broadway Street, surrounded by gardens of flowering Oleander and fragrant groves of orange and lemon trees. The Strand, on the north side of the island where the wide harbor faced the mainland, was crowded with brick business houses and the traffic of port commerce, while the sand beach on the south of the island was filled with the carriages of pleasure-seekers enjoying the balm of the Gulf breezes. In fact, if it hadn't been for the lingering legend of the Karankawas, civilized Galveston wouldn't have seemed like wild Texas at all.

The Karankawa Indians were cannibals, so the story went, roaming the Gulf islands long before the shipping trade had turned Galveston into the leading port city of the West, and even before the legendary pirate Jean Lafitte had stopped by to bury his stolen booty. When the fishing wasn't good, the Karankawas turned to eating human flesh, and it was rumored that their campfires were heaped with the bones of their supper guests. The fact that they had stalked around the island stark naked, their bronzed bodies glistening in alligator grease to ward off mosquitoes, only added to the allure of their legend. Galveston was, after all, a beach and bathing resort where even very proper Victorians went nude into the waves.

John Henry learned about that surprising island custom on one of his first nights in Galveston when a drink in a Strand saloon led to an invitation to join an outing of men and ladies for a swim in the ocean.

"Though I don't have any bathing clothes with me," he remarked, and one of the other men answered with a laugh.

"Don't need 'em! City Ordinance says you can swim in the altogether between ten at night and four in the morning. They figure all the children are asleep by then."

"You mean you swim naked with ladies along?" John Henry asked in amazement. While he'd grown up going skinny-dipping in the green waters of the Withlacoochee, he'd never gone undressed in open public view – and certainly not with ladies.

"Well, I wouldn't call 'em ladies, exactly!" the gent replied. "It's usually only these saloon girls who are bold enough to accept the invitation. But once they've got their pantaloons off, the barmaids and the ladies all look pretty much alike, anyway. Care to come along?"

And that was how John Henry Holliday found himself in the company of several young sports and a few of their female friends, riding out in a hired dray toward the sand beach on the south side of Galveston Island. They could have walked the two miles to the shore, as it was a warm and brightly moonlit night, but the dray would be a convenient place to stow their clothing while they did their bathing in the surf.

The other young men seemed accustomed to watching women disrobing at a hardly discreet distance, although with the moon shining down so bright no distance would have been quite discreet enough. But John Henry was not accustomed to such a sight and had a hard time averting his eyes, as a gentleman should. The spectacle of those laughing young women loosing their hair and shedding shoes and stockings, skirts and bodices, petticoats and corsets and shimmies and pantaloons until they were standing bare-skinned under the summer moon took away all his mannerly reserve – though it wasn't just the eroticism of the scene that compelled him to shed his own clothes and join them in the waves. It was the freedom of the night, the wild abandonment of the life he'd left behind and the thrill of the world that lay ahead, that made him dive naked into the warm waters of the Gulf. It was Texas that made him do it, not the girls, and he felt not the slightest bit of remorse because of it.

No remorse, but a little regret later on when morning neared and the party tired of the ocean frolic, and found that the dray had disappeared with all of their clothing in it. There was momentary laughter over the missing horse and buggy until they all realized that they would have to make their way back into town on foot – and wearing nothing but their sandy, salty nakedness. Next time, John Henry vowed, he'd leave his own clothing somewhere more reliable than in the back of a rented dray. But in spite of the embarrassing early morning walk back to the livery stable where the horse had taken itself and the dray full of discarded attire, he wouldn't have traded away that night of emancipation for a lifetime of proper memories.

He was in Texas at last, and glad of it.

The rest of his days in Galveston were less romantic as he turned his attention to the more mundane matter of finding employment, which turned out to be a harder task than he'd thought it would be. Although he had a fine education as a graduate of the Pennsylvania College of Dental Surgery and professional experience with one of the most respected dentists in Atlanta, he had no way of proving it. And at one Galveston dental practice after another, the conversation was always the same:

"I'd be happy to have some extra help, busy as things are these days. Could use another trained man in the office, if you did indeed have the credentials…"

"Too bad about the diploma, and all. I've been thinking of advertising for a qualified partner…"

"One can't be too careful in our line, of course. My patients would want to know the background of someone new to town. It's all about trust, in our profession…"

Then would come the polite apologies, adding that when the doctor received his diploma that had been mistakenly left behind in Georgia, along with a letter of recommendation from his former employer, he'd be welcome to come by and inquire after a position again…

But John Henry couldn't afford to wait on the arrival of his diploma or anything else, short on money as he was. So he took the first job that seemed at all suitable: working for a Market Street barber who advertised bloodletting, leeching, and tooth extractions "promptly attended to" on the side of a hairstyling business, and who had a room to rent in the back of his shop, as well. John Henry did the work, took the money, and consoled himself that he wasn't planning on staying in town long, anyhow. As soon as he made enough to outfit himself properly for the journey to come, dressing like a gentleman instead of a ragged refugee from the law, he would leave the barber business and travel on to the Brazos River plantation of his wealthy Uncle Jonathan McKey, where he could live a life more befitting his station.

Of course, along with the new clothes, he'd need to have a new scabbard made for his Uncle Tom McKey's big knife that had come to Texas with him. Since the Hell-Bitch had started out as a plowshare on the McKey plantation before being forged into a sidearm, his Uncle Jonathan might recognize it and wonder how John Henry had come to carry it unholstered – and begin to ask questions about why his nephew had left home in such a hurry. In spite of the family connection, his uncle would be under no obligation to take in a man on the run, and might even turn him away if he knew the circumstances of John Henry's hasty departure from Georgia.

His earnings from the barbershop were slow in adding up, however. What he needed was some seed money, just a little loan to get himself started – and he knew just the person to ask. His Uncle John Holliday, a doctor in Atlanta, was the most well-off man he knew and could certainly afford to share something with his favorite nephew, if John Henry could just find the right words to say in asking him.

It took all the skills of composition he had learned in his school days at the Valdosta Institute to craft a letter that said just enough without saying too much, asking for the loan without explaining why he couldn't ask his own father for the money. But he must have done well in writing it, for within two weeks he received a reply – the small loan he had requested, along with a letter of introduction to a dentist living in the north Texas town of Dallas.

The dentist was a Dr. John Seegar, a former Georgian and old friend of the family. Dr. Seegar had married a girl from Campbell County, just over the line from Fayette County, and had made his home for a while in the Holliday's hometown of Fayetteville. Uncle John was well acquainted with him and was pleased to offer a letter of introduction which John Henry might want to use should he ever find himself in Dallas. But John Henry had no intention of using the recommendation, having heard enough about Dallas to know that he wasn't much interested in presenting himself there. Dallas was just another upstart farm town enjoying a little boom from the arrival of the railroads, but nothing much to brag about beyond that, and he had another kind of life in mind for himself – one of ease and comfort on his Uncle Jonathan's big cotton plantation on the Brazos River. So he put the letter away in his traveling bag and spent the loan money buying a new wardrobe for his trip: a vested wool suit and two white linen shirts, two stiff collars and two pairs of paper cuffs, a pair of soft leather ankle boots and a new felt hat, promising himself that he would repay the loan just as soon as he got settled again. And by the time he stepped aboard the Houston & Texas Central Railroad headed northwest toward Washington County, he almost believed that he really was just a young gentleman traveler off to see the world.

He was lucky to get out of Galveston when he did, on one of the last trains across the railroad bridge before a Yellow Fever quarantine went into effect. The city had reason to be wary: the epidemic of 1867, just six years before, had killed nearly a thousand people, and since no one knew what caused the fever, no one knew how to stop it. The only certainty was that the Fever always followed a season of heat and rain, and that early summer had been particularly hot and rainy. The oyster shell streets filled and flooded, the open ditch sewers overflowed, and the city reeked of human waste and stagnating tide water. When the rains finally cleared and the island dried out in the summer sun, pools of fouled water remained in all the low-lying places breeding mosquitoes that hatched and swarmed and made life miserable for the citizens of Galveston. The city fathers tried every known remedy to remove the noxious fumes that rose up from those mosquito pools, even spreading lime powder on the streets as a disinfectant, but the Yellow Fever came anyway. By the time the quarantine was ordered, seven souls had already died and the newspapers were reporting a new death every day, and fear stalked the island.

So John Henry was glad to be gone, leaving the sand beach and the Oleander gardens behind as the steam engine rumbled across the Galveston Bay Bridge and over the swampy mainland into the piney woods and Post Oak belt of east central Texas. He didn't even bother getting off the train in the little village of Houston, quaint on the banks of Buffalo Bayou, for Washington County was only another sixty miles past that and he was eager to get there.

He knew something of the place already, as he knew of Davy Crockett and Jim Bowie, as he knew of the Texas fight for freedom and the war cry, Remember the Alamo! For Washington-on-the-Brazos was the birthplace of the Texas Declaration of Independence from Mexico following the massacre at the Battle of the Alamo, something every school boy knew about. The Declaration had been signed in a wooden shack on a muddy track that led up from the Brazos River, as primitive a beginning as there ever was for a new nation. But Washington County didn't stay the seat of the new government for long. The Mexican General Antonio López de Santa Anna was hot on the trail of the rebels, and five days after its birth the new government moved to the safer, more settled regions of east Texas.

When the Texans finally won their freedom at the Battle of San Jacinto, the Brazos River country started to fill up with settlers planting cotton and corn in the rich river bottoms. The Brazos was a natural passage through the unsettled countryside, and soon steamers and freighters were carrying thousands of bales of cotton from the new plantations along the river to the coast and Galveston. By the time the Republic of Texas voted to become part of the United States of America, Washington County was on its way to being the leading cotton growing region in the entire South. Although secession and Civil War put a temporary end to the cotton prosperity and the big slave-run plantations were broken up into smaller farms, cotton was still King along the Brazos and there were still wealthy landowners sending barges downriver heavy-laden with raw white bales.

John Henry got off the train at the county seat of Brenham, asked around for directions to the McKey plantation, then hired a horse for the ride out to the Brazos River. He'd imagined his uncle's place in every detail: the tall white house facing the river, the acres of cotton fields stretching beyond, the horse lots farther out where long-tailed Texas mustangs waited impatiently for riding. But when he got to the end of the road where the McKey plantation ought to be, he saw nothing but a tangle of trees along the river's edge with a rough wooden farmhouse fronting furrowed fields. In the field nearest the road, two young girls in worn cotton dresses were working at the crops, and they stopped to stare as he reined in the horse.

"'Afternoon, Ladies," he said, tipping his hat. "Can you tell me the whereabouts of the McKey plantation? I seem to have taken a wrong turn somewhere."

He waited for an answer, but the girls just kept staring up at him in silence, so he asked the question again.

"I said, can you point out the way to the plantation of Mr. Jonathan McKey?"

The older girl answered then, looking up and shading her face with her hand. "What do you want to know for?"

"I have business there," he replied, uncomfortable at being interrogated by a child. With her thin body and old rag of a dress, it was hard to guess her age.

"What kind of business?" the girl asked.

"That is my own affair, Miss," he answered sharply. It was clear the girl came from poor circumstances to be so rudely inquisitive of an adult. "Now can you point out the way to the McKey place or not? It's gettin' late and I've been travelin' a long way."

"Maybe I can, maybe I can't," she replied. "If I knew what your business was, I might could say. How do I know you're not a Yankee revenue agent or somethin'? We don't like Yankees much in these parts."

"Do I sound like a Yankee?" John Henry drawled.

"Well, not exactly. But you don't sound like you're from these parts, neither."

He took a slow breath, trying to hold back his irritation. "I have come a long way to find Mr. McKey. Now, if you don't know where he is, maybe your folks do. Is your mother at home?"

"Ma's dead," the younger girl blurted out, then hung her head.

"Hush up, Eula!" the older girl chided. "How do we know he's not a Yankee, anyhow? Pa'd whip us sure if he thought we was talkin' to a Yankee."

"I am not a Yankee!" John Henry repeated, about ready to give up on his search for the afternoon and ride back to Brenham and try again in the morning. But as he pulled back on the reins, he saw a tall man come out of the treeline along the river, shotgun in hand.

"That's Pa," little Eula said. "He don't like Yankees."

"And he don't like us talkin' to strangers, neither," the older girl said. "You better git, Mister, unless you're a better shot than my Pa."

"I doubt he'd let loose with y'all standin' right here beside me," John Henry answered coolly, the sight of the shotgun not bothering him nearly as much as those two unmannerly children.

"Eula! Lottie!" the man called as he walked toward them through the cornfield. "You girls get inside right now!"

The younger girl turned quickly and ran toward the house, but the older girl – Lottie, John Henry reckoned – hesitated a moment, almost smiling.

"Better not be a Yankee, Mister. My Pa don't much like Yankees," she said again. Then she turned, too, and ran through the fields toward the shelter of the farmhouse.

The girls' father was a tall man, thin like most farm workers but better dressed than most, and he wore a felt hat that looked like it had once been meant for better things than farm work. He stopped short of the edge of the road, the shotgun held loosely in the crook of his arm.

"What can I do for you?" he asked, as he closed the breech of the gun.

"I'm lookin' for Mr. Jonathan McKey. I understand he owns a big plantation down this way."

"He used to, 'till the damn Yankees stole it away."

"Then can you tell me where I might find him?" John Henry asked, afraid that his journey had all been for nothing, that he had come west only to find his uncle moved on or dead.

"That depends on who's askin'. I don't recall you introducin' yourself."

John Henry sighed. These Texas country people were a difficult lot, almost as suspicious as Georgia folk had been after the War.

"Jonathan McKey is my mother's older brother. I'm his nephew, John Henry Holliday. I've come all the way from Georgia to find him. Do you know where he is?"

The man pushed the hat back off his face, and for the first time John Henry could see the man's eyes clearly, sandy lashed and china blue like his own. "Why, you're lookin' at him, son. I'm Jon McKey. And I sure never expected to meet family out here in Texas."

John Henry was speechless. His uncle was nothing but a poor dirt farmer, no better off than any Georgia cracker! But more surprising than Jonathan McKey's poverty was the look of age about him. Though Jonathan was only a couple of years older than his sister Alice Jane, he somehow looked much older than John Henry had expected he would. His thick sandy blond hair was heavily streaked with gray, his face tanned to leather from long hours of working in the hot Texas sun, his blue eyes wreathed in wrinkles. He looked to be nearly sixty years old, though he must have been only in his late forties that year, and John Henry realized with a start that his own mother would be getting old now, too, if she had lived. He always liked to remember her the way she looked in photographs – her white brow smooth and unlined, her eyes clear and serene – before the illness that had overtaken her and drained her life away in that hard, bloody cough.

"So you're Alice Jane's son, are you?" Jonathan said. "Why, I haven't heard from her in years, seems like, not since she moved down to south Georgia during the War. I'm a poor correspondent, I'm afraid. How's she doin' these days?"

John Henry cleared his throat, holding back the cough that suddenly tried to come up from his lungs.

"She's passed on, Sir. She died in '66 after the War."

"Ah, poor Sis!" Jonathan McKey said, shaking his head. "I reckon the War years were hard for her. You favor her, though there's somethin' of your father in your face, as well. What brings you all the way to Texas, John Henry?"

"I'm here to practice dentistry, Sir," he said, giving as much truth as he dared. "I graduated from the Pennsylvania College of Dental Surgery last year. Heard tell Texas is full of opportunity for a young man like myself. I'm aimin' to set up somewhere around these parts, so I thought to pay a visit on my kin along the way."

Jonathan looked at him carefully. "I'm surprised you could find us way out here."

"I almost didn't. Those girls didn't seem too happy to give me directions."

"They're just mindin' my orders. We've had our share of trouble with Yanks here, so I make them be careful."

"But there wasn't any fightin' all the way out here was there?"

"Not durin' the War, no. Our trouble came after, with the Reconstruction. The Yankees near to ruined Washington County, burned half of Brenham then took our land and gave it away to the Nigras." He nodded to the farm across the road where fields of cotton fought against the encroaching line of trees. "That used to be my land over there. Had two-thousand acres, mostly all in cotton, before the Yankees came through. They stole most of it away, gave it to the coloreds I had working on my place, like they had a right to it. What was left they sold to some German immigrants. Mighty hard to see my land run by Nigras and folks that can't even speak English – land my father's inheritance money paid for."

He stared off into the distance, then shifted the shotgun in the crook of his arm.

"I hate them Nigras," he said sullenly. "But I hate the Yankees worse, dirty land-stealin' bastards. I'll get my land back one day, or there'll be hell to pay. Well, come on in the house, then, John Henry. Can't leave my own kin standin' out in the road all day."

It was clear that Jonathan McKey was a bitter man, but he had good reason to be. He was the oldest son of the oldest son of a wealthy Southern family and had been raised to expect that life would treat him well, and for a while it had. When his father, John Henry's grandfather William

Land McKey, had died, Jonathan took his inheritance money and went west to Texas buying up those two-thousand acres of prime cotton land along the Brazos River. But then the War came, and Jonathan signed on as an officer with the Second Texas Cavalry, leaving his wife behind with two small children and another on the way. When the War ended, Jonathan came back to Washington County to find his plantation ruined, his wife Emma and her baby both dead of Yellow Fever, and his two small daughters being tended by neighbors.

Lotti and Eula, Jonathan's girls, must have taken after their mother, John Henry thought, since they didn't bear much resemblance to the McKeys, though they had enough McKey in them to give them that natural Southern pride he had taken as arrogance. Jonathan never let them forget that they were Southern ladies, though his circumstances were too poor even to send them into Brenham for schooling. Still, he had hopes that they might find good husbands and help to raise the family back up from poverty. Lotti was fifteen that year, close enough for marrying age, and shy little Eula was thirteen and would be old enough soon. But the possibility of them finding well-off husbands in that part of Washington County was pretty slim, and chances were they would both end up married to sons of German immigrant families with almost as little as they had. Until they did marry, they kept house for their father and helped out in the fields, and looked less and less like Southern ladies every year.

But they did their best to entertain their new-found cousin in a genteel manner, even setting the supper table with the few remaining pieces of their mother's china dinnerware. And if it weren't all so pathetic, John Henry might have laughed at the irony of it. He had come all the way from Georgia looking for a hand-out from his wealthy uncle, and Jonathan's family was so destitute that they hardly had enough food to pass around the table. It was funny, all right, and too sad for words.

There were only two beds in the McKey house: Jonathan's downstairs in a little bedroom behind the kitchen, and the one the girls shared upstairs in the attic. John Henry would have been content to just ride on back to Brenham to spend the night in the hotel there and forget all about Washington County, but Jonathan insisted that he had to stay the night at least as he was family and all. So the girls made themselves a pallet out of blankets by the kitchen hearth, and John Henry took their bed upstairs.

But he found it hard to sleep on that lumpy old mattress, with the rope-strung bed creaking every time he rolled over and tried to get comfortable and the air so close in the windowless attic that he could hardly breathe. It was no wonder that he started to coughing, with that stale air and the dust of the attic and the summer heat sweltering in.

He had a strange dream that night as he tossed and turned in his troubled, fitful sleep. He dreamed he was back in Georgia again, a fair-haired boy sitting beside his mother at the piano in the parlor. She was young again too, and as beautiful as the Franz Liszt music she played.

"Here, honey," she said, laying his little hands on the keyboard. "You try it. You know how Mother loves to hear you play."

But before he could make a sound, he heard his father's voice calling to him from somewhere outside, and the music and his mother both disappeared.

"Leave that nonsense now, there's work to do," Henry Holliday said, and John Henry followed the sound of his father's voice. Henry was busy building a sapling box and he handed John Henry a hammer and nails. "See if you can make some use of yourself," his father said, as John Henry began to hammer at the wood. And as he worked, the sound of the hammering grew louder and louder until he wasn't a boy anymore, but a man, full grown, and standing at the end of a long drive of trees in front of a beautiful home.

It was his own home, he knew, though it looked like some Peachtree Street mansion, and he walked up the drive toward the wide front stairs. The door was open and he stepped into a house full of light, sunlight reflecting off oiled wood and polished brass, with every long window open to the air. But the beautiful rooms were empty, still and silent as a tomb.

Then another sound came out of the silence, a sound sweet with memory and affection: Mattie's voice speaking from behind him in the open doorway.

"You've come home, John Henry!" she said, but when he turned to face her, it was an auburn-haired child who looked up at him with Mattie's eyes and Mattie's smile. He reached out to touch her, but she turned and ran away from him back down the tree-lined drive and into the wild fields beyond, laughing and calling him to follow.

He ran after her, laughing too, but when he reached the end of the drive, he saw a railroad track stretching out between him and the field. The child Mattie stood in the tall grass beyond the track, smiling and waiting for him to cross over to her, but he was too winded to run any farther and stopped to catch his breath.

And then he heard the train coming, the sound of it growing louder and louder until it filled his ears with a roaring and rushing, and he tried to call out to the child to wait for him. But when he opened his mouth to speak, his words turned into a pain that tore at his lungs like a fire in his chest. He stumbled to the ground, coughing and gasping as the train roared on by.

When he could finally lift his head, the train was gone and so was the child. And all that was left before him was an open, empty field that stretched out forever, endless, alone.

He woke with a start. Someone was standing over him in a dim shadow of light and it took him a moment to realize where he was. The light came from the attic stair, and his little cousin Eula was by his bedside, a candlestick in her hand.

"You sick, John Henry?" she whispered. "You been coughin' all night long."

"No," he started to say, but he had to clear his throat just to get the word out.

"You sure sound sick to me," she said, leaning closer, and as she did the light of the candle fell over him.

"What's that all over your face, John Henry?" she asked, then she pulled back and gasped. "Why, you' got blood all over you!"

And in the flickering light of the candle, John Henry looked down and saw that his pillow was splattered with blood, dark red and drying where his head had been. Then he put his hand to his face, wiping his mouth. Tell me if there's ever any blood, his Uncle John Holliday had told him once, and the hand that touched his mouth was streaked blood-red, too.

"I think maybe you're real sick, John Henry," Eula said, slowly backing away from him. "You want me to get Pa?"

But John Henry didn't answer her. He was staring at the blood that stained his pillow and remembering how his mother had coughed up blood that stained her bed linens blood-red.

"No," he said, "I'm not sick. I am not sick."

"But you're bleedin'," Eula said. "I'll go get Pa."

"No!" he said, pulling himself up. "Get my horse, I'm leavin' here!"

"Right now? But it's hardly daybreak even."

"Get my horse!" he said, the words rasping out, and Eula took the candle and hurried down the attic stair.

He was not weak. He would not be ill. Illness was weakness, and he was not weak. But there was blood all over his pillow, blood on his hand.

It was the sea voyage that had made him sick, he told himself, or the Yellow Fever that had quarantined Galveston, or the choking black smoke of the steam engine on the ride to Washington County. Anyone would get sick breathing in all that coal smoke. Or maybe it was the air in that stuffy little attic room, or vapors from the Brazos River. Vapors brought on the Yellow Fever, vapors could make a man cough up blood...

But when he tried to get up, he found that he was drained of all energy like he'd coughed up part of his life with that blood. He had no choice but to stay in bed in that airless little attic while Eula and Lotti brought him broth and tea and sponged his head with wet rags. And every time he closed his eyes to sleep, he had an awful fear that the train would come back again and take him with it, coughing and gasping his life away.

It was days before he was well enough to travel again, and by then he'd convinced himself that it was indeed the Yellow Fever that had caused the bloody coughing fit and he was lucky to be away from Galveston before the Fever killed him. And blaming his troubles on Galveston and the Fever, he decided to follow his Uncle John Holliday's advice, after all, and take himself off to Dallas to ask for a position with Dr. Seegar. What other option did he have, anyhow? He couldn't go back to quarantined Galveston, nor could he stay with his Uncle Jonathan McKey on that miserable remains of a cotton plantation. So once again, he was on the run, buying another train ticket north and heading on to Dallas.

CPSIA information can be obtained at www.ICGtesting.com
Printed in the USA
LVOW08*1012290614

392201LV00003B/10/P